THE VIANDEN DECEPTION

The Vianden Deception

Copyright @ Tim Byers 2024
Published by Gray Squirrel Press
A subsidiary of Gray Squirrel LLC
Manufactured in the United States of America

PAPERBACK ISBN 979-8-9912390-0-4

For Mary,
Who never gives up.

Historical Note

The Second World War began on September 1, 1939, when the German Army invaded Poland, and Great Britain and France declared war. With the help of the Red Army of the Soviet Union (who was aligned with the Nazis at this time), German forces overwhelmed the brave but overmatched Poles, and the country fell in a matter of weeks.

Once major operations had ended in Poland, an almost eight-month period of relative quiet began, called the *Sitzkrieg* or Phony War, with only minor engagement between the forces of Germany, France, and Great Britain. Both sides were gathering strength for a decisive battle in the West.

By the spring of 1940, the German Führer Adolf Hitler was convinced his forces were ready. Like in Poland, the Wehrmacht would strike a decisive blow, another *Blitzkrieg* using carefully coordinated tank, infantry, artillery, and air forces. However, unlike Poland, substantial numbers of French, British, and Belgian troops were positioned along the western border. German generals needed to find a weak point, but where? The answer required a bold plan, a strike through the Ardennes Forest....

A Map of the Grand Duchy of Luxembourg on the eve of war in the West, May 1940

Chapter One

Luxembourg City, May 10, 1940

Sharp, urgent raps on the door to the flat roused Hansi from his light sleep. He awoke on the cold floor; off the blanket he had positioned beside his mother's bed. Somehow, in the tossing and turning of another restless night, he must have dozed and rolled off. His arm was numb, draped across his suitcase, the sharp corner pressing against the veins.

He sat up. The glowing dots on the clock at Maman's nightstand showed a quarter past midnight. The blackout curtains were parted in the middle, but outside it was completely dark, as it had been since the previous September, when Germany's invasion of Poland brought France and Britain into a state of war.

More knocks. A bolt of fright shot through him. Papa must have called Dr. Schenk. Could this be it?

He listened. His mother's breathing was shallow, as always, but at least regular. Still, he knew. She was dying.

Hansi got up and untwisted his tangled shirt. He had grown used to sleeping in his clothes; he had for weeks. Papa said war would come any day and to keep the suitcase close by. He heeded Papa's words and had it stuffed to its limit. The plan was that if Maman rallied, they'd go to Aunt Milly's in the north. They would be safe at her farm, with plenty of room to care for Maman and most importantly, out of the invader's path.

But Maman's rally never came. In the last few days, things had gotten worse. The pain grew intense, Hansi knew, because Dr. Schenk's visits had become more frequent. He taught Hansi and his father to give the morphine injections. They eased the pain, but not without a cost. Maman's eyes seemed to leave her, replaced with glazed globes that stared into nothing.

Hansi bent over the bed and kissed his mother's cheek. The skin was thin and clammy. She didn't stir.

Beyond the bedroom, the front door creaked open. Hansi tucked the quilt around her shrunken frame, sighed, and crossed the room.

He cracked the door open, expecting a burst of light. The hallway was dark and empty. Hushed voices drifted from the kitchen, where a faint light glowed. Hansi padded to the doorway and stopped. The Italian accent was unmistakable, the hulk of a frame immediately recognizable. Not Dr. Schenk, but Manolo, his father's close friend. The two men sat on either side of the small table. At the center, a flashlight stood on end, shooting its beam to the ceiling.

"*D'Boche kommen*," Manolo said. *The Germans are coming.*

"They're across the border?" Papa asked.

"Not yet. But the message comes from Pierre on the radio. It's time. We go now."

Hansi took a step onto the cold tile. Manolo saw him first and managed a half-grin greeting. Papa, though, never looked up. His face was taut with worry.

"What's wrong, Alain?" Manolo finally asked.

Hansi could hear Papa's hard breathing. "I'm sorry,

Manolo. Marie is near the end. I cannot leave her.”

Terror stabbed Hansi through the heart. He had never heard his father speak so directly. *Near the end?*

Hansi moved to his father and touched his shoulder. It trembled like a frightened dog. Hansi had never seen Papa this way.

“How long, Papa?”

Papa looked up through glistening eyes. “Any time now,” he said. “The Germans are coming today.”

Hansi’s legs went weak. He sat down on an empty chair.

“I meant Maman. How long before—”

His father looked away. “I don’t know, son. But soon.”

Hansi pushed the chair back with a loud scrape and flung himself against his father. He buried his head into Papa’s shoulder, taking in the smell of a long day’s work and constant worry. His father held him tight. Strange, but in his grief, Hansi felt some measure of relief. His father had finally acknowledged the truth. Still, Hansi was afraid.

He looked up. Manolo filled the doorway. “I’m sorry, Alain. Very sorry. But I must go.” He took the flashlight and aimed it toward the door. He stepped around the table and crossed into the hallway.

Papa jumped up and grabbed his arm.

“Manolo, you can’t go alone. It’s too dangerous. You might cross the wires and then—”

Manolo smiled. “Don’t worry, Alain. I practiced in the dark.” He tossed his head at Maman’s door. “I knew I might have to go alone. I worked it out. Everything will be all right.”

Papa shook his head. “Someone must hold the light. If you wire it wrong, it won’t work. The bridge won’t blow.”

“I know.”

“But we agreed, we go together. One to do the work, one to keep watch.”

“I will be very careful, Alain. I promise.” Manolo’s characteristic grin had returned, the one Hansi knew from the restaurant he owned across from the train station. He winked at Hansi. “The moonlight will guide me.”

“Don’t be silly, Manolo. If you stumble in the dark, that bag of blasting caps will rip you in half. You’ll bleed to death while the Germans march past.”

“Alain, you talk like my mama. Someone must go. Pierre will be waiting.”

Manolo was at the door now and had it open.

“Please, Manolo, I beg you. Don’t do it alone.”

Manolo gripped his friend in a great hug. When he released him, his eyes were bright. His chin jutted out of the round padded face. “I will see you in Wiltz. Three, maybe four days.” He turned to Hansi and squeezed him with his massive arms. “You tell your mama that Manolo prays for her. God will be with her.”

He pulled down on the black felt cap he wore and nodded goodbye. He turned and left.

Hansi looked at his father, whose face seemed frozen in agony. Manolo’s steps echoed in the outside hall.

A strange idea snuck into Hansi’s mind. He flew out the door.

“Wait!” he called. Manolo was halfway down the flight

of stairs. He stopped.

"Take me," Hansi said. "I'll help you."

Hansi sat alone in the front room of his flat and stared out the window through a slit between the blackout curtains. His village, called the Grund, was no more than a thin strip of apartments along the Petrusse River at the base of the cliffs of Luxembourg City. It was nearly invisible in the shadow of the ancient Casemate walls, lit only by slivers of moonlight between some of the buildings. Street lamps had been darkened for months.

Hansi's offer had brought Manolo back in from the stairway. The words caused some unspoken message to pass between the two men. Manolo came back inside, gave Hansi another smile and a quick pat on his cheek with that wide padded hand of his, and the two men disappeared into the kitchen. The longer they discussed it, the more Hansi was stunned that they had not dismissed the offer out of hand.

Hansi scanned the sky for any signs of movement. He expected wave after wave of black ravens, German Stuka dive bombers, to rise in the eastern sky and sweep overhead at any moment. Instead, all he could see was the jagged silhouette of the village, the purple sky, and pinprick stars.

He was jolted from his thoughts by the sound of the telephone. In the darkness of the room, the bell sounded a shrill alarm. He jumped off the sofa and crossed quickly toward the end table by the hall.

Dr. Schenk? More invasion news?

The handset seemed to bounce off the receiver with the last ring. It was heavy to his hand, which was shaking.

"Hello?"

The voice on the far end was distant, garbled, but urgent.

"Alain! This is Pierre. Something is wrong."

"Excuse me, sir. This is Hansi, his son. Please wait. I'll get him."

The voice didn't stop.

"There's no time. Tell your father—the Germans, they… come… somehow, they… "

Hansi squeezed the receiver with both hands. "I can't hear you!"

"… do you understand? … the bridge is…"

The line went dead.

Hansi's suitcase was halfway under Maman's bed. It wasn't heavy, though it contained everything he was allowed to take in such an emergency—two shirts, two pairs of socks, two underwear, a single pair of trousers and a small kit of toiletries. He would wear everything else— belt, shoes, hat, and a jacket. Papa allowed one personal item, but Hansi couldn't decide on just one. He made no habit of deceiving Papa, but along with his prized sketchbook and charcoal pencil, Hansi stashed a special letter penned the previous autumn from his friend Karin. The envelope was imprinted with the black Nazi eagle clutching the Hakenkreuz in its claws; taken, no doubt from her father's desk. There was no time for the memories right now. He slid the letter halfway between two pages of his sketchbook and paused. This would not do. He slipped his fingers under the fold of the envelope and tore the corner away.

With Papa and Manolo, Hansi had repeated the phone conversation as accurately as he could. A man named Pierre, something very wrong, the mention of a bridge. Papa talked it over with Manolo. They had decided to proceed.

In the hallway, Papa's voice was stern. "Do exactly what Manolo tells you, understand? Nothing more, nothing less. He will take you on to Wiltz once the sun has come up. I'll meet you at Aunt Milly's as soon as—" He hesitated. "As soon as we can manage."

Manolo smiled confidently and slapped Hansi on the back. "We make a fine team," he said.

Hansi was swept up by a surge of excitement. Nervously he grabbed his jacket and cap from the hook in the hall and fumbled putting it on. Half finished, he had taken a stride toward the door when he felt a hand on his shoulder turning him around.

Papa's expression caught Hansi off guard. He looked worried. Deep creases flanked his glistened eyes, and he fought back a tremor in his chin. A lump choked Hansi's throat and he looked away. He needed to be brave. He needed to help Manolo, not worry Papa. They all seemed to know it.

"Remember, exactly what Manolo tells you!"

"Yes, Papa, I promise," Hansi replied.

Hansi turned to go.

A faint voice echoed from behind them.

"Hansi!" his mother called, from beyond the bedroom door. Hansi dropped his things and rushed to her bedside. She was waving her arm, the one nearest him, back and forth, as if trying to reach something on her nightstand.

Hansi adjusted the pillow behind her head to help her raise up.

"Are you feeling better?"

Her lips parted but the sound was faint and scratchy. Hansi found the glass of water on the table and held it to her mouth. She sipped weakly, but never stopped moving her arm. The water spilled down her chin and neck.

"What is it, Maman? What do you need?"

Her hand found the lace cloth that covered the nightstand. She tapped around and clasped onto something. Hansi couldn't see it in the faint light from the hallway until she drew it to her chest. A silver chain hung from her fist. She panted and let her eyes fall shut, as if exhausted from the effort.

The other arm came up, weak with tremors.

"Hansi!" she rasped.

He bent down and placed his ear close to her mouth. She found his shoulder with her free hand and slid it down to his hand. In the next instant, she was forcing the object into his.

"Remember me," she said.

The words plunged deep into his heart. Somehow, she knew what was happening. *No!*

He glanced at the object. A small silver crucifix hung at the end of the chain. Maman had always worn it. Her faith was strong. She was giving it to him.

"But Maman—"

"God protect you," she whispered.

Weak as she was, Hansi embraced her. She turned her head and kissed his neck. Hansi choked back a sob. He wanted to crawl up in her lap like he had always done as a little boy, after a fight, or a skinned elbow, and let her comfort him. But he couldn't. He had to be strong.

Hansi felt Papa's hand on his shoulder once more. He rose up. Maman's eyes were closed. Her chest rose and fell with large, labored movements. Yet her face was peaceful, her lips upturned in a gentle smile.

Hansi rushed out of the room. Without another word or glance, he was out the front door and down the stairs. Manolo's truck waited at the curb.

Chapter Two

The truck coughed awake like an ancient, angry beast disturbed from its sleep. And a nearly blind one. The headlights were masked off but for small slits due to the blackout rules. At the bottom of the steep grade to the Upper City, Manolo downshifted. The transmission, stiff and stubborn, shuddered. Burnt diesel fumes swept over them.

"Get on with you!" Manolo urged. The beast obeyed and began the ascent.

Part way up, Hansi turned back. The valley, swallowed in the shadow of the cliffs, dissolved behind him. He had expected to leave for weeks. But not under these circumstances. Barely a kilometer from home, he felt homesick already. He had to be brave.

At the top of the hill, the city was like a cemetery, the truck a disrespectful intruder. The gears ground hard at every turn and the engine rattled. Familiar landmarks, like the Cathédrale Notre Dame, once basked in bright lights. Now, because of the government-enforced blackout, it lay dark and still like a deserted ruin. The faintest light, it was said, would guide bombers to their targets. Hansi had seen the newsreels. They would come at first light. How would a few sandbags protect that spire from the Stukas?

Hansi's mind was never far from the tiny flat in the Grund. He knew. He would never see Maman alive again. Papa had only let him go with Manolo because of the war, not because of the mission.

They passed through the silent city, and Manolo found the road north that would take them to the Ardennes Forest. Beyond the city limits, the road straightened out. The truck settled down. The landscape of farms and forest seemed less haunting, the moon shadows less threatening. Hansi settled back in his seat and let the cool air wash over him. Manolo also seemed to relax; he took a deep breath and twisted his head back and forth to stretch. But his eyes never left the view ahead.

Hansi broke the silence.

"Who is Pierre?" he asked.

Manolo glanced over. "Pierre is a Frenchman. He tells me and your Papa what to do."

"I don't understand. Do what?"

"Blow up a bridge."

The truck bounced over a crack in the pavement. Nerves intensified the jolt, and Hansi found himself braced against the dashboard, every muscle tense.

Manolo smiled. "Relax, Hansi. I prepared everything in advance."

As they lumbered on, Hansi wanted to ask about the phone call. Pierre had been frantic.

Manolo must have read his mind.

"Pierre likes to worry. That is good for a leader. We'll take extra care."

"What if he was trying to warn you and Papa? He said something was very wrong."

A slight crack appeared in Manolo's normally pleasant demeanor. But only for a moment.

"Your papa and I discussed it. If Pierre wanted to stop the mission, those would have been his first words. But he didn't. Whatever was wrong, he wanted to discuss it. He trusts your papa. So do I."

About twenty kilometers north of the city the farmland gave way to forest. They wound between, over, and around hills covered with a mix of budding and evergreen trees. The houses, barns, and sheds were infrequent in the forest, and small meadows appeared suddenly between stands of thick forest. Another thirty minutes on, the truck crested a hill. Manolo braked and the truck rattled to a stop. The broad valley, bathed in broken moonlight, spread out before them. The forest stretched in every direction. Hansi's eyes followed the road until it disappeared behind a hill. Further down, gray mist settled in the gorge that meandered east to west.

"That's the Sure River down there," Manolo said, setting the brake. "And our bridge."

Hansi's pulse surged.

"The explosives are in place," Manolo continued. "I will finish the wiring. Then, we continue to the village." He pointed north and a little east. "Of course, I forgot—heh, heh, the bridge will come down in a great crash. We will meet Pierre at the hotel in Vianden. And then we wait. Tomorrow, the next day, we go on to Wiltz." He slapped Hansi on the leg and smiled wide. "See your papa and mama again."

Hansi returned the smile, but only to be polite. The next time he saw Maman, he was sure, would be at her funeral.

"Oh, one more thing."

Manolo reached between his knees toward something on the floor. He retrieved an object, triangular and cloth-covered, and placed it on the seat between them. He unwrapped it, a pistol. Hansi held his breath.

Manolo took it in his right hand and held it up for Hansi to see. He might have been presenting a bottle of wine at his restaurant. His eyes were bright, not serious. He tugged on his belt.

"I have my own. You take this one."

Hansi's heart raced. He hesitated and then took hold of it. It was cool to the touch, heavy. He pointed it forward. He couldn't believe what was happening.

"On the side, see that bump. That's the safety. In that position it is on. It will not shoot."

Trying not to tremble, Hansi focused on the small tab of metal above where his thumb wrapped around the stock of the pistol.

"Go ahead," Manolo said. "Flip it off, but be careful. Don't pull the trigger or you'll kill the windshield." He chuckled.

Hansi held the pistol in his right hand. With his left, he reached for the tab.

"See if you can use your thumb."

Hansi could. The safety catch clicked off.

"Then—well, if you need to, you just pull the trigger. But not now. Switch it back off. That's all you need to know."

Hansi flicked the safety back on. He cradled the pistol in both hands, examining it along its length.

"It was for your Papa. Give it to him when you see him."

Hansi ran his fingers along the smooth round barrel. He turned it over, measuring its weight in his grip. It was substantial. He felt...substantial.

"Don't get too excited," Manolo chuckled. "We're not planning to use it. But just in case."

Hansi couldn't help it. He was exhilarated. Every hair on his body seemed now to stand on end, every rumble of the engine clearer, the air cool and sweet through his nostrils.

Manolo turned his attention back to the road ahead. The brake released with a sharp thump and he revved the engine.

"What will I do at the bridge?" Hansi asked.

The truck began to roll forward. Manolo's eyes were fixed ahead.

"You'll wait with the truck. Of course."

Hansi's heart dropped.

"But Papa said something about wires...and the danger of being all alone."

"There's nothing to worry about. Everything is nearly ready. I just have to place the timer and we're done. I promised your papa I'd keep you safe."

Hansi sank back into the seat, his adventure short-lived. The gun in his lap was nothing but a prop, a deadweight. He wasn't to participate after all. He'd been a fool to think otherwise.

The truck dropped into a thick pine forest. Mist, seeping out from the trees, swirled around them, swallowing what little light passed through the slits. Manolo switched on the wipers to fight condensation. As the road grew steeper, the truck accelerated. Manolo compensated by pumping the brakes, and the truck's suspension groaned and rocked. Hansi's disappointment turned to alarm as they picked up speed.

"Steady!" Manolo growled, the cheer gone from his expression.

Pines disappeared from view as the road plunged into the cut of the hill. Sandstone walls, a jagged blur, rose on each side. The truck hurtled down. Vibration hammered at Hansi's eardrums. One violent shock popped the mirror off its bracket, and it exploded on the metal floor, sending silver splinters like shrapnel through the cab. It seemed the entire vehicle might come apart at any instant. And now Manolo gripped the wheel like they were the horns of a bull.

He braked again, the wheels locked, and the truck slid over the pavement. Manolo had to let off.

"This mist! It coats the road like butter!" he was yelling at the top of his voice.

Manolo tried the brakes again. The truck jerked and skidded more wildly than before.

Hansi felt it in his hips. They were losing control.

WHAM!! Metal met stone. Sparks shot from the rear of the truck, and it ground against the jagged cut in the ridge. Hansi slammed against the door, elbow first. A jolt of pain shot up through his shoulder.

Manolo fought hard. He twisted the wheel and the truck veered left. The vehicle returned to smooth pavement, but only for a moment, when Hansi heard a loud *PAAAP!!!* And the truck jerked right again. The front tire was gone, and in front of them, the wall rose up quickly into view.

Manolo wrenched the wheel once more, but this time the truck didn't respond. They hit the stone wall again, this time at a sharper angle. The truck shuddered violently, the cab lighting up in a fresh shower of sparks. Hansi was sure they would be crushed.

But the truck slowed. The shudders and sparks settled. The truck came to a stop with the sound akin to a rusty lid scraping on a trash can. A cloud of dust and chewed rubber followed them down the hill and swept past. Then all fell still.

Hansi's head lay against the door frame, only centimeters from the red molars of the stone wall.

Manolo, exhausted from wrestling the beast, draped his arms over the steering wheel and rested his chin. He sat still for a long moment while his shoulders heaved up and down. In a matter of seconds, steam from body and breath had clouded the windshield. A moment later, he pushed back, looked up, and while mouthing a silent prayer, made the sign of the cross. Finally, without turning his head, he spoke.

"Are you all right?" he asked.

Hansi rubbed his elbow. He felt lucky to be alive. He could only manage a nod.

They were halfway down the hill, Hansi judged, amidst a gathering fog.

Manolo gave the engine a try. The motor cranked;

then, after a spasm of coughs, sputtered to life.

He slipped it into gear and tried to turn the wheel back toward the center of the road. Despite his powerful arms, it wouldn't turn. Letting it go, he revved the engine. The truck groaned and rocked backward but could not free itself. Manolo tried a few more times. The beast groaned and strained but would hardly budge. Manolo slammed his hands against the wheel.

"Ti buono a niente!" Before Hansi could guess what he was saying, Manolo had thrown the door open. He flew around the truck, front to back, bending, staring, waving his arms, and cursing in Italian. In any other situation, it might have been funny.

Since Hansi's door was smashed against the sandstone wall, he had to climb out Manolo's side.

The truck's front corner was missing, like a giant monster had chewed it off. The tire on Hansi's side was torn off the rim, the axle bent up so that the bare wheel was wedged into the well. The truck was finished.

Manolo came alongside Hansi and let his shoulders fall. He swept his fingers through locks of black curls and sighed.

"That's that," he said.

Manolo retrieved a rucksack from the back of the truck and started down the road.

Hansi clomped after him, a half step behind, dejected. Carrying a suitcase on a mission to blow up a bridge felt silly. He was just a spectator along for the ride, or, more correctly, the walk. Possibly a long one.

The road grew steeper. Hansi felt it in his thighs as

they walked. The air was cold on his cheeks. In the heavy mist, even the smallest pebble crunched and echoed off the wall. His mind returned to the Grund. Better to have stayed home, he thought. *At least I could help Maman.*

The moon cast its unsteady glow on the road ahead. In the damp swirls, the beginning of a curve emerged and Hansi realized they were lucky. The truck would never have made that turn.

"How will we get to Wiltz now?" he asked.

Manolo hardly glanced over. The breeze was breaking up the mist.

He pointed ahead. "The bridge."

Chapter Three

At the last moment, the cut in the hill fell away to reveal a broad valley and narrow gorge. The mist, thick in the forest, gathered in every low spot and drained into the gorge. The mass surged downstream like a flood, splashed over the stone abutments on the upper side of the bridge and washed over the roadway. The sky above sparkled with stars and their view extended all the way across the valley to the ridge beyond the river. There the road rose gradually through the forest. Hansi sucked in a deep breath and relaxed a bit. He had never seen this part of the country at night. Its beauty had a quieting effect on him, and the sense of adventure returned. The bridge's destruction would be quite a spectacle, even if he only watched from the safety of the far hill.

Manolo paused, turned, and raised a finger to his lips for Hansi to be quiet. Hansi nodded. Holding Hansi in place with an upturned hand, Manolo went on. Hansi wondered, why such precautions suddenly? With the timer safe in Manolo's pouch, was there a hidden danger? He dared not ask. It was easy to trust Manolo, and so he stood firm.

Manolo crossed the bridge, scanned the scene, and then ushered Hansi to follow. Manolo's eyes, set deep behind narrow slits, never rested on anything. When Hansi completed the crossing, Manolo positioned Hansi by the stone guardrail while he continued with a quick circuit around the area. He'd take a step, listen, and continue, his head darting toward the faintest sound. He studied the underbrush at the edge of the dark forest, the steep, rocky riverbank, and the curved road ahead. They were alone but for the sounds of nature—tree frogs, insects, and the river itself. Mist swirled everywhere. Manolo was like an animal. Hansi couldn't understand the concern. As they ascended, he would pause every minute or so, listen again, and look back toward the bridge before continuing on. Hansi guessed he was measuring how far away they needed to be to remain safe from the blast. About a half kilometer up the valley, they passed through an outcropping of sandstone. Manolo stopped.

"Wait for me here," he whispered. He grasped Hansi by the arms, and pulled down, as if to plant him firmly on the spot.

Hansi looked back. His disappointment boiled over.

"You can't even see the bridge from here!" They were in thick forest. The valley was completely blocked from view.

"Shhhh!" Manolo snapped, his head darting around again. His voice was firm.

"You stay here. I will return in thirty minutes. We will see a great show."

Hansi knew it was no use arguing. He found a clump of boulders nearby and climbed up, hoping for a better view. The disappointment stuck to him like the damp air. The view was only forest and fog. Manolo had already disappeared back down the road.

Hansi had no way of telling whether his wait was five

minutes or fifty. It felt like the latter. He laid back on the boulder and let the light breeze pass over him. Above, the sky was vast, the spread of stars like sparkling dust cast to the wind. He knew little of constellations, but enough to find Ursa Major, the Great Bear, that looked more like a large ladle. He knew to follow the two points that formed the front edge of the ladle across the sky to bright Polaris, the northern star. But that was about it. Stars had never been easy to see under the bright lights of Luxembourg City, that is, until the blackout. An unwanted benefit.

Thoughts of the city drew him back to home, where Maman lay dying. *How would Papa go on without her? How would I?*

His stomach sunk into a sour pit. Trying to free himself of the thoughts, he sat up. The gun pinched his gut. He drew it out.

Suppose I have to use it? Will I?

The pistol was heavy in his hand, unsteady. He slid off the rock, touched onto the grass facing downhill, and stationed himself with feet apart like a guard at the Grand Ducal Palace. His left hand joined the right one on the grip. Slowly, he brought the gun to eye level. He squinted and looked down the barrel. He squeezed the trigger. The safety held as he had set it in the truck. The pistol remained silent.

His focus extended to the backdrop of trees. Nothing in the shroud of fog presented itself as a target. So he raised his aim above the treeline. Among the spray of stars he found a bright one and lined it up in the sight. It danced like a diamond at the end of the barrel.

That's when he heard it. The sound was faint at first, a low rumble in the distance. *A truck? No, the sound was heavier, and higher.*

He lowered the pistol and opened both eyes. *A plane! It had to be a plane.*

Hansi scrambled up on the boulder and climbed higher. Still, he could not see over the trees to the river.

The sound grew louder. Hansi twisted his head, one way and the other, straining to locate the source with his ears. The breeze rustled the trees nearby, mingling with that of the new sound. *Was it just the breeze playing a trick?* He rotated his head back and forth, listening intently. *There it was again!* From the south. He was sure.

Hansi jumped off the rocks and started running down the road. Then, when the roar grew close, he stopped. A shadow passed overhead. The thunder swept through the trees as a long slender plane, completely black, slid across the sky and banked south in a wide curve. Hansi ran again, trying to keep it in the narrow view above the road. In a moment, it was gone. The sound lingered as the pitch fell, the rattle faded, and then everything returned to how it was before. Silent and still.

Was it a German plane? Why here? What for? Where are the other planes?

Hansi pondered what to do, if anything. Manolo should be returning soon, but Hansi had no way of telling how long the man had been gone. And what of the plane? He'd heard no bomb, no machine guns. *What could it do to Manolo from up there?*

His heart pounded. Surely Manolo heard it too.

Hansi felt foolish. Papa had said the Germans were coming. Of course, they would have planes, many of them, more than anyone could count. They were going to have to get used to the idea. They had been waiting for this since September, when Germany invaded Poland and France and Great Britain declared war.

Better to do what Manolo said. Wait.

Reluctantly, he returned to the rocks, where he put the pistol in his pocket and took a drink from the bottle Manolo had brought along. He climbed back onto the boulder and looked up. The sky was empty. The chill of sweat trickling down his neck and back was pleasant. Manolo would show up any minute now. In the meantime, perhaps he could rest.

PAP! PAP! PAP-PAP!

Echoes rushed up the valley. Hansi snapped awake. Gunfire!

He sat up. A giant vice had seemed to clamp down on his chest, making it hard to breathe.

How long was I asleep? Where's Manolo?

He scrambled down the boulder, hit hard on the ground, and tripped over something. *That blasted suitcase!*

In the fall, the pistol came out from his belt and thumped on the ground. On his knees, Hansi scrambled and rescued it from the dew-covered grass. He gripped it tightly with his left hand. It was warm from being held so close to his body, and still very heavy. He lifted it and took aim at the horizon again. Hard as he tried, the thing wouldn't hold still.

He shifted his gaze down the road. *Was Manolo trying to signal for help?*

This time, there was no hesitating. And no worrying about the suitcase. Manolo needed him. Hansi took off down the road, accelerating fast on the downward slope. He pumped the pistol up and down with every stride. The grade helped him cover ground fast, and soon he reached the limit of his balance.

What if Manolo was hurt? Who was shooting?

He ran as fast as he could without falling. His feet slapped the pavement in a furious rhythm matched only by that of his heart. Soon he was sucking in huge gulps of air that burned the back of his throat, and yet the bridge was still out of view. One more bend?

Finally, the trees thinned enough for him to catch a glimpse of the bridge. It looked just like before, bathed in mist and moonlight. But deserted.

He rounded the bend and slowed. Breath, like steam from a locomotive, blew in long, billowing streams. His throat tasted of metal and blood.

Careful now!

About twenty meters from the bridge, he stopped. Fear swirled all around him.

What if Manolo had already set the timer? The bridge might blow at any instant!

Feeling suddenly exposed in the middle of the road, Hansi darted right and dropped down into the drainage ditch at the roadside. *If the bridge blows, perhaps I'll be protected.*

Rising to a half-crouch, he continued.

The edge of the canyon emerged through the hazy mist as he drew near. He climbed out of the ditch and moved into the first line of trees. Less protection than the ditch, he thought, but better than open ground if the bridge goes.

Tree by tree, he crept on. The bridge lay quiet, resting on stone arches sunken in fog. Hansi's focus moved along the curves and stopped. Wooden crates, lashed with rope, clung to the underside of the span.

The explosives...

Hansi's heart leapt. Manolo's burly figure emerged from the shadows. He was working on something in the space between the arches.

Hansi thought to call out but was interrupted by movement out of the corner of his eye. He looked toward the river.

What was that?

A bush on the riverbank stirred the mist. Then, a dark figure appeared, creeping toward the bridge. The movements were strange, slow and halting, like the thing was dragging some heavy but invisible object.

The breeze cleared the view for a moment, and Hansi saw him clearly. A German soldier, with high boots and a small steel helmet strapped tightly around his chin, was doubled over. He carried a machine pistol slung over his shoulder with a leather strap, steadied by one arm. The other hung lifeless at his side. The heavy object he dragged behind was his leg.

He's injured! Those were the shots I heard!

The German moved again, short puffs of breath pouring out with each step. He came to a boulder, one of the many that littered the ravine, and fell against it. He was only meters from Manolo, whose back was turned.

Hansi jumped out from behind the tree, sliding on the soft needles that carpeted the slope. He fumbled for the pistol and thrust it high in the air. He had to warn Manolo.

Hansi pulled the trigger—it wouldn't budge.

The safety! The safety is on!

He lowered the pistol and wormed his thumb over the hilt. He couldn't find the switch. The soldier took another step, and then another.

Hansi's entire body was quaking.

Where is that switch?

He pressed against a tree to steady himself. Drawing the pistol close, he tried to focus. *There it was*—with a click, the switch was off.

When he looked back, the soldier had risen up. With his good arm, he was bringing the machine pistol up and wedging it between himself and the boulder.

Shaking, Hansi lowered the pistol and took aim down the ravine. The end of the barrel found the dark figure of the German.

Manolo was still working on the explosives, unaware of the danger.

Hansi's heart pumped molten liquid. It shot up his neck, over his face, and into his ears. He wanted to throw up.

Now! Do it now!

The voice inside urged him on, but Hansi couldn't

comply. His entire body shook, but especially his arms and hands.

The German faltered. His gun barrel scraped against the rock, but the sound was swallowed by the distance between them.

Manolo, however, must have heard it. He spun around. The German rose to fire. Manolo leapt at him.

The two men smacked together in a crash of flesh and metal. They tumbled in an indistinguishable mass of churning limbs, stirring up the fog all around.

Hansi left the cover of the trees and approached the lip of the bank. He would slide down and…

A muffled shot flashed in the mist below him. The wrestlers didn't move. Hansi's heart stopped too. Then slowly, a figure rose from the mist.

Manolo! He was hunched over his enemy, steam rising from his head and pumping out his mouth like a dragon. He wiped his forehead with the back of his sleeve and looked up.

Hansi nearly lost control on the bank, which was very steep, but managed to land upright on the soft sand of the riverbank. He was at Manolo's side in no time.

He expected Manolo to be relieved; his expression was the opposite.

"I told you to wait for me!" he growled.

"The shots! I heard the shots and thought you were in danger."

Manolo grabbed him by the collar. A bolt of anger shot across his face. "We've no time. I had to shorten the timer. We must go!"

Piled on the shame of paralyzing fear was that of disobeying Manolo's orders. But at least Manolo was all right. He had beaten the paratrooper.

They scrambled up the bank. Hansi was driven by the new fear of the bridge. Manolo clawed at the bank and followed, but slowly. All at once he seemed exhausted.

"Are you hurt?" Hansi asked, offering a hand from the top.

"Go on! Run!" Manolo's voice was urgent, even scared.

Hansi hesitated, and then took off up the hill. The pavement was smooth, but the grade was steep. He was winded quickly.

Hansi paused to look for Manolo. He looked like a bear climbing over the top of the bank—hunched over, lumbering, snorting hard breaths. He caught Hansi's glance and waved him on.

Hansi retreated to his side. Manolo was furious, shaking his head and swatting at Hansi.

"I promised your papa. I won't have you die on this road" His voice was gravelly now, but Hansi ignored him. He ducked under Manolo's arm, reached behind his broad back, and lifted. Together they moved up the road. *Would fifty meters more be enough distance between them and the bridge?*

Manolo grew heavier and heavier. Hansi's every muscle burned. But he churned his legs with all his strength.

In a spasm, Manolo's hand slid up to the back of Hansi's neck, and he pulled him close.

"The ditch," he said, his voice barely a rattle.

Hansi knew what he meant. Time was up. He pulled Manolo to their left, took a step off the pavement, and set his eyes on the dark line that formed the drainage ditch beside the road.

It was too late. From behind, an ear-splitting *CRACK* swept past them, followed by a shock wave that lifted Hansi from the pavement. He experienced the momentary sensation of floating before being slammed against the bank with such force that popped every molecule of air from his lungs.

For a moment, Hansi could hardly move. Some great weight pressed down on him. His ears were ringing, and cool water trickled along his back. Then he smelled the earthy scent of the warm body above him and realized he was at the bottom of the ditch, and Manolo was on top of him.

With great effort, he squirmed out from under the great hulk of the man. He looked back toward the bridge where the bridge had stood only an instant before, as a dirty cloud rose from the center of the valley.

"You did it!" Hansi exclaimed. "It's gone! You've stopped them, Manolo!"

What's more, they had made it far enough up the hill that, other than being knocked over, they were unhurt.

Hansi turned around and his heart stopped. Manolo lay back against the grass, his head flopping from side to side. He seemed to be fighting to come awake—his eyes blinked and he searched the bank with his hands as if trying to regain touch with the world. His midsection was soaked in a broad, dark, and shiny stain.

Manolo wasn't wet from water in the ditch.

"Hansi," Manolo whispered.

The boy flung himself down on the bank beside his friend. He unfastened Manolo's jacket, unbuttoned his shirt, and drew back at once. Blood, dark and sticky, oozed from a small hole in the center of his stomach, covering his large belly. Hansi realized now—in the struggle at the bridge, the German must have got a shot off. Manolo hadn't said anything, and Hansi was blinded by the apparent success of their mission. But now, as his life leaked down his torso onto the spring grass, Manolo's pained expression and loss of strength brought reality crashing down onto Hansi like the bridge itself.

"Go to Vianden," Manolo said faintly.

Hansi began to remove his own jacket. "We'll go together."

"The hotel there."

"Hold on, Manolo. You're coming too." Hansi took his own shirt off and began to dab at the hole. When the flow continued, he wiped in a wide stroke across Manolo's stomach. As quickly as he wiped, the hole supplied enough fresh blood to replace Hansi's effort, and more.

Manolo began to shiver. "Ask for Pierre."

"Don't talk that way! You'll ask for him yourself. I'll get you there." Hansi's shirt was soaked.

Manolo began gesturing toward the sky. "No, Hansi. You go."

"The angels can wait," Hansi blurted. "We'll get you to a doctor. They'll patch you up and you can get some rest."

Manolo shook his head. "The Germans." His voice was a gurgle. He gestured again. "There could be...others."

Manolo meant paratroopers. When there was one, there were likely others. Roaming the woods now, ready to avenge their own fallen comrade.

"I won't leave you, Manolo!" Hansi said, drawing close to the man.

Manolo was fighting. He bit down on his lip to try to stem the shaking. He had bitten so hard that it, too, was bleeding.

Hansi took Manolo's hands and pressed them together between his own, folding them at the elbow as if Manolo were praying. His friend, whose grip had always been that of a wrestler, was without strength. But still, he resisted. Something was bothering him. Hansi let go.

Manolo's right arm fell to the ground. His hand fluttered, fingers curled, leaving a half-bent index finger as a hint.

"My pack," he mumbled.

Hansi scrambled over the grass. Manolo's pack was in the ditch. He retrieved it in no time and returned to Manolo's side, fumbling at the fasteners.

Manolo's eyelids fluttered. Hansi felt an entirely new level of fear seize him. Fear, mixed with overwhelming shame. He had had a chance to save his friend, when the German was readying himself, but failed. He could have warned him with a shot of the pistol but didn't. Hansi's own fear had paralyzed him in the moment of greatest need, and now his friend would die for it. Molten guilt penetrated every limb.

"What? What is it? Manolo! Don't go! Please!"

Manolo's lips quivered. Hansi bent down.

"Box," he said in a barely audible whisper.

Hansi clawed at the pack and got the flap open. Among the pliers, rags, and wire, he felt the edge of a corner within the folds of cloth.

"What is it?" he asked, pulling the bundle free, but his friend didn't answer. Manolo lay completely still, his face turned downhill, and jaw sagging awkwardly. Steam, rising from his bare head and torso, rose to join the fog-filled breeze, but Hansi knew at once. Manolo was dead.

Chapter Four

Hansi fell back against the bank, clamping his head in his own arms.

Manolo dead! It couldn't be true!

The burning fire erupted again, this time from deep inside his guts. In a violent wretch, they exploded onto the wet grass, covering the blades in a shimmering web of goo.

Hansi doubled over, clutching his midsection. The heaves continued, yielding nothing. He rolled on the ground like one struck by a sudden seizure, his eyes pressed tight to shut out the image of his dead friend sprawled out on the bank.

The moments passed without reckoning, their agony unbearable. Hansi wished he had been vaporized like the stone pillars beneath the bridge. Lost forever in the mist, without memory. Without guilt. The spasms gripped with the unrelenting force of a great invisible beast. He opened his mouth to scream, but there was no air inside to make the sound.

The battle between his stomach and his throat continued longer than Hansi could comprehend. Then, all at once, he fell still. His abdominal muscles throbbed in pain but were exhausted. The great monster had let go. In its place, a chill crept over him. He lay against the bank. Sharp-edged grass blades cut into his bare back. Stars still loomed overhead, but a sour taste in his mouth and the cheese-like smell of stomach acid penetrated his consciousness.

He sat up. A string of vomit, trailing off his chin, flapped in the breeze. He wiped it with the back of his hand.

All was quiet. The road up the hill was empty. Hansi's mind flashed awake.

I can't stay here.

Manolo's body lay where he fell. Steam from his head, still warm, rose up like a funeral pyre.

But I can't just leave him.

Hansi crawled over to the body of his friend. No longer did Manolo's expression bear the strain of danger. Yet it was not at peace either. The eyes stared blankly ahead; the mouth was parted as if caught in the middle of a word. His face was a mask, frozen unnaturally like a store mannequin.

Hansi expected the Germans to come down this road from up the hill. *Why else would Manolo have blown the bridge? But what good would one bridge do against the Wehrmacht, the massive armed forces of the Third Reich?*

He calculated that if the Germans found Manolo's body, they'd know he had blown the bridge. Eventually, they'd learn his name. His family in Luxembourg City would be in danger.

Hansi looked up the bank to the woods. He could hide Manolo there, but the top of the bank, though only a meter and a half above the lowest part of the ditch, might have been the top of the Matterhorn. Manolo was a large man. Hansi couldn't lift him.

The only way that remained was down. The ditch led to the river.

There is soft sand along the bank. I'll bury him there.

Positioning himself between Manolo's legs, he squatted down, gathered an ankle under each arm, and pulled. The slope, damp grass, and mud at the bottom of the ditch worked in Hansi's favor, and soon he was moving. But the tremors through the body, arms splayed behind, and bouncing head were a humiliation Hansi could not bear. He twisted his gaze away and pulled, his throat closing again. But the tears would not come. He had to do this.

At the approach to the bridge, the drainage ditch emptied into the river over a berm about three meters above the river's edge. Hansi pulled Manolo's feet to the lip of the bank and set them down. Then he moved to Manolo's upper half, dropped down to his knees, and slid his arms under his friend's shoulders.

The indignity of what he had to do next gave him pause. All that remained was to push the body and let gravity finish the job. Unaware of the hour, the presence of paratroopers was nonetheless evidence that the Germans would be coming soon. Hansi closed his eyes and pushed. The body slid, and Hansi let go. Only the sound, a soft thud, told him Manolo was down.

Down on the riverbank, Hansi pulled the knife from the sheath in his belt. Hansi had retrieved it from Manolo's knapsack, knowing somehow it would come in handy.

The river, curving slightly above the bridge, had deposited a large volume of silt in this spot. Hansi was surprised it wasn't flooded this time of the year, but gave it no further thought. The blade sunk easily into the soft earth. Within minutes, he had dug out a shallow pit. The soil, bearing the smooth edge of the blade, piled up like chunks of soft cheese.

It was not long before his bare torso was completely covered. The blackness clung to him like a layer of dead skin, and smelled that way. Decayed and fishy.

Enough.

Manolo's body had come to rest in an ugly heap below the spillway. He lay on his side, his back arched in an abnormal position, the lower arm caught under his body so that it looked as though he had been bound by the hands from behind. His legs were splayed out randomly like a ragdoll tossed to the ground.

Hansi rolled Manolo over on his back to gain enough leverage. The sight of his friend's ashen face, staring up at him in a terrible scold, stopped him short. Blades of grass were glued to his friend's cheeks and forehead, clods of dirt collected unnaturally in his open eye sockets. Once more, Hansi's stomach wretched.

Hansi brought Manolo's feet together and pulled him by the boots like before. The body shuddered. Manolo's head snapped backward. Hansi's stomach spasmed again. But the body moved. Hansi kept on, straining to his limit. Finally, he wrestled his friend into the grave.

And not an instant too soon. Up the valley, Hansi heard a rumble.

They're here.

Manolo's order echoed in Hansi's mind. *"Go to Vianden. The hotel there."*

Hansi spread the clumps of dirt hastily over the grave and scrambled up the bank. The road was empty. Above the trees, still only stars, cold and uncaring. In the distance, the sounds of the motors rose and fell, pushing away the nausea and guilt, making room for fear.

He began to run. His speed gathered and arms pumped. Mud, already dried and crusted in spots, cracked off his arms and shoulders and skittered down.

My suitcase. I need my suitcase.

Without a shirt, he might not freeze, but he would certainly stand out. He could never approach the hotel.

As he ran, Hansi's heart thundered. The thick metallic taste choked the back of his throat again. But his attention was fixed on the thin gaps between the trees.

Just then, a motor roared.

Hansi looked up. Through the trees, up the hill, a flash of movement. Then another.

Motorcycles!

A shiver rippled down Hansi's bare back. He closed the distance to the boulder and took cover, putting the boulder between himself and the road. The surface felt cool against his bare skin. No sooner had he knelt down than a motorcycle screamed past, its engine ripping a sharp popping sound as it coasted down the valley and around the curve. Others were sure to follow. He needed that suitcase.

As he remembered, it lay somewhere at the base of this very boulder, but on the road side. Perhaps even now it was visible in the growing light. He could dash now and risk being seen by a second rider. He could wait for others, let them pass, and then dash for the case. New sounds echoed up and down the road. They sounded like they were up the hill, but the way sound traveled in the trees and broken terrain, he could not be sure. But he had to act.

Hansi looked up to the last of the stars overhead. Not an hour earlier, at this very stone, he had been bored, feeling sorry for himself. Manolo was truly courageous. He had known everything—the danger of blowing the bridge, the risk of paratroopers. Most of all, Manolo had surely known he couldn't rely on Hansi. That's why he had tucked him safely at the rock.

Courage had blown the bridge; fear had cost a man his life. And now all Hansi could think of was how cold he was, and how badly he wanted a shirt from his suitcase. And yet how afraid he still was.

He stepped out from behind the rock. The suitcase was situated just where he thought it would be, in the strip of grass between the boulder and the edge of the road. He took another step forward, letting his eye drift up, and his heart stopped. A German soldier stood in the middle of the road, just downhill from where Hansi stood, not ten meters away. Beside him sat his motorcycle, silent. The soldier faced down the road, his knee-high boots spread wide apart. A machine pistol hung by a leather strap over his shoulder. He swung it slowly from side to side, presumably watching after his comrade, whom Hansi had seen only moments before.

Frozen in place, Hansi's mind churned at how he had missed this. He had seen two motorcycles higher up the hill. But in his haste to find cover, had lost track of them when he slipped behind the boulder. The sounds had deceived him. And now Hansi stood exposed beside the boulder. The moment the soldier turned, he would be discovered. A giant grip closed around Hansi's throat.

The suitcase was only centimeters away. Hansi glanced at it and then back at the soldier. He pondered his next move.

Forget the shirt.

He paused to calculate his retreat. Then another, more terrible thought popped.

My sketchbook. If they see the suitcase, they'll find my sketchbook. My name!

The forest was not far behind him and would provide cover in the darkness. But snatching the suitcase would alert the soldier. Hansi could dive behind the boulder, but would still have ten meters to the trees.

Enough time for the soldier to shoot me.

He was trapped.

The soldier continued to stare down the road, giving Hansi precious seconds to think. The sound of his companion's motorcycle fell away in the distance. He would be almost to the bridge.

Then Hansi's eyes settled on a small object at his feet. A stone, the size of a small potato. He had an idea.

Hansi knelt slowly, his eyes never leaving the soldier in the road. His fingers touched the wet grass and groped ahead. He found the stone. His fingertips climbed the smooth surface and dropped over the broken edge. He gripped it.

The soldier let out a long sigh and let one hand fall

from his machine pistol.

Hansi raised the stone and hurled it across the road as hard as he could. It sailed in silence for a brief instant, and then crashed into the brush on the far side.

Hansi didn't wait for a reaction. He was already moving for the suitcase. The German, surprised, snatched his machine pistol and spun toward the sound.

Hansi grabbed the handle of the suitcase and took off. A second later he was behind the boulder. The trees were not far. He leaned into the bank and churned his legs like pistons.

BRAT-AT-AT-AT!

Hansi's heart jumped. The rounds thudded into the bank and splintered in the trees. He ran like never before with energy from an unknown source. The grass and small shrubs swept underneath as if he was a galloping steed. Yet because of the early hour, everything was damp. The grass was slippery, his strides too frantic. Then came a spot where the ground dipped unexpectedly. Hansi lost his balance. His foot caught something hard. He slammed to the ground, headfirst. A bolt, white hot, reverberated from his chin out through the rest of his body, extending to his fingers.

The suitcase!

Dazed and panicked, Hansi flailed to get up. The soldier would be right behind. At any instant, the next burst might find their target. Hansi wondered what he would feel when bullets ripped through him. At the bridge, he had been afraid. He had frozen when Manolo needed him. Now there was no time.

Get up!

He found his hands and knees. The world spun without mercy, but he could make out the silhouette of the boulder against the starlit sky. The road was deserted.

Where was the soldier?

Hansi turned in the opposite direction. He was stuck in a no-man's land between the road and dense forest, his vision clouded. He staggered to his feet, determined to go on, but the ground sucked him back. Everything swirled. He wanted to clamp his eyes shut but to do so was certain death. He had to keep going.

At the edge of the trees, something moved.

Did the German race ahead? How?

Hansi pushed off the ground once more. Splotches of light flooded his vision. He couldn't tell whether what he had seen was real or imagined. But the German soldier had to be nearby, and Hansi had not imagined the bullets. Of that he was certain.

He crawled forward, expecting a hail of gunfire at any instant.

Then *WHAM!!!* Something smacked hard into his shoulder. It pressed hard and forced his face to the dirt. And wouldn't let up. The pressure increased, sending a shooting pain deep inside. Something was on him, holding him to the ground.

Then, a voice from the road.

"Er ist meine!"

Hansi could barely move. Still, he caught a glance. A shoe, not a boot, and a straight pant leg, wrapped in a blood-stained bandage and bound with a crude splint that had been fashioned from a pine stick. The smell of fishy mud, like the riverbank.

Then *CRACK!!!* The pain to the back of his head was sharp and short. And everything went black.

Chapter Five

Hansi smelled smoke. Yellow light splashed against a rough overhang of reddish rock. He wondered for a moment if he was on fire. His body felt like it.

He blinked to sharpen his focus. The fire was somewhere beyond the edge of what he realized was a cave.

What happened?

He rolled to one side and felt scratchy wool on his still bare shoulders. A layer of pine needles crunched beneath him as he moved.

Hansi tried to raise up, but his body erupted in searing stabs of pain. The top of his skull felt like someone had drilled a fist-sized hole and then filled it with sharp stones. That's when he remembered the shadowy figure by the edge of the forest.

He hit me.

Fighting through the pain, Hansi retracted his arm and tried to sit up. His vision washed white for an instant. He waited a moment, and the wave subsided.

He pushed up enough to see that he lay inside in a wide-mouthed cave. A campfire burned in the shadow of sandstone walls. The sky showed just the hint of dawn.

The flames drew his gaze. A handful of seated figures, dark in shadow, ringed the fire. The voices were muffled at first, then an explosion of laughter that sent the shadows racing back and forth across the cave wall.

Who are they?

Someone shushed the group to be quiet. Hansi adjusted his position on the wool blanket, which sent another tremor through him. He groaned. A figure stood up.

"He's awake." The voice was that of a boy.

The shadows fled and before Hansi could react, the group from around the campfire had filled the cave. Hansi counted at least six boys, mostly his own age, dirty-faced but smiling. One in front, apparently the leader, wore a flat-brimmed campaign hat from under which blonde locks spilled out. A red kerchief around his neck told Hansi who they were.

Boy Scouts. Did they know about the invasion?

A light clicked on, blinding Hansi.

"Put that away." The command was in French, not Luxembourgish, and the voice of a man, not a boy.

The light clicked off, leaving Hansi in near blackness.

"Can you stand?" the man asked. The voice was nearer, but the man remained hidden in shadow.

Still blinded, Hansi raised an arm for balance and twisted on the bedroll. Though his body rebelled, his will prevailed. He came up on one knee. The jolt to his head was nearly unbearable. He found the cave wall, steadied himself, and then rose to his feet. The blanket fell away. The cool air in the cave sent a shiver up his back.

"Give it to him," said the young leader. An instant later, one of the boys handed Hansi a shirt. It was the khaki of a scout uniform. With extreme care to keep the tremors at bay, Hansi pulled it up one arm and then the other. It was short in the sleeves and tight around the chest but covered enough to help against the cold.

"Thanks," he croaked.

A step was needed to keep balance, but it brought a torrent of throbs. Hansi wondered if his head, teetering on top of his body, might snap off his neck, leaving his lifeless body to wilt to the cave floor. He had to push through. A hand on the cave wall helped.

He edged a toe off the bedding onto the smooth stone. Every crunch and scrape seemed to be amplified by the stone chamber.

After some delay, a series of very careful steps brought Hansi from the shadows of the cave into the full light of the steamy fire. It hissed at the darkness, mingling the smell of smoke and moist earth with the cool night air. He raised his face to the light rain and remembered the grave of his friend.

"Where am I?" he asked, to no one in particular. The boys took the question as an invitation to close the circle around him. They seemed excited to see their visitor awake, but no one answered. They looked at each other as if waiting.

The man stepped forward, and for the first time, became visible in the light of the fire. He was not what Hansi would have expected in a Scoutmaster. Rather than the portly woodsman in field jacket, campaign hat, and binoculars that Hansi remembered when he had camped with his friend Georges's troop, this man had a muscular frame and sharp features. He wore a black leather jacket and matching beret tilted down across his forehead. A close-cropped mustache ran above the thin line of lips; yet his most distinct feature was his eyes—dark and serious. He leaned on a crutch fashioned from a limb, and his right ankle featured a bandage and home-made splint that stirred a distant memory.

"Please sit down," the man said. He directed Hansi to a canvas stool while he bent down and retrieved a blackened pot from the edge of the fire. The scouts seemed to react by instinct. The next moment they produced an enameled cup, which the man filled with something steamy and hot and one of the boys handed it to him. The heat brought relief to Hansi's swollen hands, and the strong scent of the coffee transported him to Manolo's restaurant. The pangs of guilt returned.

"The Boche bastards nearly got you," the man said, continuing in French. The accent seemed different than his French teacher Madame Dubois and took some getting used to.

"Let's hope that soldier rides his motorcycle better than he shoots. He hit everything but you. Sure, you've got a nasty bump on the head, but consider yourself lucky. Those men shoot first and ask the questions after. Another millimeter and, well, you'd be on the other side now."

The other side. Where I belong.

"How did I get here?"

The scouts exchanged proud glances and knowing smiles.

"Introductions, first. Boys?" The man nodded to the eager faces surrounding their visitor. The boys introduced themselves in turn. Hansi heard Heng, Mill, Charel, and a few others before he lost track. His head throbbed a steady beat that drowned out the details.

There was a stretch of silence before the man extended his hand. "And you are?"

Reflexively, Hansi took it. He instantly regretted it, because his other hand, the one holding the cup, was weak and unsteady. Scalding liquid splashed on his legs. He bolted upright, at the same time as he let go of the cup. The boys jumped back like he had dropped a grenade. The man bore the worst of it, but he never flinched. His hand, rough and muscular, never let go. His eyes remained fixed on Hansi, strong behind the disarming smile.

Some of the liquid sizzled on the fire. A column of steam, strong of the smell of wet ashes, rose from the fire. The boys began dusting themselves off and tried to stifle their laughs.

"My apologies," the man said. "You needn't have bothered. Please, sit down."

The man hopped and sat down heavily on a folding canvas camp stool and the boys followed. One of them reset the one Hansi had knocked over when the coffee proved too hot. Hansi sank down, trying to fight back the never-ending waves of pain, not to mention the embarrassment.

"So, what is your name?" one of the boys asked.

"Hansi."

"Our pleasure," the man offered, retrieving a pipe and leather pouch from his pocket. He tapped it against his palm a few times and then packed it with shreds of tobacco. With careful deliberation it seemed, he lit a sprig from the pile of branches and brought it to the bowl. An earthy aroma mixed with the ash, coffee, and rain. Hansi's body clamored for rest, but his mind tried to remain sharp in the presence of this mysterious stranger.

"Heng, why don't you tell our guest how he came to be here." The man tossed the sprig back into the fire.

The boy with the wide-brimmed hat stood up, confirming what Hansi thought earlier. Heng was apparently the leader. Athletic-looking, his chiseled features and blonde curls across his forehead reminded Hansi of the pictures he'd seen of Germany's Hitler Youth. Pristine, strong, and confident. Hitler's future warriors in Boy Scout uniforms. Heng looked to be a year or two older than Hansi. His was the most complete uniform among them, from the kerchief to the khaki shirt and matching trousers. When the man called him, he had jumped up, not quite at attention, but like one does when called on to speak at school.

"We heard shots," he began, evidently proud. The boys' eyes were wide. He laughed. "We had no idea the war had started. We thought it was hunters, or poachers. When we got to the river, we practiced our tracking skills. We crept carefully down to the river, and that's when we saw everything."

Another pang of guilt sliced Hansi's heart.

"The most incredible explosion—" Heng seemed at a loss for words. "From below the bridge. It was—" His mouth hung open.

"Start from the beginning!" a voice cried out.

"Let Roby tell it," said another. "He's better at stories anyway."

Heng nodded, apparently unembarrassed at his failure to capture the magnitude of the tale. He ushered a boy forward with a sweep of his hand.

Roby nudged forward while the other boys made way. A short, round, unassuming figure stepped into the light, his face a mix of surprise and pride at the recognition from his peers.

"We were asleep in the cave, some around the fire. That's when we heard the shots—*POP POP. POP POP POP!* Everyone froze." Roby's eyes were round like him. "Peter says, *'That's no hunting rifle!'* So Heng makes the plan. He gives strict orders. Single file. Three second intervals. Tree to tree. A real scouting expedition."

Hansi studied the other faces. The boys were enraptured. This wasn't just an excellent camp story; it was an epic tale in which each one played a part.

"Heng plunges into the forest. Our hearts are racing. We follow, one by one, as he gives the signal. Each one passes it along to the next. We were silent as Indians."

"Near the river, Heng spreads us along a line. Mill anchored the far left flank, I the right." Roby exchanged proud glances with one of the boys. "The younger ones in between us."

"I wasn't afraid!" one of the voices called out.

"You followed orders," Heng interjected. "That's the important thing. That's what makes you brave."

Roby continued. "We saw two figures clamber up the north bank. A big man. And someone else—was that you?"

Hansi nodded. He didn't want to hear the story. Roby went on.

"Then the bridge went off. The sound broke our eardrums. The shock wave flattened us. We couldn't imagine what would have happened to you two. The forest fell down on us. Branches, sticks, rocks—it pelted us like a hailstorm."

Hansi's throat closed as he saw the picture in his mind. The main blast missed him and Manolo but was channeled up the canyon toward the cave and the troop.

"We figured you both were blown to bits. But it was too dark, and we were caught in a cloud so thick we could hardly breathe. My face was pressed in the mud, it was so awful. Heng sent word down the line to stay put. Naturally we obeyed. We waited twenty, maybe thirty minutes. Without a sound."

Hansi felt sick at the memory of what happened next. Roby seemed oblivious.

"Finally, we could see the faint light of dawn in the sky ahead of us. The mist rolled back down the valley and there you were, down by the river. Bent over, digging. Were you hiding something?"

Hansi shook his head, determined. He would not be made to tell the story. There was nothing exciting about it, nothing to be proud of, no part of it he ever hoped to speak of again.

Roby gave Hansi a curious look and paused, but not for long. "You climbed out again, and headed up the hill."

Someone nudged Roby from behind.

"Don't forget the part about the shirt."

"Oh yes," Roby said. "We noticed you were no longer wearing your shirt."

"It was me who noticed!" the voice called out from the dark. "I saw it first."

Roby seemed flustered for a moment. "Ok, Pauly, it was you who noticed."

"Give the boy the proper credit!" someone else said.

Light laughs rippled among the boys.

"Who cares?" another, louder voice shot out. "He was there. He knows all this. Get on with it."

The troop fell silent. Only the breeze, vibrating the young spring leaves above, could be heard in the night. The words had the effect of breaking a spell. Roby's shoulders sagged and he sighed.

It was then that the man stepped forward.

"That was a fine tale, Roby," he said. "But Charel's right. Hansi *was* there. He knows this part."

He turned to face Hansi.

"What happened to your companion?"

Hansi felt as if his face had been shoved in the hot coals. He stood up and stared out into the darkness.

"He's dead."

No one said a word. Not one breath seemed to escape.

The man's hand came to rest on Hansi's shoulder.

"You continued north up the Vianden road. German advanced units were already across the border. Motorcycle troops, heading south, intercepted him."

He paused as if for effect. Hansi looked up. Their eyes met. Hansi got the feeling he should be quiet and listen carefully to the next part. He had no interest in saying anything more.

"I was at the edge of the forest. The Germans had

Hansi in their sights. But they had no reason to pursue him. Soldiers of this kind are trained to keep the roads clear, to scout for resistance. Hansi was injured, but no threat to them. I pulled him to safety."

The boys erupted in chatter. The story had reached its climax. To Hansi, the facts weren't exactly right. Something was missing.

But what?

He tried to piece the scene back together in his head. The boulder, the German on the motorcycle—the suitcase! Yes! That's it!

He remembered grabbing the suitcase, turning to run, and—

"Let's get you something to eat." The slap on his arm, from the man, was like an earthquake. Hansi's head split open. Searing pain like hot lava gushed from the fissures. He had forgotten he was standing, and now realized his legs were about to give out.

"Are you all right?" the man asked, now helping Hansi back to his camp stool. "Heng, your canteen. Boys, give room. He needs some air."

The world, already dark, faded further away. Hansi let his head sink down to his knees and closed his eyes. Though the fire had dwindled to deep orange coals, its heat radiated over Hansi's neck and shoulders and down his back.

When Hansi lifted his head, the boys were gone. Only the man remained, the canteen open and ready. Hansi took a sip. It was the best drink he had ever had. He sucked down more. Next came a sandwich of thick ham and butter. He hadn't realized how hungry he had become. It hurt to chew and swallow but was a welcome gift.

"Now that we're alone, I need to ask you a few questions." The man's voice no longer carried the light, confident air of a scoutmaster. It was serious.

Hansi wiped the last drops from his chin. "You don't look like a scoutmaster," he said.

The man's dark eyes sparkled. "Nor you a scout. But you are perceptive, that I grant you. And by the time we finish our discussion, I think you'll be glad for that."

The man drew in a breath. The tobacco glowed in the pipe's bowl, illuminating his features from below. Like Heng, the man's face was sharp, the cheekbones high and strong, his nose an efficient use of skin and cartilage. When he wasn't running his fingers over his mustache, he was adjusting his beret or pulling at the collar of his sweater, almost as if he were unaccustomed to it.

"What time is it?" Hansi asked. "What day?"

The man glanced at the glowing dial of his watch. "Not quite four-thirty. It will be light soon."

"Friday?"

The man nodded. Hansi felt like he left home a month ago, not four and a half hours ago.

"I know something about you already, Hansi. Your father is Alain Broussard, yes?"

Hansi's heart jumped. *How did the man know, unless—*

"You know him?"

"Never met him. Although I expect to."

Pierre?

The man paused and lowered his voice. "Unless that was him you left at the bridge."

"No! My father didn't come. He sent me in his place."

The man's face sharpened for an instant and then relaxed. "Well then, I'm glad he is well. Your companion—he must have been Manolo then."

Hansi nodded.

"I was to meet your father and Manolo earlier."

"Then you are Pierre? Manolo told me to find you."

Hansi's memory sparked. Manolo had said to find him at the hotel in Vianden.

"Yes, Pierre. I'm with the French Resistance. Manolo, your father, and I are working together."

"That was you on the phone?"

Pierre paused. "When?"

"Last night. Remember, I picked up the phone. You thought I was my father. Our voices sound similar."

Pierre slid his jaw sideways and looked right at Hansi. "Yes. That was me. Of course. So much has happened—and gone wrong—I'd forgotten. Speaking of that, what went wrong at the bridge?"

Hansi looked out past the cave's mouth at the silhouette of trees, just becoming visible against the predawn sky. Mist in the undergrowth was disturbed from time to time by puffs of breeze.

"It doesn't matter now."

"It does indeed," Pierre said. "The mission was to be routine. The bridge is not on the border. It's not on the strategic route from east to west, which will soon be flooded by troops and tanks. And yet German paratroopers arrive to try to disrupt the operation. Don't you find that strange?"

Hansi returned his attention to the conversation. Strange was well down any list of words he would have for his past few hours.

Pierre continued. "That means someone on the inside, someone in the Luxembourg or French Resistance, is sharing plans with German intelligence."

"Gestapo?"

"Any number of groups. But they knew exactly where to land and exactly where to strike. So, I need to know exactly what happened. Every detail."

"What does it matter?"

"The more I know, the better I will be able to uncover the mole, whoever it is, and neutralize it before it disrupts the next phase of the operation."

Hansi's interest spiked at the mention of *the next phase*. The more he pondered Pierre's question, the more it made sense to him. There had to be a good reason for blowing up a bridge that, on a map, would have been the last bridge in Luxembourg the German Army would cross on their way to France.

"Tell me, Hansi. Everything."

By now, the warmth of the fire, the fatigue, the injuries—perhaps even the hint of some larger purpose behind Manolo's mission, conspired against Hansi's inhibitions. Truth was, he needed to tell someone what had happened. But when it came to the exact details of Manolo's death, Hansi was paralyzed by shame. Something inside wanted to scream what he had done. How he had tried to be a hero, but the result had been disastrous. But Pierre was no priest. Father Jean was someone Hansi could have confessed to. But he was gone too, dead at the hands of the same Germans that tried to kill Manolo. *And would have killed me in the woods, if they could.* The alloy of guilt and anger boiled in his gut like molten steel. His sinuses tightened and clogged.

He told Pierre the basic facts. Crashed truck, a plane, shots, explosion, Manolo dead and buried. A German soldier by the boulder. Pierre knew the rest.

When Hansi finished, Pierre pulled the pipe from his mouth, and let his shoulders fall. "I'm sorry about your friend," he said.

Hansi let the words drift past. "What happened to you?" he asked.

Pierre's eyes darted. "Oh, it was foolish really. Running around in the dark, these rocks. I stepped right into a crack."

"Is it broken?"

"I don't think so. Hurts like the devil, though. These boys were only too anxious to try out their first aid skills. Not a bad job of it. I should be core-healthy in a day or so."

The phrase "core-healthy" struck Hansi as odd, but he figured it was a French idiom he didn't know.

"So, what happens next? What is this next phase?"

Pierre let out a faint smile, returned the pipe to his pocket, and stood up.

"When we started this conversation, I told you you'd be glad I wasn't a scoutmaster. Something else you'll be glad of, which you may not believe when I tell you, is that it is better if you don't know the details of the next phase."

"Why not? I made it this far. I watched my friend die. The Germans did it. I'm going to pay them back. I have a right to know." Hansi was standing now too, facing Pierre. His head was punishing him for it, but anger was stronger.

"Of course you do, son. I respect all that you have done. You have been brave beyond your years. Your father must have known that or he wouldn't have sent you. But right now, and perhaps always, you must not know what happens next."

"Why not?"

"You saw how narrow your escape was last night. Suppose the Germans catch you next time. They ask you questions. You make up answers. They ask more. You lie more. They don't believe you. Why? Germans never ask questions they don't already know the answers to. They will torture you. And you will tell them everything I would tell you about the next phase. Things you never needed to know. Things that will not only cost you your life, but the lives of others involved too. That's why I can't tell you."

Pierre had lied. Hansi wasn't glad for this answer, or for Pierre's confirmation that he was no scoutmaster. But there was still a measure of relief in his words. Hansi could find his father and join Maman for whatever time she had left. Pain returned and pushed back the anger. He slumped back down on the stool.

"But that doesn't mean I don't need your help," Pierre said.

Chapter Six

As dawn lit the forest, Hansi left the camp and its strange leader behind. With nothing but their compass to guide them, two scouts, led by Heng, marched straight into the dense darkness below the pine, elm, and maple canopy.

On any other morning the forest would have still been asleep under the heavy dew. But now, even before the sun had peaked over the horizon, it was alive with sound. Not the sounds of nature. Overhead, endless formations of warplanes, like thundering black ravens, streamed west toward France. Nearly invisible through the canopy of foliage overhead, the constant drone spread a wash of dread through the woods.

"We must avoid the trails," Heng counseled, his eyes jumping up and down from the mass of trees ahead to the compass cradled in a hand pressed against his stomach. He extended the free hand toward some point out in front, squinted like he was aiming a rifle, and then studied the compass. Occasionally, he would mumble something to himself before setting off. The process was a mystery to Hansi. But Heng seemed confident, so they trampled on. Every hundred meters or so, he would stop to take another reading.

After several stages, Hansi's curiosity woke up.

"What are you doing?"

Heng took a moment for the question to register. He continued a few more steps and swatted at a branch. Then he turned to Hansi.

"Well, since you know we're taking you to the main road, I assume you're asking how I know the way. Pierre showed me a map. The bridge is that way." He pointed to his right, which Hansi calculated was east. "He wants us to head west-northwest for about a kilometer. Two-hundred ninety-two degrees or best I can reckon." He looked down at the compass and then down the slight slope. He pointed ahead. "Pauly— see that pine down there, growing at an angle. That's next."

He held out the compass for Hansi. It was round like a pocket watch, but instead of a tapered edge, it had a cylindrical band that formed the edge. The band was painted black except for the narrow rim of silver.

"Hold it flat against your stomach and be real still. Let the needle settle down."

Among the several hands in the compass, Hansi fixed his eyes on the one that spun freely. With every twitch and jiggle, the needle danced nervously. Hansi concentrated. The point settled almost straight ahead from where he stood.

"That's north," Heng said. "Now carefully rotate the compass until those two dots at three-sixty line up with the needle."

Hansi obeyed, and the needle leapt to life until he had calmed himself once more.

"Now Pierre showed me a map. The shortest path from camp to the Vianden road is two-ninety-two. That's west-northwest."

Hansi looked up. The needle reacted. "How do we go that way?"

"Simple. Rotate that knob on the side of the compass. Point it to two-ninety-two."

Hansi found the small protrusion on the band of the compass.

"Pull it out like you do to wind a watch."

With only minor tremors, Hansi extracted the tiny wheel with his fingernails and began to twist. A second needle, which rested flat against the compass face, rotated around the dial. Hansi found the halfway spot between the two-eighty and three-hundred marks, and then the first hash to the right. Heng leaned over.

"That's it. Now carefully turn your body in the direction of the arrow."

Hansi complied. This time the needle seemed to better behave.

"Now look up."

Hansi let his eyes float up and there it was—the bent-over pine tree Heng had identified to Pauly.

Hansi felt a surge of pride at the accomplishment. He gave the compass back to Heng.

"How much longer?"

"According to the map, the road should be about two kilometers further. Lesson over. Let's get a move on."

They hiked down to the listing pine tree, and Heng made Hansi take the next one. As they hiked, Hansi wished he had been a Boy Scout. He would have enjoyed camping. Sleeping outside, cooking his own food over an open fire, learning how to live in the forest—it all sounded adventurous. But the dream couldn't take up residence now. The boys seemed unaware of the real danger all around them. As Hansi watched Heng and Pauly, true comrades enjoying themselves with the task, he envied them. If only they knew what he had seen and done the night before. How he had watched while Manolo was ambushed by the paratrooper. How he had frozen with fear at the moment his friend needed him most. The guilt and shame rose inside like bile that corroded away the lining of his stomach and throat. It made him nearly sick again. When Heng offered Hansi another chance to use the compass, he refused.

"Suit yourself, city boy," Heng laughed. The words penetrated, and embarrassment gurgled up inside Hansi.

He lost count of the stages. The joy of the task was replaced by a heavy fog of misery. He trudged behind the pair in silence, shaming himself now for how quickly his mood changed and wanting now nothing more than to disappear in the woods. They crossed the river upstream from the bridge, at a place where it was wide and shallow. The cold water rippled over flat sandstones. Hansi let his thoughts be absorbed by the rushing sounds.

They continued on, up the far side valley. The climb grew steep, Hansi worked hard to keep up with his guides, and he felt the sweat gather on his back and forehead. The sky above grew brighter and brighter, a pale blue. The sun would appear soon, he thought.

Finally, at an outcropping of sandstone boulders, stacked up like blocks of cheese, Heng stopped. He studied the course they had just completed and made a count on his fingers.

"That should do it. You can make it from here."

"What?" Hansi said, closing the distance, winded.

"Pierre doesn't want us going any further," Heng explained. "The Germans, he says, are on the road just north of here. About another kilometer or so I'd say. He doesn't want us raising any suspicion. Just head that way."

Hansi studied the woods ahead. He tried to pick out something unique like Heng and Pauly had.

The pair emptied their rucksacks of a few pieces of fruit, some cheese, and a section of a hard baguette. Pauly slung a canteen over Hansi's head. The canvas strap dug into his neck.

"You're almost a proper scout, now, city boy," Heng laughed. He reached in his pocket.

"Here, that should do it." He thrust an object in Hansi's hand. The compass.

"We got you close enough that if you just head straight north you should hit the road without a problem."

Hansi looked down at the dial. The north-marking dots shifted back and forth like a pair of nervous eyes staring at him. His hands could not steady it. The needle wagged left and right, as if a finger scolding him.

Heng took it from Hansi and twisted the dial. When he gave it back, the directional needle was pointed at one-eighty.

"Don't forget. Tomorrow night. Find the spot and head south. We'll meet you right here by this dead tree."

Hansi looked at the fallen pine. It lay wedged between two smaller trees to form a large triangle. At the base, roots clumped with dirt hung upright. Needles still hung from the branches; the tree had only recently been plucked from the soil. Everything reminded Hansi of Manolo.

"How will I see the compass?" Hansi asked. "I have no flashlight."

Pauly stepped forward. Up until now, he had been Heng's silent partner, moving out in front. His face was red and shiny from exertion, his wire-rimmed glasses, which Hansi had not noticed until now, were smeared with sweat and dirt and hung at the tip of his nose. He pointed at the compass face.

"The dots and dial are like a watch. Radioactive paint. They glow in the dark."

Hansi knew about watches that could be seen in the dark. The clock beside his mother's bed was like that.

"Radioactive? Is it dangerous?"

Pauly chuckled. "Not that I know of."

Heng slapped him on the back. "Get going, city boy. Before it gets dark and you need those dots."

It was barely past sunrise. Hansi didn't appreciate the humor. He took another look at the compass, found a tree to the north, and took a step.

Struck by a thought, Hansi stopped.

"Does Pierre seem—well, kind of strange to you?"

Heng flashed a grin at Pauly, and then back at Hansi.

"He is French, you know."

Pauly huffed a laugh.

Hansi pressed on. "But I don't get it. Your troop is camping in the forest, this stranger shows up, and all at once you do whatever he asks."

Heng stooped over and grabbed a stick. He snapped it in his hands. "I guess I never thought about it much."

"We never met a spy before," Pauly offered. "And sure, he's a bit odd. But the war is here, and he wants to kick the Germans out. We're too young to head off to France and join the Army. So I guess we're just trying to help."

"Our duty," Heng said. "As scouts."

Hansi stretched his neck and rubbed a hand across it. He admired the boys and their confidence. All he knew was doubt and shame and fear. He thanked them, turned, and trudged off into the trees.

Orienteering the last kilometer wasn't as bad as he expected. He moved from point to point, tree to tree, just as Heng had taught. The longer he hiked, the more he concentrated on the landmark ahead, the more Hansi's mind edged away from the pit in his heart. But never far enough. A crease in the hillside reminded him of the ditch where Manolo died. The faintest crack of a branch hearkened back to the gunshots. The shimmer of the dark rivulets of runoff through patches of mud brought him to the terrible sight, forever stained in his memory, of the uncontrollable blood that covered Manolo's chest.

The sun had crept over the roof of the forest when Hansi came within sight of the road. The rumble of motor traffic came almost as a relief until he caught sight of the road. He may as well have stepped onto another planet.

The German army was a giant, rumbling, gray, articulated monster. It stretched as far as the eye could see both east and west along the road to Vianden. Every manner of motorized vehicle moved in the center of the road. Slower foot soldiers and horses marched along the edges. The beast ambled west like an undulating dragon, leaving no room for traffic east except for single-file pedestrians, of which there were none. Tanks, supreme in the formation, scraped over the pavement, belching diesel fumes in swirls behind them. Commanders, perched atop the turrets, served as the eyes and ears of the steel monsters. Black headsets clamped over their ears. They spoke into microphones and the beast would respond. Clumsy turns, accomplished by stopping one track and spinning on it, kept the beast within the confines of the narrow forest road. But only barely, it seemed.

Here Hansi caught his first sight of the planes in the open sky above the road. Waves of twin- and quad-engine bombers soared highest in slow, diamond-shaped formations. Stukas, the single-propellered dive-bombers with claw-like fixed landing gear hanging below their fuselages, drifted in tight V's like hawks riding the drafts. But the most impressive machines to Hansi were the Messerschmidt 109's, speed-demons of the skies. These sleek craft sliced through the sky almost in advance of the sounds of their engines. They bounced along the treetops so low Hansi caught sight of a white scarf around the neck of one of the pilots. By reflex he ducked when the first few passed over, until he realized no one else on the road seemed concerned.

He had to focus his attention back to earth to avoid stumbling into the road.

Giant open-cabbed trucks, whose back wheels had

been replaced with tracks like a tank, pulled enormous wheeled guns. Hansi knew from the newsreels these were the notorious 88's, named for the 88-millimeter shell they shot. Like an oversized hunting rifle, the gun could drop its target whether it flew in the air or crawled on the land.

Other canvas-topped trucks, that looked like everyday delivery trucks except for their gray coat of paint, bounced obediently in formation. Interspersed among the tanks, halftracks, and Opal trucks were the smaller vehicles—motorcycles with machine guns mounted on their sidecars, like Hansi had seen the night before; and the strange-looking kübelwagen, the flat-paneled command car with a folding windscreen.

Soldiers and horses marched on either side of the vehicles. Dark steel helmets, stretched in a line down the road, bobbed up and down like the legs of an enormous centipede. The soldiers' rifles jutted in the air as they marched. Their backpacks, lashed with charcoal gray blankets, rode high on their backs. Canteens, ammo belts, knives—every piece of metal seemed to clink together. This army would not sneak up on anyone; it would crush it by the sheer bulk of its size.

Hansi couldn't move. Bumps had formed on his arms and rippled down his back. It was the most terrifyingly awesome spectacle he had ever seen.

"Wie Gehts?" a voice shouted.

Hansi snapped awake. A handful of soldiers, broad smiles beaming through their dirt-smudged faces, were waiting for his response as they marched past.

He was caught by surprise. Why would the soldiers

notice him? Was he gawking?

Hansi stared as the soldiers marched by, necks straining as they wheeled past.

"He's about to piss himself!" one of them said, to a roll of laughter. Hansi spun away and moved quickly down the road in the opposite direction. From then on, he hardly looked up at the passing army.

The road swept around a hill and began its descent toward the village. The army stretched as far as Hansi could see. Around the next curve, the valley opened up, and he beheld a wide expanse, anchored by a steep berg to his left, upon which sat the ruins of the old Vianden Chateau that looked down on the tidy village on the other side of the tiny Our river. The narrow ribbon of water appeared from behind the berg, wandered south along the western edge of the village, and disappeared behind the rise of hills to Hansi's right. A tiny spire marked the center of the village, and a sprinkling of homes and buildings that followed the contours of the hills east of the river. Yet as the chief feature, the vast German army wound down the hill, through the town and south along the main road. The mass of men, beast, and machine cut a path through the countryside without opposition. Yet, almost supernaturally, it defied gravity as it swept uphill through the forest; an unstoppable hoard both magnificent and ominous. Hansi's legs weakened at the sight.

To make his way down the hill, Hansi had to keep to the ditch alongside the road on the opposite side of the chateau. Halfway down, he noticed a small, gravel road that peeled off the main Vianden road and disappeared in the woods. He had never been to Vianden before, but guessed this road led to the ruins. Straight-faced soldiers stood guard at the road. Occasionally while he descended, a command vehicle or motorcycle would zip up alongside the column and take this road. Atop the peak, a collection of vehicles surrounded the ancient chateau, whose lone tower, moss-covered and jagged against the blue sky, stood unaware of the soldiers crawling like bees below. The brick and stone buildings that ringed its base and formed the outer wall were largely intact, and these were the center of activity. Men in and out, carrying desks, chairs, file cabinets, and boxes. Some sort of command post, Hansi guessed.

He approached the stone bridge at the edge of the village. Traffic had paused at the far side. The foot soldiers were held back by a military policeman in black boots that rose to his knee. He held a pair of paddles. The red one held the line of soldiers. With the green one, he waved at the commander atop a tank to cross. His movements were urgent, and he bobbed his head in rhythm.

"Mach schnell! Mach schnell!" he urged.

Hansi looked beyond the bridge, past the queue of soldiers and line of vehicles waiting to cross.

There it was! A mustard-colored silhouette to his left, with bold brown lettering: *Hotel d'Vianden.*

Without thinking, he took the opportunity to cross what at the moment was an empty bridge. He jogged, keeping to the wall that rose on the bridge's edge. The stones, round and smooth, were cold to the touch as he swept over. The tank roared and leapt forward onto the bridge. Startled, Hansi slammed his knee into the hard stone and looked up. The tank clawed up the bridge. It had not lined up parallel to the road and was heading straight for him! The commander caught sight of him and screamed into his headset. The tracks locked, the metal monster rocked forward. The steel suspension screamed, but was surprisingly nimble. The tank stopped but a meter from where Hansi stood pressed against the wall. An instant longer, and Hansi had no doubt the beast would have crushed him, bashed through the side of the bridge, and plunged into the river.

The commander stretched toward him like the head of a turtle straining out from its shell. He was screaming again, this time at Hansi. The sound was lost in the thunder of the tank.

The commander barked another order. The track nearest Hansi clawed at the pavement, spitting bits of asphalt out behind it. It belched an oily cloud. Hansi covered his nose and pressed against the wall.

Then the track found its grip. The giant beast twisted away. Nearly straight on the road now, it thundered again. With a sharp crack of the gears, it jerked forward, passing within a meter of where he stood.

Hansi ran down the far side of the bridge. Soldiers, log-jammed behind the military policemen, followed his movements. Frantic, he burst through their line, head down, clawing past them. Somehow, despite the press of bodies, dark, woolen, metal, the sea of gray parted in front of him. He crossed an intersection just beyond the bridge and found the safety of a sidewalk on the far side, filled with civilians. They were bunched together, filling the sidewalk from the front of the dress shop to the street, and spilling into it. But they were facing south, away from Hansi, toward the center of the village.

Hansi came up to the edge and discovered why. The commotion was up ahead, just outside the Boulangerie Vianden. The entire length of the shop, as well as several meters beyond in either direction, had been cordoned off by military police, who held back the onlookers. Positioned at the far edge of the space was a tripod, upon which sat a camera, with twin film canisters affixed on top.

Someone grabbed Hansi and pulled him from the edge of the crowd. A man, about sixty, wearing a navy blue beret pulled down to his bushy eyebrows, maneuvered Hansi to the front of the line.

"Hurry, son, your chance to be in Hollywood!"

"What's going on?" he asked.

The man raised his arm, but Hansi could see only gray wool, as the man's coat appeared too big for him. Then the hand emerged, bony and knotted. He pointed to the scene ahead.

"You'll see!" he said.

A soldier Hansi hadn't noticed before, standing next to the camera, raised a black megaphone to his mouth. The other hand, which held what looked to be a rider's crop, raised high in the air.

"Action!"

There was a brief pause, and then the tinkle of a bell. The door of the boulangerie opened, and out stepped a young woman, in a bright spring dress. She carried a bouquet of flowers in the crook of her arm and swung out the door with the sweeping movement of a dancer. A young man, who was just as smartly dressed in a dark suit and stylish fedora cocked just to the side, like Hansi had seen on the manikins through the windows of the fancy clothing stores along the Grand Rue in Luxembourg City, followed with graceful steps just behind. The woman's face lit up when she caught sight of the column in the street. She beckoned her companion, and together they waved in perfect unison. The joy on their faces was as real as Hansi had ever seen—in a Hollywood movie. They skipped to the curb, the camera following their movement. The thin soldier with the megaphone snapped his riding crop toward the street. A line of soldiers Hansi hadn't noticed before, but which had been waiting along the curb, began to march. The couple met the first of the line and, with mock spontaneity, the woman raised the bouquet. The soldier paused. The woman handed him a blossom, which he inhaled with a grand breath, a contented sigh, and a respectful tip of his helmet. The man produced a sack of apples and began to pass them to the soldier's comrades. Smiles and nods of thanks all around. The column moved on.

"Cut!" boomed from the megaphone. The director trembled in place.

"*Ausgezichnet! Simply wonderful!*" he echoed.

Hansi turned back to the older man. His face was twisted in anger, and he was gnawing at his bottom lip.

"What is this?" Hansi asked.

"Propaganda! Propaganda, pure and simple!"

Heads snapped around. Faces drained of color, frightened at the man's outburst.

"Mind your own business!" he snarled. "Their blasted machines and all this march, march, march is too loud for my old ears. Besides, they're drunk on their own power to care about a shriveled-up old man like me. Turn around all of you! Leave me be!"

Hansi tugged at his coat. "I don't get it. Why are they filming?"

The old man spun back around. His eyes, veined and yellow, strained out of their sockets. "You missed it, son. They all climbed off the back of a truck. The director, the soldiers, those two with their presents. It's all pretend! The *volk* back home will watch this on Saturday night at the movie theater and think we Luxembourgers couldn't wait for the Boche to march in. They'll send it to England, America. The world will think we Luxembourgers are nothing but German cousins. Just what they want."

Someone pushed up against Hansi from behind. Hansi stepped sideways to narrowly miss bumping into the old man. Then all at once, the source of commotion was apparent—a boy, about seven or eight, green cap bent forward as he burrowed toward the front of the crowd. He held something in his fist as he plowed ahead. In an instant he, had broken through the line and was free in the space reserved for filming.

"Filthy Boche!" he yelled, then drew his fist back and let fly. The stone sailed in a perfect arc over the open space. Before anyone had realized what the boy had done, the projectile smacked against the megaphone which hung at the director's side. The stone skittered harmlessly away, but the effect was like a grenade. The director jumped back, terror gripping his already tightly drawn expression. The megaphone bounced and rolled toward the sidewalk. The director's foot caught a leg of the tripod; he continued down, the camera staggered and fell on top of him. Stunned, a shock wave knocked the crowd back.

Hansi was struck by instant fear.

The old man burst out laughing. He stepped out from the line. "Bravo, young man! Well done!" He slapped the boy on the back and continued to congratulate him while the crowd eased further back.

Hansi felt the hair on his neck jump to attention. Something terrible was going to happen. He watched, unable to move, as the director collected himself, righted the camera, and snapped an order.

The response was swift. Real soldiers with real rifles, led by a military policeman with his pistol drawn, formed a circle around the boy and the old man. The crowd seemed to collectively stop breathing. The old man hardly noticed until the policeman stepped forward and clamped hard on the boy's arm. He raised his hands in protest.

"Leave him alone! He's just a boy!"

Just as it exited his mouth, the last word was cut off by the butt of the policeman's Luger. The old man fell, instantly unconscious from the blow. The hollow sound of his head striking the sidewalk horrified Hansi. Blood began to drain from the man's mouth onto the stones. The crowd froze.

When the boy saw what the policeman had done, he

dropped down to the old man's side and began to roll him back. The man was unconscious, and blood covered the lower half of his face.

"Look what you've done!" the boy yelled at the German. His cap had slipped off, revealing sweeping locks of rusty red hair. "You probably killed him!"

The accusation seemed only to inflame the policeman. The eyes of every soldier at the scene turned to him, waiting for his response.

Hansi was amazed. While his own terror was white hot on his face, the boy seemed completely fearless. The German was going to strike him, but he either didn't know or didn't care. He seemed driven by justice. He would suffer worse than the old man.

The soldier stepped closer and raised his pistol. The boy drew his hands up.

"Wait!" Hansi cried, leaping free of the crowd. All at once, he was in the open on the sidewalk, exposed. He strode to the ring of soldiers and pushed through the perimeter.

The policeman held his blow.

"*Entschuldigen! Entschuldigen!*" he begged, hoping the German would impress the officer. "*Meine bruder ist ein enfant!* He doesn't know any better. Please, sir, let me take him home. I'll give him a good thrashing! I'll teach him some basic respect. Please, sir, don't trouble yourself any further. Surely your men have more important concerns than this child!"

Hansi didn't know what had come over him, but he found his hand taking hold of the boy by the hair and shaking him.

"Owww!" he cried, trying to break free.

"There's more of that waiting at home for you! Just wait 'til Papa hears about this!"

"I don't have..."

"Silence!" Hansi gave another shake. The boy howled again.

One of the nearby soldiers elbowed his comrade and laughed. "He should be in uniform, that one!"

"In a year or two, he will!" the other replied. Others joined the chorus of chuckles.

"Enough!" snapped the policeman. "You two—take them both into custody! And get this man off the sidewalk."

The smiles fell off the men's faces, replaced now with uncertain, confused stares. The second soldier, a smooth-faced boy who seemed only a few years older than Hansi, pushed his steel helmet back a centimeter or two and stepped forward.

"But Herr Oberst, where will we take them? They are *children* after all."

The policeman jutted his pistol up in the air, pointing vaguely west. "Up the mountain. They are holding terrorists in the chateau for now. As soon as the invasion traffic subsides in a few days, they will be sent east to Germany."

Hansi's blood froze. Concern for the boy evaporated. He imagined himself in a cold dark cell. But far worse was the thought of vanishing into thin air—disappearing without seeing or speaking to his mother or father again.

Papa, if he survived the invasion, would follow his son's steps and find not a single trace. He would stand at the ruins of the destroyed bridge and conclude that something had gone terribly wrong. He would spend the rest of his life searching for his son and his friend. He would die without knowing the fate of his only son.

The thoughts filled Hansi's stomach with a sudden sickness. He felt light-headed and wondered if he might pass out. His hand relaxed. The boy's red locks slipped through his fingers.

The boy bolted. He burst through the ring of soldiers and headed for the curb. Stunned at the sudden action, they watched as he ran along the street against the flow of the invading column.

"Halt! Halt, I say!" the policeman was enraged. He thrust his pistol toward the path of the boy. The civilians, watching in awe, drew back with cries of terror. But the boy was fast. And short, which made him hard to see darting along the crowded and curving street.

At the next intersection, the street rose just enough that the crest of pavement showed between the buildings. The street squeezed to its narrowest such that vehicles and men had to take turns passing through the gap. The medieval two-story structures rose on each side like old trees that had learned to lean toward each other over a farm lane.

Hansi's heart jumped when he saw the boy dart into the middle of the street. The dark silhouette of a Panzer Mark III tank rose just beyond him. Driven no doubt by fear, the boy had not calculated the tank's speed. Barreling as it was, it would never stop in time. Hansi clamped his eyes tight and waited for the screams to echo above the noise.

They never came, perhaps lost in the hard scraping sound that drew Hansi's eyes back open. The tank filled the space between the buildings; the boy was nowhere to be seen. Then unexpectedly the giant beast jerked to its right. The commander, previously perched atop the turret, lost his grip on the steel ring and fell over sideways. A wave of soldiers and civilians rushed forward to avoid being crushed. The tank plunged headlong into the side of the townhouse, crunching its stucco-covered wood wall like it was made of saltine crackers. The building offered little resistance; Hansi knew that was what a tank was designed for. Indeed, the panzer might have eaten all the way through had not the driver jammed the tracks into reverse. The beast churned for a moment, like a tractor slipping in a muddy field, and then came to rest, just short of the turret ring, where the tank commander had half-climbed out. A few centimeters more and he would have, at best, had his legs pinched off; worst, been cut in half by the building's upper story. A cloud of debris followed, filling the street and pelting both soldiers and civilians alike with splinters of stucco, wood, glass, and plaster.

The boy was gone.

All eyes turned to the accident. The tank sat at an angle to the street, blocking three quarters of its width. Within seconds, as the debris cloud settled, soldiers appeared on the street and began to gather at the spectacle. Soon a great mass had gathered. A handful of

Luxembourgers also drew near.

A troubled look swept over the policeman's face. He looked down at Hansi and then back at the gathering chaos and then back at Hansi again.

He's going to let me go!

The policeman's eyes narrowed, and he bit down on his lower lip. Then he snapped forward, startling Hansi with the sudden movement. He had Hansi by the collar and jerked him close. The man's breath was stale tobacco.

"I should shoot you on the spot," he snarled. "But consider the goodness of your master. Next time, don't count on it."

He shoved Hansi away. He fell over, smacking his elbow on the pavement. The pain was nothing compared to the relief that swept over him. Scrambling to get up, his hand slid through something wet. Blood, sticky, and still warm.

My own?

He remembered the old man. A mouth full of blood. He should have been right here. He must have vanished into the crowd. Hansi got up and ran to the curb. The street was empty now. All the military traffic had moved on toward the bridge; the wrecked tank had slowed the invasion to a trickle.

Hansi crossed the street. Coming down the hill he had seen the Hotel d'Vianden north of the main road. It could not be far. Never had Hansi been so glad to leave the noise and crowd behind. The side street fell empty quickly. Hansi realized he was soaked with sweat. His heart was racing. The street rose up in front and he paused to rest against a fence.

Breathe. Relax.

If only he could leave the war behind. Never far from his thoughts, or from his gut, were memories of the night before. Manolo should have been with him. They'd have been at the hotel by now, waiting for Papa. Manolo's face, pale and sticky, dirt crumbs gathered in his eyelids and nostrils and the lines on his face, would never leave him. And Maman. Hansi felt a fool for leaving her. So near to death, perhaps. He scolded himself for leaving. It had seemed so prudent in that moment. Even heroic.

What a waste. A stupid bridge, a dead man.

The world would never be the same.

Chapter Seven

Berlin, May 10, 1940

Fifteen-year-old Karin Blik awoke with a start, a sense she had overslept. Her room was full of light, sure evidence she had missed the alarm. But how? Her bedtime routine was as reliable as the timetable at the Berlin Hauptbahnhof— a twist and a half on the key at the back of the windup clock that sat on her bedside table the last thing before climbing into bed. In the morning, as the bell clanked sharply to penetrate her heavy sleep, the glowing hands guided her no matter how dark the morning. She would punch the plunger and relieve her ears of the clamor. At six in the morning, she had plenty of time to wash, dress, and down a bite of breakfast before school. Today, something was clearly wrong. For in the broad light of the morning, she noticed at once that the bedside table was empty.

She wrapped herself in a light cotton robe and padded across the polished wood floor, ignoring the cold beneath her bare feet. Of all days for this to happen, today was not ideal. Herr Zoeller was giving a pre-final practice exam in biology, and she had stayed up late the night before to prepare. And while this practice had no effect on her final grade by itself, missing a look at the types of questions he was going to ask on the final certainly would. Damaging her biology grade now would damage her chances for university later, narrowing her paths to only those chosen for her by the regime.

Karin heard the tinkling of porcelain from behind the door of the kitchen down the hall. The opening of her bedroom door brought the scent of coffee, another surprise. Karin was used to waking alone, well before her mother, whose own rising, time seemed to be a well-guarded secret, but well after her daughter had left for school. Karin wondered, as she moved up the hallway, what time it really was, and what had caused her mother to rise before her.

"Karin, Darling!" Her mother beckoned, when Karin had pushed through. "What a sleep you've had! I'm so glad. You really must have needed it."

"What time is it?" Karin asked, still blinking away the fog from her slumber.

"Barely eight," her mother replied, with a trace of disappointment.

"Then there's still time," Karin said, instantly calculating the change to her schedule. Then she saw her alarm clock on the table. "Did you take it?"

"Don't worry about school today, dear."

"My exam!"

"It's been taken care of."

"I don't want it to be taken care of."

"Why not dear? It's kind of a holiday."

Holiday? Karin scanned her memory. Hitler's birthday had been weeks earlier, but the Nazis had invented all sorts of days she was still unfamiliar with, having spent most of the previous ten years somewhere other than Hitler's Germany, the Third Reich.

"Well, not an official one, but a holiday nonetheless. We're going to celebrate."

She poured Karin a cup of coffee while Karin sat down at the table. She took an urgent sip, burning her lips and tongue, hoping to accelerate its effect.

"Celebrate?"

"We'll go to an early luncheon, dear. And then shopping. I want to see a new line at the KDW. And something for you, too." Her mother laughed. "I suppose I said that backwards. Something nice for you and perhaps for me if it happens to catch my eye." She chuckled again and lowered her voice to a whisper. "The Nazis have ruined fashion, I'm afraid, though I'll deny saying it. Still, it's worth a look, don't you agree? I forget just how beautiful a girl you are, Karin—well, that is, I neglect to tell you as much as a mother should. I left that kind of thing more to your father, I suppose." Her voice trailed off and she sipped her coffee. "It's going to be a beautiful spring day."

Karin had little time to parse her mother's contrition. Shopping was one of Ursula Blik's many distractions. The mention of Father, however, was unusual. She didn't speak often of her husband and Karin's father, the late Maximilian Blik. She was too preoccupied, not only with shopping, but with social engagements in the bustling capital. The frequent parties brought the attention of various suitors, who, in Karin's estimation, had little respect for a widow's grief. Ursula was quite beautiful herself, and it seemed to Karin there was no lack of men telling her as much. Another distraction. Mother seemed quite willing to take advantage. So, a shopping trip held little appeal.

"I'm not following," Karin said. "What's there to celebrate?"

"The army has thrust toward France," Ursula said.

Karin felt the coffee cup slip in her hand, splashing hot liquid on her hand. The pain and the news worked faster than caffeine on any lingering sleepiness. "Where? How?"

"The army crossed the border this morning. Paris is already in panic."

Karin's face tightened. She placed the cup down and put a hand over her mouth. In history class back in March, they had discussed how Germany might invade France if the Wehrmacht turned west. Professor Herbstreit drew a map of Europe on the board, and students took turns arguing for their strategic plan. Most agreed that France's Maginot Line fortifications along the southwest border would prove too difficult to penetrate, and so, just like in the Great War of 1914, Germany should strike through the neutral countries of Holland, Belgium, and Luxembourg to the north.

"Don't worry, dear," her mother said. "Luxembourg has no army to speak of. They will simply move out of the way and let the tanks pass."

That was no encouragement. Her mother oversimplified everything, especially when the subject was Luxembourg.

Karin didn't reply. Her thoughts were never far from Luxembourg, the charming fortress city built on the cliffs, the last place she had seen her father alive, and the last place she had seen her friend, Hansi.

"And besides, there's nothing there but bad memories. Today is a day of celebration, victory. Let's not cloud it over with dark thoughts."

"I'm going to school," she said, and got up.

"Oh Karin, don't be such a party grouch. Today is a great day for Germany. Live a little, enjoy it. Don't take yourself so seriously."

"I'm not like you, Mother," she shot back. "What I lost in Luxembourg cannot be replaced by anything—or anyone—in Berlin."

"Someone's coffee is quite strong this morning," Ursula said, lifting an eyebrow. "You think you know. Young people always do. I don't blame you for that. A beautiful young girl like you has dreams, hopes, even ideals. Heavens, do they have their ideals." The last statement seemed directed beyond Karin.

"And you're trying to teach me the truth, Mother? The real truth? What is that? What happened to Father in Luxembourg? What happened in that tunnel?"

Karin had last seen her father outside the entrance to the tunnels of the Bock Casemates in Luxembourg City the previous autumn. Maximilian Blik was an attaché to the German Embassy in Luxembourg. The afternoon she saw her father for the last time was also the last time she saw Hansi.

"Your father was a hero," Ursula said, though the tone carried less confidence than usual.

"That may be true," Karin said, "but isn't all of the

truth worth knowing."

"We'll never know," Ursula said, and leaned forward. "Only *he* knows."

"On that we agree," Karin said. "Why don't you ask him?"

Ursula drew back, tensing her forehead in confusion. "Who do you mean?"

"Him, of course," Karin replied. "He was with Father, or should have been, and yet conveniently survived. And what's more, now you and him, together, it's—" Karin wanted to say "disgusting."

"Schlinge? You meant Heinrich Schlinge? For heaven's sake, don't speak of this to him. He wakes up every day to that regret. And never for a moment can he forget what happened when that bomb went off in the Luxembourg Gare, nearly ripping half his body away."

"If you expect me to feel sorry for him, I can't. He's done very well for himself back here in Berlin. A top-level position with the black coats, a black Mercedes with a driver, everything black. Oh, and the most beautiful woman in the Reich on his arm at parties. He'll get no pity from me."

"I suppose there was a compliment in there," Ursula said, "but you'll do well to respect him. And to try to appreciate him."

Karin ignored her. "Earlier, who did you mean?"

"Your friend, whatever he was, that Luxembourg boy."

"Hansi," Karin supplied.

"I won't speak his name. He was in the tunnels when

it happened. He knows the truth. He—" she hesitated.

"He didn't do it, Mother!"

"And how do you know that?" Ursula asked. "Have you spoken to him?"

She hadn't. They had left Luxembourg City the night her father was killed, returning to Berlin. She had only enough time to have Fritz, their butler, post a letter. Her mother had found Karin's weakness. She didn't know Hansi's role in her father's death. She didn't know the truth. It was a matter of faith alone.

Ursula reached across the table and touched Karin's arm.

"Believe it or not, Karin, I was once your age. So, you'll have to trust me on this next point. If you have any lingering feelings for that boy, you'll do well to try to get rid of them. Meet some new friends. Give these Berlin boys a chance. Study your schoolwork. Anything to take your mind off the past. And if you want to help that boy, whatever you do, don't mention him to Heinrich. Now that the German Army is on the move, Heinrich will be quite busy. You'll do well not to remind him of any unpleasant memories associated with—," she paused, "your friend."

Karin heard the words, disagreed with the wisdom, but lingered on the advice. Hansi and the endearing fortress city were still deep in her heart. She was not like her mother, not soothed by the attention of new boys. Karin could only temporarily be distracted by schoolwork. And Schlinge was not someone to be pitied; rather, someone to be feared. Despite his broken body and scarred face, he was a very powerful force in the Gestapo. He would not need reminding what happened in Luxembourg. Mother said it herself; he woke up to it every morning. He would be bent on revenge, even now.

And so, as Karin left the kitchen and quickly dressed for school, thoughts of her excuse for being tardy, or what might be on the biology pre-test, were far from her mind. She moved, driven by a single desire: *I must warn Hansi.*

Chapter Eight

Hansi approached the quaint structure that was tucked tight between the river and the road that led north out of town with it. It featured a long porch on the south end, still shrouded in winter's canvass. Fixed on the lower side of the building, it sat above a brick-enclosed beer garden which was wrapped around to the back. The inn's upper floor was mustard-colored stucco, a common material, but punctuated along its length by neat and narrow windows, each one bracketed by gray shutters, and underscored by dark wooden boxes currently filled with green ivy since it was too early for flowers. Giant lettering on the end of the inn above the porch left no doubt: *Hotel d'Vianden*. Despite the madness down in the village, the quaint old inn seemed inviting to Hansi.

Still, he wondered who he was supposed to meet and how he would let them know. Manolo had not been able to say. Pierre, for an odd reason, didn't know either.

The front door squeaked on its hinges and tinkled a tiny bell when he opened it. A pleasant aroma of herb-scented broth met Hansi's nostrils when he stepped into the narrow lobby. It was dark inside but for a tiny lamp at the far end. Hansi strode across the well-worn carpet to a small desk tucked beside the steep stairway. Finding it deserted, he turned to his left, where a hallway stretched along the length of the inn. Shadows flickered behind a pair of translucent glass doors. Hansi took a step.

"May I help you?"

He jumped and spun around. The voice had come from right behind him, but he couldn't see anyone.

"Bonjour," he stammered.

A face emerged slowly from the honeycomb of nooks, where the room keys and messages were kept. A girl. Her face remained half-shrouded in shadow. The portion that met the light was nearly covered with her flowing brown hair. It fell in sweeping cascades, like a waterfall, and curled below a delicate chin. Her eyes, large and dark, shone like an animal in hiding.

"Good morning," she said. The eyes fell. "Well, not really. It's a terrible morning if you think about it."

Hansi stepped closer. The girl, about his own age, perhaps a year or so older, kept to the half-shadow. What he could see of her wore a gray sweater that hung loose over a petite frame. Her arms were crossed as if she was cold, but to Hansi, the inn was cozy and warm compared to the chill of the morning air outside. The mention of yesterday opened the pit in his stomach again. It stole his breath and nearly erupted.

"Are you all right?" the girl asked. "You don't look well."

Hansi put his hand out and leaned against the desk. He felt suddenly light-headed, and beads of sweat erupted on his forehead.

The girl swept out from around the desk and took Hansi by the arm.

"Here. We'll get you something hot. You look like you've seen a ghost. Come down to the dining room. You'll be more comfortable there. Can you walk?"

"I'm fine," he said, shaking his head. He wished he had seen a ghost. If she only knew what he'd seen.

They walked down the hallway together, the girl steadying him. She pushed through one of the glass doors with her shoulder and pulled him in the open space.

"Sorry about the soldiers," she whispered, pulling close. "They're noisy, but their lieutenant keeps them mostly under control so far. Here, take this table."

She helped Hansi to a small round table in the back corner of the dining room. It sat at the end of the inn, just behind the covered porch, which Hansi could see beyond the wide glass windows in wooden frames with cleats that looked like they could be removed in warm weather, expanding the porch. The tables along the windows were filled with German soldiers and tall glasses of beer and plates of bread, sausage, and cheese. They were devouring it all, chattering and laughing.

Hansi sank down on the chair and let his elbows hit the table, disregarding the bad manners. He let his head fall and closed his eyes. The white cotton was smooth and smelled clean. How he wished for his bed back in Luxembourg City.

The girl patted him on the shoulder. "Rest yourself. I'll be back in a moment with something to warm you."

He could not protest. When she left, he noticed for the first time that she walked with a distinct limp on the right side. She favored her left arm, compensating for a weakened one on the right. He sat up and their eyes met. A look of embarrassment flashed in hers and was gone in a blink.

She padded off and left him alone and ashamed for embarrassing her. When she returned, her voice was defiant.

"Look at him," she said. "I told you he looked like he'd been playing with the rats in the alley."

A woman stepped out from behind the girl. She shared the dark hair, fine features, and penetrating brown eyes of the girl. Wiping her hands on the smudged apron, she bent down and drew near to Hansi, carrying with her the scent of the kitchen and the aromatic soup. She swept the hair away from his forehead and placed the back of her hand against it. It felt ice cold against his skin.

"He's burning up. Michele, get a cloth and fill a pitcher. Meet us upstairs. Room six."

"Yes, Maman," the girl replied and retreated toward the kitchen.

The word took him back to his flat in the Grund.

Maman.

Chapter Nine

Despite oversleeping, Karin managed to get to school only seventy-three minutes late, five of which were spent negotiating with her mother, who reluctantly wrote an excuse note in exchange for a promise to accompany her to the KDW after school. Seventy-three minutes late was egregious in the moral economy of a German school unless one was mauled by a bear on the way to school, which was unlikely in urban Berlin. But seventy-three gave Karin a full twenty-two-minute cushion before biology. The day might still be saved.

"You look fine enough to me, Fraulein Blik," the assistant principal had scolded. Karin shrugged and said nothing, agreeing with him.

She slipped into second class history for its final minutes, where her late entry was met with curious stares. But silence, thankfully, since Professor Herbstreit was finishing his lecture, and from the tone and volume, apparently building to a big finish.

"Today represents the beginning of a triumph over the humiliation of Versailles. Our national shame is over, thanks to Herr Hitler and our brave soldiers."

He continued, little different than the voices one would hear at any given moment from their living room on the Peoples' Radio. He extolled the virtues of Hitler's fresh decision to strike west against, as he put it, "the pathetically weak French and their ill prepared partners, the British."

"They thought they would smash us, punish us, in

their smug self-righteousness after the 1918 war. But they underestimated the will of our Führer and the will of our people. But it is they who will be smashed."

Karin had heard it a thousand times before. The only remarkable part was that so many of her classmates still fell under its spell.

"So when you go home tonight, bow your heads in thanks to God, who in His Providence, has chosen our nation and our leader to exalt the German people over their enemies."

The bell rang as if on cue. Enraptured as each one had been, they were students through and through. The bell's call broke the spell, and they were on their feet.

Karin got up with the others, the professor's words still echoing in her mind. She had spent little time at church in her fifteen years. Like her fellow students, she had sat through compulsory religious education until her family left Germany with Father's work in the diplomatic corp. Even so, Karin immediately thought of her grandmother, the only person in her family that spoke of God more than as a swear word. Karin knew something about his speech was off, and not just a little. Grandmother didn't think God had chosen Germany, much less this Führer, Hitler, for anything, except perhaps to punish Germany. Karin didn't think very much about it except on these occasions. But she would not be bowing her head in thanks on this night, or any other.

Karin was relieved to enter biology on time with the other students. *Get through this hour, and you've made it through the toughest part of the day.* And then she remembered her promise to her mother to go to the KDW together.

The practice exam began easily enough, featuring a set of numbered questions requiring short answers on a variety of topics. Karin had studied concepts of heredity, which were especially important to German educators. For example, one question asked, "Two boys live next to each other in a neighborhood. One boy's father is an alcoholic. The other boy's father is not, but his grandfather is. Which is more likely to pass the trait of alcoholism to his own son?" It struck Karin that reality was more complex than the expected answer. Nevertheless, she could navigate these and her investment in study would pay off. What would prove more challenging was the exam's last question. Professor Zoeller pulled a curtain away from a chalkboard, where he had drawn a chart that looked like a thick-trunked tree growing sideways from a vertical line on the left side of the board. The tree stretched to the right, spanning other vertical lines and dividing into smaller branches, some of which stopped midway on the board. Two major branches continued all the way to the right edge of the board, splitting further into four branches each. Karin knew this chart at once—the Relation of Man and Apes Chart, but Professor Zoeller had numbered various places that in the textbook would have been labeled. The test challenged the students' knowledge beginning with the Paleocene Era in the Age of Mammals, through the Pleistocene Era in the Age of Man, all the way to the Current Era, where four branches represented the Human trunk, and four the Ape trunk.

Having recognized the chart, Karin felt anxious. She

had seen the chart in her book, drawn it for herself in her notes, but not memorized the labels. She stared at it for a moment, grappling with the shock.

Remember, this is a practice exam.

She knew one answer with certainty, number fifteen. The top-most branch of the Age of Man. She knew the answer because it struck her as more political than scientific: *Aryan.* She filled in two of the other three branches with *Chinese* and *Negro,* but couldn't remember the third. Another branch by itself she knew as *Jew.*

Having spent most of her school years outside of Germany, she had never been taught this kind of biology. She knew two things for sure. First, any doubts concerning the chart's truth or value must be kept to oneself. And second, *I have work to do.*

At the lunch break, she caught up with her friend Leni. Leni was her best, if not quite only, friend. They had more or less found each other as a result of somewhat common circumstances. Leni had lost her father, a soldier, in the first weeks of the war in Poland near to the same time as Karin lost her own. Leni's father had died in a suspicious drowning accident. The school nurse, knowing Karin had lost her father in similarly mysterious circumstances, had put the pair together at the beginning of the school year. Unlike Karin, Leni was decidedly more patriotic, which was true of almost all students. Still, she was sympathetic and open to Karin, and the two shared a sincere bond due to their grief, no matter how it was understood or interpreted. They had lost their fathers, and now faced a future where they would be asked to trust their Fatherland instead.

"It's not like you to be late," Leni said, her bold, brown eyes lighting up her face.

Karin explained, but Leni cupped her pink-kissed cheeks in her delicate hands.

"Well, I just don't understand," she said. "I would have traded a day at school for a day of shopping in a spark."

"You don't know my mother," Karin said with a half-laugh.

They sat at the end of their table of eight, but Karin moved as far to the edge as she could manage, trying to ignore the chatter and laughter of the others. She pushed the noodles around on her plate.

"What's wrong, Karin?"

"Nothing."

Leni took Karin's hand. "I understand. Everyone is excited today, but it hits me the opposite way. I can't help but think of my father. Everyone is celebrating. Triumphant. But Mother and I just stare at his picture on the wall. You must feel that way about your father."

"It's not that, no," Karin replied. "I mean, I do miss him, or at least part of him. It's not him. But I am worried for someone."

"Who? You've never said. Do you have a relative in the Army?"

Karin shook her head. She paused, and then took a chance.

"I met a boy when I lived in Luxembourg."

Karin felt Leni's squeeze tighten and looked up, as she

had been staring into the nothingness of the food on her plate.

Leni's lips curled in sympathy. She let go, and clutched her sweater, pulling it tight in a self-embrace. "It's so romantic, Karin, I had no idea!"

Gretchen, who was beside Leni, was a sandy-haired girl with a rounded face that was sprinkled with freckles. At the word "romantic," she spun around and leaned in.

"Oooh! What's romantic?"

"Nothing," Karin said.

Gretchen's question was loud enough to draw the attention of the others. Suddenly all eyes were on Leni and Karin.

"What's romantic?" Karla, next to Karin, repeated.

Leni's face tightened. Karin was trying, and failing, to ignore them.

"One of you has a boyfriend," Gretchen declared. "Confess!" she ordered, evoking a round of laughs from the others.

Leni shook her head anxiously, unable to speak.

All eyes fell on Karin.

"Karin? You?" Gretchen's tone was laden with surprise.

"No, it's not like that," Karin said. "Not exactly. I don't know."

The girls shivered with delight. Then came questions in rapid fire: "Is he a soldier? Where did you meet him? Tell us everything!"

"No, he's too young. He's in Luxembourg."

"Hold on!" Gretchen interrupted. "Karin, this is quite

some news.”

“Bigger than the invasion,” someone said, to a round of mocking gasps.

“Start at the beginning,” Gretchen said.

“There’s no time,” Karla interjected. “The bell is about to ring.”

“Then let’s get to the good stuff,” Gretchen said. “Do you love him?”

“That’s not the good stuff,” Karla protested. “Have you kissed him?”

Karin didn’t hear the second question.

“I…I don’t know,” she answered.

Karla closed her eyes, leaned forward with lips puckered for a kiss. “He must be an angel! You don’t even know when he kisses you!” The girls squealed in mock drama.

Karin was embarrassed.

“So what’s the problem, then? A boyfriend in Luxembourg. It’s not exactly next door, but can’t you go see him?” Gretchen asked.

“Pardon me,” Karla said, “but there’s a war going on. Of course she can’t.”

“What do you mean? Luxembourg, isn’t that Germany?”

“No!” Karin said.

“Well, if Poland is any measure, it will be very soon,” came the voice from the other end.

“That’s not funny,” Leni said, finally having recovered her courage. “This is serious. Karin has been through a lot. War is not anything to joke about, as you should all know.”

"We're just happy for you, Karin, that's all," Karla said. "And a bit jealous if we're honest."

"Speak for yourself," said Eva, sitting on the end.

"It's all right," Karin said, genuinely. "I appreciate your concern, I really do. I suppose I just feel, well, hopeless."

The playful mood among the girls had slumped by now. There was a pause, and then Gretchen spoke up.

"I have an idea! My grandmother helped me one time when I was little. My brother found our pet rabbit Mitzi dead in its hutch one morning. I was devastated. The next time I saw my grandmother, I told her all about it. She said I should write a letter to Mitzi, to tell her all the things I would miss about her, and to say goodbye. I did. I cried and cried, but the letter did me good."

No one said a word. Gretchen looked at each one, confused, until a realization dawned on her face.

The bell rang.

Chapter Ten

Central Berlin showed little evidence of the invasion news. Honking cars, thundering trams, the tinkle of bicycle bells, and even the occasional clop of horses accompanied a cityscape already accustomed to war. Soldiers, bureaucrats, tourists, and shoppers filled the streets adorned with red Nazi flags and banners, emblazoned with the ubiquitous swastika. Karin was unimpressed, but Ursula was buoyant with the joy of shopping, no matter that it was delayed by Karin's school. The car bounded down the Kurfurstendamm with Karin and Ursula in the back.

"You'll thank Herr Schlinge the next time you see him," Ursula said. "He arranged this car for us."

I'm sure you'll thank him enough for the both of us, Karin wanted to say, but held her tongue. "He's awfully generous," she said instead, and counted it as a peace offering.

Shopping was the furthest thing from her mind. She thought only of the soldiers streaming over the border and Hansi. Was he safe? Was the city under attack? She had seen the newsreels at the theater, same as everyone, of Germany's move into Norway the month before. She doubted the pictures she saw of friendly locals greeting the German soldiers with flowers and cold drinks of water, bread, cheese and kisses. No doubt similar scenes were being staged in Luxembourg. If only she could reach out to Hansi. Surely he would have taken precautions, she hoped. His father and mother would not take chances. Perhaps even now they had fled to France like Hansi had offered before their last time together at the casemates.

"Before we try on the new clothes, there's something else I want you to look at," Ursula said, interrupting Karin's thoughts.

"Sure," Karin replied, "but shouldn't we be…serious?"

Her mother laughed. "You look like your father just now. He would have said: 'It's war, not a celebration.' Of course you're right, dear, but there will surely be tough days ahead, no doubt. Today is not one of them. Today is a day full of hope and possibility."

Karin tensed, drawing away. "And that doesn't sound like you. Hope and possibility? Since when did you become so…so political?"

"Goodness, Karin, I don't mean them in any political sense. Well, at least not in their way. I have my own politics, I suppose, but it's not about blood or race or armies and guns like them."

"Like *him*." Karin countered, not saying his name if she could help it.

"Schlinge?" Ursula laughed hard. "Oh heavens, I suppose so. He and your father were so alike on those points. So like all of them, really. They don't like any variety on those subjects."

"Then what do you mean?"

"Hmmm, a good question." Ursula paused, letting the car rock them for a half block before something changed in her playful expression.

Her attention left Karin to a place in her mind, Karin could see, by the wandering eyes. And then the tension in her mother's brow seemed to relax, if just a little, as though she had come upon a truth. Karin hadn't seen a look like that before. Her mother seemed so unaffected by anything, especially anything serious, and particularly the death of her own husband. Ursula had never shown grief to Karin. She was never sad. As Karin thought about it, she realized her mother wasn't sad, but more afraid. People took it for grief, but it wasn't that. And so this look of knowing was to Karin a transformation of the fear that hid behind her mother's playful smile and light-hearted banter into a look of something stronger, something harder.

"It's about survival, Karin. We can't trust these men. You must never forget that. They have big plans, big dreams, and big weapons. We are not part of that. Mark my words. And yet all is not lost. We can take advantage not just to survive, but to thrive."

Karin had never heard her mother speak in such a way. Strong, confident, and yet still upsetting. Cold.

"How?" Karin asked.

"By not letting them take us for granted, and by keeping them off balance."

"Is that what we're doing now?" It was beyond Karin.

Ursula's smile returned. "Heavens no, dear. We're just out enjoying ourselves. A day may come when we can't do this, but today we can. Let's just enjoy it, huh?"

They arrived at the entrance of the KDW, which occupied almost the entire block, just before five. Traffic was heavy from workers heading home. The driver of their car opened Karin's door and helped her to the curb with a crisp nod and click of the heels. Her mother slid over and joined her. They passed a boy at a newsstand waving a copy of the Berlin newspaper. A big headline read, "GERMAN ARMY BLAZES WEST." Down at the corner, Karin noticed a crowd had gathered around a group of soldiers and a band of musicians, starting up a patriotic song.

Inside, her mother led her past a forest of display stands to the elevators in the center of the structure. At the third level, they strode through the children's department. Karin had been to the KDW only one other time, during the Christmas season. She remembered the smells of the roasted nuts, the mulled wine, and the fine perfumes. Her memory recalled a picture of a handsome couple, and happy together. The mannequins on display now wore spring and summer clothes for boys and girls going on summer holidays to the Bavarian mountains or the Baltic seashore.

Past these offerings they turned the corner, and the merchandise changed. Ursula's eyebrows lifted in hope. Karin's heart dropped. Before her, the stone-faced girls wore white blouses and long navy wool skirts, black leather belts, straps looped diagonally over their shoulders. In their flat shoes, red kerchiefs, and red armbands with the white circle and black swastika, they stared upward toward some National Socialist utopian future.

"Is this some kind of joke?" Karin asked.

Ursula exhaled heavily without answering.

"Your idea of a surprise?"

"Now, Karin, hear me out. It's time for you to join."

Her mother was speaking of the BDM, The League of

German Girls. The female equivalent of the Hitler Youth. Karin had never joined the Catholic youth groups, the Girl Scouts, or any group. She was not a group-joiner, and certainly not the Hitler Youth.

"They're responsible for Father's death, in case you forgot," Karin said.

"Oh, Karin, don't be so dramatic. How do you know it wasn't that boyfriend of yours?"

"Goodbye, Mother. Enjoy your new clothes and all that hope and possibility."

She turned and left.

Mother didn't come after her.

Karin knew she wouldn't. There was too much left to explore.

Chapter Eleven

The busy streets of Berlin absorbed Karin in her disgust. Her departure, however abrupt, was not unusual. She and her mother sparked more often than they got along. The rift had been growing for years, only to be fully exposed when her father had been killed. Despite Karin's shock upon learning what her father's role had been in Luxembourg, she knew he loved her. He noticed her and listened to her. Which made his death even more difficult to bear. So much was left unresolved.

Why did you agree to plotting against the tiny country? When did you first agree to such a job? Where did you find a man like Schlinge? How could you have risked so much? Did you not think of us? Of me?

Karin strode down the broad avenue. Shoppers, workers, bureaucrats, soldiers. Diesel, manure, cigarette smoke, street vendor sausage, and sauerkraut.

At the corner of Unter den Linden and Wilhelmstrasse, she waited for the policeman's signal to cross. The crowd gathered around her. Everyone carried on like before, smiling, laughing, or just going about their business of traveling home, stopping at shops along the way. She had an idea.

On Orienburger Strasse, the imperial-looking stone Haupttelegraphenamt, the Main Telegraph Office, cast a long shadow over the cobblestone plaza in front, where pigeons flapped and scattered just beyond the reach of passersby.

Karin pushed inside and scanned the interior, polished marble floors and brass-framed glass walls. To her right, a row of stalls stretched as far as she could see, where people crammed into the corner of each booth. They pressed their ears against the black telephone receiver and plugged their other ear with a finger. Lips seemed to caress the horn-shaped receiver as people talked. Karin had no idea how one would use one to make a call, so she stood still among the tempest to study the procedure.

She noticed that nearby, people were waiting in lines like at a bank. At the head of each line, they spoke to workers behind glass windows, paid money, and received some sort of ticket. And then they walked to one of the numbered booths where people talked. After an interval, they would hang up and leave just before the next person in line arrived at the booth, lean into the receiver, and begin their conversation.

Karin got in line. Hers might have moved more slowly than the others, or it might just have been her growing anxiety's perception. Because of the noise in the hall, she could not hear what was being said at the front of the line until she was quite close.

She heard a customer say, "I'd like four minutes to this number," and watched as she slid a slip of paper to the clerk. The clerk consulted a chart of some kind and replied, "Two marks, fifty."

The customer paid. The clerk returned a receipt. Booth Seven.

The customer nodded and headed for Booth Seven.

Karin was next. She stepped forward, suddenly

overcome with panic.

"What number?" The clerk snapped.

"I'd like to call Luxembourg," Karin said.

"What number?"

"I don't know it."

"I can't make a call without a number."

"How much for two minutes?" Karin asked.

"What number? I have to have a number."

"I'm sorry, I don't know it." Karin felt her plan collapsing in on itself before it had even begun. "I'm sorry," she repeated.

She felt a nudge from behind. Someone anxious to take her place, no doubt. Everyone making urgent calls on the first day of the invasion, just like her. They'd be angry at her for wasting time. But when she turned around, she encountered a middle-aged woman in a gray raincoat who had a kind face.

"If you ask her to look it up," the woman said, "she's obligated to help you. But only if you ask."

Karin's eyes widened. *"Vielen dank,"* she said.

When she turned back to the clerk, the woman's irritation was set in the stretched lines around her mouth.

"Will you look it up for me, please?" Karin asked.

"Tell her the city," came a whisper from behind.

"Luxembourg City, please."

The clerk exhaled heavily and glared over Karin's shoulder. She paused and then pushed away. She got up from her chair and disappeared through a door. A moment later, she returned with a thick black volume and plopped it dramatically onto the counter.

"Name?"

"Broussard."

The clerk stuck a finger in the front and began searching. Karin searched her own memory…Albert…No!

"Alain."

The clerk looked up. "French?"

"Luxembourgish."

The clerk lifted a nostril and continued searching. She thumbed another page and slid her finger down a column. "Rue du Grund?"

Karin didn't really know. "*Ja.*"

"Have her write it for you," the voice behind her said.

"Can you write it, please?" Karin asked.

The woman set her jaw again, but scribbled the number down. "Ten marks," she said. At this, a slight grin appeared.

Karin's heart sank. She had three marks in her purse at best.

"How much for one minute?"

"Three minutes is the minimum charge, *fraulein*. Ten marks. People are waiting."

Karin's plan crumbled, and her face grew hot with embarrassment.

"I'm sorry to trouble you," she said, just as a hand shot across the counter from behind her. Underneath the fingers was a ten mark note. Karin turned. The woman was smiling.

"I don't know what to say," Karin began.

The woman tossed her head back to the clerk, as if to urge Karin to keep going.

The clerk, defeated, took the money and scribbled the number on the paper, which she slid back over to Karin. "Booth Eleven," she said curtly.

Karin thanked the clerk, and then the woman, who by now was more interested in her own phone call than receiving thanks. Karin rushed to the booths and found number eleven.

She picked up the receiver and pressed it to her ear. It was warm to the touch, a matte black plastic with a lingering smell of the innumerable callers before her. There was no sound at first, but then a series of clicks with no pattern to them. Dead air, a few more clicks. She waited, fearing something was wrong. Seconds passed. A few clicks more. Karin's heart thundered, her hope flagged, then sank completely.

Would someone tell her to give up? Or would they wait for her to realize it on her own? She looked back at the row of clerks for help, but they were busy with other callers. It had been a stupid plan, Karin concluded. Of course, the lines to Luxembourg would be down. Bombs smash things, soldiers cut wires.

Her disappointment gave way to panic. Bombs smash houses, flats, shops. She had seen the pictures, watched the films. The German army was without equal if the propaganda was to be believed, and the images seemed to prove it. *How did Hansi stand a chance in his tiny apartment?*

She had just pulled the receiver away from her ear when she heard another sound. A short burst of clicks followed by a faint series of buzzing sounds. *Brrrrr, brrrrr, brpp, brpp.* Ringing! Her heart soared. The call was going through! She pressed the earpiece tight to her ear and nearly kissed the mouthpiece.

More rings, the series continued, and Karin's ear strained for the final connection, the clicks, and the voice. It never came. The ringing continued past her counting. Finally, a voice came on the line, "No answer. Take your receipt to the booth and collect your refund."

The line went dead, just like Karin's hope.

Chapter Twelve

Hansi awoke with a start to the sound of the door opening. It was the girl, carrying a tray. The smell of broth wafted in. She set the tray on a small cloth-covered nightstand and switched on a short brass lamp. The windows were dark, the blackout curtains drawn. He must have slept all day.

"Are you hungry?" she asked, the hard edge of her earlier tone gone.

Hansi sat up. His chest was wet and cold, like a fever had broken. The soup, chicken broth with vegetables, was hot and delicious. It was better than medicine. He ladled it down quickly and slid to the edge of the bed. As much as he might have wanted to stay and rest, or even escape the war outside, Hansi remembered why he had come. He needed to speak with the owner, or manager, Pierre hadn't known, but someone at the hotel would know what to do next. He had to find him.

"This is excellent," he said, cleaning the last drops off the bottom of the bowl with his last crust of bread. "Tell your mother I'm grateful." He moved to get up.

"Where are you going?"

"I've got to go."

"You're not well."

"I'm fine," he said, though whether it was true, he really couldn't say. The soup had revived him, but for how long, he had no idea.

"Wait," she said.

He looked at her. Her eyes were full and glistening with tears.

"I don't even know your name."

"Hansi," he replied.

Without warning, she touched him on the arm, leaned forward and stretched to the limit of her one strong leg. He thought she was going to whisper something in his ear, but instead, kissed him on the cheek. "Thank you," she said.

He stood frozen, every fiber alive and on edge. "I don't understand," he said.

"Jacky told me everything. The film crew, the old man. Thank you for saving my brother's life."

The scene in the village flooded back. The boy had nearly been the end of all of them.

"Your brother was a fool. He could have gotten all of us arrested."

"He hates the Germans." She caught herself and glanced at the open door, lowering her voice too late. "But he's that way. Acts before he thinks. He's always getting into trouble." She tried to laugh.

"It's one thing to be a little mischievous," Hansi said. "But now he'll have to be careful. The Germans don't know how to take a joke. Where is he?"

"Maman's put him to work. We're going to be full tonight."

A voice rang out from downstairs, calling Michele. She became suddenly self-conscious, looking down at her feet, backing away.

"I must go. The German soldiers are quite demanding. Maman must feed half the army it seems. There's a mountain of potatoes half as tall as the chateau. Jacky and I will be at it all night."

"Let me help," Hansi said, rising off the bed. He slipped his shoes on, which someone had removed for him, and picked up the bowl of soup. He began ladling it in like coal in a locomotive.

"No, you must rest. Maman won't hear of it."

"Michele! Where are you?" the voice was nearer.

"Coming Maman!" Michele spun toward the door. Because of her limp, she stumbled and crashed to the floor. Hansi stooped down to help. When he touched her arm, it was like he had shot her with electricity.

"I'm fine! I can manage on my own! I don't need your help!"

Hansi stood back. The girl rolled on her strong side, the left side, and pushed up with her strong arm, balancing on a bent knee until she was able to sit back on her leg. Then, with an amazing display of strength, lifted herself with the power of a single strong leg, as one would rise up from a squat. Michele achieved it with a single powerful spring. Her eyes were full again, but this time she dared not to look right at Hansi. She rushed out of the room.

He didn't follow.

Hansi stared out the window. It looked west where the valley rose sharply. The sky held the faintest glow of the day's last light in a pink shroud behind the ancient chateau, where tiny pinpricks of lights traced an outline around the ramparts. In a previous year, the lengthened day would have lifted his spirit with the hope of warm days to come.

And long summer days hiking in these very hills. But now, darkness rose like a ghost, and the German army swarming through his land was a shadow Hansi could feel under his chin, rising as a knot in his throat. Manolo, Maman, Papa. And himself, far away.

Chapter Thirteen

"Mehr bier! Schnell! Schnell!" The red-faced soldier held a foamy glass over his head, waving it in a wide circle. His close-cropped hair and fleshy ears gave him the look of a snub-nosed elephant. He bellowed like one. "Where is the beer? How do you Luxembourgers expect to join the Reich if you can't keep the glasses full?"

His comrades burst out laughing. They were jammed around a line of tables along the window, shoulder to shoulder. Weapons were everywhere—rifles in the corner, pistols on the table. And grenades, each one like a tin can attached to a wooden handle the length of Hansi's forearm. They were nicknamed "potato mashers." One man hung a pair on his belt, like six-shooters. Another had stowed his in the top of his tunic so it jutted out like a metal corsage. A third had crammed one into the top of each of his boots.

One of the men stood up. He was tall and broad-shouldered, the kind of warrior Hansi had seen in the newsreels. The bars on his sleeve, Hansi knew, indicated he was a man of rank.

He turned and interrupted Hansi's stare.

"Junge, komm."

Hansi complied.

"You speak German, *ja?*"

Hansi shrugged. *"Ein bischen."* A *little*. More than a little, in truth. All Luxembourg students studied German from the first grade, but his was the standard response.

Schmidt smiled. "Good. You have a nice inn here.

And the beer is good, despite what the men might say." He wiped his hands on the tablecloth and extended one toward Hansi. "Allow me to introduce myself. Heinrich Schmidt, *Obersturmbannführer* of these men. What is your name?"

Hansi hesitated and then shook Schmidt's hand. It was large, strong, and rough, just like Papa's, he thought. Shriveled and cracked from years of hard work at the steel mill. Perhaps Schmidt had been a laborer before the war.

"I'm Hansi."

Schmidt's face lit up and he slapped Hansi on the shoulder. "Short for Johannes, *ja?* A good German name."

Hansi knew Schmidt was technically correct. Some of Hansi's ancestors had immigrated from across the Sure River in Germany and had married a Luxembourgish Broussard. One of the few remaining traces of the family history was his name, Johannes, rather than Jean, which was more common for Luxembourgers. It didn't matter; everyone he knew shortened Johannes to Hansi, and it stuck.

"How old are you? Sixteen?"

"Fifteen."

"Ah, to be fifteen again." He took a long drink. "Enjoying life, no cares. Summer will come soon. Roaming about the hills, enjoying the fresh air."

Hansi didn't respond.

"Yes, of course. You're worried about the war." He patted Hansi on the shoulder. "This part will pass soon enough. We will not stay long. Things will quiet down." He rubbed Hansi's hair. "You'll have your summer, you'll see."

Hansi tried to nod in agreement, but all he wanted was

to retreat to the kitchen.

Schmidt finished his glass. He pulled his chair closer to Hansi.

"Look," he said. "You've nothing to worry about, Hansi. We are not animals. We are flesh and blood just like you. I have a wife and young son at home. Willie is eight. I see the boy in the kitchen and I miss him."

Hansi said nothing.

"I don't want you to be afraid," Schmidt continued. "And don't listen to the French propaganda. Luxembourgers are not the Poles. Did you know, Hansi, how many Germans lived there? The Poles tortured our German women, and children too." Hansi had indeed heard. The previous September, Germany marched into Poland. Throughout the autumn, the stories came. Rumors and reports told of German soldiers shooting Polish civilians without so much as a second thought. Yet he dare not argue.

"You Luxembourgers are like us, you'll see. Just try to think of us like…" he searched for the word, "cousins."

Bully cousins, Hansi thought. Invading and conquering cousins. Cousins that grab helpless girls for their own amusement. Manolo's dirt-caked face rose up in his mind. Ruthless relatives who demand absolute obedience.

The door to the dining room burst open. A dust-covered soldier, wearing riding boots, gloves, and goggles across his helmet crossed quickly to Schmidt, saluted, and handed him a message. Schmidt ripped it open, scanned the contents quickly, and let a smile stretch across his face.

"Thank you," he said. "You may go." The messenger saluted once more, cracked his heels together, spun around, and tore off.

Schmidt turned back to the men and raised his glass high in the air. The smile had grown in proportion to the inflation of his chest.

"Comrades! Comrades! *Achtung! Achtung!*"

The room fell silent.

"Let us raise our glasses on this most glorious of evenings! First, to our hosts, our Luxembourg cousins." He nodded to Hansi; for the moment, the only Luxembourger within earshot. "*Vielen Dank* for your hospitality. Second, to our first success today! Clearing the tank from the road. Your effort keeps our march on schedule, and the Führer will be most proud when he hears of your exploits. I salute you! *Prost! Prost! Prost!*"

They clinked their glasses and took deep drinks. Schmidt beamed with pride. If only he knew that the boy that caused the accident was hiding in the kitchen, plotting his revenge. The thought was almost humorous to Hansi.

"Drink it down, boys. Leave not a drop!" He waited while the men obeyed. It was a strange end to a toast, as indicated by the curious looks on some of the men's faces. The room fell silent again, and every eye turned on the officer.

"Grab your weapons and your gear, comrades. We have new orders. Not far from here, just west of the village, terrorists have destroyed a bridge." Hansi's heart jumped. "As you can see, traffic is slowed. The terrorists are being sought at this very moment. You may rest assured that they will be dealt with harshly and swiftly."

"According to the messenger, our equipment is not twenty kilometers away, just over the border in Kleindorf. The military *polizei* are redirecting all traffic so that it will arrive tonight! This time tomorrow, we will return to celebrate completion of the repairs to the bridge. I salute you! Now let's get going!"

Now everything was clear, Hansi realized. These men were combat engineers, and Schmidt their leader.

Cheers rose to a roar. Hansi's heart sank. The men congratulated each other with slaps, shakes, and hugs. In the clink of a glass, they were gone. Hansi fell onto a chair, wracked with terror.

Chapter Fourteen

The silence left in the wake of the soldiers' exit was more startling than the commotion they had made in the dining room. Thoughts flooded Hansi's mind. They were off to repair the bridge before he even had made contact! Who was he supposed to meet? Where was the owner? Had he fled the hotel, leaving everything to the kitchen staff? As he watched the men march down the hill towards the village, Hansi fought the urge to give up. Let someone else complete the "mission." It was senseless. And hopeless. His energy, what little remained, would be better spent trying to get home, to Maman and Papa.

"Who are you?"

Hansi spun around.

Michele's mother had come from the kitchen while Hansi was frozen in thought.

"And why are you here?"

Her tone was neither angry nor suspicious, but cautious. She had removed the fastener that held her auburn hair back so that it fell to her shoulders.

"I'm looking for the owner," he replied.

"What do you want?"

"I've a message to deliver."

"From whom?"

"I'm sorry, it's private."

"He's not here."

"When do you expect him?"

Tears had gathered in her eyes.

"Never."

"I don't understand. Where is he?"

"Enough with the questions. Tell me, what is the message?"

"I'm truly sorry, madame, but I have been instructed only to deliver it to the owner. If he's not here, then I will leave. *Merci.*"

Hansi turned away, wondering what had gone wrong. Pierre had been clear. Go to the hotel and make contact with the owner. He didn't know his name. Manolo hadn't time to explain. He had barely enough strength to hand Hansi the leather pouch. It was supposed to be simple. It wasn't fair to be left like this.

Despair, never far from his throat, rose up like bile. Manolo died for nothing.

A botched mission, a missing contact, an uninformed French spy. Everything a total failure.

Hansi could go home now, but there was little relief in the prospect. The war was barely two days on and Hansi couldn't imagine how he was going to survive it.

"Wait."

When he turned back around, the woman hadn't moved. Tears had fully formed, however, and made their tracks down her cheeks. The rag she held was being wrung to death.

"I wasn't expecting someone so...so young," she said.

"I'm afraid I don't understand."

"Are you not Resistance, then?"

Hansi stopped short. He had never fully considered himself that way.

"Yes."

"Sit down."

Hansi tossed a look back toward the windows.

"It should be all right now. They won't be back for a while. I am Paulette Poulet."

They sat at one of the small tables that had not been used by the soldiers. Michele's mother seemed to have gathered herself now. The tears were wiped away, and she moved with the confidence he had seen when he first arrived.

"You have come from Luxembourg City?"

He nodded. Pierre had warned him not to discuss the mission beyond his next task. But it was inescapable now that the woman knew what she was doing.

"By yourself?" Her tone carried a hint of incredulity.

Now Hansi felt the lump once more. He wasn't sure what to say. This had nothing to do with why he had come.

She patted his arm and smiled. "It's all right. I'm sure you have been told not to talk about anything but why you're here. I don't understand the secrecy. This is war. The Grand Duchess has fled the country and we are going to need each other more than ever."

Hansi was stunned. "The Grand Duchess, gone?" He remembered the palace, the dignitaries, the gleam of the polished floor, and the kindness in the eyes of Her Highness when she greeted him. A world ago now.

"I don't mean to add to your troubles," she continued. "It's just that with what we have to do next, I'd like to know why—" She paused.

"Why they sent me? A boy?"

She laced her fingers together on the table.

"My last contact was with a man from the city. He wasn't Luxembourgish. Spanish, or Italian, I think."

Hansi's face flushed.

"You know him? Why did he not come?"

Hansi tensed throughout his entire body. He sat frozen, unable to put words to what had happened.

"This man, was he your friend?"

Hansi nodded.

Madame Poulet got up from her chair, knelt beside Hansi, and took hold of him. "You poor dear, I'm so sorry. No wonder you seem like a ghost. I'm sorry, so sorry."

She held him like a mother would, rocking him back and forth. A voice inside hissed that he was nearly fifteen and didn't need a mother's comfort. But Hansi was exhausted and could think only of Manolo. And home, where his own mother, too weak to comfort him, lay dying.

Hansi didn't protest. He didn't pull away until she was ready to continue.

"I won't ask you to speak of it," she said. "But tell me, Hansi, what comes next? Your friend, what did he tell you to do?"

Hansi swallowed hard and pushed the knot down once more. He reached into his pocket and retrieved the felt pouch. He loosened the string and let the object slip out. A small wooden case, with lacquer finish, ebony, with finely painted golden scrolled trim. On the box lid, a hand-painted scene: three horses pulling an old-fashioned sleigh. The driver and passengers wore large fur hats.

"The Russian troika," she said, reaching. "May I?"

Hansi nodded. "Manolo said to come to the hotel. He must have thought you—well, the owner—would know what to do with it."

Madame Poulet examined it, turning it over in her hands with the same care as Maman with her Villeroy and Boch teacups.

"I wasn't entirely truthful with you, Hansi. My husband owned this hotel. He inherited it from his father, who inherited it from his father. And when Jacky is old enough, it will belong to him."

It was at that instant Hansi noticed the ring on her finger.

"For now, I guess you could say that I am the owner."

"I'm sorry, Madame."

She smiled, though it was mixed with pained eyes. "He went to the city last month for a part to fix our boiler. We had finally saved enough. The heat was off and on all winter. He was on his way back. It was during that cold snap the first of April. He had nearly made it. Just south of the bridge, the one you and your friend blew up. There was no grip on those old tires."

Hansi couldn't speak, couldn't move.

She set the box on the table.

"It is quite an extraordinary piece. Beautifully painted. Handmade in Russia, I believe, for the Tsars to hold their jewelry. I've read about them in a magazine. They are very rare, very expensive. But I'm afraid I have no idea why your friend wanted you to bring it to me," she said. She opened the lid, revealing an interior painted red. Completely smooth and empty.

"Are you sure he said nothing more? No further instructions?"

Hansi shook his head. He looked at it again while searching his memory. Everything at the end had happened so quickly. Manolo had faded so fast he had nearly missed giving the pouch to Hansi altogether. Still, there was nothing Hansi could remember about it other than the simple command: *take it to the hotel.*

Michele came in from the kitchen, where she had been washing the dishes. Her brown hair curled to form a frame around her slender face, whose cheeks were flush from her work. She came to the table and noticed the box.

"It's beautiful," she said. Then to Hansi, "Yours?"

He hesitated. "It is now."

Michele was confused and began to turn the box over in her hands, examining its detail. She slid her finger slowly along the edge of the base. "The craftsmen were known to create secret compartments, for the Tsarina's to hide their most precious treasures. Oh my! Look!"

She showed them a section of the base where, nearly invisible before, a rectangular line formed a segment at the corner. She pressed on it and it gave way. An audible *click* signaled a change in the nature of the box.

Michele turned the box upright again and opened the lid. The bottom, a glossy red lacquer, was loose inside. She carefully lifted it out.

Hansi saw a white slip of paper revealed below it. By instinct, his hand reached to take it.

"Of course!" Michele gasped, handing the assembly to

Hansi. "I'm sorry. I shouldn't have."

Hansi shook the box roughly. The false bottom clattered on the table while the slip of paper fluttered down like a falling leaf. He snatched it out of the air.

"I don't understand." He handed the paper to Madame Poulet.

She retrieved a pair of glasses from her blouse and studied the sheet. It was a portion of a printed page from a book. The left edge was a mostly straight line, as though it had been sliced from the binding with a blade. But it had been torn in two pieces, and Madame Poulet held the top half or so. It had been ripped in a diagonal so that leading edges of sentences hung on the page as if at the edge of a cliff that had been swept away by the surf.

"It's Hugo," she said. "From *Les Misérables*." She handed it back to Hansi. "Does this mean anything to you?"

Hugo, Hansi knew, had written massive novels. Some teachers required *Les Misérables* for advanced French. But Hansi hadn't read it. As he scanned the page, he shook his head in slow frustration.

Michele asked for a look. Her large brown eyes darted over the surface, alight with interest. She murmured the French under her breath, as if savoring the sounds to herself.

"I know this. Here's a familiar quote—or at least part of it: *'mourir n'est rien.' To die is nothing.* I wish I could remember the rest of it. Hugo visited Vianden frequently, in this very hotel."

"What does it mean?" her mother asked Hansi.

"I wish I knew. My friend didn't tell me." He took the page from Michele and shoved it in his shirt pocket. Then he replaced the false bottom in the box and shut the lid. "What a waste," was all he could say. "What a waste."

He felt the hand of Madame Poulet on his shoulder. When he glanced up at her, her jaw was set in a confident expression. "I know who to ask. I'll go to Father Mathieu. Perhaps he can help."

After hiding the box under the corner of his mattress, Hansi returned to the kitchen. Though only a handful of guests remained in the hotel after the Germans crossed the border, the Poulets were glad for the extra help. The evening meal would be simple, but Madame Poulet put Hansi to work on the next day's midday spread.

Hansi welcomed the distraction. He peeled potatoes with Jacky—they filled the most enormous steel pot Hansi had ever seen—while Michele set the dining room. Madame tended to everything else—first braising the beef with butter, chopping onions and carrots, and then bathing everything in red wine. Between each phase, she rushed in and out through a wide swinging door back and forth to the dining room, carrying dishes, sweeping floors, arranging chairs. No detail escaped her attention.

When the last peel hit the pail, Jacky dumped it out back. In the meantime, Hansi lifted the pot full of potatoes onto the stove and filled it with water from a faucet built just for this purpose. Then came the dining room. Tablecloths needed changed, silverware set, candles lit. Jacky seemed to enjoy the help the most, because the longer they worked together, the quicker his responsibilities were discharged.

Despite the hum of aircraft, which from time to time vibrated the dining room windows and served as a constant reminder of the war, everyone, Hansi concluded, seemed to enjoy the routine—in a small way and but for a few moments, it kept the sense of dread at bay; the feeling of fear and despair from knowing that less than a kilometer away, the German Army was smashing through the village.

When they were finished, Hansi noticed Jacky had positioned himself at the doorway between the dining room and the lobby. He was watching for his mother to return.

"I'll not be far, Maman!" Jacky called when she pushed through the kitchen doorway. She was distracted by a sudden thought, a forgotten detail, Hansi reasoned, and spun back toward the kitchen. A vague wave and she was gone. Jacky had a wild and delicious look on his face.

Hansi caught up with him on the front steps. He clamped down on his arm and swung him around.

"Where are you going?"

"To watch the tanks," Jacky replied, as if there could have been no other reasonable answer. "Why don't you come with me?"

Hansi jerked his arm. "You stay away from them, do you hear me?"

Jacky's brow shriveled. He jerked even harder. "Leave me alone. You're not my father."

"If your father was here, he'd lock you in your room after what you did down there today."

Jacky's face puffed red.

"If my father were here, he'd be proud of me." Jacky twisted and threw a kick that hit Hansi across the shin like a wooden plank. Hansi let go.

Jacky paused for a fraction, staring down at Hansi as if proud of his accomplishment. Then, with a slight grin, turned to go.

"Jean Jacque Poulet! Don't you take another step!"

Hansi looked up. Behind him, Michele stood at the door of the inn, wagging her finger at her brother. His grin melted away. He didn't move.

Michele closed the distance, holding Jacky by the power, it seemed, of only her stare.

"If you take another step toward the village, I'll thrash you harder than Father ever dreamed!"

A look of horror swept over him. His lip quivered and then wrinkled as he fought a sudden wave of emotion. Jacky burst between them through the front door, slamming it behind him, disappearing inside.

Tears had filled Michele's eyes. They stood for a moment in silence together on the sidewalk.

"He doesn't understand," she said, "why Father isn't coming home."

"I'm sorry," was all Hansi knew to say.

Michele moved closer and slipped her arm inside Hansi's. At her touch, his arm tensed, but he hoped, somehow, she couldn't tell. Together they turned back toward the inn and began the walk to the door.

"We are glad you have come. Even if you don't know why."

Hansi was surprised that Madame Poulet had shared information with Michele. He thought all details had to be kept secret, with only those directly involved needing to know. Pierre had said as much. Manolo and Papa hadn't shared much. Thinking about it, though, Hansi realized there was not much, if anything, to keep secret. Sure, Manolo had blown the bridge, and passed on the box. But it was empty. *A dead end.* And so, apparently, was his mission. It didn't much matter, he concluded, whether Michele knew or not. In the end, the reasoning brought a greater relief than Hansi anticipated. He liked their family. He liked Michele. She was strong. She had reason to expect help from others but asked for none. If anything, she resisted special consideration. Yet a part of her was like Jacky. Very much in grief. Very much on the edge of losing control. He would stay if they let him, Hansi decided, until Papa arrived. There was plenty to do around the hotel. The work would be a nice distraction.

Hansi sat with Michele at the front desk as the last of the day's light leaked away. They both seemed content to let the darkness seep in. For Hansi's part, it was the toughest part of the day. A time when, as the day turned to night, he enjoyed the quiet moments at home. Supper with his mother and father, followed perhaps, by a radio program in the front room. A detective mystery or American western, dramatized in incredible detail, particularly in the sound effects—the tinkle of keys in a lock, the clicking of ominous footsteps. Unlike the movies, in which every detail was seen as well as heard, the radio left the listener to imagine the world in one's own way.

Staring out the window at the dark silent street, he realized how much he missed the pleasure. Only the companionship of Michele made the situation bearable.

He glanced her way. She seemed locked in the same sad stare. It was easy to know why. The face of Maman rose up in his mind's eye. The stone in his stomach began to burn.

"I think I'll go see if Madame needs a hand with the guests."

"Please, Hansi, stay." Michele spoke softly. "I'd feel better if you'd sit here with me. Maman will be fine. She always is. The work distracts her I think."

"Your hotel is very nice. And clean. Not that I've ever been to a hotel before," he added, "but it seems very comfortable. Like someone's flat."

Michele laughed.

"A flat? So, it's as nice as an apartment?" Her tone was sarcastic. "Thanks! I'll be sure to tell Maman. She'll be so pleased."

Hansi was confused.

"I meant it as a compliment, really, I did. You see, I live in a flat."

"You're from Luxembourg City, then?"

"It's an average flat I suppose, probably below average really. But it's nice enough."

"And clean."

"Yes. Hah, I see. I'm just trying to make conversation."

"I'm just teasing you, Hansi. I'm glad you're here to appreciate Maman's hard work. At least someone does.

Jacky makes the messes I think, just so Maman will get the pleasure of cleaning them up."

Hansi grew serious. "You're going to have to keep a close eye on him, Michele. The Germans don't care that he's just a boy."

Michele didn't reply.

Hansi felt a freeze in the air. "I'm not trying to scare you. Truly I'm not."

"Too late. I'm already terrified."

"I'm sorry," he said.

"It's not your fault. I have been scared ever since—."

"Your father was killed?" Hansi finished, instantly regretting it.

"No. Ever since I got sick."

Hansi suddenly realized the way she moved, the way part of her body seemed out of sync with the other part, was more than just the way she was.

"I remember the day like it was this morning," she said. "I woke up with a terrible fever. At first, I was glad not to have to go to school. But there was something different about this one. It seemed to have attacked my entire body. By midday, I couldn't move. I thought I was going to die. Maman called for the doctor. They talked in the hallway, outside my door. I'll never forget it. That's when I got scared. They took me that afternoon to the hospital in Luxembourg City. Every bump in the road was like getting stabbed with a knife."

"What was it?"

"Polio."

Hansi tensed. He knew of a boy in his apartment

building sent away for treatment, never to be heard from again.

"What did they do?" he asked.

"Not much, really. I lay in bed for months. They wouldn't let me get up. The fever would come and go. Not as bad as at first, but off and on for weeks. Finally, it went away. By itself. It spared me. But I was left with this."

It was dark, but Hansi could see well enough. Michele twisted her shoulder in such a way that her weakened arm flopped out from her body. And then she presented her cheek to him, the side that sagged.

"They said that I was one of the lucky ones. Lots of kids would be in the ward with me one day, gone the next. If the polio went into your lungs, it was the Beast for you."

"Huh?"

"The iron lung. A giant machine. Like a locomotive boiler. They put you inside it, and it presses down on your chest. Makes you breathe. We called it 'The Beast', because it ate most of its visitors."

"This contraption is at the hospital?"

She nodded.

"What happened? How did you get better?"

"The polio—it kind of just leaves. I guess it's like a plague of locusts. It eats some fields more than others. It spared my life but ate my arm, leg, and part of my face."

"It's hard to imagine, Michele. Can it come back?"

"You can see why I'm still afraid, Hansi. The doctors say it never attacks the same person twice, but I don't believe them. They seem to know very little about it. How would they know?"

She leaned over toward him, as if to whisper something in his ear, and then, just before speaking, jabbed him in the ribs with her finger. He nearly fell off his chair. She burst out laughing.

"And it's not contagious! At least that's what they tell me."

Hansi let out a grin and felt an ache rise back in his molars. He liked her.

The bell danced to life as the front door swung open. A rush of cool air met Hansi's face as he looked up and saw a man whose silhouette filled the frame. The figure paused, stomping his feet and brushing the dust from his overcoat. He stepped forward just as Michele found the switch to the small light on the desk. The man's head was dipped forward, covered by a wide-brimmed hat. Hansi tensed. He had seen that garb before. The dark, knee-length trench coat, leather gloves, and wide-brimmed hat signaled not a businessman, but an officer of the German State Security, known to everyone as the Gestapo. The reputation of Gestapo men preceded them into every territory the Germans invaded, and the reports of ruthlessness wrought palpable fear.

The man let his hat fall into his cupped hand and lifted his face to reveal a smile.

"*Guten abend,*" he said. *Good evening.* "I would like a room, please."

Hansi didn't move.

Michele seemed unaware of the man's pedigree. Hansi had learned firsthand, the year before, when the Gestapo had temporarily assisted the Luxembourg gendarmes with anti-terrorist investigations. She retrieved the register from the drawer and pulled up on the ribbon that marked the day.

"Let me see here," she began, thumbing along the slots. "How many nights will you be staying?"

"One week for now. I require quiet, and I will take my meals in my room. I am not to be disturbed. You will clean in three days and then after I leave. What is the rate?"

She scanned the book and looked up at the keys along the wall.

"Here, room thirteen. It's upstairs, at the end of the hall. Should be nice and quiet. It's 425 francs per night."

The man rifled through a wad of bills he had produced and put the money down in front of her.

"I'm sorry, sir, but we only take Luxembourgish or Belgian francs—."

"I will pay in Reichsmarks. Here's one hundred marks. Soon enough there will be no francs, and you will thank me for my generosity."

Michele opened her mouth to speak, but Hansi warned her not to with a touch on her arm.

Later, when dinner had been cleaned up, Hansi sat with Michele and Madame Poulet in the kitchen.

"He's Gestapo," Hansi said. "I'm sure of it."

"And how do you know?" Madame Poulet asked.

Hansi wanted to tell the whole story. Of his father's disappearance the year before. Of the Gestapo's subversion of the gendarmerie, and near overthrow of the Luxembourg government.

"They are all the same. The trench coat, the hat, the air about them. They own the world and don't take 'no' for an answer."

"Why would he come here?" Michele asked.

"You must do everything he says and give him no reason to suspect anything about anything," Hansi said.

"Perhaps someone told him," Madame Poulet suggested, her eyes searching her memory.

"We must be very careful," Hansi said. "I must tell Pierre."

"Where is he?" Michele asked.

"At a camp west of the river."

"Be careful."

"I will. He will know what to do."

Michele touched Hansi's arm.

"What happened out there, Hansi?"

"What do you mean?"

"I can see it in your eyes. You are afraid too. And something else."

He waved her off. "You can see it for yourself, Michele. There's an army over there."

"No. It's more. Something happened. Tell me."

The vice tightened around his throat. Everything got hot. He looked down.

"Please, Hansi. We're friends. Tell me. This war will be bad enough. Don't carry it alone. Tell me. Please."

Her touch was tender, and powerful. He tried to swallow, but the knot was enormous.

He told her. He explained it all, from start to finish, holding nothing back. The bridge, the woods, the German.

And Manolo.

"I was right there. I froze up. I could have saved him."

His head felt that it might burst. He wondered if he would leave his body and drift away. His molten guts wanted to erupt again, and only the embarrassment held his dinner down.

Michele sat in silence at his side, holding his hand. Then, after a moment, simply leaned forward, and rested her head on his shoulder.

Chapter Fifteen

At seven in the evening, a full two hours before curfew, Hansi set out. He joined the line of travelers down in the village and followed them west across the river, up the cut in the ridge below the chateau, and into the forest. He needed to be positioned to find the trail the Boy Scouts had taught him before nightfall.

About halfway up the hill, with the village still in view behind him, a road split north. It followed a wide sweep on a steeper course up to the ruins. Here, the parade of pedestrians thinned to just a few farmers heading home from a day in the town. Here, Hansi caught sight of a small figure behind him that had been trailing just far enough behind to avoid detection amongst the crowds. Here, at a distance too far for him to return to the village and back before dark, and curfew. Hansi stopped, turned, and positioned himself like a sentry. The boy, seeing now that Hansi recognized him, ran to join Hansi.

"Go home, Jacky." Hansi was not asking.

The boy's grin, that of anticipation shared between co-conspirators, vanished.

"Mother sent me to keep an eye on you," he answered.

Hansi guessed Jacky had been thinking about this in advance. "You're lying. Your mother would thrash you a good one if she knew you were here. Now turn around and go home."

"I won't make it before curfew."

"You can if you run."

"Where are you going?"

"None of your business. You need to get out of here. I can't be late."

"I'll go with you." Jacky moved past Hansi and continued up the road.

"You can't, Jacky."

"How far are you going?"

Hansi had to run to catch up to him. He grabbed Jacky by the front of his jacket and spun him around.

"Listen to me! I'm telling you. You've got to go home. This is no place for you."

"The forest? Are you heading to the forest? That's got to be it."

Hansi was surprised. How did he know?

"What if something happens to you, Hansi? Somebody will need to warn the others."

"What others?"

"Mother. And 'Chele. You've stirred them like a pot of leftover stew. If you don't come back, I need to tell them."

Without realizing it, Hansi had followed Jacky to the top of the ridge, where the road had begun to level off. He was winded from the walk and the argument. Jacky was right about one thing. The sun was slipping fast. He would be in danger trying to make it home now.

"Pay attention, Jacky. You must do exactly as I say. Where I'm going, I must be alone. If they catch you with me, who knows what will happen. Do you understand me?"

Jacky almost leapt with excitement. He agreed, showing it by bobbing his head up and down like an obedient dog. An instant later, he produced a pair of apples from his pockets and offered Hansi one. "Hungry?"

Not more than half an hour later, with bright streaks of rose-colored clouds in the sky overhead, Hansi found the spot where he had exited the woods the day before. They were the only civilians in sight. The German army marched and rolled past, oblivious to their presence. The stream of vehicles and men seemed endless, Hansi thought, as if the country had been drained of every last man and was pouring them through this road.

The French don't stand a chance.

Keeping his thoughts to himself, Hansi pulled Jacky down into the ditch, and together they slipped into the trees.

As darkness fell quickly in cover of the woods, Hansi hurried down the path. He found a fallen tree, whose bark and branches had long been withered away, and sat Jacky down. The rumble of vehicles could still be heard in the distance, but they were out of sight of the road.

"Wait here," he commanded. "Your mother will be scared to death when she realizes you are not there. Don't make it worse by wandering back to the road and getting yourself arrested for violating curfew."

Jacky looked suddenly afraid. "How long will you be?"

"Not long. But we have to wait until it's completely dark now before we go back. And we'll have to stay in the woods to avoid the traffic."

"What if you don't come back? What will I do?"

"I'll be back. I promise. In the meantime—" Hansi

paused. "I don't know—say your prayers."

As he turned and bounded deeper into the forest, Hansi was surprised at himself for the advice he'd just given. It had just popped out. Jacky was worried—it showed in his pressed eyes and twisted mouth—and the expression made Hansi think of Maman. She had a sincere faith. At night, when Hansi was younger, she'd tuck him into bed and sit beside him. He would tell her about the things that happened that day—the perils of a hard test, an argument or fight at school—all the trials of a young boy were laid in her lap. And she would listen. She would nod and hum a simple acknowledgement: *Uh huh. Yes, dear. Of course.* He could talk as long as he wanted or until sleep took over, whichever came first, and it was normally the latter. But no matter how late or how tired, Maman seemed to know the right moment to end the conversation. The simple phrase—*say your prayers*—came without even the hint of scolding. She meant it as a way of directing Hansi's cares beyond herself. He would eke out the feeblest of prayers, often through the fog of fatigue, but they were effective. The day and its cares were left behind.

Hansi moved along with a sense of sadness and guilt. Such times with Maman were distant memories and bound to grow even more so. And his counsel to Jacky had been nothing like that of his mother—Hansi had nothing of her compassion and patience. And so Hansi had swung the advice like a club, and now he felt ashamed.

"Who is the boy?"

The voice caught Hansi by surprise. Pierre appeared

from behind a tree, his face floating ghostlike in the darkness above the red glow of his pipe.

"No one. He just followed me."

"I told you to return alone."

"I didn't want him to come. He just followed me. He'll wait by the road."

"Followed you from where?" Pierre's tone was nothing like before. It carried none of the charm and persuasion. He seemed irritated and urgent.

"The village."

"Where in the village? Why did he follow you? Who is he?" The questions came like a jackhammer.

"H-h-halfway up the hill. I noticed him."

Pierre leapt forward and grabbed Hansi by the front of his shirt. "You spoke to him by name. You must know him."

"Jacky," Hansi croaked. "His name is Jacky. He lives at the hotel."

Pierre let go and stepped back. He sucked in again on his pipe and let the sweet smoke swirl in the space between them.

"So, you've been to the hotel. Excellent." Pierre's voice had changed in a heartbeat back to that of the sophisticated spy.

"I appreciate your effort, Hansi, I really do. But it is critical that you hold nothing back, nothing at all. You must tell me everything even though you think you are protecting someone as harmless as a boy. The Nazis are very clever, you see. You would be surprised at who they can use."

"Jacky hates the Nazis. I've seen it firsthand. You have nothing to fear with him."

"Very well. Then let's leave it at that. You have been to the hotel. You've met your contact?"

"Not really." Hansi explained that Madame Poulet was part of the Resistance, but that she had no idea about the next step. He told Pierre about the Russian box and the half-page from *Les Misérables*. That Madame Poulet would ask Father Mathieu. "The whole thing is stupid if you ask me. My friend is dead, and we have no idea what he was up to. I've done my part. I'm going to go find Jacky and head back."

Hansi turned to leave.

"Father Mathieu. He's part of the Resistance?"

Hansi shrugged. "I suppose so. Madame Poulet seemed to think he might know. But I want out. I did what you asked. I'm finished."

The words, finally spoken rather than just rattling around in his mind, surprised Hansi. But they were true.

"I need to find out. You can still help."

"It's too dangerous," Hansi replied. "I'm not suited for this kind of thing. Come to the hotel and do it yourself. You can take care of the Gestapo agent while you're at it."

"What?"

"A Gestapo agent checked into the hotel. Everybody seems to know what's going on but us. I'm done with it, Pierre. I'm finished."

Pierre moved close again, but he didn't grab Hansi's shirt.

"Think of your friend, Hansi, please. He gave his life

for this, whatever it is. He died for nothing if we stop here. There is something going on, and we must find out. It's too dangerous for me—they'd spot me in an instant. Just ask the woman, Hansi. Find out what the priest tells her. Come back here tomorrow as soon as you can. It will be enough, I promise."

The only part Hansi heard was the part about Manolo. He had died for something else, not the bridge. It must have been important. Pierre was nobody. Manolo was his friend.

"Tomorrow and that's it, then. No more."

"No more," Pierre agreed.

Hansi hiked back toward the road using the compass the Boy Scouts had given him and a card deck-sized light Pierre gave him. It was fitted with a special cap over the lens to permit but a tiny slit of light to escape, allowing just enough light for Hansi not to run into the trees. He navigated the way he had entered until he reached the trail off the road. But when he found the log where he had left Jacky, the boy was missing.

Hansi waited for a moment and wondered what to think. Now that it was dark, Jacky could have headed for home. It was the least worrisome outcome, Hansi thought. But he couldn't be sure. So, he switched off the light, let his eyes adjust to the starlit surroundings, and decided to search. He would check the road first in case Jacky had gotten scared and headed there. If he wasn't there, Hansi would return to the log and search onwards.

He didn't go far. A branch snapped from behind.

Hansi spun around, flicked on the light, and there Jacky stood, as if he sprung out of the ground.

"Where were you? I told you to stay at the log and wait for me there."

Jacky rubbed his nose with the back of his hand and sniffed. Hansi shone the light on his face and saw that his cheeks were shiny, his nose dripping. He was breathing rapidly.

"You followed me!" Hansi snatched the boy by the collar and shook him. "Pierre might have shot you. Or both of us. Didn't you hear me? I told you to stay put!"

Jacky twisted free. He was defiant.

"You're not my boss. And besides, I don't trust him. You shouldn't either."

Hansi turned away and stomped up the path. "What do you know about it? What do you know about anything?"

Jacky ran to catch up. "I know that if Pierre was so important, he'd help you. He wouldn't hide out in the woods like a scared rabbit. He'd come out in the open and fight the Germans."

"Oh right," Hansi huffed. "I almost forgot—you fought the Nazi propaganda battalion. I hear the Germans are thinking about canceling the invasion. All because of you."

"And what have you done? I hope I ruined their stupid film."

The accusation stung. Hansi said nothing more as they trudged back up the slope to the edge of the road. Jacky was a fool, and Hansi couldn't help but think the boy's impetuousness would cost him dearly if he didn't heed the warnings. But the lingering thought—the one that tormented Hansi as they worked their way along the edge of the forest back to Vianden—was that Jacky possessed raw courage Hansi could only envy.

Chapter Sixteen

Upon their return to Vianden, the pair kept to narrow garden paths and dark alleys to work their way back to the hotel. It was shrouded in darkness and seemed lifeless from the outside.

They ascended the stone path that bisected a narrow strip of lawn along the back of the hotel. At the steps to the kitchen door, they were met by the smell of manure. Just off the edge of the porch lay the carcass of a hog, sprawled out on the grass. Its head was marked with a peppering of holes about the diameter of Hansi's thumb. The underbelly had been sliced open from snout to tail. The cuts were rough and jagged, as if the beast had been butchered with an ax.

At the door the smell of roasted meat mixed with that of manure. Although he didn't know what time it was, he knew it was late and expected the hotel to be quiet, the few guests asleep. Instead, the kitchen was alive with bright lights and activity. Potatoes boiled in huge aluminum pots. Pork sizzled in cast iron skillets. Hansi slung his jacket over a hook and moved further in. Jacky slid past him and disappeared through a narrow door that bypassed the dining room for the interior of the hotel.

An instant later, Madame Poulet appeared through the swinging door with an overloaded tray of empty dishes rocking on her shoulder. An explosion of sound— masculine shouts and laughing—crashed in behind her.

She tossed Hansi an anxious look, and he could tell

from the loud German voices that Leutnant Schmidt's men had returned.

Hansi took the tray from her.

She sat the tray onto a table between the stove and a large sink. "Anything?" she asked.

Hansi shook his head.

"I spoke with Father Matheiu. He wants to see the page," she said, her voice barely audible.

"What about the special guest in room thirteen?"

"He's been invisible. I don't think he's left his room since checking in."

The dishes went into a large sudsy basin and Madame Poulet motioned Hansi to follow her to the stove. She ladled potatoes and odd-shaped chunks of meat into a collection of odd-shaped dishes stacked beside her.

"If the soldiers hadn't brought the hog, I don't know what I'd have done. They ate my entire week's order of meat the last time they were here." She shook her head and wiped a lock of hair out of her eyes. "I don't know how they expect me to keep up."

"Don't worry, Madame. Everything will be all right. I'll help you." The words came out slowly with a weight that extended beyond serving food. Why he spoke that way, Hansi wasn't sure. But he was glad he did.

"Take this," she said. "I'm going to go find some old dishes and check on Jacky." He took the tray and hoisted it up while the woman slipped out the same door Jacky had used.

The tray weighed more than he realized, but he would manage. He headed for the dining room, pushing backwards through the swinging door. The floor was covered with boot prints and mud clods. For an instant, he wondered if something had caught fire. Smoke hung low and stung his nose and eyes. The tables were arranged in a long line and encircled by soldiers crammed twice the normal density. Bottles rose like chimneys and every other centimeter was covered with plates, serving dishes, and glasses. Hansi twisted in and let the door slide off his backside. When the soldiers saw him, they erupted in a spontaneous cheer.

The air assaulted Hansi's nostrils—a mix of sweat, food, beer, cigarettes, belches, and farts. He coughed and nearly lost control of the tray.

"Open a window!" a voice nearby shouted. Hansi watched a grimy-faced soldier, whose tunic was unbuttoned to his waist, stand up, snatch a rifle from the wall, and smash open the closest window. The platoon erupted in their endorsement.

At the head of the table, Michele fought a losing battle to keep the glasses full. Her face was taut with tension pouring beer as fast as she could.

She squeezed between two soldiers and drained the last of her pitcher into a glass that was filled less than a quarter full. Her chin was trembling.

In a flash, Hansi discovered the source of her terror— a sweaty, red-nosed, leathery-faced soldier whose tunic was unbuttoned halfway down his torso waved an empty glass like a signal flag.

Schmidt was nowhere to be found.

"She may be crippled, but she's still a sweet little

Mädchen!"

Michele tensed.

"I'll return with more, Corporal Bultmann," she said, but it was too late. Bultmann snatched her around the waist and pulled her onto his lap.

"Das macht nicht!" he bellowed. "I'm in no hurry!" He squeezed her close and made knowing eyes at his comrades. They roared in approval.

Michele twisted free, and hit Bultmann in the lip with the elbow on her strong side. His head snapped back at the force of the blow, and Michele was free. She jumped up, pitcher in hand, and fled. Bultmann's lip gushed blood, and he leapt up in a furious rage.

Michele flew past Hansi into the kitchen. Bultmann was only steps behind her, screaming. He thundered past Hansi, but his bulk and the effect of alcohol transformed him into a lumbering beast. The tray exploded, sending plates and potatoes and sausage everywhere. The man lost control. Hansi spun around and slipped on the mud or a piece of potato, he wasn't sure. He went down with a hard bump and found himself on a burning bed of potatoes and pork, broken porcelain, and tangled legs of angry soldiers.

Michele disappeared through the kitchen door with Bultmann close behind. Hansi twisted in the mess, found his knees, and had risen among a chorus of curses and shouts when Michele screamed.

Hansi slipped, slid, and clawed his way through the throng. He burst into the kitchen. It was empty but for the cool breeze wafting in.

"I'll teach you to make a fool out of me!" The

German's voice came from outside.

Hansi ran through the kitchen and out the open door. Bultmann had Michele in his grasp, clamping her in place with powerful arms so he could force a bloody kiss. Her frenzied twists did nothing but fuel his rage.

Hansi came upon the German from behind and realized he had snatched the only thing suggestive of a weapon from the kitchen on the way through—a wooden paddle the length of his arm, used for stirring the enormous pots. He squeezed it with both hands, raised it high, and swung hard like he was splitting a log. It cracked on the German's head and disintegrated in an explosion of splinters. The German spasmed in surprise, but only for an instant. He let go of Michele and whirled around to face his attacker. His eyes were wide and yellow.

Without thinking, Hansi lowered his head and charged straight ahead. He hit the German just below the breastbone with the side of his head and shoulder. Though the soldier was nearly twice Hansi's size, the force compensated for the difference and was sufficient to send both of them off the edge of the landing.

They hit the sidewalk with a hard *clunk* and the sound of air being let out of a bag. The German fell still. Dazed but unhurt, Hansi rolled off, climbed to his feet, and was back at Michele's side on the landing.

"Did he hurt you?"

Tears streaked down from her eyes. She shook her head back and forth. Hansi reached out for her, but he was interrupted by a soldier bursting through the door. The man still had his napkin tucked into the top of his tunic.

His face was greasy from the meat. He looked at Michele and Hansi before his attention was seized by the figure at the bottom of the landing. He jumped down to Bultmann's side.

The rest of the platoon spilled out. Soon, the narrow strip of lawn behind the hotel was filled with soldiers clumped around their comrade.

Madame Poulet came last, her face twisted with horror, and then, seeing Michele safe on the porch, drained in relief. She collected her daughter and pulled her inside.

Hansi moved to follow. He took but a step before he was jerked by the arm like a dog at the end of his chain. Leutnant Schmidt took up position between Hansi and the door.

His stare froze Hansi in place. Then, as his gaze shifted to the men at the bottom of the steps, Hansi couldn't help but turn too.

The soldiers were huddled over their corporal. The one with the napkin in his collar had his ear to the fallen soldier's chest. Then, without warning, he snapped upright and spun around. His face was pale, his eyes huge circles. The others followed, their stares like a dozen shotgun barrels aimed at Hansi.

"He's dead."

Chapter Seventeen

Karin had little time to grieve her failure to call Hansi. That night after an evening of not speaking to her mother, whose BDM ambush Karin had thoroughly rejected, she hunkered down in her room, reading a book of poetry her grandmother had given her. Debussy's "Clair de Lune" played quietly on the phonograph. Karin had liberated the machine from their living room, where it was gathering dust since they had moved back to Berlin the previous autumn. It was her father's. He'd listen to Wagner and Beethoven. Karin preferred Mozart and Tchaikovsky, who were mostly out of fashion—the former for being too joyful, the latter for being too Russian. Ursula never used it, leaving Karin to incorporate it in her private sanctuary on the top floor of their townhouse. She would wind it up and listen to scratchy discs of various artists, including the forbidden Felix Mendelssohn and American George Gershwin. Her enjoyment of the classical pieces put her out of step with any of the people her own age, and most of the people her parents' age too. But they had belonged to her father, who had inherited them from his mother. And so, without consciously realizing it, the music connected her with the time without war, when both Grandmother and Father were free to enjoy them with a smile.

Karin was having trouble with the lines on the page of her biology text when the front door buzzer sounded at the edge of her notice. The hour was far too late for Karin's own sensibility, but not for Mother.

Moments later, a knock sounded at her bedroom door.

Mother. *A peace offering?*

Karin bid her to enter, but not only was she empty-handed, but the narrow-set eyes showed concern.

"Heinrich is here. You must come at once."

"At this hour? I'm just going to bed."

"He must speak to you. Now."

Karin put her robe on and cinched it tight around the waist.

"I'm not joining," Karin muttered as she followed her mother downstairs.

Schlinge was waiting in the parlor. He had not removed his black leather coat. It had recently been cleaned, Karin observed, from the fresh black tone and buffed shine. But like him, it still bore the marks of wear and wounds. The blast at the Luxembourg Gare had nearly killed him, ripping across the right side of his body. Perhaps the leather had saved him. Perhaps that was why he had kept the coat, when anyone else would have replaced it long ago. The tattered appearance diminished his authority, Karin thought. But she knew not to trust in appearances. Not only in general, but especially when it came to Heinrich Schlinge. He had some mysterious role in her father's death, she was sure, but he had not only survived, but escaped blame for the failure of their mission, whatever it had been.

Her attitude toward him was not quite ambivalent. On his own, he was to be feared as any of the power-driven Gestapo men. As a friend of Mother, she was both disgusted and yet somehow assured that, as long as her mother led him around, Karin herself was safe. Sort of.

Schlinge skipped the greeting. "What were you doing in Berlin this afternoon?"

"You know perfectly well if you've spoken to Mother. We were," she paused, unable to withhold the look of contempt. "Shopping."

"After that."

"I went home by myself. We had a falling out."

"What about?"

Karin looked at her mother. "Have you two not spoken? I'm not joining."

"Not now," her mother offered.

"Not ever," Karin said.

"On your way home, where did you go?"

"Nowhere," Karin lied. "I just needed to walk."

Schlinge took a deep breath and let it out slowly. He flipped Ursula a disappointed look, and then turned back to Karin. He forced what he probably thought was a smile but looked more like he had stubbed his toe on something. Or banged his shin on a railing.

"Karin, please. I can understand you have not quite become accustomed to me. Being closer to your life, and that of your mother."

Not quite. Karin wanted to laugh.

"But you must grow to trust me. I can make things better for you in the days ahead."

"Better," she repeated. "Are they bad now? Are they going to get worse?"

"A girl like you without a father is quite vulnerable,

you see." He chose his words carefully. "I can protect you."

"What does that have to do with anything? With Mother and me shopping and me walking home?"

"You must tell me the truth," he replied. "No matter how difficult or embarrassing it must seem. I understand you more than you know, and can help you."

"Help me now, then," she said. "Because you're talking in riddles."

"You went to the PTT, did you not?"

"You know I did. So why did you ask?"

"And whom did you call?"

"You seem to know everything, so you tell me."

"Karin!"

Her mother's slap stung Karin's cheek.

"You'll show him more respect."

Karin fought back tears, both from the slap and the humiliation.

"I called Hansi in Luxembourg."

"That's right," Schlinge said.

"That urchin!" Ursula blasted. "After what he did?"

Karin glared at her. "What *did* he do, Mother?"

Ursula folded her arms and shook away the question. "I don't know other than that he is responsible for your father's death."

"Oh really? Do you know, Herr Schlinge?"

"I wasn't there," he said.

"Of course you weren't. How convenient." Karin turned to Ursula. This time, her anger held her mother's hand at bay. Ursula hesitated.

Schlinge continued. "It was both a profound tragedy and a profound mystery. The exact circumstances, and indeed, the actions of the young boy are unclear even to this day. Officially, he is responsible. I have no doubt of his intention to harm your father. Unofficially, I appreciate your perspective, Karin. Your father was a very capable man, and I doubt that the boy would have been any trouble for a man of your father's quality.

Karin rolled her eyes.

"Now you must listen to me for your own good, Fraulein Blik. You must not try to contact him. Truth or not, he is considered responsible. But I assure you, when German authority is fully established in the new Luxembourg, I will do everything in my power to make sure he is treated fairly."

"I know what that means!" Karin said.

Ursula sprung forward. Schlinge blocked her.

"Karin. You must not pursue this any further. You must forget that you ever knew him. Is that understood?"

Karin was seething, her body on fire, it seemed, the cinch of her robe slicing her torso.

Fists clenched and trembling, she managed to speak. "Perfectly clear," she said.

Without so much as a glance at her mother, she added, "Good night, Herr Schlinge," and left.

Chapter Eighteen

Leutnant Schmidt ordered a pair of soldiers to guard Hansi in the dining room. Madame Poulet was permitted to give Hansi a cup of tea, which helped calm his frayed, adrenaline-raddled nerves. As he settled, fear rose and brought tremors like being caught in the cold without a coat. Madame Poulet brought more tea and a blanket. Still, when the military police arrived about an hour later, Hansi was a shivering mass.

Through the window, Hansi saw a trio of men arrive outside. Trailing a pair of corporals in steel helmets and brandishing shoulder-slung machine pistols was an *unteroffizier* whose cap was tilted so far forward his eyes were mere slits in shadow beneath the brim.

Schmidt met them in the lobby and began to speak to the *unteroffizier*, who quickly brushed him aside. Without a word, the corporals crossed directly to Hansi. They swung their pistols behind their backs, and one of them jerked the blanket away with such force, Hansi fell to the floor.

They snatched him up. Hansi let his legs extend, but when they let go, his legs could not hold him. They had to drag him out of the room.

In the lobby, Madame Poulet and Michele clung to each other behind the desk. As he was dragged across the carpet toward the front door, Hansi twisted back, afraid to lose contact with the family that had taken him in. His eyes met Michele's. She burst into tears and buried her face in her mother's embrace. Then Jacky, who had been hiding behind the desk, popped up and flashed two fingers in a "V" for victory sign. The gesture did more for Hansi than the tea and blanket, until he saw movement in the stairwell. A figure appeared, hidden mostly in shadow.

The Gestapo man?

An instant later, he was out the door, chilled to the bone by the cold outside air.

Chapter Nineteen

Hansi lost track of what exactly happened next. He remembered the scuffing sound of his shoes on the gritty pavement, the scrape of a metal door swinging open, cold wet steel on his hands, the smell of urine and worse, and a jerky slamming ride in the back of a vehicle. The strain of the gearbox, being whipped from side to side as the vehicle navigated narrow turns at high speed, and then a stop. They dragged him out of the truck, where the air was colder than in the village, thrust something over his head to blind him, and dragged him over rough ground. The sounds, lost in the open air, suddenly grew close. He was in a narrow passageway, the smells musty now, some orders snapped in German. And then they let him go.

He fell onto what felt like a bed of razors. Sharp stones slashed at everything they touched—his elbows, face, shoulder, back, knees, thighs, and rear. A metal door slammed behind him. He rolled and squirmed, hoping for some relief from the jagged surface, but could find little. The torture seemed unbearable, clawing at his whole body until finally he found a sandy spot that rose above the chards.

He took off his mask and peered into the darkness. His heartbeat sounded throughout his entire body, overwhelmed by the breaches up and down its length.

After a few minutes, Hansi's eyes adjusted to make out the outlines of the walls around him. The chamber itself was quite large, and cold, and smelled like a kind of cellar.

Unlike a cellar, however, the walls stretched up three times his own height. And high up on the wall opposite the door, a small square, quartered by cross-shaped iron bars, opened to a handful of stars. Hansi knew immediately. He was in the ruins of the Vianden Chateau.

He tried to take stock of his injuries. His clothes had provided some protection against the sharp stones. Still, he had fallen hard enough that they had sliced through his pants at the knee, his shirt sleeve moving up from his right elbow, and apparently the mask above his right eye. These three were the major sources of pain and blood. The cool of the chamber helped, especially on the cut above his eye, which, after pressing with his shirt sleeve, quickly became sticky and seemed to have stopped.

He heard the tinkle of metal outside. The door scraped open. A bright, flickering light blinded him. He drew back and covered his eyes. An instant later, he was taken, this time without a blindfold or mask. The same gray-uniformed guards he had seen before dragged him out to the corridor and turned deeper inside the chateau.

They pulled him into a smaller cell and dropped him onto a chair that was positioned beneath a single bulb hanging from the ceiling. The bulb swung for a moment, dizzying him, until one of the guards grabbed it and steadied it just over Hansi's forehead. The heat felt good until it began to burn.

They bound his hands roughly around the back of the chair. Hansi had no intention of trying to escape. The Germans seemed superhuman, with their overwhelming size, strength, and well-oiled weapons. The arrest had sapped Hansi of all his strength, both physically and emotionally. Beneath the lamp, all Hansi could see was his knees, wet from blood and the dampness of the chamber, and the tips of his shoes, blackened and glistening with slime mold from being dragged through the corridor.

Then a voice, like a train station announcer, but more ominous: "Do not move or you will be shot. Do not speak unless you are asked a direct question. Answer the question and only the question. Do you understand?"

Hansi nodded. The sound came from in front of him, he could tell, though the speaker was invisible in the blackness.

Then the sound of footsteps, the scrape of wood on the floor, and the shuffling of papers.

Tap, tap, tap. Hansi strained against the darkness and thought he saw the outline of a slender hand, and a fountain pen.

"Name?" The voice was businesslike, carrying no anger or urgency.

"Hansi—" He paused. "Poulet." His voice was scratchy, almost foreign to his own ears.

"Explain your whereabouts the night of the ninth of May."

The night before the invasion?

"I was at home," he answered.

"Where is that?"

Hansi paused.

What did the man know? Was he the Gestapo agent from the hotel? Would he believe my story?

He pondered what to answer.

"At the Hotel de Vianden."

A loud crash in front of him made Hansi jump. The binds held him to the chair, chewed into his wrist, but kept him from tumbling over.

"The prisoner will answer with the truth! Where were you at midnight, the ninth of May?" The voice was surgical.

Everything felt weak. Hansi was sure the lie burning his cheeks was visible under the lamp. These were the kind of men impossible to fool. Hansi had encountered the Gestapo the year before, starting with the day he met Karin in the air raid shelter and overheard Schlinge whispering in the Casemate tunnels. Schlinge chased them all the way to the Gare and would have arrested Hansi if not for the explosion. He might have killed Hansi if not for Karin's butler, Fritz. The Gestapo was behind Hansi's father's arrest and disappearance, and the attempt to destroy the Grand Ducal Palace. Men like Schlinge only asked questions to which they already knew the answers. But Hansi couldn't give in. Surrendering would be a death sentence.

He's just testing me, that's all. Trying to keep me off balance.

"I was at home. Our family runs the Hotel de Vianden. At midnight I would have been asleep. You can ask my brother, my sister—."

"Silence! You will answer directly, only what is asked, nothing more. I instruct you not to test my patience."

Hansi nodded and ran his tongue along the roof of his mouth, teeth, and lips. There was little moisture, and his body was quaking.

"What was your role in the sabotage of the bridge on

the Diekirch road?"

The question hit like the butt of a rifle in the center of his chest.

The blood left his head, and everything started to go white. Hansi was seized with the certain knowledge that they knew everything, that they were just toying with him, and that he was as good as dead already. A tremor rose inside. He wanted to let go a wail, relinquish control to all he felt, and simply sob everything loose.

Something inside urged him to hang on. He squeezed his eyes shut, clenched his fists, and strained against the ropes. The pain directed his focus. He twisted them harder, sure the flesh was tearing.

"Do I look like a saboteur?"

"Silence! Further insolence, and you will be punished! Answer the question!"

A soldier penetrated the circle of light from Hansi's left. He struck him across the face with the back of his gloved hand. Hansi's head spun sideways as the pain exploded through him. The force knocked the chair over onto two legs, teetering, and then crashed sideways. Hansi's face slammed into the stone floor. The surface was cool and felt strangely relieving compared to the hot bulb. Then came the taste of blood, metallic and warm. The pain was so pervasive Hansi had no idea if he had busted his lip, broken teeth, or cracked open his forehead. Because of the binding on his hands, he could but lay there.

After a moment, powerful arms lifted him back to an upright position. He was fully alert now, the pain sending adrenaline coursing through his body, and back beneath the bulb.

"Did you shoot the German paratrooper?"

"No."

"What are the names of your co-conspirators?"

"I had nothing to do with it."

"Thill, Poulet, Henckel, St. Pierre? Did any of these participate in any way?"

The names were strange to Hansi, except for Poulet.

Hansi guessed that the others were on Pierre's list. Manolo had never mentioned anyone else, and now Hansi appreciated why details of the operation were kept secret. The less he knew, the less the Germans could learn by interrogation.

"No."

"But you know these names?"

"No, unless by Poulet you are speaking of my mother. This is the only name I know."

"Pierre Montagne. Do you know this man?"

They know everything. How?

"No, sir. I don't know anyone by that name."

There was another pause. Hansi braced for another blow. The bulb drifted slowly back and forth overhead. The strike didn't come.

Instead, Hansi heard the sound again of papers rustling and being thumped on the surface of the table.

"How old are you?"

"Fifteen."

"In time of war, the Wehrmacht must do everything to ensure its own safety to conduct military operations. It is authorized to bypass normal legal process to that end. In the Third Reich, the legal age of adults is sixteen. But saboteurs, at any age, will be shot. Do you understand?"

Hansi shuddered.

"I understand. I had nothing to do with any sort of sabotage."

"Does this belong to you?"

Hansi stared into the darkness. An instant later, something plopped on his lap. He looked down. The sight made him weak.

My sketchbook!

"Is it yours?"

Hansi stared at the name inside the front cover: *Hansi Broussard.*

"Yes," he answered. His mind raced for an explanation. "Where did you find it?"

"You don't know? We thought you would tell us."

"I have no idea. I've been looking all over for it."

"Indeed! And where have you been looking?"

Hansi scrambled for an idea. "All over the hotel. It's been missing for days."

"That's curious. We found it in a suitcase along the Diekirch Road. The same road at the end of which is a sabotaged bridge. The suitcase is full of things I'm pretty sure fit a boy of your size."

A shirt and a pair of pants hit him across the lap and face.

"Are these yours?"

"Yes," Hansi replied. "They're mine. I can explain."

"Please do." The voice was patronizing.

Hansi paused to think, overwhelmed by the frenetic

sense of panic. Everything inside wanted to shrink down to nothing and disappear into an atomic particle.

"We all had suitcases packed. Just in case."

"In case of what?"

"The invasion. We knew it was coming any day. We had packed suitcases in case we needed to flee. But mine got lost. Two days ago. I figured it must have gotten mixed up with one of our guests. Perhaps they took it by mistake. That explains why I couldn't find it anywhere in the hotel."

Hansi was surprised, but proud of his answer. It had popped into his mind like a gift.

There was silence in reply. Alarming silence. Hansi's joy was snatched away as quickly as it had been given.

"Anything else?" the voice finally asked.

"I don't understand."

"Did you lose anything else?"

Hansi shook his head.

"Are you sure?"

Every muscle clenched. *What did he mean? He's leading me to something, but what?*

"I'm sure," Hansi answered.

"I'm glad," the voice said calmly, "because by the look of that sketchbook I thought perhaps you had misplaced your family name—Broussard. A moment ago, I thought you said your mother's name was Poulet."

The trap snapped shut with deafening silence. Invisible teeth clamped around Hansi's throat and squeezed out his breath. He'd been caught in a lie, and the rest, he feared, would pour out like wine from a cracked bottle.

The voice waited.

"Broussard is my artist name. Poulet is my real name." This twist came in the same kind of flash as before, but without the sense of being a gift. With each lie, Hansi knew he was digging a deeper and deeper pit, from which there might be no escape.

"A pseudonym. Hmm. Very convenient for a fifteen-year-old. Very convenient indeed. Imagination is vivid for one so young, *ja?*"

The voice fell silent again. Hansi took the moment to breathe, to regroup. His explanation was beyond imagination. Pure fiction, but an answer all the same. A question and an answer—a few more seconds alive.

"Corporal Bultmann. He died last night at your hotel. Surely you know something about this?"

The question came as a relief. Hansi told the truth. Bultmann was drunk. He grabbed Michele. Hansi hit, and he fell. It was an accident.

"Do you also realize that attacking a German soldier in the discharge of his duties is an offense punishable by death?"

"No, sir."

"Why did you strike Corporal Bultmann?"

"He was hurting Michele."

"Don't you mean 'your sister?' The other witnesses say he and Michele were friendly. She addressed him by name, after all."

"She wanted to stay away from him. She busted his lip open."

"You fail to understand something. The German soldier is attractive to women. Young girls are given to infatuation. In some cases, they virtually throw themselves at our soldiers. Only training and discipline ensures their purity. You were jealous of the corporal, ashamed of your own inadequacies, and driven to impress the fraulein, whom you claim is your sister. So you took advantage of the situation to attack and murder the corporal."

Hansi exploded against his bindings. "No! I didn't want to kill him, I swear! You're making this up! He was drunk, a disgrace to your army!"

The guard swept in and struck Hansi from behind. The force toppled Hansi and the chair together to the stone floor, chin first. Hansi was furious and began to thrash about like a chained beast.

The soldier put him upright a second time. Everything hurt. But the rage inside Hansi overwhelmed any sensation of it.

Leaning forward to the limit of his restraints, Hansi spoke quietly but firmly straight into the darkness. "For the last time, I'm telling you. I didn't mean to kill him." Then his voice fell to a low growl. "But I'll tell you something— if he had hurt Michele, I would have killed him."

"Enough! Get him out of here."

The soldier jerked Hansi's chair backward and pulled him away. Out from under the harsh light, Hansi could finally see his accuser, a shriveled-up man with bony features and round spectacles. With a too-big tunic that cut into his chicken neck, he looked more like a clerk at the Postal and Telegraph Office than a soldier.

The door slammed behind, and Hansi was given a short but bumpy ride down the corridor. At his cell, he was tossed back onto the sharp stone floor, which stung with fresh stabs all over his body. He collapsed against the wall and tried to let the cool dampness relieve some of the pain of his back and arms. Throbs echoed in his ears and inside the dark chamber, it seemed, as if to emphasize how alone he felt.

Despair crept up from the depths of the cold and seeped throughout his entire body to every extremity. Arms and legs, knees, fingers, shoulders, neck, feet and toes seemed to go numb. What remained, he wondered, was the end of everything. As the feeling intensified, the earth below issued two words that slinked between the jagged stones. They slithered up his back and around his neck, slipped into his ears and burrowed deep inside his mind, enveloping him with a growing blackness. They sucked the air from his lungs and life from his soul. The words consumed him: *firing squad.*

Chapter Twenty

Saturday morning, Karin awoke to the familiar sound of her alarm clock, which she had made sure was returned to its place after the strange surprise the day before. But today, she woke up wishing she could ignore it. School leaders were planning a day of support for the war, which Karin could only imagine would be full of flags, songs, marching, and sports. On the best of days her heart would not be in such events, and today, her mind was six hundred kilometers to the west, in the tiny Grand Duchy.

Was Hansi safe?

Like yesterday, the smell of fresh coffee had ascended to the top of the townhouse. And Karin quickly discovered, from the sounds below, that her mother was up well before her usual and mysterious hour. Ursula not only had a fresh pot of coffee waiting for Karin, but a plate of Berlin Jelly rolls. Surprise was not the accurate reaction. Suspicious hit the mark.

Karin sat down at the table and braced herself while her mother, also uncharacteristically, served her.

"Dear, I need to apologize."

Karin stopped mid-bite. She had never heard that word escape her mother's lips. That word, as far as Karin knew, had never formed in her mother's mind, much less rumble from her throat. Karin resumed chewing, but cautiously, as though sudden movement would scare her mother away.

"What for?" Karin asked, her own words dripping out

slowly, lifting at the end, as if she wasn't even sure the question was appropriate.

Ursula paused and swallowed hard. She was wrapped in a silk robe which flowed gracefully over her shapely figure. But her body trembled beneath her gown. And though her eyes were set in deep sockets and lines had formed along her temples and forehead, Karin still saw her mother as one of the most beautiful women she knew.

Why do you attach yourself to these men?

Her mother's expression, which to Karin displayed something far more genuine than she was used to, softened Karin's posture, if only just a little.

"For many things, I suppose," she finally said.

Karin didn't speak, hoping she would continue.

"For starters, I'm sorry for the surprise yesterday. It's just…" She caught herself before the rationalization came.

She regrouped. "I shouldn't put pressure on you that way."

Karin agreed fully, but remained silent, hoping for more.

"I've also realized that I'm not much of a mother to you, at least not in the way you need me."

Karin swallowed, but the bite went down slowly. She set the roll on the plate. Something was working its way inside. The words. No, *the truth*.

Truth from her mother was as unfamiliar to Karin as the strange homeland she had returned to from Luxembourg. In Karin's judgment, her mother worked very hard to maintain her own version of the truth. Mother's version kept her happy and entertained, which in

Karin's mind was calculated to also keep her fears at bay. This present admission was not just surprising, but unsettling. This kind of truth gave Karin a feeling she hadn't experienced for a long, long time, if ever. She didn't trust it.

"Your father's death is also my husband's death," she said.

There it is. The Turn, where the conversation would return to Ursula and her suffering.

"No, I said that backwards. Good heavens! I mean my husband's death is your father's death. I grieve it in my own way, and frankly, well, I have no idea how a daughter grieves."

Karin felt a sting in her eyes. She didn't want to cry. Mother had ambushed her with the truth. Humility. Sincerity. Trust was not easily restored, yet how could she not accept what her mother offered? Karin's heart wavered. Let her in or shut her out. The silence hung between them. Karin wondered if her mother's statement had been intended as a question. Perhaps she expected Karin to speak.

"I miss him," Karin said finally. "And I'm also upset with him. Furious, in fact."

"He was a good man, Karin," Ursula said. "He loved you more than anything."

Karin wanted to snap back. He had deceived them both. He had deceived the Luxembourg authorities and had been willing to put her friend Hansi in mortal danger. If Karin wasn't careful, the fragile peace her mother offered would explode like always. It hurt and burned so badly.

"I don't want to fight, Mother," Karin said.

"But you disagree. You're saying he didn't love you?"

"No, but that doesn't mean he was…" She stopped.

"He was a hero," Ursula said. "He died for our fatherland."

"That sounds like your precious Heinrich talking, not you," Karin replied.

"How dare you!" Ursula snapped. "He has been good to me. To us!"

"To you. I don't like him, and he's no good for you. And you know it deep down inside too."

"It's none of your business, Karin. People grieve differently."

"They do? Then let me experience it my way."

"I'm trying to make peace here."

"Oh really? How? By making me surrender what I feel? By ignoring what I've lost? Not just Father, you know."

"Your friend?" Ursula's tone seemed dismissive.

Karin got up.

"No, no, Karin, I'm sorry. Please don't leave. I'm trying. I am."

Karin stopped, only the tiniest thread of hope holding her there.

"I wanted to suggest something," Ursula said. She looked at Karin tentatively, eyebrows lifted and mouth crunched to one side.

"Perhaps a holiday is in order," she offered. "You and me away from Berlin, away from all of this…" She was unsure of the word. "Well, all of this."

"I haven't finished the term, in case you forgot."

Ursula reacted genuinely, as if she hadn't even considered the notion. "Hmm, I see. Well, when do you finish?"

"Good heavens, Mother! June 22nd."

"Oh, that long. In my day, it seems like we finished well before then."

Karin was off balance for a moment before recovering. "I appreciate the offer, Mother. I do." She could at least give her credit for the attempt. Imagining the two of them on a holiday together was nearly impossible, however. But it spawned a thought.

"I have another idea," Karin said. "Now that my pre-final exam is over, how about I go visit Oma and Opa?

Ursula's face fell, but only slightly.

"Didn't you just say the term wasn't over?"

"Yes, but they're going to be parading all day today, and probably next week too. Perhaps a few days away would do me good."

"A little distance perhaps?" Ursula asked, pondering the idea. Then, after hardly a beat, the idea seemed to lift her expression.

The change was so fast that Karin wondered whether her mother had concocted the holiday idea just to plant the alternative idea in her own head.

Had Mother wanted the time apart all along? There was no way to crawl inside her mind to know for sure, but the fact that Karin wondered gave her pause.

"Perhaps you're right," Ursula continued, with a slight

smile that did nothing to allay Karin's suspicions. "We can still do the holiday in June," she added.

"Of course," Karin said.

"Rail travel is under restriction right now, given the needs of the army, naturally, but perhaps I can speak to Heinrich."

Karin tensed. *He had to know?*

"I can take the bus. No need to trouble him."

"Long distance bus service has been suspended, haven't you heard? The army has taken the buses and the petrol. Besides, who wants to cram into a bus when a train is so comfortable? I'm sure Heinrich won't mind writing you a pass. In fact, I think he'll be pleased you're asking him."

"We are good citizens of the Reich, Mother; we shouldn't be asking for special favors."

"Whose daughter are you?" Ursula teased. "Surely not mine. It's not like they're running the train just for you. It has to go its way whether you're riding or not. You might as well be on it. Heinrich will tell me if it's not allowed. He's more like you. Rules are meant to be followed. To me, rules are like rabbits; they multiply quickly. Best to take advantage while we can."

For Karin, the argument seemed lost. "Still, Mother. I don't like him knowing our business."

"I wish you'd give him a chance, but I won't argue the point right now. Peace and harmony is what I prefer between us."

"Your business is yours, and mine is mine," Karin pressed.

Ursula let her shoulders fall. "I can see you are my daughter, after all. You know what you want and stay after it. I happen to admire that in you, Karin, I do. But I'm afraid that in the long run, now that we're at war, that quality will fail us both."

The humor had left her tone, replaced by a sudden gloom.

Why? What did she know? What did she fear?

Karin wanted to know what her mother meant with her prophecy, but at the same time, didn't want to endanger her plan. The wrong question might drive the conversation into a culvert. So she left her mother's comment unchallenged.

"Can you speak to him today? I'd like to leave tonight."

"Tonight? That doesn't give you much time with them. You'll scarcely get there by the time you have to turn around and come back."

Karin sucked in on her lower lip. "Perhaps you could excuse me from school for a few days?"

Ursula's eyes grew large and playful. "Who is this speaking?"

Karin was ready with a smile and an answer. "This is *your* daughter speaking now. Perhaps you are right. Who knows what the future holds. I learned what's coming on my exam, and we won't cover much new material before then. Everyone seems to be distracted by the war. And I can study with Opa. I'll tell him about all the new knowledge I've learned in the Reich schools, and he can get mad and argue with me. It'll be great fun!"

Ursula laughed.

"I'm meeting Heinrich for lunch this afternoon, and, if I can persuade him, afternoon cocktails at the Hotel Kaiserhof—a bit boring, but the most exciting places have disappeared. Then home to change, and then there's a reception at the Italian Embassy."

"A new dress?"

"Our trip to the KDW yesterday wasn't a total loss."

"The Italians will do whatever you ask them, I'm sure."

Karin finished her coffee and got up to leave.

"So, it's agreed?" Karin asked. "After school, I'll come home and throw my things together. Can you have the pass at three? I want to get the earliest train I can."

Ursula nodded.

For Karin, it was a small but significant victory. And a glimmer of hope in the gloom.

She bent down and gave her mother a kiss on the cheek. And then, leaving Ursula in a state of shock, turned, and left.

Chapter Twenty-one

Hansi felt sticky wetness on his right cheek and opened his eyes to a forest of grass blades. He snapped upright to a seated position on the gentle slope of a hill whose shadow stretched beyond the meadow to the forest. The morning light was behind him.

Blinking awake, he climbed unsteadily to his feet. The breeze swept over his back from the top of the hill. Hansi turned, and the sight sent a shock through him. He dove to the ground. The chateau stood barely a hundred meters away, silhouetted against the pre-dawn sky.

How did I get here?

Hansi quickly surveyed the scene. The stone wall stretched across nearly his entire view. Above it, the jagged outline of ominous dark towers stabbed the morning sky. There were no guards or dogs, nothing to indicate an active presence of the army, Gestapo, or anyone. He concluded he was on the back side of the ancient castle—the side that faced away from the village.

Why did they let me go? The Gestapo seemed to know everything.

Behind him and down the hill, he discerned a faint clicking sound. He twisted to look. The sound grew louder and sharper, like that of the kind of metal cricket he had won at the fair. It paused and then started again and then paused again.

He descended the slope to investigate. Only meters from the edge of the woods, the sound became as clear as if it were beside him.

A figure emerged from behind a tree.

Pierre!

He shot a glance up the hill and motioned for Hansi to come quickly. Under cover of the trees, he pulled him deeper in before he spoke.

"Good boy, Hansi! Let's hurry."

Pierre moved down among the trees, where the forest was still heavy with night air. They descended into the valley, turned to the right, and moved along a level path that eventually rose again. They came to a lane through the woods. Pierre stopped next to a pole. He produced a canteen, opened the spout, and handed it to Hansi, who before that moment had not been aware of his intense thirst. He sucked down hard on the cold water, letting it splash over his face and down his shirt.

"What happened? Why are you here?" he asked.

"You are both lucky and courageous," Pierre replied, with a glance up the pole. "Normally, if a civilian strikes a German soldier in time of war, they are shot. No questions, no trial. It is considered an act of terrorism and dealt with swiftly and conclusively."

"It was an accident. He attacked my friend and I pushed him. He broke his neck falling down the stairs."

"The Germans make no such distinction. To them, you attacked their soldier. Like I said, you were extremely lucky. You know this sergeant's superior, Leutnant Schmidt?"

"He wasn't there," Hansi said.

"But he came to your defense. He put his career—yes,

his life—on the line for you. After you were taken, he stole a motorcycle and drove up to the prison on his own initiative. He spoke on your behalf." Pierre started to dig in his pack. He withdrew a small leather case the size of a dictionary.

"They listened to him? That's why they let me go?"

"It's highly unusual, but yes. He could have been arrested himself. Court-martialed and sent to prison. Or worse yet, shot. Very curious, very curious. We took advantage."

Pierre opened the case and withdrew some kind of instrument—a small block of wood, to which was attached a brass apparatus with two stubby legs connected by a bar. Connected to the bar was a short lever with a black knob. Copper bolts rose from either end with securing nuts. Pierre bent down on one knee and sat the instrument on his thigh. He withdrew a spool of wire from the case and attached two strands to the instrument. Hansi realized it was a telegraph key used for sending and receiving Morse code.

"Wait a minute!" he interjected. "They knew everything! They asked about the bridge, and my friend Manolo. They had my suitcase. I was as good as dead!"

Pierre rose. "Hold this, will you?"

Hansi took it while Pierre unspooled a considerable length of wire. He clamped the free end between his teeth and secured a leather strap around his waist and the pole. A moment later he was climbing the pole. His injury showed when Pierre bit hard with every step. At the top, Pierre took the wire from his mouth and exhaled a heavy, steam-filled breath. With a knife he retrieved from his pocket, he scraped at the overhead wires and then clipped the ends of his own wire to it.

"Tap it!" he called.

Hansi found the device at the bottom of the wire and pressed the knob. The key clicked.

"Again! Rapidly!"

Hansi tapped in succession—*click, click, click, click!* An electrical force seemed to be assisting.

"Do you feel it?" Pierre asked. "Can you feel the magnet?"

"Yes!" Hansi said. Pierre descended.

"What is this for? Who is on the other end?"

"You'll see," answered Pierre. He retrieved another instrument from his pack. It looked like a telephone that had been taken apart. With no handset, its distinguishing feature was the circular dial. Pierre attached a pair of wires from this device to the key and leaned down against a small earpiece.

"It's ready," he said, taking the key back. "So now I can tell you. Once the commandant of the prison had agreed to your release, we took an opportunity." Pierre cleared his throat. "To test you. I had the Abwehr agent ask you those questions in order to see if you could be trusted for the next phase of the mission."

Hansi felt a liquid acid rise in his throat. The memory of the German soldier striking him was fresh. The taste of blood was still sharp in his mouth.

"It had to be done," Pierre offered.

The questions stacked up in Hansi's mind like the

German tanks, trucks, and guns.

"Abwehr? Ask me questions?"

"The Abwehr is German intelligence. Not all of them work for Hitler. Some of them work for us. We have a man here who happens to have a decent enough relationship with the Gestapo—a miracle of its own note—to have worked it out to let us question you. We had to know."

"Know what? I've done everything you've asked, and more. And you have me beaten for it?"

"I'm sorry for the rough treatment, but I cannot control the Gestapo. Remember, you should be grateful to be alive. We had to know if you could be trusted to keep secrets. And now you know why I said you were both lucky and courageous. You are ready."

"I'm ready to go home. I'm done with you. And don't worry, I won't tell a soul. The whole thing has been a ridiculous waste of time from the minute I left the city. Goodbye, Pierre. Have a good war."

Hansi didn't wait for Pierre's reply. He didn't know where he was, or which way to return to the village, but he could figure it out. He would return to the chateau if that got him away from Pierre.

He started down the road, hoping he had chosen well. Ten paces later he was already starting to feel relief.

"Hansi!" Pierre's voice echoed down the road and swept past. "What should I tell him?"

Hansi spun around. Pierre was holding the telegraph key above his head.

"What shall I tell your father?"

Chapter Twenty-two

Karin was correct about school. After morning attendance, they crammed into the gymnasium for patriotic speeches. A military band arrived and played. They all sang songs. The Hitler Youth and Deutscher Mädel marched with flags and pledged oaths to the Führer and the Fatherland. A film was shown, supposedly shot the day before, showing German soldiers marching happily, being greeted with flowers and refreshments by Luxembourgers, Belgians, and Dutch.

Karin ordinarily would have been bored, but she would have endured it like she had so many times before. As she stared ahead and mouthed words she didn't believe, anxious thoughts began to unravel her plan. She imagined Ursula sitting down to lunch with Schlinge at the Café Europa. She would explain to him Karin's plan to visit Köln, barely four hours from Luxembourg City. She would smile and ask for the travel pass. Schlinge would do what she asked, how could he not? How could any man refuse her?

But Schlinge was not stupid, not by a long stretch, and the request for a ticket would certainly alert his suspicions.

As the band droned on, panic took hold. She had to come up with another plan. She had to do something, or her plan would die before it started.

Her friend Leni was next to her, clapping, stomping, and singing with gusto.

Karin tugged at her sleeve and spoke into her ear.

"I don't feel well," she said, "I'm afraid I'm going to be sick."

Leni responded as Karin expected and put her full attention on her friend. She touched Karin's forehead with the back of her hand and then looked quizzically at her.

"It's warm in here, but you're cool."

"It's my stomach," Karin said.

"We're about to go outside for races and games. Perhaps you'll feel better then."

Karin bent slightly forward, clutching her midsection, and feigned a gag. She shook her head.

"I don't think I can wait. I've got to go."

"But we need you for our relay team!" Leni lamented. "You're our fastest runner!"

"I can't stay," Karin said. "I'm going home."

Leni took Karin by the hand and began to guide her through the crowd. Karin pulled away, drawing a frown from Leni.

"It's all right," Karin insisted, pushing Leni back. "You enjoy yourself. I'll be fine."

It was enough of a nudge. Karin could tell Leni wanted to stay. She would provide Karin a good excuse when others would ask later.

Once beyond sight of school, Karin put her speed to use and ran most of the way home. The morning mist had given way to bright blue sky, another fine spring day that failed to match the anxiety inside. She was relieved to find her mother still at home.

Ursula was in her room, sitting at her dressing table in

a flowing silk robe, attending to the details of her appearance. She dabbed with her makeup sponge and touched various areas of her nose, cheeks, forehead, and chin, pausing, examining, turning, swabbing. Karin came up to her from behind, and their eyes met in the mirror. Ursula was looking through gold-rimmed spectacles.

"Are those new, Mother?" Karin asked.

Her mother pulled them off and snapped them closed, half embarrassed. "Sadly, no," she replied. "You're the only one who has seen them. You must keep my secret."

Her mother worked hard to avoid the appearance of her age, and for the most part, Karin decided, she was successful. Such an accessory made no difference to Karin.

Ursula turned away from the mirror.

"You're home early. Are you unwell? Your face is red. Is that sweat?"

"I ran from school. I wanted to catch you before you left for lunch."

"German girls and their athletics!" Ursula said. "At your age, I would have died sooner than sweat. Boys were not interested in the smelly ones!"

"Oh, Mother, I don't care about any of that."

Ursula held her tongue. Karin knew she meant to say, *well, you should.*

Karin would not be put off by her mother's old-fashioned opinion. It was another of their differences, unimportant for the moment. Karin was glad to have arrived in time.

"I've changed my mind, Mother," Karin announced with a smile. "Instead of Köln, I'd like to go east to Cousin

Gertrude's in East Prussia. I'll see Oma and Opa at the term's end, when Oma's strawberries are ripe."

"Oma and Opa will be so disappointed," Ursula said. "Your grandmother misses you especially."

"But I think Gertrude might understand my situation better."

Karin's logic was unassailable. Cousin Gertrude was three years older than Karin and the daughter of Ursula's younger brother. She lived in a village near the capital, Königsberg, where her father worked as a doctor at a nearby military hospital. While Ursula and her brother were not close, Karin had a fond relationship with Gertrude, who was the distant big sister Karin never had. Trudi, as Karin called her, would sympathize with Karin's plight. Her older brothers had gone off to war in Poland. One was already dead, the other had survived and was probably part of the invasion force driving West.

Ursula would think Karin wanted to share in her niece's grief. The explanation was perfect.

Mother would understand.

Schlinge's suspicions would remain dormant.

Trudi would indeed sympathize with Karin's concern for Hansi in Luxembourg, if she ever got the chance. Karin had other plans.

"That's a long journey for a weekend, isn't it, dear?" Ursula asked with a pitying expression.

"Trains run to Königsberg all day and all night," Karin replied, knowing that the city was home to much of the professional German military staff. "I'm sure I can make it. That is, if Herr Schlinge would be so kind to write me a pass. But you had a big evening planned. How will I get it?"

"I'm sure Heinrich can send a courier," Ursula sighed. "We'll think of something. Now you better get your things together. And I'd better get this face together!"

"Thank you, Mother!" Karin said, and for the second time in as many days, gave her mother a kiss on the cheek.

"You are quite beautiful," Karin added, and left.

As she put a few things in her knapsack, Karin began to feel hope anticipating her journey, despite so many challenges that remained in the hours ahead. Deceiving her mother was not a course she entered into lightly, but after all, as Mother had agreed, *you know what you want and stay after it.*

More thought was spent on Schlinge. Karin guessed he would write her travel pass strictly for Berlin to Königsberg. Could it be altered? She had never seen one and had no real idea. Yet if that was what was required, she was determined to try. She would take a parcel of supplies: an eraser, an ink pen, tiny scissors, slips of paper, a jar of glue, and do her best if it came to that.

Chapter Twenty-three

Hansi's heart raced while his mind caught up. Pierre was telling him he had Papa on the other end of the line.

He ran back up the lane. Pierre was clicking away on the key.

Questions sparked across Hansi's mind. *How is Maman? Is she—? Where are you? Are you coming? Do you know about Manolo? What do I do now?*

"Do you know Morse Code?" Pierre asked.

Hansi shook his head. He knew what it was—a series of clicks that represented letters, forming words and sentences. But he didn't know the code itself.

"I tapped into the phone line. But the Germans might be listening. So, we use Morse Code. It's more secure."

He tapped out a series of clicks with either a short or long pause in between each one.

"I've said hello for you already." Pierre lifted his hand off the key. "We'll wait for his response."

Not long after he had said this, the key clicked by itself. Pierre concentrated while the series rattled off.

"'I am coming to the hotel,' he says, 'as soon as I can manage. After you return.'"

"How is it possible?" Hansi asked, overwhelmed by what was happening. "Is it really him? He never said anything about having such a machine."

"Secrecy is essential in this kind of work. He wouldn't have told you about it unless you needed to know. Now what is your reply?"

"Ask him, 'Return from what?'"

Pierre tapped. Clicks echoed back. Pierre looked up with a look of confusion.

"'Go to church.' Does it mean anything?"

Hansi needed no time to think. "Father Mathieu, the priest in Vianden."

"Is he part of the Resistance?"

"Madame Poulet must think so. She thinks he will know what comes next."

Pierre smiled and rubbed his hands together, warming them in satisfaction.

Hansi tossed his chin up defiantly. "Tell him I don't want to go. Tell him you'll take things from here. I'll just wait for him at the hotel."

"We've come too far, Hansi. This is the breakthrough we need."

"The breakthrough *you* need. You can finish on your own."

Pierre waited, calculating. He sucked in a deep breath and then let it out slowly so that the steam billowed out in a stream.

"I can't repeat all of that word for word, but I'll tell him." He began to answer, conveying his feelings by keying slow, disappointed taps.

After a moment of silence, in which both stared at the device, the key rattled in a furious stream.

Pierre mouthed the words to himself as the message poured out.

"What did he say? What's the message?"

Pierre pinched his face. "He says to do your duty.

Honor Manolo. Honor your mother. I am coming soon."

The words were sharp arrows in Hansi's heart. *Maman—gone? No! It couldn't be true! Not now, not yet!*

Despite being caught between guilt for failing Manolo and rage at Pierre, he couldn't help but feel manipulated. Pierre had seemed to anticipate Hansi's reaction to the staged interrogation and planned accordingly—arranging for Papa on the telegraph was without conscience but brilliant. Hansi couldn't go against him. To refuse now would not only dishonor Maman and Manolo; it would dishonor Papa too. Why was this mission so important to him?

Pierre nudged Hansi with his boot. "The day beckons. You don't want to spend any more time at the chateau than you must. The Germans may change their minds."

The words sounded like a threat. Hansi pulled himself up and looked around.

"This road heads north," Pierre instructed. "But the only traffic on it is for the chateau. So, I wouldn't use it. Any soldiers or Gestapo agents will be suspicious. Follow it from the woods for about a kilometer, where it will leave the curve of the mountain. Go east deeper into the forest until you get to the river. Follow it down to the bridge."

Without a word or even a look, Hansi stepped out from the edge of the woods.

Pierre reminded Hansi to meet the priest and wait for further instructions.

"Get some rest if you can. You've earned it."

The words bounced off him.

Chapter Twenty-four

By half-past ten, Karin couldn't believe her good fortune. Ursula had called Schlinge about the pass, and he wholeheartedly endorsed the idea and signed an order immediately.

"It's coming with the car he's sending," Ursula said, after hanging up with him. "A seven-day pass, for anywhere!" she added. "Are you sure you want to go to Königsberg? Perhaps Bavaria and the fresh air is more to your liking?"

"That's a nice idea, but I'm really looking forward to seeing Trudi," Karin answered.

"Well, you have time to think about that. The car will arrive at a quarter till four. That way you'll have plenty of time to make the four-seventeen to Königsberg."

Karin could hardly contain her elation at the news. Full authority to travel anywhere! No need to paint over or erase the printing somehow, or to mimic a typewriter's letters with a fountain pen. And instead of the eastward departure to East Prussia, she could head west to Köln, then Koblenz, Trier, and then…take her chances. The pass seemed too good to be true, but then again, Schlinge was a busy man and seemed eager to please Ursula.

Just before the appointed time, Karin was waiting in the sitting room of the townhouse when Ursula descended the stairs.

"Mother!" Karin said.

Ursula wore a trim, a-line dress made of deep red chiffon, which hugged her mother's figure from shoulders to waist, before relaxing at the hem. A simple black leather belt accentuated her narrow waistline, as did the elegant white faux pearls and earrings. Her blonde hair was gathered neatly behind, leaving attention on her round face and red lips.

"You look positively radiant!" Karin said.

Ursula looked genuinely pleased.

The doorbell rang.

Karin opened the door.

Schlinge stood there, while the black Mercedes idled at the curb. His gaze left Karin and fixed on Ursula. Karin was glad, for perhaps he had missed her disappointment.

She greeted him cordially while her mind raced ahead.

They got in the car, Schlinge and his driver up front, Karin and Ursula in the back. Karin could hardly speak but knew she must.

"I cannot thank you enough for making this possible, Herr Schlinge," she said. "And for the car. It's too much, really."

"It's essentially on our way," Schlinge replied.

Minutes later, they pulled up at the Hauptbahnhof.

"Call me when you've arrived," her mother insisted. Karin had anticipated the request but had not quite worked out how she would comply. Trudi's house would be quiet. Karin would have to call from a noisy train station or PTT office, risking exposing her deception.

"Of course," Karin said. She would have time on the train to plan and would think of something. Some excuse to not tell her right away, for example. *I forgot; we were having so much fun.*

"Are you all right, dear?" Ursula asked. "I should think you'd be excited to go. You seem nervous."

"I'm sorry, Mother. I'm just wondering if I remembered everything. Goodbye."

"Give my love to Trudi and my sister-in-law."

"Yes, Mother, I will."

Karin kissed her mother, whose perfume included the scent of schnapps.

"Thank you again for driving me, Herr Schlinge. And especially for the pass," she added.

"I was thinking." he replied. "Königsberg is lovely this time of year. I thought about accompanying you." The working side of his mouth raised in what Karin could only imagine was a grin.

Her heart fell into her stomach.

Then, after a pause, he added, "But holidays are for the young, I'm afraid. Perhaps another time."

The shock, she realized, was deliberate. He would be thrilled to have a weekend without her underfoot at the townhouse. And while other adults saying the same thing would be interpreted as playful teasing, Schlinge's words always seemed calculated.

Chapter Twenty-five

Karin's train left Alexanderplatz Station on schedule at 4:37 p.m. A surprising legacy of her father was the ability to read a railroad timetable. Rail travel was endlessly fascinating to him, and he shared his discoveries and knowledge with the only one in his life interested in listening—his young daughter. She had fond memories exploring the French countryside with him by rail, and with it, this unusual gift served her now when she needed it most.

From Alexanderplatz in central Berlin to Schliesischer Station on the eastern edge of the city was thirteen minutes, an ideal stop to disembark and catch a westbound train through the capital and beyond. She would have preferred to execute the deception further from the city, but the next stop east of Schliesischer was two and a half hours later, in Poland, which would have cost her five precious hours in total.

Measuring the thirteen minutes with every heartbeat, it seemed, Karin did her best to steady her nerves as the carriage slowed and stopped. She pushed past the throng of boarders, surprised and grateful for the anonymity afforded by the afternoon crowd. She checked the board. They had arrived on time, ten minutes before five, giving her a full twenty minutes to find the westbound train that would not only return to Berlin, but continue on to Köln.

The terminal was busy with Friday afternoon travelers getting a head start on the weekend. Berlin was always full of soldiers, most of whom were traveling on leave, and today was no exception. Karin consulted the main board and found the train for Köln waiting at its track.

The conductor, a gray-templed man with a glistening, round, red face, was at the door of the first-class carriage checking tickets as the passengers entered. Karin's chest tightened. At Alexanderplatz, Schlinge's presence—black leather coat, gloves, and fedora—was clearly seen in the way the conductor there had treated Karin. Here at Schliesischer, that presence was gone.

She approached with as much confidence as she could muster and showed him her travel pass.

He looked at it for a few seconds longer than the conductor in Alexanderplatz. "Hmmm," he said. "I haven't seen this one before."

He glanced at her, back at the document, and repeated the sequence. He checked a notepad.

"Where are you going, then?"

"My Oma's in Köln," she said with the lie she practiced a hundred times the night before.

Like the conductor at Alexanderplatz, he folded the paper, smiled, and extended his hand. But then he hesitated.

"You're from Berlin?"

She nodded.

"It says here you are from central Berlin. So then why are you here at Schliesischer, east, when you are heading west to Köln? Wouldn't Friedrichstrasse or Zoologischegarten have been better?"

The questions slammed like a trap around Karin's

throat. Fire erupted on her face and her hands broke into a sweat. How quickly he had seen through her plan! He would notify Schlinge, and the plan would be dead before it was born.

How foolish I've been.

"Uh, my mother and I were shopping this afternoon for something for Oma and ended up nearby."

He was already looking past her at the next passenger waiting to board the first-class car.

"Of course. Compartment seven may be to your liking, Fraulein Blik," he said. "Do you need help with your luggage?"

Karin shook her head. Her knapsack was easily managed.

Unsurprisingly, the train left on time. Karin felt the tension melt from her neck and shoulders as the train accelerated. For some reason known only to the German planners, her train would pass through Alexanderplatz without stopping. This alleviated any remaining concern, however small, of Schlinge discovering her deception by lingering at Alexanderplatz. He wasn't a man to linger. Ursula would be anxious to get to the reception. Karin's reason prevailed.

Still, there was a long way to go. She retrieved her notes from her bag and reviewed the schedule: Hannover at 7:31 p.m., change trains to depart for Köln at 8:32 p.m., arriving just after midnight. From Köln the journey south along the Rhine would take longer. Unless special trains were running that weren't published in the timetables, she might not make it to Trier until mid-morning.

How quickly would Schlinge move against Hansi in Luxembourg? He could have already made calls. He could already be planning to arrest him himself. Karin was thankful that he was with Ursula for the evening. The head start might just prove to be the difference. But there was no time to lose. She could call Mother from Hannover or Köln. This would keep Mother's suspicions at bay, and perhaps even give her some information about Schlinge. If she couldn't find a quiet enough place to call Mother this evening, she would have to go on to Koblenz and then Trier. She could stretch calling until about midday tomorrow before her mother would become concerned. Would Mother care enough to call, or would she be preoccupied with Schlinge? Karin couldn't let her disgust cloud her judgment. She would have to make that call.

Chapter Twenty-six

When Madame Poulet nudged Hansi, he awoke as one having been frozen in concrete. The blackout curtains were drawn.

"What time is it?" he asked.

"A little before nine," she answered. "You slept all day."

She set a plate of bread and cheese, and a glass of apple juice on the table beside his bed.

"Thank you, Madame," he said, and sat up.

"No need, dear boy. You are a part of our family now. We are so grateful that you are safe."

Hansi raised his arms in a stretch, which sent a stab of pain through the top of his shoulder.

"Did they hurt you, Hansi?" Madame Poulet seemed hesitant to ask.

He evaded, but the question served as a trigger. "I'm worried about the Gestapo agent. He is bound to find out."

"Why? Why do you say that? What happened?"

He dipped his chin. "Nothing happened. But he's so close. Why, he's right here in the hotel. Don't you find that to be a strange coincidence?"

"He asked to use the house phone this morning. He wanted strict privacy, so I had to seal off the lobby. He couldn't get through."

"How do you know?"

"I have a friend at the PTT. After the Gestapo man returned to his room, I called her. All the lines outside

Vianden are down. The village is cut off."

"That's it? He couldn't get through, so he went back to his room?"

The agent's behavior seemed odd to Hansi.

"I haven't seen him since." she said. "I'm not even sure he uses the bathroom. But one thing seems strangest of all."

"That he sleeps all day?"

"His phone call. I would think that if he's calling his superiors for further instructions, he would contact them in Germany."

"Where did he call?"

"Luxembourg City."

"Are you sure?"

"My friend is an operator. She knows the exchanges by heart."

The news struck like a hammer blow. *Who would he be calling there?*

"Is he here right now?" Hansi asked.

She shrugged.

Hansi waited inside his door, which was left cracked open. He heard Madame Poulet's footsteps in the hallway come to a stop. She knocked on a distant door.

"Monsieur! Monsieur! May I offer a change of linens?"

Hansi waited. The hallway remained silent. He stuck his head out the doorway.

Madame Poulet held up a key and motioned him to come. A moment later, he was at her side.

She inserted the key—her eyes shot wide open.

"It's unlocked."

She pushed the door open and stepped inside. Hansi followed. The room was empty.

Madame Poulet knelt at the bedside and ran her hand over the duvet. She paused it just before the pillow, feeling the place where the mattress sagged slightly.

"It's cold, and made up as if no one has ever slept here. And see this," she added, lifting the corner of the duvet at the foot of the bed and pointing at the tightly tucked sheet. "Unless this guest was once a hotel maid, he would not make the bed like this."

It was as if the man were a ghost.

Chapter Twenty-seven

Across the valley, on the German side of the river east of Vianden, a house on the plateau was the only spot where the sun still shone when he left the hotel with Madame Poulet. Avoiding the direct route down to the Vianden road, they took small lanes and alleys among the houses in the village to their destination. St. Joseph's, a typically Luxembourgish church, rose no higher than the shops and townhouses among it. Only the gray stone and simple wooden crucifix distinguished it as an enduring fixture in the village. Madame Poulet led Hansi to an opening in the stone fence that surrounded the small cemetery at the rear of the structure. They moved quickly through the withered stones to a space of grass that separated the graves from the building. A short flight of stairs cut down through the strip to the cellar door. Madame Poulet rapped in a coded sequence, and within seconds the door was open.

Father Mathieu was exactly what Hansi expected in a priest. Hansi guessed him to be in his eighties, round, with splotchy puffed cheeks, a hedge of white hair at the base of his bald head, shrubs for eyebrows, and wild sprigs in his ears and nostrils. Round wire spectacles constantly slipped down his nose because of perspiration. The opposite of what Hansi expected in a Resistance leader.

"Welcome, welcome," he said, the nerves evident in his voice. They entered a dark cellar whose air smelled as old as the church itself. A single bulb, affixed to one of the ancient beams, hung so low that Madame Poulet, who was taller than either Hansi or the priest, had to stoop down to avoid it. They sat around a small table that occupied the space between wine racks that stretched from the floor to the ceiling.

"May I offer you some wine?" the priest asked. Hansi decided the priest was not so much nervous as that his voice had the characteristic that it was always near to breaking.

"Where are the others?" Madame asked.

Despite the heavy perspiration on his face, Father Mathieu's lips were dry. He licked them and bit down. "I don't know," he answered. "They seem to have vanished."

He poured a glass for Madame Poulet and then one for himself, and then, when Hansi refused, poured more for himself. He gave the glass to Madame and gestured quickly before taking an oversized drink.

"Old man Thillman wouldn't answer his phone. No doubt he's busy with spring cleanup at his farm. Then I tried Paul in the village. He didn't answer, so I went there on my way to see Claudine at the PTT. Paul's shop was open and so I went in. I waited a few moments, but Paul did not appear. I supposed he had gone to the back to retrieve something he repaired for a customer, or a tool or something else, but he did not come. I waited a few more minutes and then called for him. I even went upstairs to his flat. He lives alone and sometimes we share a drink. He repairs my shoes, I know him well!"

"Perhaps he was delivering a repair," Madame suggested.

"He would not desert his shop in the middle of the

day! His bed was unmade! There were dishes in his sink."

Father Mathieu took his spectacles off and cleaned them on a fold in his shirt.

"I'm sure there's a reasonable explanation," Madame offered.

"It doesn't make sense," he said. "And to top it off, there's Claudine."

"I spoke with her this morning," Madame Poulet said. She explained about the Gestapo man's call from the hotel. Claudine worked at the PTT.

"I went there after Paul's. Just about an hour ago. They told me she had fallen ill. We're in grave danger," he said, "I fear the worst."

"The war," Madame Poulet said, "gives all of us reason to think twice about what we're doing. Heaven knows I have. I don't think we know what we're up against."

Hansi knew. He was sure of it.

"Forgive me," Father Mathieu said. "What kind of *resister* am I, blabbing on about our work in front of a stranger?" The priest looked quizzically at Hansi.

"This is Hansi," Madame said. "He has come from Luxembourg City. The operation has begun. Show him, Hansi."

Hansi produced the page from Manolo's box and explained how he had found it.

"My friend gave me the box and told me to go to the hotel. Perhaps he was supposed to meet you there. We hoped you would know what it means, or at least what comes next."

Father Mathieu put his glasses back on and studied the page carefully. Then, he took them off again and shook his head.

"It means nothing to me. I've been told nothing about it." He folded his pudgy fingers together for a moment, rubbed them together, and pushed his glasses once more.

"Not that it isn't important," he continued. "Hidden as it was in the box, it's obvious to me that it is intended as some kind of code. That much is clear." He took the page again and held it up to the light.

"Just a moment," he said as he got up.

A moment later, he returned with a short candle in a brass holder. It had a thick cascade of wax at the base. The priest set it on the table and lit it with a match from his pocket. He took the page and held it just above the tip of the flame.

Fearing he was going to burn it, Hansi shot up from his chair. "What are you doing?"

Startled, the priest drew back. "Sometimes there is a code in the letters printed on the page. But you must mark them somehow, so that the message can be extracted. I've heard of using lemon juice as a kind of invisible ink. To reveal it, you heat the paper, like this."

He took the page again and held it just above the flame. The white of the paper began to brown in tiny dots around the letters. He tried several places until the page was splotched like it had been pelted with muddy water drops.

The priest fell back on his seat. He was sweating faster than his handkerchief could keep up. He handed the page to Hansi. "Nothing," he said.

"Then what next?" Madame Poulet asked.

"I don't know," the priest said. "Your friend Claudine, because she worked at the PTT, received telegrams from French intelligence in Paris. They were sent in code, which I was not privy to. The last message I know of was two days before the Germans crossed the border. It said to await 'visitors from Luxembourg City.'" He turned to Hansi. "Are you that visitor?"

They were interrupted by sharp raps on the door. The sounds sent a shockwave through Hansi's body and sucked the breath out of everyone.

"Are you expecting anyone else?" Madame Poulet asked in a whisper.

The priest shook his head. The raps came again.

"Quick. Behind the racks there."

He rose from the table and paused while Hansi and Madame Poulet found a place among the wine racks. They were hidden in darkness.

"The church is closed," the priest said from inside the closed door.

"I am not here on church business, but I must speak to the priest at once."

Hansi stepped out of the shadows. "Let him in—quickly!"

The priest complied, and the door scraped open. Pierre stepped in.

"Well, what have you all got?" Pierre asked once they had gathered around the table. The bulb on the rafter provided Hansi his first good look at Pierre. His face was thinner and features sharper than Hansi recalled from seeing him in the dark and half-light of flashlight and campfire. Graying temples enforced his serious demeanor. Faint lines that spread out from his eyes like tiny fissures on a dried creek bed intensified his expressions. Hansi judged him to be suited to his ruthless work—the equal, in fact, to any Gestapo agent. Seeing Pierre at the table taking instant command, Hansi's confidence grew with every passing second. He was surprised at the feeling.

Everyone looked at each other as if they expected the other to answer. Pierre turned to Father Mathieu.

"We were told to go to church. And here we are."

The friar frowned. "I can only help you spiritually it seems. I've received no instructions other than to wait for others. And here you are. But you know nothing apparently either."

"Then is that it?" Madame Poulet asked. "The mission is finished?"

Hansi felt despair. The journey to the bridge and Manolo's death were for nothing. He had left his mother for nothing. The time, effort, and blood were no different than the pile of potato peelings rotting in the garden.

Pierre paused for a moment and then stuck a hand into his jacket. For a brief instant, Hansi wondered if he was reaching for a pistol. Instead, it was a piece of paper. When Hansi saw it, his eyes grew wide and his face flushed. Pierre had spread on the table a page from a book. The missing half of Hansi's page, with the numbers 5-1-1 handwritten near the tear.

"Does this mean anything to you?" Pierre asked the priest.

Father Mathieu looked terrified. "Not in the slightest. Should it?"

Before he had finished his answer, Hansi had produced the missing half and slid it into place. The complete number read 5-1-1-9-8-9.

"Where did you get this?" he asked.

Hansi braced himself for Pierre's wrath.

"I brought it from Luxembourg."

"It was hidden in a box," Madame Poulet came to Hansi's defense, as if by instinct.

"What does it mean?" Father Mathieu asked.

Pierre turned to the priest. Ignoring his question, he asked instead, "How do you receive your instructions?"

"Normally from Claudine at the PTT. But she's been arrested."

"And the lines are down," Madame added.

"I have a radio," the priest said. Hansi noticed Madame Poulet's surprise. "It's for emergencies only," he added.

"This is an emergency," Pierre said. "Show me."

Father Mathieu got up from the table and turned toward a rack of wine bottles along a darkened wall. He grasped one of the uprights of the rack, leaned in, and shoved with a grunt. The rack slid sideways, revealing a lectern that was covered by a red silk cloth fringed in gold. He pulled the cloth away, revealing what was not a lectern but a narrow table, on which sat a radio the size of a small fruit crate. A wire ran up the side of the stone wall and disappeared in the rafters above.

"I've only used it once, when the man installed it," he said. He flipped on a switch, which lit a small dial in yellowish light and emitted a faint hum. He picked up a small notebook that was stashed nearby and thumbed to an important page. Then, bending forward toward the dial, he squinted through the spectacles and turned the dial. Satisfied that he had matched the entry in the notebook, he took the earpiece from the top of the radio and held it close with one hand. With his other hand, he began tapping on the key.

He tapped a sequence, paused, and then repeated it. After the third try, he was answered in the form of clicks. He tapped again, something different, and upon receiving a reply, recorded the answer with his pencil on a separate piece of paper.

"Give me that sequence," the priest whispered.

Pierre gave him the two pages, and Father Mathieu tapped out what Hansi understood to be the numbered code from the torn pages.

There was another pause, longer, and then a series of clicks, which the priest recorded. Sweat had gathered on his forehead and begun to drip from his nose, adding to his gyrations.

Finally, he removed the earpiece and switched the radio off. He carefully replaced the cloth over the radio and returned to the table. Hansi was anxious.

The priest flipped to another page in his notebook and set it beside the code. Character by character he compared the written letter with one in his book, and eventually a message emerged.

"What did they say?" Hansi asked.

Father Mathieu sat up proudly, the anxiety gone from his countenance. "Kleindorf, stop. Hotel, stop. Worker's entrance. Stop. Protocol twenty-three. Stop. Ask for Hilde. Stop. Return with Package. End."

"A package? What kind of package?" Hansi asked.

Pierre let out a faint smile that was tinged with condescension. "Package I take to mean a person. Someone, rather than something."

"Hilde? The package is Hilde?" Madame Poulet asked.

"Just that the contact at the hotel is named Hilde. That's all."

Pierre sat back and folded his arms, thinking. Madame Poulet and Father Mathieu just stared at him, waiting in silence. Pierre stood up and looked at Hansi.

"In other circumstances I would go myself," he said, "but I'm afraid my leg will not cooperate. It was all I could do to make it here. What's more, the Gestapo seems to be closing in on your little group, and I must think of a way to deliver the package safely to Paris. Not to mention, it is extremely dangerous for a man of soldierly age and my appearance to move in public view. Every able-bodied man in Germany is in uniform, and my presence would immediately arouse suspicion."

Father Mathieu cleared his throat. "How far is Kleindorf? I have a car."

"Cars cannot get through," Pierre said. "Thank you, Father, but this is not your task."

"I'll go," Hansi said.

Madame Poulet's head snapped up. Her expression was pained as though ashamed. When she opened her mouth to speak, strands of saliva stretched at its corners, but no words came out.

"I would never let you go," Hansi said softly. "Jacky and Michele need you. Pierre's right. This calls for someone less noticeable. I can move in the open. My German is passable, I suppose."

Pierre stood up.

"It's settled, then. Well done, Hansi. Your father will be proud." The words stung, and Hansi wondered whether Pierre intended them to.

Pierre pulled out a map from his pocket and spread it out on the table.

"Here's Vianden and here's Kleindorf. You can't take the main road because it's the main invasion route and the border is closed to civilian traffic. The hotel is here, just south of the fountain at the center of town. Enter the village from the north, along this road, where there should be little or no traffic. You'll have to cross the invasion route but hopefully in the middle of the night, it will be quiet. If not, at least you'll have darkness to help you find a gap in the traffic."

Hansi drew the map in his mind. The town was like so many he knew, with a small square where all the streets met.

"A study of the map suggests a good place to cross north of here. Take the road that runs beside the church until the village thins out. There's a farm lane here that runs up the ridge to a wide meadow. The border cuts right through it. You can cross here, move through what might be an orchard, and find the road to the village."

Hansi studied the map a moment longer before Pierre withdrew it and stowed it back in his pocket. He buttoned his jacket, stretched his shoulders back, and then pulled back on a sleeve.

"It's eleven twenty-three. Gather anything you need and be ready to leave by midnight. That will give you three hours to get to the hotel, one to retrieve the package, and three to return. If you're lucky, you'll be back before—"

"Breakfast!" Hansi finished, but no one was in the mood for a joke.

Pierre looked at Father Mathieu.

"Prepare a place for our guest. Depending on the Germans, we may not be able to leave right away. When we do, we may have a long journey. Can you gather a knapsack, food, water?"

"I'll help you Father," Madame Poulet offered.

"Good," Pierre said, and then to Hansi, "Return the package here. Make sure you're back across the border before daylight. I'll meet you here and your work will be finished. Or I suppose you could accompany me on to France."

Hansi couldn't dare imagine that if he endured until morning, the ordeal would be over. Yet as he considered Pierre, supremely confident and thoroughly prepared, Hansi couldn't help wondering that, despite Pierre's ruthlessness—or perhaps because of it—the operation just might work.

"My father told me to wait for him here, or to meet him in—" Some instinct caused Hansi to cut himself off.

"Good boy," Pierre said. "You're learning."

"When you arrive at the hotel," he continued, "go to the service entrance in the rear. Ring the buzzer three times. Find Hilde and tell her you are there to collect your wages. That will confirm to her that you are there for the package. Got it?"

Hansi nodded. "How do you know that I should ring three times and all the rest?"

Pierre smiled. "Protocol Twenty-Three."

He snapped his heels together—an odd gesture, Hansi thought, and shook everyone's hands. *"Vive la France, Vive la Luxembourg. Bon chance!"* He dipped his beret, passed through the door, and was gone.

Chapter Twenty-eight

Hansi pressed against the stone wall of the stairwell behind the church and waited for his eyes to adjust to the darkness. The stones were cool and smooth to his touch. Michele, right behind him, tapped him on the arm. After the meeting concluded, Madame Poulet had gone back to the hotel and sent Michele back with a satchel of sandwiches and bottle of water for his journey.

"I know the farm," Michele had said. "I'll take you to the border." She ignored his protests until he realized it was no use.

Now Hansi was reluctant to leave the protection of the church. The shadow and stone were strong, immovable, secure. And in the hours since the meeting, Hansi's confidence had melted like the wax of a candle.

Michele stepped around him and ascended the stairs nimbly despite her limp.

Hansi could wait no longer. Sucking in a deep breath, he finally pushed off the stone and severed his attachment to the solid certainty of the life he once knew.

She led him along the narrow street that ran north along the east side of the cemetery. They crept carefully along the silent street, away from the town center, pausing every minute or two to check for others in their path. Although Michele moved with a distinct gait, she was surprisingly hard to keep up with. Soon they had risen away from the densely squeezed townhomes of the village. Smaller houses with yards and wooden fences spaced out along the road. In the open now, Hansi could make out the outline of the V-shaped valley they ascended, with Michele's slight silhouette in the middle. Despite everything, he was glad for the company and let the breeze wash over his damp forehead.

After about a half an hour, Michele slowed. Her head rotated back and forth across the road in concentration. She found what she was looking for—a stone fence, along the right side of the road, with upturned slabs along its top. A hundred meters more, Michele stopped. They were at a corner of the fence, which trailed east for some distance up the hill. With a wave of her hand, Michele made Hansi wait while she moved along this adjacent section. She disappeared in the darkness for a few unsettling moments before appearing from Hansi's left as if from thin air. He jumped.

"Don't worry," she whispered, very close to his ear. "This is the way. It's clear."

They followed the fence along a grass-covered farm lane until it came to an end at the edge of the woods. The lane quickly grew steeper as it wound its way back and forth up the ridge. The sweat was so heavy that Hansi wanted to strip off his jacket, but Michele pressed on and there was no opportunity. Another half hour's climb and the trees began to thin out. Here the breeze could be felt and Hansi welcomed it.

All at once, the forest came to an end and the lane curved north. Michele stopped again. Ahead, a wide meadow stretched as far as Hansi could see. The expanse of stars cast a faint glow across the landscape. She pulled him close.

"The border is about a half kilometer to the east." She pointed across the open space. "On the far side of this field, you will come upon a lane just like this one. Follow it to your right. It will descend through a valley and cross a stream. Another kilometer more, at the farmhouse, find the road. Follow it south, all the way to Kleindorf."

Hansi's mind scrambled to visualize what Michele had said. He drew the rough map in his head—*downhill, stream, farmhouse, road.* He wondered if she shouldn't go in his place.

He faced the broad meadow, split by the invisible border. He had been to Germany countless times—Trier, the ancient Roman outpost just a thirty-minute train ride from Luxembourg City, was the destination of an annual school trip. With the war, everything was different. They were the enemy now, and he was sure he'd stand out like a mule among horses. Facing the open space alone, his chest seized up.

Michele seemed to sense his fear. She came close, pulled the lapels of his jacket together and smoothed unseen creases. Her voice was soft, almost affectionate.

"You'd better hurry. You'll need every bit of night. I'll be waiting for you when you come back." She leaned forward and kissed him on his cheek. "Now go, my dear!"

A motor turned over. Hansi froze. Then *WHAM!* Michele smashed into him at the waist and pulled Hansi to the ground. He had underestimated her capabilities, for she had delivered a powerful blow. He was thankful.

The sound came from the north. The engine rumbled

to life with loud and heavy slaps, like a jackhammer. *Some kind of tank?*

From his position face down in the grass, Hansi could only guess, but they had to be very close.

The vehicle cranked and clanked. It was moving, the sound rising until, just as suddenly as it started, it stopped.

Then a voice, and a sharp hiss to be quiet. But the hiss was too loud, and what followed was a series of snorts and stifled laughs.

"You'll wake the whole mountain, you idiot!"

"Shhhh!"

"Your *shhhhing* is louder than my talking. Shut up, Hans."

Michele crawled close to Hansi. Her breath warmed his ear.

"A border patrol. They're drunk," she whispered.

Drunk soldiers could still be dangerous, Hansi knew. Perhaps more dangerous, in fact, than sober ones.

He twisted his head sideways and stretched for a look. Through the grass, he could make out the outline of the vehicle against the night sky. He recognized the shape of the turret and protruding machine gun barrel from the films of German equipment used in the Spanish Civil War and the *blitzkrieg* in Poland. The vehicle was not a tank but an armored car. He had seen several on the road out of Vianden. It stood like a tortoise shell against the starry background. Two heads bobbed up and down on top of it.

Without warning, a light beam split the darkness. Hansi was nearly blinded. Surely, Hansi thought, he and Michele were exposed in the glow. Then he realized the beam was to their right, across the meadow toward Germany. The soldiers swept the light back and forth over the field along the border in jerked movements. Had their attention settled south, they would no doubt have been surprised to see what lay just in front of them. Their movements were wild, however, causing the shadows from Michele's beret to dance across her back.

A flash of light and the crack of a rifle echoed across the meadow like thunder.

"Congratulations, Hans! You killed a blade of grass! Every rabbit from here to Berlin now knows they are safe from your rifle!"

"Shut up, Willie. You should try to take proper aim in this sardine can. It's so tight up here my toes are numb."

"Fine supper you've found us. We'll starve to death at this rate."

So, these soldiers were guarding the border with a second purpose, Hansi reckoned. And apparently a more important one. Still, their presence so close threatened everything. For all Hansi knew, the soldiers might shoot them for dinner as well as for breaking curfew. Terrified, he found himself unable to move.

Michele pressed close. "Count to twenty and run," she whispered.

"What?"

"Do it, Hansi. Count and run. For the border."

"We'll just wait. They're bound to move along."

"They turn this way, and we're both dead. Now do what I say." Her voice left no room for argument, and she had a clamp on his elbow. Her grip dug in so hard it hurt.

"Do it!" She slithered sideways, away from him.

He forced himself to count. *One, two, three, four...*

Michele snaked forward, straight for the armored car.

Five, six, seven. What is she doing?!

Eight, nine, ten, eleven. Michele was near enough now, Hansi thought, to reach up and touch the beast.

Twelve, thirteen. She was out of sight now, sneaking past the vehicle on the Luxembourg side. The soldiers were still facing east. They sounded lost in a discussion on the recipe for a meatless stew, pondering the best wine for it.

Michele kept moving.

Fourteen, fifteen, sixteen.

She was out of sight beyond the vehicle. Hansi's heart leapt. She could make it if she kept going. He might too. But he would be crawling into the soldiers' line of sight.

Seventeen, eighteen, nineteen.

Without warning Michele sprung up in the distinctive one-legged manner. The Germans didn't notice at first. She started shuffling down the path, away from the vehicle back west as fast as she could.

The noise startled one of the soldiers. He yelped.

"There! Look!"

The light swung over Hansi's head.

"It's... it's... a girl?"

"HALT!"

The realization struck Hansi like a lightning bolt. *Michele! No!*

The words echoed only in his mind. A stronger voice rose up. *Run for the border!*

Hansi jumped up. Without another thought, he leapt

across the path and plunged into the tall grass in the meadow beyond. He crossed right in front of the armored car. He ran with all his might. The meadow fell quickly down the slope. He slipped further into the darkness and the cool air in the crevasse. A tree line rose up ahead of him. The path would be nearby. He charged on.

CRAAACK!

The sound knocked Hansi off his feet. He fell forward, the momentum of his speed and the downward slope carrying him like a boulder. Over and over, he tumbled, rolling over the tall grass until the ground rose again. He stopped with a thud near the far path, his hands and face sliced by the moist blades.

Dazed, he stood up and turned back up the hill. The glow of the beam shone at the very crest of the meadow. He had covered a great distance in a short time. The light swayed back and forth.

Terror pierced his heart. The thought of Michele wounded or worse was so strong he wanted to run back, despite the soldiers. He strained to listen. He was too far to hear the voices. He hoped for Michele's silhouette to appear along the horizon. It was a foolish thought. If she was still alive, she would be flying back down the ridge without another thought. Her job was to deliver Hansi safely to the border. His job was to cross and head for Kleindorf. She would not come looking for him. He was alone.

The engine roared to life. The light swung back toward him, randomly, but Hansi dropped down. He couldn't wait here long. Michele had sacrificed herself for him. If Hansi allowed himself to be captured when she had created the chance for him to escape, her sacrifice would be for nothing. Perhaps the drunken soldier had missed again.

Keep going. Honor the dead with your life. The same thoughts as when Manolo died. Hansi would do the same for Michele.

Hansi turned away from the meadow and started down the path. Soon, he had disappeared in the darkness of the path. On German soil.

Chapter Twenty-nine

Karin's journey across the northern plain of the country, through farmland and fields, proceeded under the cover of darkness. At Hannover, she changed trains and continued to Köln, the home of her grandparents on her late father's side. Aboard the trains, Karin was surprised at how normal life seemed for a nation at war. Businessmen, on their way home from a week of work, stared at their newspapers. Students teased and laughed and ignored the scolds of their elders. Soldiers, on weekend leave from duty, caught up on their sleep.

Karin enjoyed the simple pleasure of blending into the background of a typical Saturday evening as part of the world's most modern and efficient transportation system.

After dark, she tried to get some rest, and even sleep, but her nerves were too alert. She tried distracting herself with a magazine she had bought in Hannover, but everything triggered the challenge in front of her. Every aspect of German life, from fashion to fiction, music and movies, was colored by the regime, and everywhere she turned she was reminded that they, not her, were in control. Her deception had to succeed beyond her mother and Schlinge; in a real way, she had to fool the entire the Nazi system. She was never free from the forms and passes, procedures and rules; ears, eyes, and noses designed to prevent her from doing something on her own. And to insert herself into the mighty flow of forces pressing west just to reach a single boy in tiny Luxembourg seemed, in her most vulnerable moments, ridiculous.

And so, even a magazine, which told about the good life in Hitler's Third Reich, with its brown and gray fashion and its shapeless and functional forms of perfect men and beautiful women, who were not only uninspiring and unattractive, but were completely repulsive, served to keep Karin on edge as the train steamed on.

She tried to occupy herself with letter writing. A note to Trudi, another to Oma and Opa, who would be sleeping only kilometers from where she would sit in the Köln terminal.

And then—a late thought—a letter to Hansi.

The blank page was like a mirror in her mind.

What to say after months of silence? I miss you? I wish I would have fled to France when you offered me the chance?

She remembered one of their last times together. He told her he was sending his mother to France in advance of an invasion. He pleaded with Karin to join her, and they would all be together.

Had he meant it?

She tried to imagine such a scenario coming true. He had asked her to leave her own family behind. He was convinced her father was behind something terrible threatening Luxembourg.

What did I feel toward Hansi then?

A voice inside whispered, and her heart stirred.

Love? Marriage? Family?

Another voice howled. *You were fourteen, and only fifteen now!*

She tried to write.

My dear Hansi,

Are you real or just a creation of my dreams and desires?

The pen floated over the page. Hansi wasn't like her German classmates—showoffs for the most part, practicing to be heroes, desperate to please and be noticed. Not bad boys really, just misled. In other circumstances there were surely kind and considerate ones among them. But everything now was poisoned. Nothing was normal. Hansi was free.

Karin switched off the small light in her compartment, raised the curtain, and stared into the rushing darkness beyond her window.

If only I could speak to Oma. She would understand.

Chapter Thirty

In the darkness of a narrow street, Hansi reviewed the mental map of Kleindorf he had drawn earlier. He had approached the village from the north and found an alleyway that bisected the invasion route that ran more or less northwest from the center of Kleindorf toward Vianden. At the center of the village was a circle and a fountain. The invaders would approach the circle from the south and exit on the road northwest. The Hotel Kleindorf overlooked the circle from the southwest quadrant. This meant that now that Hansi had crossed the invasion route, he could approach the hotel by continuing south some distance and then turn left, following any of the streets that led to the circle.

The narrow streets were still. He crept as quietly as he could manage at a brisk pace, peering ahead into the gloom. After five minutes, he judged he was far enough south to make the turn east. He came to an intersecting street that featured streetlamps covered in canvas and seemed a bit wider than the one he had been on. He turned left and followed the street's slight rise and curve to his right.

The circle appeared ahead. Pinpricks of light sliced through a cloud of dust that in quick slices revealed the outline of the fountain. Hansi slowed and saw ahead a narrow street that ran in a concentric circle with the one at the fountain. Keeping to the shadows, he moved along a row of shops, stopped at the corner, and checked the view.

Ahead, the circle was now in almost full view. On the right, there was enough light to reveal a porch draped with Nazi flags that looked dark purple in the moonlight. The hotel! Retracting his view, he could just make out the rear edge of the building, and the alley. Just as Michele had described.

Hansi scanned the street one more time before crossing. He stepped into the moonlight and trained his eyes at the shadows. His heart thundered, and for a cool night, he was covered in perspiration.

Across the street, he kept to the sidewalk opposite the hotel where he could remain in moon shadow. He crept slowly, careful with each step, as though he was stalking a nervous beast. He drew closer and closer to the hotel, fighting to control his breathing. The alley behind the hotel drew into view, in almost complete darkness. Hansi needed a brief rest before the final approach. An alcove just ahead fell away from the street level to the lower entrance of a shop. Hansi pulled himself past the corner of the opening and stepped down into darkness.

"Es ist du, mein leiber?" A soft voice came from deep in the alcove. Hansi's heart spasmed.

The girl giggled. "You are late tonight."

Before he could think, Hansi leapt up and onto the street, in the bare moonlight.

"Erich?" The girl called out. "Is it you?" A head broke out of the shadow, a girl with dark hair in braids.

Hansi ran, caring no longer for the noise or the darkness of the alley ahead. He found the hotel's back entrance Michele described. He slipped down the short slope that led to a loading dock. The heavy air reeked of rotting food and soured milk. He was out of breath again, so he paused and cast a glance back across the street.

A second figure appeared on the sidewalk near the alcove. A boy, about Hansi's height. It was hard to see in the dark, but he looked to be wearing shorts and had sharp shoulders, as if in uniform. The girl met him, and they embraced. She said something Hansi could not hear and then giggled again. The boy pushed her away for a moment and scanned the street. The girl pulled at him, but the boy was on edge. Hansi hunched down behind the cover of the wall. The boy took a few steps into the street. In the moonlight, Hansi saw that indeed he was in uniform, but not that of a German soldier. The boy was too young for the army. His short shorts, leather belt and red kerchief were like those of a Boy Scout but unmistakably different—he was a Hitler Youth.

"Erich," the girl pleaded. "Do you want to be caught?"

No wonder the boy was nervous, Hansi thought. He was breaking curfew to see his girlfriend. She tugged at him from the shadows, but he resisted. Finally, he disappeared, but not before their eyes met—the Hitler Youth and the Luxembourg boy—staring at each other across the dark street.

Hansi heard a door open behind him. Still crouched down, he spun around. A woman's figure was silhouetted in the doorway by a faint light deeper inside the hotel.

"No soldier boy tonight, Inge? *Ach*, just as well. There's a colonel on the loose. Can't get enough to drink. Come in now."

Hansi gave no answer.

"Inge? Don't play games now. Show yourself."

Hansi edged forward. His instructions had been clear. Go to the workers' entrance at the rear of the hotel and meet the housekeeper.

He stood up. The woman's gaze narrowed, and she retreated. Hansi closed the distance quickly, his finger to his lips. A moment later, he was inside.

The woman, middle-aged, plump in every dimension, wore a black and white maid's uniform that bore the tension of many years of hard work. She leaned back against the table in shock.

"Excuse me, Fraulein," Hansi said in accented German. "I didn't mean to frighten you. *Bitte...*" He remembered Pierre's instructions and spoke very carefully. "I've come to collect my wages."

The woman's shoulders relaxed, but just a little. Her brow expanded, and her eyes grew. She took a breath and tucked a graying curl back behind her ear.

"Sit down," she said, her voice low. Hansi took a seat at the table. He was in a small workroom. The air was hot and humid and smelled of soap and fresh laundry. Canvas carts, stuffed with white cotton towels and sheets, lined the far wall like a convoy of trucks. In the corner, the giant washing machine hummed.

The woman remained standing. "What is your name?" she asked.

"Is that necessary?" Hansi countered.

"It is if I'm to...pay you." She emphasized that last part of the phrase, confirming that she understood his purpose for coming.

"I'm Hansi," he obliged.

"Are you German? I was told to expect a Frenchman."

"I am a Luxembourger."

"You are, well, so young."

There was nothing spy-like about her, Hansi decided, until he realized she probably held the same impression of him. On second thought, no one he had encountered since leaving home fit any notion he would have had about being spies. Everyone, from Madame Poulet to Father Mathieu, to this woman, seemed, what was it—Too casual? How could they ever expect to stand up to the Nazis with such little concern for keeping to the task at hand? Everyone wanted to know what everyone else was doing. To validate everything by knowing everything. Pierre was the only exception. He knew the consequences of too much talk. This woman wanted an explanation.

All the same, a realization struck him. Had Maman not been ill, Papa would have likely come in his place. Manolo's role had been to blow the bridge. His German was terrible, Hansi knew. Papa worked with Germans every day at the steel mill in Differdange. His German was flawless. Why did they send a boy? Why did it matter now? He was here and that was it!

"They sent me," he replied.

"I am Hilde. Are you hungry? Boys are always hungry. I can get you something to eat. The chef here is famous for his schnitzel."

"No thank you," he answered. "I've come for, well, I'm not exactly sure. But you have something for me? A package?"

She raised an eyebrow. "Not a package and not a something. A someone."

The words rattled around Hansi's mind before settling into recognition. "Someone? I'm here to take someone back to Luxembourg?"

"Yes, but there's a problem. Come with me."

Hilde led Hansi past the line of carts to a second door that swung on a spring hinge.

"Wait here. Let me make sure it's clear." She pushed through the door and stopped. "By the way, if Inge returns, tell her you're my nephew." She chuckled. "I'm your *Taunte* Hilde."

She continued and let the door swing back on Hansi. Through the window, he watched her move up a plain hallway and slip through another door, where the finery of the hotel's decor could be seen. Red carpet and glossy hardwood.

Inge didn't return. Hansi could guess why. A few minutes later, Hilde came back.

"Let's go."

She led him through the hallway into what was the lobby of the hotel. It was well lit by a brightly sparkling chandelier but deserted. Hilde shook her head when they came to the elevator and turned left, where a narrow stairway rose up.

At the third floor, Hilde paused. She checked the hall and waved Hansi forward. At the far end she stopped. Room 315. A key appeared in her hand, and she worked it quickly.

The room was pitch dark. The air was stale and carried the smell of body odor and a twinge of something sweeter. Out of the darkness rose a sound, slow and rhythmic. Breathing like the slow drag of a saw across a board.

Hilde moved deeper into the room, leaving a wake of the sour air. A light came on. A small lamp on a nondescript bedside table. Sprawled across the bed, on top of the covering, lay the lump of a man, draped across it like he had been thrown there. An arm dangled off the edge nearest the table, along with a bare foot. Otherwise, the man was in his day clothes.

Hansi crossed cautiously. A mostly empty bottle cast an amber glow on the bed table. Hansi knew at once—the man was passed out drunk.

Hilde reached across the bed and rolled the man on his back. Hansi saw that he was old and skinny. With his head rolled back, his nostrils looked rat-like.

"Do you know who this is?" Hilde asked.

"A drunken old man who snores," Hansi answered.

"And the most important scientist in Germany."

Chapter Thirty-one

Hilde gripped the old man up by the shoulders.

"Help me," she grunted.

The old man's arm was bony. They pulled him upright.

"Who is he?" Hansi asked. "What kind of scientist?"

"I don't understand it," she said, and loosened the old man's tie. "He tried to explain, but it was lost on me. Something about atoms." She unbuttoned the top of his shirt. "'Nuclear fishing?' I know that's not correct but he's slurring his words. I don't understand it at all."

Hansi had heard stories on the radio about scientists around the world working in the field of atomic science. Their goal was to build a terrible superweapon, capable of destroying entire cities with a single explosion.

"It's nuclear 'fission,'" Hansi said. "It means splitting an atom."

"Aren't you the smart one? Hold him up while I get some water." Hilde crossed the room to the dresser with a wide ceramic bowl and pitcher. Hilde poured hastily and soaked a towel from the hook. After a quick wring, she returned and began to wipe down the old man's face and hands.

"Time to wake up, Dr. Salzmann! We need you to wake up now!" She dabbed roughly at the bony cheeks and beard, a patchwork of silvery stubble. She shook him. "Dr. Salzmann, please! You've got a visitor! Wake up!" She glanced at Hansi, frustration growing in her expression. The old man's head bobbled like a rag doll. His eyes remained closed. Hilde jerked harder. The old man squeezed his eyes tight.

"Leave me alone!" The words came out like a cough. "Let me die alone!"

Hansi was surprised.

"He's a dramatic one, that's for sure. Now come on, Herr Doktor. You can't die just yet. That would be bad manners." She winked at Hansi. "You've got a visitor. A young man with something important to tell you."

The old man twisted against their grip. "Where's my vodka?"

"I poured it out the window. Now wake up before I call the Nazis."

He grunted and moaned and tried to break free from her grasp. But Hilde was strong, stronger than Hansi, and kept him firm in her grip.

"Get the bowl. Quickly!"

Hansi crossed the room and took the bowl. There was a tray of half-eaten food, shriveled and sour, sitting on a chair next to the dresser. Clothes were scattered everywhere.

Holding the doctor with one hand, she took the bowl from Hansi with the other and flipped it straight into the old man's face.

His head snapped back; he sputtered, gasped, and spit. But it did the trick and he exploded with life, flailing his arms in wide, wild circles like he was swimming.

His eyes shot open. "*Mein Gott!* You'll drown me, woman!"

"As soon as you wake up, Herr Doktor Salzmann, I'll

stop."

A pained look flashed across the old man's face. His eyes disappeared into tiny slits, and he clutched his stomach.

"Stand back," Hilde commanded, her voice utterly calm.

Hansi stood up and stepped back. Hilde was ready with the bowl. Dr. Salzmann wretched with all his might. She caught most of it. The rancid smell filled the room, causing Hansi to gag.

"You old fool," Hilde said, wagging her head. "See what you've done now. In front of your guest."

Salzmann heaved for the third time, and the crisis seemed to have passed. He blinked a few times and fell back on the bed. But he was awake, staring up at the ceiling.

"The atom is like that pattern on the tiles," he said, pointing. His voice had changed, measured now, like a professor. "They interlock in a discernible pattern, but you can't precisely say where one tile ends and the other begins. When you trace the path, you sense everything has shifted."

Hilde exchanged glances with Hansi. "He must be sobering up. I can't understand a word he says. But I was told he is a genius."

Hansi studied the old doctor's face. The light eyes darted back and forth across the ceiling. The bony finger, like a crooked stick, traced an unseen line around the ceiling. Occasionally his lips formed silent words.

"Is he all right?" Hansi whispered.

"Do you mean, *am I crazy?*" the old man barked. "No. It's the Nazis who are crazy. They are crazy for not believing me. Let them build the thing on their own. They're wandering like a child lost in the forest, and it's right under their nose. If only they'd have listened to me."

"He's talking nonsense again," Hilde said.

Hansi shook his head. "You mean the super-weapon."

"They call it the atom bomb," Salzmann said. "And not only me. Hundreds, perhaps thousands of scientists, in Germany and all over the world. The first one to get it will win the war. Russia, Japan, Britain, America. Yes, America certainly. Perhaps they already have made it."

Hansi looked back at Hilde, who was using the cloth now to try to clean up what had missed the bowl.

"Is he to give me a set of plans? Is that the mission?"

Hilde smiled knowingly and shook her head. "Not exactly. The plans aren't written down on any piece of paper or notebook."

She pointed. "They're in his head. To take the plans, you must take him."

Hansi's heart dropped into his stomach.

"Smuggle him back into Luxembourg?"

Hilde smiled deviously.

Dr. Salzmann sat up. "I'm much more capable sober."

"I'll die of old age before I see that day," Hilde said.

"Capable? You'll find no one more capable than me."

"No, sober. Now get up. You haven't been formally introduced."

Salzmann sat up. Hansi stepped forward and offered a hand.

"No," Hilde instructed, "see if he can get up on his own. There's not much time. He needs to prove how 'capable' he is for your journey. Don't you, Herr Doktor?"

Salzmann was lifting the wet folds of shirt away from his shrunken chest. "I'll be glad to rid myself of your nagging, that's for sure." He swung his legs off the side of the bed and touched them down on the floor. He stomped with each foot, steadied his arms on either side, and pushed off. He rose, swayed just a bit, but held on. Color rose in the old man's cheeks, and fully upright, he towered above Hansi. Despite a wet and vomit-stained shirt, baggy and wrinkled trousers, the old scientist's eyes were like green flames. Throwing up had done the man some good, and in better circumstances, Hansi guessed, Dr. Salzmann suggested the look of a distinguished gentleman.

"I am Doktor Albert Salzmann," he said in a formal tone. He thrust out his hand and then, with a sudden flash of panic, withdrew it, wiping it on his trouser leg. "My apologies—I suppose handshakes have fallen out of favor anyway. Everyone's *seig-heiling* these days." He waved the arm up in a quick salute to Hitler and then let it fall by his side.

Hilde turned to Hansi and nodded.

"Oh. My name is Hansi. I'm from—well, just recently from Vianden, across the river, in Luxembourg."

"Of course, the village where the great Victor Hugo loved to rest on holiday. And you are the French intelligence officer come to rescue me, *ja?* Well then, the war is lost already."

Hansi took less offense than he expected. He was

curious how Salzmann knew to expect a French agent. Hansi thought his father was supposed to have come.

"I'm just trying to help," he said weakly.

Salzmann wagged his head. "The French are hopeless. They send a boy. I'm doomed for sure."

"You ungrateful swine!" Hilde exploded. "Look at this boy. That bump on his head. Heaven knows what he's been through to get here. And he is here, lest you forget."

"It's all right, Fraulein."

"You ought to be ashamed of yourself, Herr High and Mighty Atomic Scientist! Why, if you're so capable, why didn't you sneak across the border yourself? Because you're afraid of the breeze in the trees! And as flimsy. This lad is waylaid, and what do you do? Curl up in bed like a baby and suck on your bottle, that's what. If the boy's got half a brain, he should turn around and walk down those stairs and head back to Luxembourg while he can. Or drop you off in the middle of the Our River. Then nobody would figure out how to build the big, bad bomb. We'd all be better off. Me, I'm done with you and your whining! Let the Nazis keep you!"

"Please," Hansi interjected, "Fraulein Hilde, please calm down. I'm not offended. If Dr. Salzmann wants to come with me, I'll take him. I'll get him safely to Luxembourg."

What made Hansi so gracious in that moment he couldn't explain. Perhaps it was because Hilde had said everything he would have said, had he thought of it. Or maybe he could hear the fear in Dr. Salzmann's voice. More than anything, Hansi was tired. He wanted to go.

With or without the scientist. The sooner it was over, the sooner he could return to Luxembourg City and see his father.

Dr. Salzmann lifted an eyebrow but made no reply.

Hilde's face was white hot. "Get your coat. If we haven't woken the entire German army, it's time for you to go." She walked to the door and turned back.

"Wait here. I'll go downstairs and check the back entrance. If it's clear, I'll call your room. Let it ring. Two times—that means it's clear. Anything else and you both stay put. Understood?"

"Very exciting," Salzmann said in a very flat tone. But Hansi noticed a tremor in his left hand.

Hilde closed the door quietly behind her and padded silently down the hall.

Salzmann turned away from the door and regarded the mess of the room with hands on his hips. He huffed and then strode diagonally across the floor. He knelt and began to gather the strewn clothes with great sweeps of his arms, like a child gathering his blocks.

Hansi moved to the nightstand. The bottle of Stolichnaya vodka was empty.

Salzmann uncovered a small suitcase and flipped open the lid. The case itself was made of plain brown leather, but the inside was unusual, Hansi noticed. Rather than the usual lining of patterned cloth or silk, this case had been stripped of its interior and painted black. Hansi knew it had been painted because splashes of paint had spilled on the outside of the case in spots, and flecks of it had fallen away. Salzmann had his glasses on and was studying the marks with great interest.

He's an odd one for sure, Hansi thought.

Salzmann wadded up whatever he could get his hands on and shoved it in the case. He seemed not to care either for the selection of items or their arrangement.

"You'll want to travel light, Herr Doktor," Hansi said. "We will run, crawl, and perhaps even swim before the night is over. Our friends in Luxembourg will have plenty of clothes for you."

Salzmann continued as if he hadn't heard a word. He filled it to overflowing, shut the lid, feeling where the pressure was distributed, reopened it, and jammed more into the corners.

"Excuse me, Doktor, but that will slow us down."

Salzmann added a few more items in and shut the lid, pressing out every molecule of air, it seemed. When he was satisfied, he closed the latches, stood up, and tapped the side affectionately.

"First of all, you have no idea what I'll want to do on this journey. I may wish to hire a lorry for all you know. If that's what I require, I will do it. Second, I have no interest in running, crawling, or swimming. I will walk or ride, that's all. And third, I have no friends in Luxembourg. It's a dirty little country full of dirty little coal miners."

Hansi felt his cheeks flush. And anger rise inside. He wondered if anyone in Luxembourg had known what kind of man they were trying to rescue.

The phone rang once and then fell silent.

Hansi looked at Dr. Salzmann.

Hilde had said twice. He was sure of it.

Salzmann bent down and lifted his case. "Let's go."

"Hilde said two rings. That was just one."

"Don't be silly. She can't control how many times it will ring. The machine does that. She just waits the amount of time she thinks it takes for two rings."

"She said two!"

Salzmann moved toward the door. "I don't expect they teach the children of coal miners how a telephone system works. But I happen to know. When Hilde dials a number, the phone exchange sends a voltage down the wire to us. That voltage causes the bell in this telephone to ring. Hilde only hears a series of clicks to represent the ring. They aren't the same thing. There can be a delay between the two. If she hangs up too quickly, which, for example, she might do if she is nervous, the exchange may not send the second ring pulse. Hilde may indeed have heard the second ring, but we didn't. I suppose this is all too technical for you, but trust me, I know. Hilde simply meant for us not to go if the phone rings on and on."

Hansi hated to admit it, but Dr. Salzmann was right. He didn't understand electricity, let alone its use in telephone systems. It sounded reasonable enough, but still, Hansi was unsure.

"She said two rings. If we wait, she'll try again."

"Are you sure the British didn't send you? I'd expect such caution from them."

Hansi wasn't sure the meaning of the last question, but knew it was an insult. *Coal miner's son*—that burned.

"Can I ask you something, Herr Doktor?"

Dr. Salzmann stopped short, as if surprised that the

student would be able to stand up to the professor.

"If you were expecting a real agent to come for you, why did you nearly drink yourself to death?

Salzmann lifted his right eyebrow like a drawbridge.

"*Touché*, young Hansi." He let out a slow breath and cleared a rattle from his throat. His voice was low. "In truth, I thought no one was coming. I thought I'd be stuck here forever."

For a moment, Salzmann's armor of arrogance had been lowered. Or just maybe, Hansi thought, it was a brittle shell.

The phone rang again. Then a second time. They exchanged tense glances. A third ring followed, then a fourth. It kept on ringing.

Hansi reached for the receiver.

"Don't answer it!" Salzmann snapped.

Hansi ignored him. Something was wrong.

"Halo," he said.

"Don't move," Hilde said. "And don't make a sound."

The phone went dead.

Chapter Thirty-two

Hansi repeated Hilde's instructions to Salzmann and ushered him to sit on the bed. The old man complied, after which Hansi retrieved a flashlight from his knapsack. He switched off the overhead lamp and moved back to the table between the beds. He switched off the lamp between the beds, which plunged the room into darkness until he switched on the flashlight. He covered it with his hand so that only orange light from between his fingers escaped.

"What are you doing?"

"Shhhh—" Hansi moved to the window and pulled back the edge of the curtain. From here he could see the circle clearly, where the fountain spit water from the mouths of four gremlin-shaped faces.

He pressed closer to get a wider view. His heart shifted to a higher gear of anxiety—a black Mercedes surrounded by at least four men in dark attire. One was directing the others with stabs of his arms in various directions. Hansi didn't need to hear him to know who they were and what the man was commanding. The Gestapo would surround the place in seconds.

Hansi's stare was interrupted by a sharp knock on the door. He let go of the curtain and removed his hand from the flashlight. He held Salzmann in place with a finger to his lips as he moved with soft strides. He leaned against the door and pressed his ear close.

"It's me, Hilde."

Hansi let her in, and she locked the door behind her.

"Gestapo, front and back," she said. "We have two minutes, no more. They'll block the exits and check the rooms, floor by floor."

"I have a cyanide pill," Salzmann offered. "But only one for myself."

"Put that away," Hilde hissed.

Hansi had heard of such things and shuddered at the thought. But he understood Salzmann's reaction.

"What can we do?" he asked Hilde.

"I'm thinking," was all she could manage.

"You'd better hurry," Salzmann said.

Hansi's knowledge of the hotel was limited. He knew for sure that there was a workers' entrance in the back. Certainly, there was another in front opening to the circle. These would be covered by the men he saw exiting the Mercedes. A jump from the third floor would be little different than swallowing Salzmann's pill, though perhaps not so quick. Hansi considered abandoning the mission and letting Salzmann, for whom he had no affection, try to save himself. But what if Salzmann really held the secret to the super weapon? What if his capture gave the weapon to Germany?

Moments, heartbeats thundered on in agonizing silence.

The door latch clicked.

"Come," Hilde said in a whisper. "I think I can buy a few minutes while we think."

She stepped into the dimly lit hall. It was empty and silent for the moment. She led them left, down the carpeted hall away from the central stairs deeper into the hotel. Hansi wondered if the entire operation had been some elaborate trap, with Hilde the chief trickster. Still, he had no alternative but to follow, with Salzmann and his stupid suitcase between them. After a half-dozen doors, the corridor came to a fork and angled left in a long stretch. To the right a short space opened in a kind of sitting area.

Hilde turned into the short space and stopped at a narrow door.

"You, in here," she said to Hansi. She already had hold of his sleeve and was tugging him past Salzmann, whose face twisted with a kind of jealous alarm. She opened the door with one of the keys from her waist and shoved Hansi inside. It was a quarter of the width of a normal elevator and the sides and floor of a uniformly gray metal. The transition between floor and cabinet was rough, causing him to stumble before banging against the back wall of the carriage. He smelled something old and stale, perhaps cabbage. The door closed behind him, enclosing him in near complete darkness.

"What about Salzmann?" he asked, surprised to be stashed in the space alone.

"I'll find him somewhere else," came the muffled reply. "Stay out of sight. And whatever you do, don't move or make a sound."

In other circumstances, the command would have seemed humorous to him, because the chamber, certainly more of a closet than an elevator, was too cramped for him to move much anyway, except to turn around and face the doorway. His body fit between the sides easily enough, but it would have been impossible to add Salzmann, and certainly not his blasted suitcase.

Keys rattled outside, and then the chamber dropped from under him, sending a fright through him. He stumbled, slammed against the wall, and then recovered by flexing his arms outward against each side to brace himself.

A motor whined and the cabinet settled into a slow descent. Hansi realized that he was in a dumb waiter. But what would he do when he reached the bottom? What about Salzmann?

He didn't have long to ponder these questions, because the carriage slammed to a stop as quickly as it had started. He estimated he had barely moved a meter down the shaft.

Had it broken?

During his short ride, his eyes adjusted. From light that leaked in from around the doors, he realized the dumb waiter had stopped only about halfway down to the lower floor. Crouching down, he peered through the small slit under the door bottom. Hilde and Salzmann were moving away down the long corridor.

Despite Hilde's instructions to be still, the confinement was so unsettling, he pushed on the door. Although the wooden door flexed a little, an unseen latch held it in place. He pounded it with the heel of his hand and realized why Hilde had ordered him to be silent—the sound reverberated up and down the core of the hotel, it seemed.

He leaned back. *Why had she said to stay out of sight?* In a dark box, no less.

He scrunched lower and pushed on the upper third of

the lower door. It was also locked. Even if it had been unlocked, it would have been a very tight squeeze.

Hilde and Salzmann had disappeared by now somewhere beyond his view. The chamber fell silent. Hansi leaned back to ponder his predicament—he was caught in a tiny box that smelled of old roast and cabbage. Trapped.

He heard footsteps and voices through the lower door frame.

"Check every room, in sequence," said a voice in German. "Wake everyone, check their papers."

"But there are officers here," a second one said.

"Everyone!" the first one snapped. "Go! Now!"

The voices and footsteps faded. Then, in the distance, sharp rapping on a door, the order being carried out.

For Hansi, the countdown had begun—they would check the rooms first and then closets, stairs, and sooner or later, this dumb waiter. He could not sit and wait to be captured.

He stood up tall and pushed again on the upper door. The bottom of the door flexed a little, but only that. Hilde had locked him in tight, and he wondered, had she intended to send him all the way down? Had she meant to hide him by lodging the dumb waiter between floors? Surely the Gestapo would not be put off by locked doors. Hilde was acting on instinct, and for that, she could be forgiven. But a more terrible idea rose in his mind—she was protecting the more valuable of the two of them! Hansi needed out, and quickly.

He pressed his face against the bottom edge of the door to get a look at the door lock. In the faint slice of light, there was just enough space between the door and the dumb waiter shaft to make out the outline of a latch handle. If he could reach it, he could release the lock, push open the door, and free himself.

What looked simple proved not at all easy. The latch handle was nearly a meter beyond the tip of his upraised arm, and the gap between the frame of the dumb waiter, while wide enough for a latch handle, was still only wide enough for his fingers and the heel of his hand to pass through. He reached for it, but his forearm wedged itself in the small space, leaving him about two-thirds of the remaining distance short. Wedged like this, the dumb waiter would rip his arm from its socket if it somehow started to move again.

Still, he tried various methods to reach further. After a few moments, he discovered that the most effective technique was to spread his legs apart and press one foot on the back of the chamber to lift himself up. At the same time, he would push against the door with one hand and reach with the other. The gap widened, and he wedged his arm further up. Sweat streamed down his face, and his calves, thighs, and stomach muscles began to quiver. Nevertheless, he had progressed all the way to his elbow.

He kept at it. Circulation began to fail in his hands and fingers. Was he a forearm's length yet to go? Climb, press, reach, and measure. The pressure was enormous. His heart thundered in his neck and ears.

Then he got another idea.

He let himself down with a heavy clunk and removed a shoe. Turning it sideways, he wedged it in the gap and began to pound it with his fist. To Hansi's amazement, it did the work of his forearm and more. Hope rose until he tried to lift up and reach through this new gap—his damp socks had no grip on the carriage wall. He dropped back down, which sent another shockwave up and down the shaft. Surely the men would hear it.

He pulled his sock off. His bare foot gripped easily. He pushed himself up again and stretched. Despite being able to freely reach to his shoulder, he was still about a forearm length away! He strained with all his might. Still, the latch was beyond his fingertips.

The unthinkable happened when the shoe slipped out of its wedge. Hansi's straining and stretching wiggled the shoe loose. It clanked on the chamber's metal floor and clamped down on Hansi's upper arm without mercy. The pain was intense, instantaneous, and sent a bolt of panic through him. He twisted with violence against the jaws of the trap.

He quickly lost the sensation of individual fingers, wrist, forearm, elbow, and shoulder. Everything was just pain. He thought he might rip his own arm out of its socket. The chamber shook with his jerking movements, emitting the sound like the banging of a giant drum.

He was losing the battle and losing consciousness. This brought another level of panic—that he would pass out or die. His body took over, acting without him now. In a final spasm, he kicked at the far wall of the chamber, wildly and without purpose other than to lash out against the gathering doom.

Later, he could not detail exactly what happened, but

he concluded by the lack of any other explanation that this last effort had dislodged something in the mechanism of the dumb waiter, causing two things to happen at once—the clamp released him, and the dumb waiter resumed its descent.

And just after he crashed to the floor of the chamber, voices rang out again.

"In here, behind this door!" a man announced. He pounded furiously. The lock on the lower door rattled.

The chamber sank down, revealing more and more of the lower door, the only barrier between Hansi and the Gestapo men.

"Open the door!"

"I have no key, Sir."

"Break it down!"

The chamber dropped further. Hansi got a proper look at the inside latch as it passed before him. A tremendous crash against the door rocked the carriage.

Hansi braced himself as best he could. If the door came open, he would run like a cornered rat and trust in surprise to give him a chance.

The door held through repeated blows, each one more terrifying than before. The chamber passed level with this door and sank further.

"Give that to me," he heard from above. "Stand clear."

The carriage kept on, only seconds away from the next floor down, and then *BAMM!*

The shot was razorlike in Hansi's ears, reverberating within the metal walls with the echo of a thousand hammers against a steel bucket over his head. Hansi opened his eyes. The carriage was still descending! Only half the upper door to go!

"There, you fool—*schnell!*"

The upper door flew open. Light poured into the chamber. A sharp sulfurous smell, the bottom half of two men, disappearing as the opening shrank.

Then, to Hansi's shock, an arm shot through the gap.

"I can't stop it!" the agent yelled. The gap narrowed. All Hansi could see was the gray sleeve of a trench coat and an outstretched arm.

Without thinking, Hansi jumped, snatched the arm, and held on with all his might. He squeezed his eyes shut for what he knew was coming. The chamber sank further, the gap closed and Hansi heard and felt the excruciating crunch when the elevator's force met the resistance of a human arm. The man's scream froze Hansi's blood. The chamber slowed, the scream intensified, and then, having caught its prey, the giant trap was now still. Its prey wriggled in agony. Hansi let go and fell back into the corner. The door below clicked and swung open. Hilde reached in and pulled him out.

The space outside the lift on the ground floor was filled with guests who, besides being awakened by the Gestapo hunters, were further terrified by the screaming above. They met Hilde and Hansi with confused, and then suspicious stares.

"Poor thing was trapped in there," Hilde said to an elderly couple. Hansi couldn't avoid the impression they were on the verge of working out that rather than him being the victim of the accident, he was actually fleeing the Gestapo.

Hilde dragged Hansi by the collar.

"You will not keep your job for long, young man, sneaking off every chance you get," she scolded.

Her timing was perfect. Her words caught the couple and others nearby in mid-calculation, disrupting their thoughts long enough for her to slice through the onlookers. She whipped Hansi past the main staircase and continued down the hallway through other guests, keeping them off balance with additional strategically placed scolds.

"And your uniform," she said. "A disgrace. I should never have listened to your uncle. Hiring family is a mistake. One must have thoroughly checked references. You have shamed us and yourself."

Hilde's performance was so effective, Hansi almost felt guilty. But most important, she had dragged him away from the guests. She opened a door to a stairway.

"Where's Salzmann?" he asked.

"Never you mind," she snapped, shoving him into the stairwell. "Now listen carefully. Go to the bottom, and if it's quiet through the door, go into the storeroom and wait. I'll meet you in ten minutes."

"What if you don't?"

She paused, as though the question was an insult. Then perception dawned on her face. "You think I was using you as bait in there?" She grinned. "An interesting idea. I'll keep that one in mind. But no, that stupid contraption has a mind of its own. We quit using it. But there's no time for this. I'll be there." She shoved him through the door. "But if I'm not, the storeroom opens up to the loading dock where you first came in—you'll have to make a run for it."

She shut the door behind him. Alone on the stairs, he descended quickly. Beyond the door at the bottom, the scene was quiet as she predicted. He slipped into the dimly lit storeroom and passed between columns of shelves full of crates, boxes, summer patio furniture, tools, rakes, awnings, flower boxes, and more.

He took a moment to catch his breath. All in all, he was grateful for Hilde's skill so far. Four or five Gestapo agents covering the entire hotel would give them a chance, albeit a small one.

He crossed the storeroom, paused at the door that Hilde said was the loading dock, and listened. It was quiet.

He pressed down carefully on the latch, and then pushed. In a slow, steady movement, it twisted quietly on its hinges. Bright light from the loading area streamed through the crack.

He pushed more to get a better view. The path of escape looked clear—the room itself was empty and the street lay in view beyond the garage bay door. He could run, find the darkness, and make his way back. No one would blame him. Was Salzmann's escape worth his own life? Was an old drunk with a suitcase going to stem the tide of tanks and troops heading West? *Surely not.*

How had events come to this? Only days earlier he was safe at home at Maman's side, thinking about the war only when he was forced to by some news or rumor that

Papa brought home. And here he was now, nearly free from a most terrifying trap.

I can't do this.

He made up his mind. He would go and find Michele, return to Vianden, then make his way back to Papa and Maman. They would endure the war together—somehow.

He imagined their meeting, the embraces. And then the explanation. A shadow crossed Hansi's heart. Manolo's face rose in his mind's eye. The gray face of death, frozen in his last, terrible stare.

I can't, Hansi's mind repeated.

Manolo's face didn't stir. He gave no answer from beneath the flecks of dirt from Hansi's last look.

The street beckoned.

A noise, the scrape of a door opening interrupted him. Hilde, pushing a large laundry cart. He had forgotten her promise already! *I'll be there.*

Hansi took a step and caught Hilde's eyes. She shook her head in a quick warning. He retreated. An instant later, a Gestapo agent appeared—apparently watching the loading dock from outside.

"Where do you think you're going, Fraulein?" he asked.

"Nowhere," she answered. "You've managed to rouse the guests, thank you, and so they start to make demands. I've got towels and laundry already piling up. I'm just getting ahead of the day's work."

Hansi was amazed at how nimble Hilde was. The laundry cart she pushed had a wooden base, steel rods forming a frame where hung a rectangular box-shaped sack of dull, beige canvas. Hansi's gaze was drawn past the puffed bulges to three sharp lines in the canvas, forming a corner.

Salzmann's suitcase!

The Gestapo man eyed her briefly and then stepped aside.

She leaned into the cart and pushed, trying to conceal the effort required to overcome Salzmann's weight. It rolled on, and the Gestapo man watched her pass.

Hansi expected her to continue down the ramp. He could wait until the Gestapo agent left and join them outside. But Hilde turned the cart right for the storeroom.

Inside, she began removing the laundry. Hansi joined in, and soon the wriggling body of Salzmann appeared, folded upon itself in a remarkably small space. He stretched out, limb by limb, still clutching the suitcase.

Hilde pressed her hand over Salzmann's mouth just as it began to move, shaking her head at him in stern command. He complied.

They got him out. He stretched and winced and rubbed his neck.

Hilde leaned back into the cart and retrieved a paper-bound laundry package. She untied the string and ripped the paper.

Hansi's eyes grew wide. A German officer's uniform!

He looked at Hilde, then Salzmann, and then back at Hilde, lifting an eyebrow.

She nodded.

They spent the next few minutes completing the task,

and the result was less than satisfactory, at least from Hansi's perspective. Salzmann looked too old and too frail to be a German officer. But Hansi had every reason now to trust Hilde and had no better idea himself. They were running out of time. Even now, the Gestapo might have freed their broken comrade from the dumb waiter and returned to the search. They would react like hornets whose nest was struck.

Hilde brushed Salzmann's sleeves and torso and straightened his collar as best she could. She whispered something in his ears. He blinked, acknowledged it in his expression, and turned.

Hilde pulled Hansi back behind a shelf.

Salzmann arched his back and lifted his chin, and then pushed through the door.

The Gestapo agent spoke first. "Excuse me, sir, but I have strict orders not to let anyone exit the hotel without explicit permission, when the search for the fugitives is complete."

"And I have strict orders from General Keitel himself to meet him in—" There was a short pause. "Paris, by morning."

Hansi saw Hilde visibly tense. Salzmann was going to fail the very first test.

"Paris?" The agent said.

"Get out of my way! A German officer doesn't have to explain himself to a policeman." There was a rough scuffling sound and then the sound of quick footsteps falling away. And then silence.

Hilde moved to the door and peered through. She

waved Hansi forward.

"Quickly! The agent's gone back into the hotel."

Hansi responded instantly, almost running to the back door. Outside, the fresh night air was delicious. The stars and moon illuminated the back alley. They had made it!

On the ramp, Hilde stopped suddenly. Hansi nearly crashed into her.

Up ahead, near the corner, Salzmann stood, suitcase in hand, held in place by another agent.

Hansi reacted by instinct and retreated inside the hotel all the way to the storeroom where he retrieved the cart. He climbed inside.

Hilde, following his thoughts, covered him with linen and pushed the cart into the alleyway, turning directly at the agent.

"Take your hands off me!" Salzmann demanded. "I'll have you shot for this."

Hansi thought better of Salzmann's performance this time, but something was still not convincing the agent. Hilde's skills would be put to the test again.

"Stop, Fraulein! Return to the hotel at once."

"But I must get this laundry delivered right away. These army maneuvers are quite unexpected, and we are full to capacity. Surely you can let me do my work." The cart rolled on.

"I have strict orders. And this general seems not what he appears."

The cart inched closer.

"Is he in trouble?" Hilde asked.

"That's none of your business. I won't say it again.

Return to the hotel at once."

The cart slowed but had not stopped.

"I'm sorry, sir," Hilde said. "Of course."

Hansi felt the sudden jolt of the cart, heard shoes scraping the payment, a firm punch, a short gasp. Then, a brief scuffle and finally, a heavy thud.

"Help me, Hansi!" Hilde's voice was desperate.

Hansi clawed up through the linen and climbed out of the cart. The agent lay in a heap on the pavement. Salzmann stood gripping his suitcase, dumbstruck.

When Hansi drew closer he learned the horrible truth behind the sounds. The hilt of a kitchen knife protruded from the agent's rib cage. Blood had already soaked his entire front and was pooling in the alley. Hansi gagged.

Together they lifted the agent into the laundry cart. Hilde arranged the linen over him roughly.

"Go!" she hissed. Hansi could see in her eyes an animal-like intensity, fright and fight together through the beginning of tears.

"Go!" she repeated.

Chapter Thirty-three

Just after midnight, Karin's train slipped across the massive steel bridge over the Rhine River and came to a stop beneath the shadow of the magnificent cathedral in Köln. Unless there were special trains unpublished on the regular timetables, here she would have the longest wait of the entire journey.

She bought a bread roll and fingered the leftover coins. They would give her about three minutes, more than enough time to report that she had arrived safely. That is, if Mother was even home. Knowing Ursula and the Nazi bureaucrats, who loved a good party, she counted on her mother not answering. But the attempt would reduce the number of lies she would have to tell later. As the phone rang, she offered a silent prayer that Schlinge was not tracking Ursula's phone. If he was, he was a bigger monster than Karin thought.

"Halo?"

"Mother?" Karin couldn't believe it.

"Karin, darling, are you all right?"

"Yes, Mother, fine."

"It's awfully noisy there, dear. Is Trudi having a party?"

"No, Mother, nothing like that. We had a slight delay, and Trudi wanted to take a walk along the river, so I thought I'd call you from the station. I expected you to still be out. How was your reception?"

"A complete bust," Ursula replied.

"Oh really?"

"Heinrich got called away unexpectedly."

"Oh, I'm sorry, Mother."

"Yes, me too. But he said it was important," she added with sarcasm outweighing sympathy. "More important than usual. A conference with you-know-who himself."

Karin knew that meant the Führer. That would be unusual and important, indeed.

"And what's worse, he left me to fend for myself getting home. His driver appeared just as we sat down for dinner—with the Italian Ambassador no less—and whisked him off like he was needed to remove the Führer's appendix!"

"Mother!" Karin hissed. "You must be careful with such talk."

"Yes, yes, I know. It's all so very important. Very important. If anyone's listening, it's all very important."

The phone buzzed, a warning that the timer was soon to expire.

"I've got to go, Mother," Karin interjected. "I'm sorry about your evening," she added, but it was too late. The call had disconnected.

Karin did not typically find pleasure in her mother's misfortunes but was happy on this occasion that she was so easily distracted. Karin was sure she had fallen for the deception.

Chapter Thirty-four

Hansi led Salzmann back across the street, past the nook Inge had used as a secret meeting place, continued to the corner, and turned west toward the main road.

Salzmann managed only a shuffle; half-limping behind. Soon they were at the crossing where Hansi had narrowly escaped the truck convoy.

The street was silent and still. Darkness hung in a damp mist. Invasion traffic had all but stopped for the night. The blackness should have been a comfort—instead it was unsettling.

Hansi looked in every direction, hardly able to believe their good fortune. Utter stillness. Only the moon and stars cast a pall over the length of the road. Houses and walls, mere black rectangles and boxes, lined the road. The village had become a ghost-town.

"Why are we stopping?" Salzmann asked, unaffected by the quiet, unaware of the need to remain so.

"Shhhh, this is the invasion route. We must cross here without detection."

"There's no one within—" Salzmann broke off. Something snapped in the garden to their left. They froze in place.

Hansi peered across the street. A low wooden fence set the boundary of another garden behind a small house whose windows were shuttered. The fence, like broken teeth, revealed dark spaces between the slats.

Hansi leaned close to Salzmann. The smell of alcohol,

vomit, and tobacco still hung over him.

"Wait here. I'll circle round and signal you when it's safe to come."

"How?"

"A bird call, I don't know. Something."

"You're being dramatic again."

"Look, if there's somebody over there, I'll draw them off. You continue west, and I'll catch up with you. If I don't find you in an hour, consider me lost. You're on your own. Your best chance without me is to cross the river about a kilometer up the main road. A kilometer after that and you should be in Luxembourg. Head north and you'll hit Vianden."

"Swim the river?"

"I don't know another way."

"Don't be silly. I can't swim."

"You'll have to."

"I've got a better idea."

Hansi waited.

"Don't get caught. Now go. *Tempus fugit.*"

Hansi stepped out from the wall. His feet crunched the tiny pebbles in the joints of the cobblestone. He paused in the middle of the street.

Was there something—someone—waiting behind the fence?

He crept on, his pulse racing. At the far side of the street, he bent down, squatting down to the level of the fence.

He slid to his right and focused his eyes on the dark gaps.

His hand touched the smooth wood. An electric shock seemed to bolt through him when another twig snapped. A shadow passed between two of the slats, then a hedgehog waddled out from under a board.

Then came laughter. It echoed up and down the street. It emanated from behind.

When Hansi looked back, Salzmann was bent over, pointing as the hedgehog slipped back into the darkness, seemingly unaware.

A second sound cut the laughter short.

A siren, faint at first and then louder. From the center of town.

Hansi shook away the shock. "Hurry!"

He waved Salzmann across. The old man slid across the road as the siren reverberated between the houses.

Hansi snatched him by the arm and pulled. He dragged him up the road, concerned no longer with the siren, but with speed.

"I can't run!" Salzmann said. "And you're cutting the circulation in my arm."

"That siren means the whole town is going to be awake. This place will be crawling with police, the army, who knows. We've got to hurry!"

The siren blared on. Hansi found the secondary road he had entered the village on and hoped the search for them would be west instead of north. As he dragged Salzmann, he could see lights flickering near the center of the village. The sound of an engine starting broke the eerie silence. The search had begun.

The road rose slightly from the village, and minutes

later, they were among the protection of the pines, birch, and elders that lined the road. Hansi kept a sharp eye behind them.

After about thirty minutes, the sirens fell quiet. Had they given up the search?

"I need to rest," Salzmann said.

"Not yet," Hansi said. "Not until we're across the border."

"How far is that?"

"Another two or three kilometers. The road curves up ahead—"

"Blast your curves! The French won't appreciate you delivering a dead scientist, I can tell you that. Especially one of my stature."

Salzmann's arrogance was a club he swung wildly. Ignoring it, Hansi looked back down the road and listened. The breeze had died off. The bugs, a constant buzzing, had finally grown tired and let up. They were in near complete stillness.

"Ok," he finally said. "Five minutes, no more. We've got to get across the border before dawn."

"Slow and steady wins the race," Salzmann replied, his tone back to that of the wise professor. He tipped his suitcase on its end and sat down. A handkerchief appeared from somewhere, and he began to pat his forehead, cheeks, and neck.

"I'm too old for this," he said after a moment.

Hansi was trying to see up around the next bend.

"And you're too young. This bloody war will rob both of us of any good years we might have had left."

The words slid down Hansi's back like a sharp slag of ice. But there was no time for this kind of talk.

"Do you really know how to build the bomb?"

The old man had his eyes closed. He was rotating his head slowly on its axis, stretching.

"No. Not entirely. But I believe I know how not to."

Hansi's thoughts raced. He could understand why the French would be interested in a scientist who knew how to build the super weapon. But why would they care to rescue someone who didn't know how to build it?

"Is that important? How not to?"

"Of course. Eliminating false possibilities is essential to progress. The Nazis don't realize this. Their scientists are not focused. They are too beholden to their precious reputations. If a man, Dr. Mannstein, for example, holds a prestigious position at Berlin University, then his theories are given more priority than that of a junior scientist. Even if—or should I say, even though—the former's theories are ridiculous. Believe it or not, the Nazis have not subdued this research with their characteristic ruthlessness. Herr Hitler is somehow jealous of their intellect and will not challenge them. For now. But hopefully the French will not be so foolish when they understand what I have to show them. Then again, to expect a Frenchman to listen to a German, well, that is asking a great deal. Certainly, the Americans will not be so parochial. They are young. Reputations count for little. They only care about the end result. They will listen."

"So, you know what the Germans are doing wrong?"

"Yes. They are wasting time collecting all this heavy

water." Salzmann spoke as though Hansi knew what it meant. "They are right in that they need to understand radioactivity, but they chase the rare isotope of hydrogen thinking that the simple atom holds the key. The British and Americans are more direct—they are trying to split an already heavy atom—uranium, plutonium, and the like. They know that the effort is more difficult than what the Germans are trying, but the results are sure to be more dramatic."

"I don't get it."

"Of course, not. I wouldn't expect you to. Think of it this way. You want to clear a forest. You don't know how. You start by breaking twigs. Simple, but you're a long way off from clearing the forest. Clearing a forest—and all at once, I might add—really has nothing to do with breaking twigs. In order to accomplish it, you must think differently. The Germans are focused on breaking twigs."

"That's the 'heavy water' approach?"

"Precisely. In trillions upon trillions of water molecules, they find one with an extra proton in the hydrogen atom. This is the twig they are trying to snap. The Americans, on the other hand, are working with the entire forest, by comparison. It is enormously difficult to accomplish, mowing down all those trees at once. But if they figure it out—wow! That will be something. Uranium is the key. If they can figure out how to split uranium, and a great deal of it, they will clear the forest."

Hansi cleared his throat. "And how did you come to know this?"

Salzmann snorted and thumped the side of the

suitcase like he was beating a drum. "That's a rude question but I suppose I should expect it from a Luxembourger. It's beneath me—hah, hah—to answer." He shot up. "You've lost track of time, my young commando. Our five minutes are up. Let's go."

Hansi was still working on the analogies of lumbering and nuclear physics and how it would lead to the super bomb. But rest had certainly restored Salzmann's ego.

No sooner had they returned to the pavement, than they heard the faint whine of an engine coming up the road from the village. Hansi grabbed Salzmann by the arm.

"Up there," he urged, indicating the line of trees up the bank.

They slipped down into the ditch between the road and the hill, and Hansi began to pull Salzmann up the bank. The slope was grassy and slick from dew.

Two pinpoints of light appeared in the road, emerging from around the curve about a half-kilometer back. Hansi realized how foolish they had been stopping in such a spot.

He scrambled up to a line of bushes and undergrowth. The vehicle drew near, but slowly. Hansi hoped the blackout covers on the headlights kept them from being seen.

Salzmann struggled, especially with the suitcase and his flat-soled shoes. Hansi leaned down.

The vehicle, a kubelwagen, moved steadily toward them. A beam of light sliced forward. Hansi made out the silhouette of a soldier, standing up in the vehicle, shining a flashlight along the road.

"Give me your hand!" Hansi rasped, reaching down.

The old man stretched out his arm, but Hansi couldn't reach it. Panic grew as the beam drew nearer, sweeping back and forth across the road, along the ditch, the bank, and back.

Hansi jumped back down into the ditch. He slid behind Salzmann and shoved him up the slope. An instant later, the old man found his grip on a shrub and had pulled himself over the lip of the bank. He disappeared into the cover.

But the light was dancing up the bank toward Hansi. He would not make it in time. The light would expose him, and they would both be captured.

"Come on!" Salzmann hissed. But Hansi's own traction now was failing. The light was nearly on him.

The kubelwagen downshifted and accelerated. Hansi dove just below the path of the beam.

Hansi splashed down and inhaled a gulp of the muddy mixture. The sudden chill sent quakes along the length of his body as his clothes absorbed their fill. His left ear filled with icy water and closed off hearing. Still, Hansi pressed himself as deep into the ditch as he could, as one dead and buried. Fear froze harder than the water. The beam passed overhead while the vehicle thundered nearby.

Hansi cracked open his right eye, which was above the water. The vehicle was moving slowly and passing right by the place he lay in the ditch. Indeed, a soldier was standing in the front seat, one hand on the windscreen, another on the light, scanning the area ahead of them.

The kubelwagen slipped past. Diesel fumes swept down into the ditch. Mixed with the putrid liquid in his mouth, Hansi fought not to cough. Then he remembered Salzmann.

Please. Stay put.

Hansi felt his entire body soak up the stream now. The chill penetrated to the core and tremors began in his teeth. The harder he clamped down, the more they moved to his body and limbs. The fight to lay still was excruciating, and he feared this would be his undoing.

The vehicle crept on, and Hansi felt a sliver of hope it might continue. But then it creaked to a stop. The motor idled. He couldn't tell how far past, but the fumes told him it had to be close.

"They can't have gotten much farther," one of the soldiers said.

"What is this alarm anyway?" his companion asked.

"Who knows. The order came from above. Something about a French spy fleeing the hotel."

The soldiers talked on. The conversation gave Hansi something to focus on other than freezing in the ditch. The pair of soldiers didn't seem particularly motivated in their search. Perhaps they would finish their search and return. He and Salzmann just might make it.

A door creaked open. A boot crunched down on the pavement.

Every muscle was at the breaking point. Hansi's body throbbed with pain.

If he looks back here...

The steps drew closer. Hansi couldn't see how close without moving his head and betraying his position. In fact, the soldier might have already seen him and was just moving with caution.

"What are you doing, Karl? We ought to keep going."

"A French spy in Germany? Do you really believe that? The French are in retreat, in case you haven't heard. Some desk-colonel got spooked and let his imagination run wild. Now we're on a rabbit hunt." He laughed. The other soldier laughed.

"Talk like that will get you in trouble."

The soldier's feet shuffled. Then a splash of water hit somewhere in the ditch above Hansi. It continued in a steady stream.

"You're an idiot, Karl."

"Ahhh—I've needed to go since we were sent out here. *Gott im Himmel!*"

The light sliced down to the ditch. Hansi jumped up. For an instant they faced each other—Hansi dripping in the ditch, the soldier Karl frozen with a mixture of embarrassment and fear, furiously fastening his trousers.

Hansi moved first. Rather than flee down the ditch; by some strange instinct, perhaps in seeing the soldier in such a vulnerable position, Hansi charged right at him. A step and a half across the pavement and Hansi hit him before the soldier had completed his fastening. The force and defenseless position gave Hansi the advantage. They crashed to the pavement with Hansi on top.

"Run, Salzmann! Run!"

Hansi was not conscious of what came over him. It was just a blind, wild desire to live. Or simply to warm himself. Whatever it was, he burst upon the soldier with speed and fury and strength he hadn't known before. He hadn't found it in the meadow with Michele. Nor in the chateau. And certainly not on the bridge, when Manolo needed him most. But here it was, in a moment of utter need. It came on him like an uncontrollable force, a chain reaction of massive proportion.

He wrestled the soldier, beat on him. Hansi's movements were that of a raving beast. He maintained the advantage and stayed straddled over the larger man. How long this continued he had no idea. But all at once, he found his hand on the soldier's holster, and then the leather flap was open, and the cool metal of the hilt was in his hand.

The soldier must have sensed it. Shock and embarrassment were replaced by fear. His strength finally engaged, and he sprung to life from arms to knees to twisting torso.

A blow struck Hansi's face from the left. His vision was unplugged for an instant, and when it returned, searing pain came with it. He tumbled off the soldier and felt the warmth of the pavement on his cheek. Cool air rushed through his fingers which had formerly been wrapped around metal.

The pistol!

Hansi scrambled to regain control in a world that was spinning. He looked up and shook his head to clear the haze. A meter and a half separated him from the soldier named Karl. Behind him, the other soldier was climbing down from the kubelwagen. Karl had managed to sit up and was scanning the pavement for the pistol. Hansi saw it first, but it was closer to Karl, between them.

A shadow flashed from the embankment.

BAM! Salzmann's suitcase served a better purpose than the dead weight of transport for vomit-soaked clothes. Karl, focused on finding the pistol, never saw it coming. He took the full weight of it in the side of his head and tumbled over.

Hansi stretched forward and took hold of the pistol.

"Hande hoch!" the soldier by the kubelwagen barked. His voice was high-pitched and fear-filled.

Hansi ignored it. Whether by rage, the desire to survive, or the memory of Manolo, Hansi ignored it. Time seemed to stop.

He stared down at his hand. The pistol pointed down to the pavement. His finger found the small switch alongside the trigger. *The safety.* He had no idea whether it was on or off. Instinct told him the soldier would have been cautious enough to keep it on. Hansi flicked the switch, raised the weapon, and squeezed—once, and then again.

The shots echoed down the road.

The soldier fell back against the kubelwagen with a hollow clank and smacked down onto the pavement.

Without a second thought, Hansi turned to the soldier named Karl and fired twice more. Karl sank to the pavement with a look of confusion frozen on his face.

Then the road was still again. Gunsmoke mixed with fog and hung all around them.

Salzmann stood rigid like a road sign. Karl looked like he was asleep on the pavement. The other lay in an awkwardly twisted lump, almost under the vehicle. Hansi let his arm fall limp, but held on to the pistol. Then something molten rose up inside. The revulsion rose like lava and erupted. Hansi turned downhill and heaved, but only water came up. The sour muddy taste of the ditch. He spit the remnants on to the road. Then a second wave of heat rose in his ears, his lips dripped with saliva, and he wretched again. Nothing came. Hansi focused on a crack in the pavement, fighting the waves of nausea. He saw himself in miniature, a toy soldier, standing at the edge of the crack. It would be cliff-sized to the tiny figure. He could pitch himself off it and plunge forever into darkness.

The slap stung through Hansi's still-wet shirt. "Well done, boy! Well done."

Hansi twisted out of range.

"Perhaps I've underestimated you. You've handled the situation very efficiently."

Hansi stared down the road, wondering if others would be following.

"Get in." Salzmann hoisted his suitcase into the back of the kubelwagen.

Hansi turned back around. Salzmann was climbing into the driver's seat. He began to fiddle with the controls. "Let's see if I remember how to drive one of these things." The engine sputtered to life. Hansi crossed to the far side and climbed in. He let his eyes drift into the indistinguishable mass of fog ahead. It suited him fine.

Salzmann found the gear lever. The engine revved, and he pushed in on the clutch. The vehicle rolled backward slightly until it came against the masses in the road. Hansi's stomach lurched. Salzmann shifted and let go of the clutch.

The kubelwagen jumped forward as if touching the dead soldiers were an unholy act. Salzmann revved hard and shifted again.

"The kubelwagen began as a Volkswagen—the people's car. For young people, I suppose, and now young soldiers. Personally, I prefer transport that's motivated by a sharp rap on the flanks!"

Hansi heard the sounds but not the words. But for the first time, Salzmann's waxing didn't annoy him.

Chapter Thirty-five

The morning sun, warming the tops of the ridges above the Moselle River, drove the night mists from the slopes. They caressed the young buds on the finely manicured grapevines before settling over the cool currents below. Karin had slept in bits but woke frequently from the concussion of passing trains, track joints, and nerves. Still, despite her fatigue, when her train rolled into the Trier Bahnhof, her spirits were high. The first phase of her journey was complete, and without complication. Luxembourg City lay only a half-hour on.

Worries about her papers had been unfounded. Schlinge's pass had been truly golden. Ticket agents seemed more concerned with the schedule than who rode the trains. A fifteen-year-old girl may have been an oddity, but not to be questioned, evidently, when credentialed by one such as Schlinge. Karin was grateful for his misplaced trust.

At the Trier station, the only trains listed for departure were those heading back into Germany through the northbound line to Koblenz, or the southbound line to Stuttgart.

She went to the ticket office.

"Are the trains running to Luxembourg?"

A white-haired old man was sipping something hot from a metal mug.

"I'm sure they are," he answered. "Just look around."

The sarcasm surprised her.

"Can I get a ticket?"

He shook his head. "Not today. Not this week. Who knows, maybe not even this month."

Karin's hope fell, but she was not finished.

"But I have this," she said, showing him her pass.

He glanced at it and then waved it away.

"That might work on some trains, Fraulein, but if you look around, you'll see that the army is running everything that crosses the border. They're not carrying anything but bullets and butts, if you beg my pardon. And not yours. Now, if you excuse me, I've got work to do."

Karin turned away without another word, but she had come too far to give up.

Back on the platforms, it wasn't difficult to tell which train was headed west. The black locomotive painted swirls of steam at the far edge of her vision to the left and stretched as far as she could see to the north, along the river's edge. Flatcars were laden with tanks, tarp-covered guns, and crates stacked two times the height of a soldier. Everything was marked by crisp numbers stenciled in white, and a black and white cross. Anti-aircraft guns, mounted on timbers on various flatcars throughout the length, pointed at morning's blue-yellow sky, where German planes streamed west.

Karin crossed toward a conductor dressed in military uniform, signaling along the train's length with a pair of paddles with red, green, black, and white faces. He would look up and down the line, glance up at a tower from time to time, and check his watch. He didn't see Karin until she was next to him.

"You can't be here, Fraulein. Get back to the first track."

"I need to get to Luxembourg, sir," she said. "Is this train going there?"

"Not with you on it. Military use only."

"I have this." She tried the pass again. He shot a quick glance at her paper but didn't read it. A whistle sounded up the line.

"It doesn't matter, and too late anyway. This train is leaving." He waved a paddle and made a last check up and down the line. Other soldiers with paddles did the same.

The whistle shrieked nearby, splitting Karin's eardrums. She stepped back. The train jumped with the thunderous clap of metal. And then squeals as the stiff bearings broke loose. The train jerked forward, then began to roll.

For a brief instant, she considered that it would have been possible to climb on to the end of a flat car where a short ladder hung down.

Something Hansi would try, she thought with a smile to herself.

The moment passed as the train had picked up enough speed already to render her idea more foolish than it had been at the start.

She would have to find another way.

When she stepped through the door of the station, the view stopped her short. The city of Trier, familiar from her many visits to the Roman-built Porta Nigra and Amphitheater, was barely recognizable since her last visit with Hansi the previous autumn. The sleepy tourist town had been transformed into a transportation hub, jammed with every manner of tank, truck, towed and self-propelled gun, car, jeep, and half-track. Some moving, some lined up to be loaded onto flatcars. The streets churned with wagons, horses, and carts, moving supplies in every direction. Soldiers were everywhere, marching, standing at attention, saluting, resting, sleeping, eating, cajoling, writing letters, and playing football. Karin had to pick her steps carefully through the crowded plaza outside the station for fear of being bowled over by the activity.

On the streets, civilians seemed to be as disoriented as her, clawing their way through the sudden influx of men and matériel. Vendors were jubilant. Their supplies of fresh bread, cheese, boiled sausages, and roasted nuts drew long lines of soldiers making last-minute purchases for their journey west.

Flags and banners were everywhere, just like Berlin. Having lived mostly away from Germany, Karin was still unaccustomed to the ubiquitous displays. Paris had been more of a home—its art, boulevards, and gardens an invitation to enjoy life. And then Luxembourg, whose ancient fortress nestled among shops, cafés, and townhouses, was so charming and comfortable. The Germany she remembered was that of her childhood, mostly defined by the four walls of her room, a beloved stuffed bear in her bed, the smell of fresh bread from Oma's oven.

The Germany of Beethoven, Brahms, Luther, and Goethe was now the land of men and machines, politics and war, raw power. It was Father's world, and apparently now Mother's too, in her way. Ursula didn't care about conquering nations, but she exercised power for survival, protection, perhaps even love.

Love? Heavens no.

Between the tracks and the shops to the left of the station building soldiers were loading trucks with boxes and equipment. Karin studied the scene for a moment. A line of soldiers was passing boxes from a large stack on the plaza to a truck parked on the street. They were laughing and joking as they worked. Full trucks pulled away and empty ones took their place.

She approached a sandy-haired, red-cheeked boy whose face was moist with sweat from his effort. He looked hardly older than Karin. She had noticed the others teasing him with jabs and rubs of his hair, behaviors Karin found annoying among the boys at her school.

Seeing her, the boy stood upright with a start, almost at attention.

"Excuse me, *leutnant*," she said.

He looked around as if to make sure she was looking at him.

"Uh, I'm just a *soldat*. Our *unteroffizier* is over there. You can talk to him." He pointed to a soldier at the back of the truck who was working a pencil and clipboard.

"I see. Excuse me, private." She smiled, evoking a deeper shade of red on his cheeks. Karin wondered if he had ever spoken to a girl before.

His comrade gave him a box, which he took and held.

"Would your trucks be going to Luxembourg?"

The private seemed to let the question sink in for a moment. "I honestly don't know. I think we're going to France. Hey, Fritz, are we going to France?"

Fritz had his back to the private, waiting to receive another box from the pile. His comrade up the line handed one to him, and then he turned to the private.

"Next stop Paris! Right, comrades?"

They cheered in unison.

Fritz held his box for the private, who had not yet passed his box along.

"Are you going through Luxembourg on your way to France?" Karin asked.

The private shrugged. "Are we Fritz?"

"I have no idea," Fritz replied. "I've never heard of it."

The interruption brought the entire line to a halt. An instant later, the soldier with the clipboard joined them.

"What's the hold up here? Hey! You didn't tell me a pretty maiden was attending us."

He bowed low. "Unteroffizier Beckman at your service, Fraulein."

The line dissolved and gathered around them. Karin felt her face flush with embarrassment.

"Anyone know where Luxembourg is?" Fritz asked. "She needs directions."

"I need to go there," Karin interjected. "But the trains won't take passengers right now."

Corporal Beckman pointed across the river. "It's right there. At least I think it is. They don't tell us much, Fraulein."

"Except to march," a voice chimed in. A few of them chuckled.

"Is your truck going there?" she pressed. "I really need to get there."

Beckman folded his arms coyly. "Our destination is a military secret," he said through a grin. "And we've been instructed to be on the lookout for French spies."

More chuckles.

"Are you a French spy, mademoiselle?" Full laughs rose now.

"Please, it's important I get there. My grandmother is ill. I have a travel permit." She flashed Schlinge's paper.

"Likely story," he said playfully. "I'd say that's a lie, however. Tell me the truth and we'll give you a ride."

"It is the truth, I swear!"

Corporal Beckman twisted his mouth and shook his head. "No, I don't think so. Try again."

"My grandmother lives in Luxembourg City. I tried calling her, but the lines are down, so I need to check on her."

He folded his arms. "Convincing, but still not the truth."

"I believe her," blurted the private.

"You're in love," Beckman said. The fellows giggled and jostled the private again.

Karin was growing angry.

"But you're close," Beckman said. "It's not you in love. It's her."

Karin's face went hot.

"I knew it," Beckman said. "Sorry, Willie. As I

suspected, it's a boy, but not you."

Karin felt like the locomotive bursting with steam, incensed by the group of soldiers who seemed quite entertained by the spectacle unfolding before them.

"Will you take me or not?"

"Calm down, Fraulein, calm down." Beckman grew serious and held out a hand, inviting Karin to step outside the circle. The soldiers parted and she stepped through the perimeter, Beckman following.

He glanced over his shoulder.

"Back to work, you swine! I'll thrash you and call the Sergeant."

The soldiers obeyed, leaving Beckman and Karin virtually alone beyond the soldiers' earshot.

"What's your name, Fraulein?"

"Karin," she answered. "Karin Blik."

"Fraulein Blik, I apologize for that—well, whatever that was. Where do you come from?"

"I'm from Berlin."

"I see. Would I be correct in assuming that you are related to someone, shall I say, powerful, someone I don't want to know, or more properly, someone I don't want to know me?"

She wanted to lie, keeping everything secret, but the corporal seemed shrewd.

"Put it this way," she answered. "I have a pass that lets me go on any train I like. It worked everywhere until now, when I really needed to go to Luxembourg. Will you help me?"

He smiled. "Yes, of course. As I said, I'm at your

service. Now, naturally, I can't just let you climb into a truck, and I don't think you're suited to being stuffed in a crate. But I need something in return, something comparable to the risk I would be taking to help you."

"Money? I have a few marks I was hoping to use for something to eat."

He took a deep breath in, placing his hands on his hips. Then he shook his head, swallowed, and smiled.

"We will be loaded here in an hour and head out. There's a baggage office just at the far end of the station, just there." He pointed. Meet me there in thirty minutes."

Karin's eyes widened.

The slap was a surprise to them both. Karin's palm stung.

"How dare you!" She fumed, and then suddenly found herself the target of the men's stares again. She spun around and ran, leaving Corporal Beckman shrugging his shoulders as his comrades howled.

Karin ran from the station, dodging soldiers, vendors, and travelers, and passed under the arches of Porta Nigra. She didn't stop until she was clear of the Plaza, where she found a less populated side street and fell against a wall in the middle of the block. She sobbed, her tears both angry and full of despair. She was no closer to her goal and had been a fool to think the soldiers would help.

Beckman's assault broke a dam of sorts, not just of her own safety, but that of the entire project. To think she could simply train over to Luxembourg City and save Hansi. Who was he to her? And who was she to him? The kilometers behind her, from Berlin to Trier were suddenly terrifying. She was far, far from home and alone in a town that had once been familiar, but now whose very air was thick with threats and hostility.

The fear morphed quickly into anxiety and flickered with panic. Her heart raced, her throat tightened, and her breathing came quick and shallow. The rising feeling turned in on itself, speaking in a whisper first, and then an inner shout: *You are losing control. The longer you go, the harder it becomes.* The spiral accelerated, feeling upon feeling.

She squeezed her eyes shut.

As a young girl in Paris, one day at the playground she naively climbed onto a large flat spinning wheel. Older boys jumped on and started to spin it. They asked her if she wanted off before they climbed on, but without fully realizing what was happening, refused to get off.

With a shrug as if to say "suit yourself," the boy put one leg up on the wheel and pushed the ground with the other. Karin held on, and for a few revolutions, the ride provided a thrill. But soon after, she realized her mistake. And now it was too late to call out. Something inside was determined to hang on. The force pulled outward. Her grip tightened. The panic rose. Inexorably, the force pried her fingers and arms from the bar. When it was over, she had been tossed, skidded, and rolled over the crushed stones. Everything hurt, everything stung.

But, as the boys laughed, she refused to cry. She pulled herself to her feet, ignoring the scrapes on her shins, knees, elbows, and chin. She ran home.

The feeling now was much the same.

"Are you hurt, Fraulein?"

The voice was that of a man, and when Karin looked up, she twitched. The soldier held out his hand.

She had forgotten that she was sitting on the sidewalk, crumpled against a downspout along a brick wall. She quickly rose to her feet.

He stepped forward to help, but she waved him off.

He retreated. "It's all right. Please. I'm sorry. I thought you were injured."

She looked at him again. Although he was in uniform, he looked too old to be a soldier. Then she noticed a symbol embroidered on his lapel. A snake coiled around a staff.

"Are you hurt?" he repeated.

"Who are you?"

"Doctor Albert Vogel. I'm with The Twenty-Fifth Medical Corps, attached to the Second Panzer Division."

Karin blinked to clear her vision and wiped some of the tears from her face with her hands.

Doctor Vogel presented a handkerchief. Karin took it. She brushed herself off and gave it back.

"I'm fine, thank you," she said, although it was obvious she was not.

"Is there anything I can help you with?" he pressed. "Directions, perhaps? Something to eat?"

He was genuinely expressing kindness, she knew, but she was wary and reeling.

"Do you know where I could get something to drink?" she asked.

"Of course," he said, his expression brightening. "There's a café just around the corner. Perhaps it seems hard to believe, but I was going there just now. My train isn't leaving for another couple of hours. I was going to get a cup of coffee, check on our supplies, and then look for some birds." He tapped on the binoculars hanging from his neck. "Allow me to show you." Panic spread over his expression. "Where the café is, not the birds."

Karin took a breath. The change of focus was helpful. She could get a drink, something to eat perhaps, and think things through.

He led her back toward the plaza to a row of shops opposite the train station. The café was narrow, featuring a display case of pastries and sandwich rolls, and beyond, a counter where hot coffee and drinks were served. The place was mostly filled with soldiers, either lined up to order, waiting for their food, or crammed along a strip of a ledge on the wall opposite the counter. There were a few tables just at the front window.

The doctor pushed his way to the window and moved a pair of soldiers off their table with a nod and wave of his hand.

"Please," he said, indicating Karin to sit.

Once she had done so, he advanced up the line, ordering lower ranked men to let him through. They yielded without protest, and he quickly spoke to the server.

The order, two coffees and two rolls, was fulfilled quickly upon his return.

"Thank you," Karin said. She welcomed the sharp

flavor and warmth of the coffee. The bites of bread began to settle her stomach. The public space, though loud and chaotic, seemed safer than a private one. She relaxed a bit.

"What's your name?" he asked. She told him. He was direct, as she expected of a doctor, but not harsh.

"You're not from here, are you?"

She wondered how he knew.

"Your bag is quite full," he said, answering her unspoken question.

"Berlin," she said, deciding it didn't matter if he knew.

"You were in distress around the corner. Were you hurt?"

"No," she said. "Well, not ill or injured in the way you were thinking."

"You assume I think a certain way. I treat many kinds of illnesses and injuries. Most of them, in fact, cannot be seen."

She looked up from her coffee. "What do you mean?"

"I'm a doctor and can fix broken bones, fevers, and the like. But the kinds of illnesses I'm most interested in are those of the heart, you might say."

"And did you think I was injured in that way?"

"I saw you crying and covering your face. That was not nothing."

"I feel better now," she said.

"Excellent. A cup of coffee can do wonders sometimes."

He gulped a few more of his own, watched the flow of soldiers in and out for a few minutes, and then got up.

"Fraulein Blik, it's been my pleasure to make your

acquaintance. I don't want to miss out on some good observation time," he said, patting his binoculars again. "Who knows if I'll be doing much birdwatching any time soon. And I do need to check on our supplies once more before my departure. I wish you all the best." He offered his hand.

"Where is your train going?" Karin asked, leaving his hand in the air.

"France, I presume. They don't really tell us specifically, but it seems obvious."

"Can you take me with you? As an assistant or a nurse?"

The question stopped him.

"Are you in some kind of trouble?" he asked.

She shook her head. "No, but I need to go to Luxembourg."

"How old are you?"

"Not old enough to be a nurse, but can you help me?"

"You realize Luxembourg is a war zone, don't you?"

"They wouldn't have resisted," she said.

"And you know this how?"

"I lived there last year. In fact, most people think that Luxembourg is a part of Germany anyway. But they have almost no army to speak of, certainly not enough of one to resist all of them out there."

"Very astute, Fraulein. But that doesn't change the fact that I can't even contemplate what you're asking. It would be illegal, immoral, in fact. Why do you want to go there so badly?"

"I have a friend there who is in danger."

"You said they had no army. What kind of danger?"

"I'm not sure I can explain, but I need to go there."

"How do you expect to help him? You said it yourself, there's no resisting 'all of them out there.'"

"I didn't say it was a him."

"You didn't need to. I was your age once."

"I need to warn him while there's still time."

"The war is already there, Fraulein Blik. I'm afraid it's too late."

She shook her head. "No, not too late," she said, mostly to herself.

He looked over her shoulder, thinking. He pulled his lower lip in and bit down.

"It goes without saying that I can't honor your original request. That would be a violation of law and my oath as a doctor," he finally said. "But if you are as determined as I think you are, you'll not listen to my advice which is as clear as I can make it. You have no business going to Luxembourg."

He rubbed his chin and adjusted the strap of the binoculars around his neck.

"But I have an idea."

Chapter Thirty-six

Salzmann struggled to find the proper gear but after a few minutes, found his rhythm. The road cooperated too, leveling out and stretching into broader, wide curves. The road through the forest and rocks near Kleindorf began to soften as they approached the higher meadows. The rise up the valley exposed them to a breeze that swept over the open vehicle and chilled Hansi in his wet clothes.

"Put that thing away!" Salzmann shouted.

Hansi looked down at his lap. The Luger was still in his left hand. He had forgotten it. The safety was still off, so he switched it back and slid the pistol between his legs, out of sight. He slid down into the corner of the hard seat and the door. The thin sheet of metal and flimsy latch was all that separated him from the pavement rushing by. He didn't care. The moon and stars seemed to stare down at him, from on high, as if in judgment.

Hansi closed his eyes to shut out the shame. He imagined flying off the seat, over the meadow, up and away from all he had seen and done. He couldn't escape the faces: Maman, pale and ghostlike; Manolo, eyes stuck open, flecked with dirt; and now the two German soldiers. Hansi shouldn't have felt compassion for them, or so he argued with himself. But the one standing by the kubelwagen had locked eyes with him for just an instant before Hansi fired. His look was odd—fear to be sure, but also surprise. Hansi imagined the soldier's last thought: *This wasn't supposed to be dangerous....*

What penetrated deeper than the cold gusts around him was what came after. Hansi replayed the scene over and over in his mind. The soldiers wanted to arrest them, not kill them. The one aiming the gun at Hansi hesitated, allowing Hansi to shoot first. And the one called Karl, stunned by the blow of Salzmann's suitcase, had been defenseless, really. They could have left him that way. Instead, something raw and terrible had been let loose. Hansi turned and fired. And again. The taste of bile in his mouth was pleasant in comparison to the poison in his soul.

"How much farther?" Salzmann asked.

Hansi's eyes popped open. Trees lined the road, but beyond, open fields.

"Up there. That farmhouse. There's a lane just this side of it. Turn left."

Salzmann squeezed the wheel and gunned the engine. He seemed to be enjoying himself. The kubelwagen whined at the speed. Hansi wondered for an instant if Salzmann would miss the turnoff until he realized this was a man who sensed the end of his fun. The old doctor, having regained his driving skill, had been enjoying the twists and turns, and now the open spaces. Soon they would leave the main road. They would cross open land. The tour would soon be over, and Salzmann was anticipating this. Strangely, Hansi was glad. Salzmann's insensitivity to Hansi's distress was almost a comfort.

A wooden mailbox marked the lane, which was little more than two ruts in the grass. Salzmann braked, the kubelwagen shuddered, and they slowed just in time to make the turn before the short, squat farmhouse. He ground the gears at the downshift and swore. They bounced forward off the pavement onto the flat part of the lane.

Hansi stopped them at the edge of a line of trees that shadowed the lane up the slope.

"The border runs through that meadow, just there," Hansi pointed. "We walk from here."

Salzmann switched the engine off and let his shoulders drop. "Ah well, it served its purpose. Driving provided an old man an unexpected pleasure. But life is that way sometimes. I shall remember this journey for a long time. Won't you, young Hansi?"

Hansi didn't answer. He climbed out of the vehicle and waited for Salzmann to collect his case.

"Listen carefully," Hansi said. "The Germans patrol across there. When I came across earlier, an armored car was waiting for us. If not for—" Hansi paused. No need to tell Salzmann about Michele. "Stay with me and do exactly what I tell you."

Salzmann drew back. "You've grown quite confident, haven't you?"

"I've come too far to get killed doing something stupid now. If we keep to these trees, we can stay hidden. Our contact is on the other side." He hoped. "But listen to me, Herr Doktor. We can't stay in the trees forever. At the top of the meadow, we'll have to cross in the open. About a hundred meters. The Germans have a searchlight and machine guns. They'll use both."

"Ok, ok." Salzmann's hands were above his head in a

gesture of mock surrender.

They stayed to the trees, half-crouched, a few steps at a time before Hansi would stop to listen. He scanned the horizon, ears tuned for any sound of the patrol or the armored car. The wind sliced through the trees behind, as if warning them. The belt of stars overhead defined the crest of the meadow, another beauty spoiled by circumstance.

They reached the end of the tree line where the meadow spread out like a broad river.

"Are they out there?" Salzmann whispered. His breath was positively rancid.

"We'll wait five minutes and see. Perhaps they patrol back and forth." Hansi started counting in his head while his eyes peered into the expanse in front of him. He studied the border of stars and grass for any unusual movement, the smallest of changes. And counted. At three hundred, the scene had not changed.

"There's a lane on the far side of this meadow, just over the crest of the hill. It's in Luxembourg. We go left, south, and it curves west back into the woods. It will take us to Vianden. If we get separated, meet me in the trees. And if anything happens to me—"

"Don't speak of it!" Salzmann's voice carried no confidence.

"If anything happens to me," Hansi went on, "follow the lane as far as you can. When you get to the paved road, turn left. That will take you all the way to Vianden. Find the church. Ask for Father Mathieu. He'll know what to do."

"A priest? Heaven forbid. I don't need a priest."

"He's with the Resistance. He'll know where to take you."

"He'll demand a confession and penance first. Let's avoid all of that by making sure you make it across."

Hansi went first. He edged into the open meadow, scanning the arc of the hill.

Michele. *Had she made it?*

He crept forward a few meters, paused, and then continued. The field was completely empty as far as he could see. With every step nearer to the crest, he got a more complete view of the entire field. Ten more steps. He waved Salzmann to follow. The old man stepped tentatively out into the light of the open sky. He strode if the mine was sown with mines. Hansi returned his gaze toward the crest and concentrated on the sounds. Only the rush of wind through the grass swept across the expanse.

When Salzmann had drawn within an arm's length, Hansi continued. At the apex of the meadow, he crept very carefully, every sense on edge.

Fwump! Pumm.

Hansi dropped to the ground. *Pumm-pa-pumm.* The sounds were dull thuds in the distance. A similar cadence repeated, and then the silence returned. Something struck Hansi in the leg and he spun around. Salzmann stood over him.

"Get down!" Hansi snapped.

The old man bent down. "Look. That's no patrol. I've heard these sounds before."

Hansi pushed off the grass. Salzmann pointed off to

their right. Hansi climbed to his feet and studied the horizon. Faint flashes lit the cottony edges of clouds far away.

"What is it?" he asked.

"Artillery. Somewhere north of here, I'd say. A night duel between the Germans and Belgians. Hard to say, but far away from here."

Hansi wiped the soft earth from his face. It smelled fresh and rich. It reminded him of the riverbed where he sliced through the earth with Manolo's knife. A tremor of despair rippled through him.

"What's wrong?" Salzmann asked.

Hansi didn't answer.

"You don't look well."

"Let's go. We're almost there."

A few steps on, there was no longer any doubt. The entire meadow was deserted, the border left unguarded. For the first time of the night, Hansi felt a measure of relief. He accelerated now, with Salzmann doing his best. The meadow lane down the slope came into view. They were back in Luxembourg. Soon they could return to the cover of the woods, descend the hill, and join the road to Vianden.

Then Hansi froze. The small dark figure cut an even darker shadow just at the edge of the lane. Hansi knew at once. He ran to her, fell to his knees, and was lost in an abyss of utter anguish.

"Hansi, my dear boy, are you all right?" Salzmann had caught up with Hansi and stopped. The girl lay on her back, a leg twisted awkwardly underneath, arms spread out.

A new series of artillery flashes illuminated an upturned face and ashen skin.

His mind rejected what his eyes beheld. She appeared as a doll, discarded and tossed to the ground for nature to consume. He shook her by the arms and slapped her face. Limp, she jerked and bounced. And refused to move. The world in all its darkness swirled and shrunk and sucked him down.

He couldn't move until Salzmann touched his hand on Hansi's shoulder.

"It's no use, son. Try not to look."

Hansi jerked away.

"Come on now. We should go. Morning comes quickly." Salzmann was pointing east. The sky had lightened just enough to notice.

Hansi wasn't interested in morning or the mission. He stared down at the grass, at the slender blades that parted like water where his footsteps had trod. His mind flew to the hotel, where Madame Poulet would be sitting at the table in the kitchen, worried to the edge of control.

How would he tell her? *I'm sorry, Madame, but the Germans killed your daughter and just left her in the meadow.*

For what? she would ask.

For a drunk scientist—no, an arrogant drunk scientist who cares more about a stupid suitcase full of vomit-caked clothes than anyone else.

Salzmann tried to pull Hansi away. He resisted but staggered to his feet. Nausea hit him like a tidal wave, but there was nothing inside to vomit.

"Help me," Hansi said. He bent over Michele and

took hold of her wrists.

"What are you doing?"

"What does it look like? I'm going to take her to her mother. It's the least I can do."

"She's a slight one, but still, too much for you alone. And I'm no use."

"Of course not. Your precious suitcase weighs you down. I'll manage myself, then." Hansi straightened her body and folded Michele's arms across her torso. He untwisted her legs and brushed the hair off her face. The touch of her skin was strangely familiar, cold and like clay. Just like Manolo's.

"Now Hansi, be reasonable. She's nearly your size. You can't hope to carry her on your own. I've got an idea. Drag her out of the open and take me to the town. You can come back. I'll even make sure to send help with you. I have money."

"She's coming with us!"

Salzmann grabbed Hansi by the arm. "There's a bloody war on! People get killed. If you're going to insist on playing commando, you'd better get used to the idea!"

Hansi should have known better by now. He should have known that Salzmann's arrogance was a defense mechanism. He should have appreciated that the old doctor was exhausted from the journey, scared by the Germans, and compromised by his desire for safety. Earlier in the evening, the offense might have been ignored, but not now.

He sprung from the ground with the force of a panther but not the precision. To his surprise, the old man was nimble enough to protect himself with the suitcase. He slid it in Hansi's path just in time. The pair smacked together, suitcase in between, with Hansi bearing the hard shell in the face. They crashed to the grass, Hansi stunned by the unexpected blow. Salzmann landed with a grunt.

I'll kill you with my bare hands.

Hansi climbed to his feet but was dazed. The hillside slipped sideways into the valley. Hansi staggered and fell to one knee.

That suitcase!

He returned to Michele, grasped her in a great hug, and lifted. She was heavier than he expected, but he was angry now, and determined. He would not abandon her now. He focused all his might and lifted. Slowly, she rose from the damp grass. He had her in his arms.

Without care for the old professor, Hansi stumbled onto the lane and trudged for the trees. It took every ounce of strength to hold her. He was quickly overwhelmed by feelings of failure. He was spent only a handful of meters from where he found her. He put her down gently near a stately oak along the lane, defeated. Salzmann was right. They would have to continue without her.

He fell to the grass, disintegrated, unable to move. A dark beast seemed to have swallowed him from the inside. As hard as he fought, he could not hold back the deep, deep howl of despair that bellowed out. The sound was unlike anything he had ever heard come out of himself—hollow, animal-like, emanating from the giant chasm that had opened down to his very bowels. He could have cared less had the entire German Army heard him.

After a few moments, Salzmann touched Hansi on the arm.

"That's enough," he said.

Hansi drew back from the touch, but the effect broke the spasms of sobs. His nostrils felt like wide-open spigots watering the meadow where he lay.

"We truly must go," Salzmann insisted. "You can grieve later."

"You don't care about anyone but yourself, do you?" The words came out in a blast of snot and spit.

"Do you want the truth?"

Hansi got up. "I already know the truth. I needn't have asked. Let's go. The sooner I get rid of you, the better."

"Listen here! Your mission, as I understand it, is to rescue me. You have accomplished half of it—getting me out of Germany. The second half—delivering me to the French spy—remains unfinished."

"You're close enough now. You can get there yourself."

"You have done more than can be expected for a boy of your age and experience. But everything you have accomplished will come to nothing if I don't make it to your spy. And the sacrifice of your friend here will have been for nothing. You can honor her by finishing your mission."

Honor. The notion seemed another world away. Nothing could honor Michele now. No mission was worth her death. Nor Manolo's. Nothing Salzmann knew about the super bomb would ever measure up against the loss of his friends. Still, as Hansi wiped his face and began the trek back down the slope, his anger toward the old man had subsided. Salzmann had not killed Manolo. He had not shot Michele. He knew nothing of the rescue plan, had agreed to nothing but fleeing Germany with his secrets. Despite all his arrogance and seeming self-centeredness, he was afraid, and it showed. In the blink of an eye, the invasion replaced the regular world with an alien hell, and in the end, Hansi had little to measure himself superior to the old scientist.

Hansi had turned to leave when from behind he heard a faint sound like a hiccup.

Chapter Thirty-seven

Karin followed Doctor Vogel's idea and walked to the southern edge of town, where she found the highway bridge across the Moselle just as he described. If she was adventurous, he suggested, she could walk about a dozen kilometers further toward the town of Wasserbillig, where the Our River joined the Moselle at the border with Luxembourg. Assuming the bridges were blocked, she could look for a shallow crossing somewhere away from the traffic and simply wade across.

She followed the flow of invaders and reached the village of Wasserbillig before eight-thirty, where a pair of motorcycle troops kept the bridge clear for troops, trucks, and horse-drawn wagons to cross. A short distance upriver, she found a spot as he described, blending in with other travelers to complete the next phase of her quest. For the first time in nearly half a year, the first time since the day her father was killed, Karin stepped into a Luxembourg far different than before.

Chapter Thirty-eight

Mist, like bony fingers of a ghost, crept along the ground as if searching for something among the shrubs, saplings, and mossy depressions of the forest. When Hansi discovered what seemed to him the miracle of Michele alive, he forced Salzmann to cross the meadow back for the kubelwagen. He would not move a centimeter further until the old man complied. And while the physicist was away, Hansi removed his jacket, wrapped Michele as best he could, and cradled her in his arms.

The back of her head was caked in a black crust that oozed red in the center. Hansi couldn't tell if she had been shot or just grazed. Truth was that fear prevented him from examining the wound very thoroughly. He bound it as gently as he could with the cleanest piece of cloth he could find—the sleeve of his own shirt.

If only Heng was here. *Scouts know first aid.*

Their descent into the valley ripped through the silence like the invasion itself. Hansi drew Michele closer. She was as cold as the ground on which he found her.

The village was deathly still when they burst upon it in the half light of the morning. Even the German Army was still asleep, it seemed. The squat steeple of St. Joseph's church rose ahead. Father Mathieu could find a doctor. Salzmann would wait for Pierre. And Hansi would run to the hotel for Madame Poulet.

The poor woman. And Jacky. Even if Michele lives, the boy will surely take revenge on the first soldier he sees.

Two opposing forces battled within Hansi. He wanted Michele to live even more than himself. At the same time, his adrenaline all but spent, he was desperate for sleep. His body held barely enough heat for itself, let alone Michele. The rushing wind over the open cab of their vehicle sucked more with each passing second. He doubted he could hold on much longer.

They came to the end of the farm lane, alongside the stone fence.

"Which way?" Salzmann called.

Hansi directed him left. They bounced onto the paved road, and Salzmann cranked hard on the wheel. The trees rushed past. Only a kilometer left to go.

Please God. Keep her alive.

The sound of the kubelwagen reverberated off the houses lined at the end in the village. Glancing ahead, Hansi saw the silhouette of the cross beyond the roofline.

"There!" he cried. "That's it!"

Salzmann eased off the accelerator and steered through a slight curve. The force sent Michele's head harder against Hansi's arm, and her face twisted in pain. She was hanging on.

The kubelwagen straightened, and Salzmann accelerated. An instant later, he gasped and stomped hard on the brakes. The wheels locked and the tires howled like demons, but far worse, Michele and Hansi slammed into the back of the front seats.

"You'll kill her!" Hansi screamed. A moment later, after the vehicle had come to a stop, Hansi saw why.

Beside the church in the street ahead sat an Opel truck. Soldiers were pouring out the back, filling the cemetery, and heading for the back entrance of St. Joseph's.

Hansi focused on the leader in the center of the squad. *The officer from the chateau!*

"Back up! Hurry! We've got to warn Madame Poulet. And Jacky. Something is wrong, terribly wrong."

"But what about me? Where's the French agent?"

"Don't worry, I'll take you to him. *Go! Go!*"

Salzmann reversed and wound his way among the narrow lanes of the village out of sight of the church. Salzmann squeaked to a halt in front of the hotel.

"Ring the buzzer! Ask for Madame Poulet!"

Salzmann complied and not long after, the door burst open. Michele's mother was dressed for kitchen work, donning an apron. Her hands and cheeks were dusted with flour. A curl of hair would not stay above her eyes. After the shock at seeing Salzmann in the German officer's uniform, she saw Hansi, and the daughter he held in his arms. For the first time, Hansi saw a resemblance to Michele he had not noticed before. While Madame Poulet's eyes had always been bright and hopeful, Michele's carried a trace of sadness. But now, in the flash of insight that came with the opening of the front door, the mother had been transformed. She flew to the vehicle and started shouting.

"Jacky! Come quick!"

She and Hansi lifted Michele out of the back of the kubelwagen and carried her inside. Salzmann followed, suitcase in hand. Jacky met them in the lobby.

"What happened? Is she alive?"

"Run to Doctor Eckert," his mother commanded. "Tell him Michele's been shot by the Germans. He'll come right away. Hurry son!"

Jacky rushed out the door.

They took Michele to her room upstairs and laid her on the bed. Madame Poulet took over, shooing them out while she removed Michele's damp clothes, covered her with blankets, and warmed her with hot water bottles.

"What are we going to do now?" Salzmann asked Hansi. They were in the foyer at the bottom of the stairs, waiting for news. Dr. Eckert had arrived and joined Madame Poulet.

Hansi ignored the question, desperate for Michele to live. He paced back and forth, his eyes never far from the windows and the street.

Jacky followed his every movement.

"Why, Hansi? Why did you do it?"

Hansi stopped and looked at the boy. His face was twisted in a snarl.

"Why did you leave her there? The Germans shot her, and you left her there to die."

"That's not it—I promise. Listen, Jacky…"

Salzmann stepped forward and before Hansi could react, snatched Jacky by the collar. "Sit down, young man." He shoved Jacky down into a chair. "Hansi was doing his duty. His mission was—*and remains*—to protect me until I reach my destination. As it happens, he also brought your sister home. You should be grateful."

Jacky seemed stunned. He wriggled on the chair for balance, his mouth hanging open. He panted like the wind had been knocked out of him.

Something inside Hansi split open. He spun around and stepped right into Salzmann. He drove himself into the old man, leaning into him as one does against a strong wind.

"*You* sit down. And don't say another word, or I don't care, I'll silence you myself." Hansi felt a rage he hadn't felt since the German road. It burst upon him easily, like a sneeze, and surprised him. Without realizing it, the pistol appeared in his hand. Hansi stabbed the muzzle between the folds hanging under the man's chin.

"I'll kill you," he said, his voice an icy gust.

Salzmann, eye's enormous, backed away. He plopped down at the nearest table and seemed to curl into a ball, suitcase between his knees. Is that what it takes, Hansi wondered?

He spun back to the boy. "Jacky, listen to me."

"Will you shoot me if I don't?"

The words cut deep. His mood swung instantly to the opposite extreme. The weapon took on an enormous weight, and Hansi almost dropped it. He shoved it back into his belt.

"I'm really sorry," Hansi said. He knelt and tried to engage Jacky with his eyes. "Michele was very brave. She saved my life."

Jacky's expression was like the stone casemates, but only for an instant. Cracks began to form in the eyes first, and then tremors swept out from his mouth. His gaze, like radiant black diamonds, drilled into Hansi. There was power deep inside the boy, power more than his years should have known.

Hansi reached out and put an arm around him. Jacky resisted at first, and then, like before, let go. He buried his face in Hansi's shoulders and sobbed. A moment later, he broke free and ran upstairs.

Salzmann stood up.

"What is your plan now?"

"I don't know."

"May I offer a suggestion?"

Hansi eyed the old man with suspicion. "Since when do you ask?"

"Since you remembered your pistol."

"I'm sorry about that. I wouldn't have used it."

"It didn't seem that way when it was under my chin. But thanks all the same. I feel much better now." The old sarcasm was creeping back in. He continued.

"The Germans are after me. And you as well. The girl means nothing to them. Now that the doctor is here, you have done all you can. Take me to Pierre, and your work will be finished."

Finished. Hansi felt the word in his limbs, like a drug.

It seemed too easy now. Deliver Salzmann and be done. Find an empty bed at the hotel and sleep for days, maybe even the entire war.

He remembered Pierre's words the first night at the campfire.

Someone on the inside, someone in the Luxembourg or French

The doctor descended the stairs with Madame Poulet close behind.

"She was lucky," the doctor said. "The wound isn't deep. Looks like the bullet grazed her. She's weak and in shock. And lying outside for so long makes that wound vulnerable to infection. She needs a hospital."

Everyone knew what he meant. Getting her to Luxembourg City was impossible.

He turned to Madame Poulet. "I have some medicine I can give you. No doubt supplies are going to dry up very soon. But she must rest."

"They are in danger," Hansi said. "Whoever knew we were in Kleindorf won't take long to figure out we're going west. If they find Father Mathieu, they'll find you, Madame."

"Where can they go?" Salzmann asked in a huff. "The Germans are everywhere."

"Can you get to Wiltz?" Hansi asked. He grabbed a postcard from the front desk, scribbled an address, and handed it to Madame Poulet.

"Don't worry about us. I'll find a way," Madame Poulet said. "Get him to Pierre."

Just then, a shadow moved in the stairway. The risers creaked as the figure descended.

"Don't move," the voice said.

The man in a black leather coat and wide-brimmed fedora pulled low to his eyes moved carefully and steadily down the steps. In his right hand was a pistol.

Chapter Thirty-nine

Karin carefully climbed the algae-covered stones on the bank of the Our River and dried her feet on the grass. The chilled water felt good. She put her shoes and socks back on and made her way along a road that followed the river down to Wasserbillig.

The village was overrun by German men and vehicles. Traffic was at a standstill, and she was able to walk faster than the jeeps and tanks and horse-drawn wagons that were frozen on the road. Only the soldiers, who marched in columns beside the vehicles, were faster than her. They strode briskly, calling and singing to keep pace, as though they were on a morning hike through German farmland. If not for the urgency of her journey, and its solemn purpose, Karin could have enjoyed such a walk herself in the morning sun, which rose steadily in her face through a cloudless sky.

She walked the road that followed a small river at the base of a broad valley of farms and forestland, putting fond memories of the Grand Duchy far away. She had thirty kilometers more to Luxembourg City, a hike that would take all day—time she didn't have.

Her fortune changed outside the village. Civilian traffic, which had kept to the farthest edge of the road, dwindled to a trickle. Seeing her alone, soldiers tried to get her attention with greetings and occasional whistles. She kept her eyes ahead. Only minutes beyond the town, she heard a honking horn from behind. A truck, half the size of the military ones, and not gray but dull brown, moved steadily toward her on the edge of the road. Behind the wheel sat an old man with a white cap that matched his bushy mustache. He was honking and waving for Karin to get out of the way.

She got an idea and stopped, facing him squarely with her hands up and waving.

He stopped but looked none too pleased about it.

"Frau, ech sinn presséiert!" His voice was thin and high-pitched. Her memory of Luxembourgish was slow to engage.

Coming to his door, Karin saw that the truck was full of milk cans. Of course he would be in a hurry.

"Et deet mir leed," she said. *I'm sorry.* "And I'm sorry to delay you, sir, but I have a small favor to ask."

His eyes narrowed and he nervously stroked his mustache.

"My grandmother is ill and all alone in the Grund in Luxembourg City. Are you going there by chance?" Karin didn't like lying, but this was a small deception among her many.

"Get in!" he said. "You can explain along the way. This milk isn't getting any colder with us carrying on."

Startled but happy, Karin ran around and climbed in. The old man revved the engine and started off again. She felt her spirit lift. With any luck, they'd be in Luxembourg City in less than an hour.

On the outskirts of the city, Karin's eyes were drawn to the sky, which was thick with German planes, low and slow over the trees.

"They've taken over the airfield in Findel," the milkman said.

The road drew alongside the field, and Karin got an up-close look at the dark birds bouncing to a stop on the runway or screaming sharply to the sky. The sounds filled the air. The milkman had to nearly shout to be heard.

"Just up ahead the road splits. The Grund is the road to the right, but I'm keeping left for Hamm and the Gare."

Karin's memory raced to the Gare. The first day she met Hansi, lost in the crowd. *The bomb.*

The milkman stopped, and Karin thanked him profusely. She was grateful for him making such good time amid the swarm of locusts.

Nearby, a sign pointed west to Luxembourg City, only five kilometers further.

An old man, dressed in blue overalls and a hat, stood watching by the side of the road, leaning against a rake.

"Are they not marching to the city?" she asked, hoping her Luxembourgish was adequate.

The old man removed his hat and wiped the sweat from his brow with the back of his forearm. He shook his head.

"The city is full enough, I suppose," he said. "Hitler is sending them around the city if I were to guess. It's been like this for days. I've never seen so many men. And those blasted tanks—they've been tearing up the fields, and you'd think they were looking for fences to plow over. If they'd stop long enough, I'd give their general quite a talking to!"

He pounded his rake and shook his fist at the parade.

The road to Luxembourg City beyond the village entered a forest and began to descend through a narrow, shaded valley. Another kilometer or two further, the valley narrowed and sunk further into a canyon of sandstone walls. The forest thinned out and she found herself among a strip of houses and sheds lining both sides of the road. Here, away from the horde of invaders, she found the quiet Grand Duchy she remembered from before.

Villagers were out attending to their daily business. At first glance, their movements seemed normal to Karin, since she supposed they had to eat, work, have clothes mended, and go to Mass, just like before. But like her, they were easily drawn to stare at the planes in the sky, quick to look over their shoulder at the rev of an engine. Like her, these people were on edge.

After several minutes along the street, she rounded a bend, and the sight stopped her. Having never walked this path before when she lived in Luxembourg, the sudden appearance of the eastern wall of the Casemates, the pointed spire of St. Michael's Church, and the silhouette of the old city against the sky stunned her. Even more, the realization that she was only minutes away from seeing the one she thought she'd never see again was too much to comprehend.

She quickened her pace and drew nearer to the steep brick and stone wall of the ancient Casemates. The road curved left, following the curve of the fortress, and then branched right, where a one-lane stone bridge crossed the river.

The Alzette! Knowing she was quite close now; she ran

across the bridge and came nearly to the base of the massive walls that rose more than fifty meters above her. Her heart jumped. Somewhere inside those walls, in the labyrinth of tunnels, her father had died. Until this moment, she hadn't admitted to herself that she had not returned to Luxembourg simply to warn Hansi about Schlinge. Her throat instantly tightened, and she held back the desire to sob again. Not the same as in Trier with Corporal Beckman, but deeper, far deeper. She wanted to ask Hansi about what happened to her father, and learn the truth, no matter how difficult it might be to know.

Fear gripped her limbs and pressed hard. The day's effort, the sunburn, the lack of food, was finally coming due. The realization that despite her kilometers, hours, plans, deceptions, and determination, she might be too late, was overwhelming.

She had only been to the Grund a single time, the night Fritz had driven Hansi home. She hadn't left the car and was not paying attention to how Fritz got there. Still, instinct nudged her to turn left. She moved along the level cobblestone street that followed the river, cliffs, and Casemate walls. Simple apartments rose up on both sides of the street. The feeling rose that she was very close.

Memories of the previous September rushed into consciousness. That first night of September 1939, that terrible night, had begun with such promise. She and Hansi had met at the annual Schoeberfeuer, a fall celebration filled with games, rides, and delicious treats. It ended after a chase by brown-shirt thugs, punctuated by Butler Fritz's intervention outside Karin's house, and finished off by news of Germany invading Poland. For Hansi, a loyal Luxembourger, committed to the national motto, *Wir wolle bleiben was wir sinn—we want to remain what we are*, the news destroyed their friendship. Fritz insisted on driving Hansi from their house near the German embassy to the Grund, and she accompanied him as he navigated the narrow cobblestone street in her father's car. Those months ago, she watched as he crossed the sidewalk and disappeared into the dark entrance to his building. That opening shrank into nothingness when Fritz pulled away and she stared through the back window. Hansi looked sad. They were cursed, forever on opposite sides of an unbreachable wall.

The cobblestones! Yes!

She leaned into the memory and found a burst of energy to run. *The building was about the middle of the block, wasn't it?* A doorway. A single lamp.

Karin looked up. The bulb had been removed, but near the entry, a tree still grew from that impossible crack in the sidewalk. *This is it!*

She entered the building with confidence, but which apartment?

She scaled the stairs to the first floor, not sure why she thought he did not live on the ground level. There were four doors at various places around a U-shaped platform that surrounded the stairs. Two doors were labeled, but neither with the name Broussard.

She ran up to the second level. Four labels, no Broussard.

She tried another door and heard movement inside. A

moment later, the door opened to a rush of the smell of fresh bread. A young woman peered out through the opening, her face flushed. A light blue scarf held her hair away from her face. A flour-dusted apron was cinched around her slim waist, and she had propped a plump baby girl on her hip.

"*Bonjour. Main numm ass Karin,*" she said. "I'm looking for the Broussards. Do they live in this building?"

"What's the name?"

Karin repeated it. A frown creased the woman's face.

"Please, won't you come in?"

The woman led her down a central hallway of the flat down into a light-filled kitchen. She put the baby down onto a blanket. Next to the oven, the fresh loaf was cooling by the back door of the balcony. The table was covered with flour and balls of dough.

"I'm Renee. Please, Fraulein, won't you sit down? How about something to drink? You look like you've been traveling."

"Thank you, yes." Karin was thirsty beyond recognition.

"You know the Broussards?" Karin asked.

"I know the son, Hansi," Renee answered. She poured Karin a glass of water flavored with elderflower. It tasted heavenly.

"They live next door in the front apartment," she continued. "Well, they did."

Karin's heart sank. "They evacuated?"

Madame nodded. "And how do you know Hansi?"

Karin couldn't move or speak. Her shock and

devastation were total. She had never considered that he would be gone. She had offered unspoken prayers to see him again and expected them to be answered. She'd been a fool. Just a silly girl chasing a dream.

"Fraulein, are you all right?" Renee asked.

Karin wanted to cry again, but held it back, embarrassed, and ashamed. Her ears grew intensely hot, and she wondered if she might vomit, although there was nothing much inside. She swallowed hard. Renee refilled her glass and touched Karin's shoulder.

"Don't worry, Karin. You are safe here."

Karin took a few tentative sips.

The baby stirred, and Renee picked her up and sat down at the table. The child was curious and looked at Karin with wide, brown eyes.

Karin was surprised to feel a smile sprout on her face. The child was at peace in her mother's arms.

"I lived here in Luxembourg for a while," Karin answered. "We met in unusual circumstances, and became unusual friends, I suppose you could say."

"You no longer live here?"

Karin shook her head.

"Forgive me, but I don't understand. I wouldn't expect an evacuee to return, especially now."

"I'm not an evacuee," Karin replied. "I lived here because of my father's work." She paused, and then added, "We had to move back home."

"Germany?" Renee's question slipped out slowly, with a sense of recognition.

Karin nodded.

Karin noticed Renee pull her baby closer and turn away, even if ever so slightly. She said nothing more.

"I'm sorry, Madame," Karin said. "I won't impose any further. I guess you've told me what I came for."

She rose from the table and quickly retreated up the hall. At the door, she turned back.

"When did they leave? How near was I?"

Renee had followed only halfway. "I don't know exactly. Hansi's mother was very ill. They couldn't leave right away. Last night, very late, the baby was fussing. I got up and heard noises. I opened the door and saw them, here for her."

Karin didn't understand.

"The doctor and, I'm sorry to say, the undertaker. Madame Broussard passed away."

Karin felt a stab in her heart.

"Everyone left after that?"

The woman nodded. "In the morning, everyone was gone. At first, I thought perhaps they had gone to church, or the morgue, but when they didn't return, I concluded they were gone for good."

Karin sighed. "Thank you," she said.

"Tell me," Renee asked. "If you are German, why did you come?"

"I thought I could warn him," she answered.

Madame 's eyes grew wide. "Then you know about him, and what he and his father did?"

"Not exactly," Karin answered. "But enough to know who would want to settle an old argument."

"They saved Luxembourg, that is, until now. You

came all the way from Germany to warn him?"

"It turns out I didn't need to. I guess he knew already."

"You love him." Renee's words were more of a statement than a question. "Pray that he stays safe in France," she added. "And please leave now. If my husband finds out I let a German into our flat...."

Just then, sharp pounding erupted on the other side of the door.

Chapter Forty

Salzmann, still in uniform, stood up from the chair and faced the man in black.

"I am a German officer, and you have no right to point that in here. I demand you lower it at once! Furthermore—"

"You are no such thing," the man snapped. "Sit down, Doktor Salzmann."

Salzmann blinked and sputtered, and then slunk back to his chair.

"All of you," the man said, waving the pistol, "to the dining room. Now."

Salzmann, Madame Poulet, and the physician seemed eager to obey. Jacky bounded down the stairs and froze at the sight until Madame Poulet reached her arms toward him. His face twisted and he ran to her.

"They had nothing to do with this," Hansi said. "It was me. Let them go."

The man's eyes widened for just an instant before narrowing again.

"Move!" he commanded, and then, as they passed, stepped in front of the physician. Color drained from the doctor's face, and he seemed to stop breathing.

"Don't say a word of this to anyone or you'll have the Gestapo paying you a visit in the middle of the night. Now go!"

The physician choked but didn't hesitate. The man's action seemed to Hansi very unlike the Gestapo.

"The rest of you, in there. *Schnell!*"

He directed them to a table along the wall opposite the patio about midway between the foyer and the kitchen. With the pistol trained on them, and Michele upstairs, Hansi put escape out of his mind for the moment.

Pierre might still save the day, but hope was fading. He was probably with Father Mathieu in the truck, already halfway up the hill to the chateau.

This felt like the end, a terrible end, after all he had endured. At the same time, strangely, it carried a measure of relief. Hansi had dodged so many traps and tricks, just beyond the Gestapo's grasp, until now. Despite it all, the tension couldn't help but drain from his body. He became suddenly aware of how hungry and tired he was.

"Where is Pierre?" the man asked.

Hansi shrugged. "Don't you have him already? At the church?"

The man shot a glance out the window, as though he was expecting to see something in the road.

"The one you know as Pierre is one of them," the man said.

"I knew it!" Jacky blurted from the safety of his mother's arms. She put her hand over his mouth.

The man lowered the gun and looked more intently up the road. "How far is it?"

"A kilometer, no more," Hansi answered, confused at the man's actions. "Who are you?"

The man turned back to them and removed the fedora. He swept a lock of dark hair from his forehead and sighed.

"I am the real Pierre," he said. "If you can believe it."

"Ha!" Jacky said.

"I don't think I can," Hansi said, although he no longer believed him to be in the Gestapo.

The man reached into the pocket of his coat and retrieved a folded piece of paper. When he revealed it, Hansi was more confused than surprised. It was a torn page from a book, just like the half that corresponded to Hansi's page.

Hansi examined it. From all appearances it was identical to the one Pierre had provided, including the written half-code. Hansi was perplexed beyond explanation. What good did this do now?

"You're too late," Hansi said. "Pierre—the other Pierre—has one of these also. With the same code."

The new Pierre turned the page over and pointed at the page number, circled in ink.

"But he didn't know how to use this," he said.

Hansi shrugged.

"The six digits formed by the two halves are only part of the authentication code," the man said. "The page number is the second part. When the impostor failed to key the second part, French Intelligence knew something was wrong. They informed me, but I still didn't know who the contacts were since neither Manolo nor Alain had arrived."

The mention of Manolo and his father shifted Hansi's disbelief. Still, how did the old Pierre get his half page? And the digits of the code?

"There's no time to discuss it," the man said. "But I can prove it by helping you."

"How?" asked Hansi.

"I'll take care of the imposter Pierre, while you find a safe place for our *package*."

The word hammered at Hansi's doubt.

"Madame, do you have a safe place to hide Doktor Salzmann? Alas, the hotel is no longer secure."

"Perhaps the old Kremer barn," she said, looking for Jacky's opinion. The boy nodded.

"The cave," Hansi said.

"What cave?" the man asked.

"Never you mind. I'll take Salzmann. Madame, you see if you can get Michele to the barn as soon as you can. Jacky, you go to the barn now."

"I'm not leaving Maman and 'Chele."

Hansi spoke to the new Pierre. "You prove yourself. I'll get Salzmann to the cave and come back to find you. If you've done what you say, I'll trust you. If you deceive me, you'll have me, but everyone else will be safe.

The man didn't hesitate. "Go. *Vive la Luxembourg and vive la France*." His French was without accent.

Before they left the hotel, Hansi had Salzmann change back out of the German officer's uniform for the hike to the cave.

"We'd make better progress in the kubelwagen," Salzmann protested. "And I've become quite good at impersonating an officer."

"Where we're going, neither will work. And that suitcase of yours will just slow us down. Might even get us killed."

"It might also save us," Salzmann said.

Chapter Forty-one

The fist hammered at the door while Karin's gaze locked with Renee's. Karin had a sense. Somehow, she suddenly knew.

"Is there another way out?" she asked.

Renee stood up, clutching the baby tightly.

"There's a small balcony there. My husband says to use it if there's a fire."

Karin leaned toward the window and saw nothing but the backs of other apartments across the river, and the steep walls of the valley behind them. She fumbled at the latch.

Renee helped her. "You're not thinking of…?"

Karin opened the door crack and looked again. The door was stiff on its hinge. She pushed hard, opening it enough to step out and look over the railing. There was no ladder, and below was just a narrow strip of walk between the building and the river.

"You can tie a bed sheet around the railing and let yourself down," Renee said.

More knocks interrupted their plans.

"There's no time," Renee whispered. "Come."

She led Karin into the bedroom, tiptoeing silently.

A second set of knocks. Harder.

"Open up before I break it down!"

The voice was shockingly unmistakable: *Schlinge.*

"Coming! I'm just finishing changing the baby."

She pushed Karin into the bedroom and pointed at the

large wardrobe in the corner. Karin shuffled past the end of the bed and opened the chestnut-colored door. The wardrobe had a stack of shelves on one side and an open section a meter wide to its left filled with clothes on hangers. She knifed her arm in the middle and pulled a gap wide enough to wedge in. She pressed in and sank down, letting the clothes swallow her. The scent of mothballs flooded her senses.

The wardrobe sat against the wall that separated the bedroom from the hallway. Karin heard Renee open the front door.

"Can I help you?" Renee said in a surprisingly calm voice.

"I'm looking for a girl," Schlinge said.

"A girl?"

Karin heard a sharp sound, and Renee gave out a yelp.

"Don't be a fool. Your neighbor upstairs saw a girl enter your flat."

"Is she in some kind of trouble?"

"That's none of your concern. Where is she?"

"I don't know," Renee said. "She was tired from her journey, and I gave her a drink. She left."

There was a pause. A good effort, Karin thought. It sounded convincing.

"Then you won't mind if I take a look around," Schlinge said, and Karin heard footsteps.

"I'm calling the gendarmes," the woman said.

"Do that, Fraulein," Schlinge said. "Tell them that the Gestapo is searching your apartment for someone resisting occupation."

Karin heard the shuffle-thump of Schlinge's gait in the hallway. He was sure to hear her heartbeat in her chest.

The steps paused at the living room, she calculated, and then continued toward the kitchen.

"Excuse me, sir," Renee said. The steps stopped.

"She escaped out on the balcony. I warned her not to. It's dangerous."

"Get out of the way," Schlinge said, and Karin heard him scuffling through the kitchen, no doubt pushing past the table to the balcony.

Karin knew this was her only chance. She pushed out of the wardrobe and crept quietly on the door, listening.

Her eyes settled on a picture frame on the dresser by the door. Renee, dressed in white silk, under a veil, stood proudly with her husband, handsome in his black suit. A canopy covered them both. Beside the frame on the dress, she noticed a brass candle holder in an unfamiliar shape, seven stems rising from a single base. Then she realized— Renee must be Jewish.

Karin slipped out of the room and padded as quietly and quickly as she could manage. Renee stood in the doorway of the kitchen, holding the baby, making herself as wide as possible. Schlinge was beyond the table, climbing over the threshold onto the balcony.

Karin didn't look back. She accelerated at the end of the hallway toward the still-open front door.

In the shadows beyond the door, Karin didn't see the man she crashed into until it was too late.

He dragged her back inside. Although he was dressed like Schlinge, with a long black leather coat, black gloves, and a wide-brimmed hat, this man was younger and not physically compromised like Schlinge. He carried a short club and wore a confident smile. His grip on Karin's wrist was like an iron vise.

"Komrad Schlinge," he said calmly, and tapped his stick on the wall.

Schlinge pushed Renee aside roughly and appeared through the kitchen doorway.

"Your mother will be so disappointed," he said.

"Lovely to see you too," Karin replied.

Schlinge spun around and struck Renee with the back of his hand. Karin shrieked. Renee staggered, sinking to her knee, and the baby began to cry.

Schlinge tossed his head back to his assistant, who pulled Karin out the door and down the steps. The numbing grip on her wrist made escape out of the question. Moments later, she was locked in the back of the same Mercedes she had ridden to the KDW and the Hauptbahnhof hours earlier, and the same Mercedes her mother regarded as a supreme privilege. In stunned silence, Karin sat in utter defeat.

Eventually, Schlinge appeared at the entrance to the building and scraped his way to the car. Taking position in the front seat, he issued another silent command, and the assistant climbed out.

Karin sat frozen as the man strode back to the doorway, twirling his club, and disappeared. A few moments later, Karin heard faint screams and thumping despite the distance to the first level. Then, a sharp sound of breaking glass, followed by a shower exploding on the sidewalk, and finally a loud crash that caused Karin to jump back. At the center of the debris lay the menorah, split into two pieces.

"You're a devil!" Karin howled.

"I am an angel of mercy," Schlinge said.

The assistant emerged from the doorway. His cold, flat expression hadn't changed.

He got in behind the wheel.

"We've got work to do here," he said, turning the key to start the car. "These Jews talk back."

Chapter Forty-two

Schlinge's assistant gunned the engine and they pulled away from the curb. The Mercedes powered up the steep road to the Old City, and Karin watched the Grund sink from view out the back window just like the previous Autumn. In some ways, Karin thought that the ride had been worse than this one, for she rode then with the dread of seeing Hansi for the last time, or so she thought, and the grief that their friendship was over forever. Now, as the car swept through the streets of a city that looked more like Berlin now than the charming capital she remembered, she had a moment to reflect. At least Hansi was beyond the reach of Schlinge, and safe.

They left the city and entered a countryside unfamiliar to Karin. During her time in Luxembourg, she had ventured outside the city only a few times, primarily east to Trier to shop and see the Roman ruins. The midday sun gave her no clue as to what direction she was traveling, but the landscape changed from a city swarming with German soldiers to beautiful farmland, gently rising meadows, freshly turned earth, and green grass. Cows flexed their winter muscles made soft from many dark days. Lambs skipped in the meadows despite the planes roaring overhead. Spring was everywhere, nature oblivious to war.

In the midst of the beauty, Karin stared blankly out of the window, unable to receive its care. The roads were full of German vehicles, the towns full of shocked faces. The interior of the car was a jail cell on wheels.

"You'll thank me one day," Schlinge finally said.

Karin refused to acknowledge his presence with even the slightest glance or change in breath.

"Despite what you think, or I should say, despite what you think you feel, you do not know the young Broussard boy."

She followed the arc of a small plane across the cloudless sky.

"He is not in France, as you were told by the Jewess. Not a surprise when you consider the nature of those people. She was probably paid to lie to us. They'll do anything for the right price."

Karin had not lived in Germany in the years leading up to the war and had been only eight years old when Hitler came to power. What she knew of racial policies of the Third Reich were, for the most part, gleaned from her father's conversations with colleagues outside the country. When talking about the Jews of France or Luxembourg, she had dismissed his epithets to carelessness and prejudice rather than anything sinister. Only when he was dead, and she had moved back to the capital, did she encounter the breadth and depth of what had practically become a Jew-free society. She had been too distracted by her grief to be curious about it. Yet, clearly Renee's Jewish identity had triggered something in both Schlinge and his driver. Beneath the calm of the driver's declaration of work to be done and Schlinge's description was something severe, intense.

"Your friend, and I consider the term to be near the end of its short life, has not rested since last fall," Schlinge continued.

He paused, but still no reaction from Karin.

"You aren't the kind of girl I would expect to befriend a terrorist. And for one so young, he's proven to be quite effective. How many more will die? Perhaps he's gotten the taste for it. There's your father…."

"He didn't kill him!" Karin finally snapped.

Schlinge showed no signs of reacting to her explosion, no twitch of the eyebrows, no reddening of his face. If anything, Karin thought he seemed pleased with himself. She regretted the outburst.

"I hope not, Karin, I really do. But all signs point to it. There's really no other explanation."

"I think you did it."

He smiled, as an adult does when a toddler accidentally splashes something on him.

"That makes no sense."

"It makes all the sense in the world," she said. "The story is as old as the Bible. You killed him…so you could take something of his." She let the end of the sentence drip out.

It was her turn to be pleased. His face flushed and he stirred in his seat.

"If not for a promise I made to your mother, I would have made you regret that remark."

"I'll be sure to thank her when I see her. Or you can do it."

Schlinge took a deep breath.

"Let's understand one another, Karin. If you can't come to appreciate me and what help I can be to you, then consider this: to the extent I help your mother, I help you. Whether you like it or not, I keep you from the hard labor of a Work Year in a Polish Farm. It is your duty, after all, as you know. And there's far worse you have yet to experience. All I ask in return is that you do not oppose me."

"It doesn't sound like you're asking."

"People who oppose me are not successful. Quite the opposite."

Karin took a deep breath.

"Then I need something in return," she said.

He leaned toward her. "The doors of this car are locked, and you are under my complete control. Hardly a position to ask for anything."

"Do not touch him," she said. "Whatever you think he's done, leave him alone."

Schlinge paused to ponder. Then, after an interval, he spoke. "If I agree to this ridiculous request, I'll have your full cooperation, not just here and now, but back in Berlin, going forward?"

She was stunned. He needed something from her, but what, really? Help securing Mother for himself? Was sparing Hansi really worth that to him? And even more, could she agree to his request, and actually keep it?

"Yes," she answered, with all the conviction she could muster. "But that doesn't mean cheering and waving flags and all of that. It just means that I won't make your life the kind of hell someone my age is skilled at. I'll stay out of your way, won't undermine you constantly to Mother, and won't poison your food."

Schlinge's eyebrow lifted for the first time in their conversation. Her tone had come off more annoying than serious, but had had its effect. The idea seemed to hold a certain appeal to him.

"My answer is yes," he said.

"You promise?"

He nodded.

"I need you to swear. You people are always swearing oaths, always trying to outdo one another to prove who is the most loyal."

"It doesn't work that way. You'll have to take my word as a man of honor."

She wanted to snort but held it back. This exchange had turned strangely satisfying, and she had accomplished something important, although at a cost she wasn't sure she was prepared to pay. But now was no time to turn back.

"Swear to me—*by him.*"

The car jumped over a seam in the pavement, as if to punctuate her request.

"Say it," she said. "Promise on the Führer."

Something in Schlinge's lack of expression, which could have been attributed to the injuries to his face, gave Karin the impression that she had overestimated the extent to which he was off balance. He set his chin and looked directly at her.

"If I do, I need something more from you. I need you to convince Hansi to stop whatever he's doing. Now."

"Stop what?" Karin asked.

"You'll see. There."

The car had crested a hill and descended through a cut in the ridge. The scene opened to a broad, forested valley, through which was cut a narrow chasm. In spots, the white foam of a churning river was visible cascading over successive ledges, from heights on the left. The central feature held her gaze. A stone bridge had its span torn away from its shoulders and thrown into the river, leaving a gaping tear in the road ahead.

Chapter Forty-three

A crew of soldiers in gray trousers and white undershirts, stained with grime and sweat, moved like ants along the jagged knuckles of the broken bridge. From the horse-drawn wagons on the far side, they had pulled yellow lumber and fashioned scaffolding from which to repair the bridge. They had spanned the gap with a thin strip of boards capable of supporting only one person at a time and were engaged in widening it. Hammers made such a racket that Karin wondered if this is what gunfire sounded like.

Schlinge's driver eased the Mercedes down the slope and stopped about fifty meters from the edge of the bridge. He switched off the engine and set the parking brake because of the incline. Schlinge got out and motioned Karin to follow.

The trio walked to the edge of the broken span. The wooden repairs were so flimsy, Karin thought, compared to the ancient stone bridge. She inched forward and looked down. The river gushed and splashed around large trunks of the former span and broken chunks of roadway now jutting out of the water.

"Hansi did this?" she asked Schlinge.

Schlinge, staring into the gap, didn't answer. Karin realized the sound of the river and the hammering was too much, and she was speaking into Schlinge's damaged side. She moved closer.

"Hansi couldn't have done this," she said.

They retreated from the edge.

"I agree with you," Schlinge said. "It seems unlikely that someone--what, fifteen or sixteen—could do such a thing. Certainly, he would need help, help his father was capable of. But that's why we need to find him. My superiors do not take resistance lightly. Nor do I. For your mother's sake, and by extension, yours, I'm willing to extend mercy to someone that, frankly, deserves to be shot."

"Am I supposed to be grateful then?"

"The point is, we need to find him before the others do."

"I don't know where we are right now," she replied, "but unless we're in France, I think we're in the wrong place."

"He's not in France, Karin, and neither are we. We are near Vianden."

"He's here?" she asked.

"We're going to find out—together."

Chapter Forty-four

Back at the car, Schlinge retrieved a map from inside and spread it across the hood for study.

"Here's Luxembourg City," he began, "and here's Vianden." He traced his finger along a line between the two. "Here's the bridge. And somewhere down there," he pointed downriver into the woods, "Hansi is making his way toward us."

"Why do you need me, then?"

"I don't," Schlinge answered. "But we have an agreement, and I'm a man of my word. Once we've got him, and what he has with him, you can assure him that I mean him no harm."

Karin's body tensed, her stomach jumping. She stared into the trees down the valley. *Could he really be out there?*

"Wait here," Schlinge said, folding the map and clamping it in his armpit. He shuffled back down the slope while the assistant uncased a cigarette, lit it, and took a deep drag. Karin, wanting as much distance as she could get away with, left the brute leaning against the grill and retreated to lead against the car's side.

She watched Schlinge try to get a soldier's attention. They avoided his gaze for a few moments until finally one relented and drew close enough to hear Schlinge's request. The soldier waved another to come, and the pair of them assisted Schlinge across the narrow planks. On the far side, Schlinge started talking with one of the men who had not removed his gray tunic, their leader, Karin judged.

As she watched, something gnawed at the back of her thoughts. Perhaps it was the sound of the rushing river and the rhythm of the hammers that somehow massaged away the tension of the entire encounter with Schlinge. Or perhaps he seemed less powerful in the face of the company of uncaring soldiers, his difficulty crossing the planks, and the powerful river that stopped at nothing. She found herself pondering the sudden bargain they had struck. Schlinge was not the kind of man, she was certain, to strike equal arrangements. Negotiating with him was foreign to her. Why did he accommodate her so easily? And then she remembered an important detail. He had failed to swear by the Führer as she had asked.

Schlinge was pointing downstream to the forest, and then at the soldiers, with forceful movements as he spoke. The officer tried to interject, but Schlinge was overwhelming him with stronger movements and words. Something Schlinge said must have convinced the soldier, because he threw up his hands and then turned to his comrades. He yelled something. The hammering stopped suddenly, leaving only the sound of the rushing river. The soldiers climbed up and gathered around them. Schlinge began to talk, pausing for the officer to talk to his men. He pointed downriver again, and Karin felt a sudden sense of dread. Something was wrong, very wrong.

Schlinge and the officer kept talking, kept directing, and without hearing, Karin understood—Schlinge was going to use the soldiers to set a trap for Hansi. The realization dawned both with obviousness and foolishness. Schlinge was deceiving her. The negotiation was nothing of the kind; he was merely placating her to preserve his standing with Ursula.

In that instant, Karin also realized that her mission had not changed, her challenge had not ended when Schlinge's monster snagged her at Renee's apartment. She had to warn Hansi, but only if she could find him. How? The forest stretched beyond the horizon. How did Schlinge know Hansi was there?

Schlinge seemed to have finished because he turned back to the bridge. The officer sent most of the men back to work but held a few back for final instructions. When finished, they ran up to the line of trucks and returned with rifles.

Schlinge approached the planks to cross back over, but the soldiers were no longer paying attention, leaving Schlinge to navigate the uneven timbers alone.

The driver, sucking on his cigarette, had been watching the scene, and realized how precarious was his leader's balance. He flicked the butt away and began to run down the road.

Karin felt it was the moment to act, but how?

The idea came without explanation. It just might give Hansi a chance.

Karin waited for the driver to take a tentative step onto the planks when she opened the driver's door of the Mercedes, reached in, and released the handbrake. The car lurched, and she jumped back just as the car snapped free with a heavy clunk.

Mesmerized by the power of her act, she staggered across the road through the space the car had just occupied and sank into the ditch on the downhill side.

She hadn't intended to kill Schlinge when she released the brake, but now it looked like she would. In fact, there seemed to be more than a fair chance she would catch them both in the middle of the span. She would be caught, she had no doubt, but would beg innocence, feign ignorance of cars and their workings. She'd blame the driver, and Mother would protect her.

The car picked up speed silently and rolled straight for them. The soldiers suddenly caught sight of the movement and realized the quarter ton of disaster barreling toward them. They shouted, but the sounds were lost in the fury of the river.

Karin had climbed out of the ditch when she saw a flash of Schlinge's coat beyond the silhouette of the car, and then a scrape and crunch and great crash. She felt no joy in the moment for she had lingered too long.

She plunged into the pines that grew among the stones. The terrain was more rugged than she had expected.

Shouts rang out behind her. She wondered if even now, Schlinge and his man were in the churning river, fighting for their last breaths. She felt no remorse, only determination.

The river cut sharply through jagged, trail-less sandstone. She swatted through pine branches and snapped dead undergrowth that slashed at her shins, arms, and face.

Barely a minute on, she was nearly exhausted. The shouts were close now.

"There! Get her!"

Chapter Forty-five

The road through Vianden was jammed just like the first day of the invasion, a kilometers long line of vehicles and horse-drawn wagons nose-to-tail that extended from the crest of the ridge in the west to the German border in the east. The vehicles moved in accordion fashion, a handful moving a few meters, opening a small gap behind them before stopping again. Single-file infantry made better progress. Hansi and Salzmann crossed the bridge and joined the flow of soldiers and civilians, the latter who seemed, in but a few short days, to have become accustomed to the traffic.

At the crest of the ridge, they saw the reason for the jam—a second column of trucks, sharing the slender lane. These belched and roared as they inched ahead. Hansi's heart dropped—they were loaded with steel girders, lumber planks, and spools of steel cable. Leutnant Schmidt would be pleased, Hansi knew. Their own journey just got considerably more dangerous.

They were above the village now, taking in the scene from the embankment at the edge of the forest. The bridging equipment trucks were navigating a difficult turn onto the road that descended toward the bridge. This was the same road where Hansi dozed on the boulder, the same road that he had hesitated to pull the trigger, the same road on which Manolo died.

"Why are we stopping?" Salzmann asked. "You said it yourself; we need to hurry."

Hansi gestured half-heartedly ahead. "That's why."

"I should have kept the uniform. We could have walked right through."

Salzmann's performances had done nothing to change Hansi's mind. He entertained not even the slightest doubt that if the physicist was wearing it now, they would be on their way to the chateau for good.

"This way," Hansi said, stepping off the road. He climbed up through a gap in the brush and found the cover of the trees at the edge of the forest. He had hoped they could hike past the road and head south directly for the cave. The jam forced them to cut the corner. They would have to find another way.

Salzmann joined Hansi under the cover of the trees. The cool air was welcome. They descended slowly through the sandstone boulders, pines, and deciduous trees.

A thin trail cut perpendicular to their descent.

"Wait here," Hansi said. "If this leads to the road, as I think it does, I'll look for a place to cross. No sense tiring yourself out exploring."

"Very sensible," Salzmann said, and took a seat on the end of his suitcase. His face was reddened from the climb. Hansi gave him the water bottle and set off.

The trail was easy and within minutes he could see the break in the trees ahead. As soon as he saw the road, his hopes sank. The line of trucks stretched in both directions, blocking the trail crossing. Soldiers moved up and down, attending to the straps, preparing to unload.

He turned back and saw a flash of movement between a cut in the rocks. He dropped to his knee and froze.

The figure stepped out from behind the boulder. *Heng!*

Hansi was glad to see Heng, but the scout didn't reciprocate the expression. Heng, with his jacket, cap, bulging backpack, and walking stick, looked like he was on a long journey.

"Where are you going?" Hansi asked.

"Home," Heng answered. "And you should too, if you know what's good for you."

"What happened?"

"A little thing called war," Heng said. "As it turns out, some mothers get concerned when their sons are camping in the woods during an invasion. My older brother showed up last night and thrashed me in front of everyone. Said he was surprised we couldn't hear our mother's moaning from the village."

"Why didn't you leave last night, then?" Hansi said.

"He's not my boss," Heng said. "I told him to tell Mother I'm fine, safer with my friends than in the village. And that I'd be home in a few days."

He looked down. "Then I felt bad. My mother worries. So, I left."

"Is everyone gone then?"

"Not yet, but I think they're thinking hard about it."

Just then, Salzmann appeared from behind a fold in the trail. Heng tensed.

"I told you to wait," Hansi said to Salzmann, but his heart wasn't in the rebuke. He should have known better.

"Who is he?" Heng asked.

"The reason I came here in the first place, I guess. For

your own safety, I can't explain, but we need a place to hide out until dark."

"It's going to be impossible to get to the cave that way," Heng said, thumbing the trail behind. He tugged at the strap of his backpack, thinking for a moment, and then unslung the pack altogether. He retrieved a map from a pocket in the top flap and spread it out on top of the backpack.

"The cave is about right here, and there's the road. We're about right here on this trail. Behind you it generally follows the river back east. Below the bridge, the river falls quickly, and the rapids are high in the spring. I've never hiked down here, but the terrain seems to level out further down. You might be able to cross about here."

Hansi turned and tried to visualize what Heng was showing on the map. The terrain fell away to his right, where he pictured the bridge and the river.

"If you can cross down there," Heng continued, "climb up to the ridge here and head back west. There are shallow places above the bridge—I've gone swimming in this wide spot here—and then you can double back to the cave."

Hansi studied the map for a moment and wondered if Salzmann could make the extra distance, descents, climbs, and crossings.

"Don't worry about me," Salzmann said, as if reading his thoughts.

Heng wished them luck and said good-bye. Hansi wanted Heng to accompany them, but wanted not to endanger him even more. He envied Heng, wishing he was going home to his mother. But in a way, he was. Just a longer way.

They backtracked east along the trail as the map had shown but were higher than Hansi had visualized. After three quarters of an hour, Salzmann was holding steady, but they had descended only modestly. Hansi was anxious to see the river and look for a place to cross, but the map hadn't shown any bisecting trails. He needed to manage Salzmann's effort. The professor would need every bit of his strength to negotiate the rocks, the slopes, and not one, but two river crossings. They kept going, Hansi trusting that Luxembourg hikers wouldn't disappoint. Sure enough, his faith was rewarded when a few minutes later, they came upon a thin trail leading down toward the river.

They took it.

At first, Hansi was glad he had waited for the trail. The path descended more sharply than before but provided them both clear places to step on boulders and over tree roots. But once the sound of the river rose to their ears, Hansi wondered if the path they followed was a trail at all. The valley grew steep through the cuts in the sandstone. Moss and ferns made the landscape beautiful but mist from the river made them treacherous. Hansi's knees were sore and sweat dripped from his forehead. Salzmann, to his surprise, was uncomplaining, and kept up better than he expected. And most surprising of all, he wielded his suitcase like a battering ram through the brush, and a pole down the boulders. The scene would have been humorous if Hansi wasn't so exhausted.

With each step, Hansi imagined the corresponding one

up the far ridge. The hike back west. Another descent, another crossing, then finding the cave.

As Hansi pondered it, an outline of the original plan formed in his mind. The purpose of blowing the bridge was not merely to deprive the Germans of an invasion route but was more specific: provide an open path for Salzmann to get to Luxembourg City.

Perhaps we should just go on to Luxembourg City.

Hansi put the question away. There would be plenty of time to consider it. For now, focus on the next boulder, the next tree, the next step. And keep away from the Germans.

Chapter Forty-six

Running down the side of a canyon was dangerous, and hurrying was foolish. But Karin did not have the privilege of a careful hike along a well-worn trail. Her descent was both careless and hurried, and for the first few minutes, she was lucky. Following close to the river's edge, she put a respectable distance between herself and the bridge. But every stride was a jackhammer through her feet, ankles, and knees. The blows had the expected effect, breaking down her strength.

She inevitably stepped wrong and caught her ankle in the fork of a fallen limb. She stumbled, twisted awkwardly, and felt the punishment of sharp pain. Still, she could not give up. She pushed up with her left leg and tried to continue. Her ankle would not comply without the severest punishment. Panic set in, making her subsequent movements meaningless but making her position even more obvious. She hopped on one leg across a final ledge and let herself fall. She hit with a thump, saved from serious injury only by a bed of pine needles. Still, her breath had been knocked from her lungs. In the grip of the spasm, she lay on the riverbank, unable to move further.

A soldier plunged into the river and instantly sank to his chest. He splashed across, climbed out, and closed the distance to her in three swift strides. He bent down and scooped her up in his arms as the water gushed from his shirt and trousers. He looked more annoyed than fatigued.

His force triggered the return of her breath in a great

heaving rush.

"Let me go! I'm a German citizen!"

No sooner had he snatched her, than he was back in the water, crossing back.

"You got my uniform wet! And you ruined a week of work on the bridge. I should tie a rock to you and throw you back in for that alone."

"I did nothing of the sort!" Karin squirmed to no effect. His arms were ten times the strength of Schlinge's driver.

"So, the car jumped into the river itself?" They were making a furious foam in the river. The water was ice cold.

"Stop your wriggling, or I might just tell them you drowned," he bellowed.

He was a powerful man and churned across the strong current easily. Reaching the other side, he dumped her on the bank and held her in place with a forearm across her chest until his companions had closed the distance.

She was sore, soaked, and surrounded.

<h2 style="text-align:center">Chapter Forty-seven</h2>

Hansi and Salzmann had just let themselves down between two large boulders, and were preparing for the next ones, when they heard shouts. Hansi crouched behind an oak trunk that angled out into the valley and motioned Salzmann to do the same. Movement flashed among the trees down and to his right.

Soldiers!

The men were shouting and pointing, but Hansi couldn't hear due to the river. He counted six men descending the valley, almost running, spread out among the trees.

Their pointing puzzled him. They were looking away from where he and Salzmann were positioned. They seemed to be chasing something. An animal?

That didn't make sense to Hansi. If they were hunting an animal, they had rifles and could simply shoot it.

"What is it?" Salzmann asked.

"Soldiers," Hansi whispered, and leaned out around the tree for a better view. What he saw stopped his heart. *Karin* was clawing through the bramble on the other side of the river.

His mind reeled.

"Wait here," he hissed at Salzman, and stood up.

"Surely you're not going down there," Salzmann said. "They'll capture you, or worse! Then what will I do? I have no idea where we are, where we're going, or how to get back to Vianden."

Salzmann was right. But Hansi couldn't simply abandon Karin after what could only be—well, what could account for her sudden appearance, here, in this forest, at this very moment, but—*a miracle*. Why was she here? Looking for him? How would she have known?

Hansi had no choice. Without warning Salzmann, he left the safety of the rocks and cover of the trees and descended straight for the gathering of soldiers. Though he could hardly take his eyes from Karin, as he approached, he recognized these men as Leutnant Schmidt's engineers.

His movement caught their attention, and before they could react, he was among them.

Karin had been facing the river and didn't see Hansi until he had penetrated the circle and touched her on the shoulder. She turned and her face lit up. Hansi fell to the ground as Karin rose, and they embraced.

Hansi thought they would never see each other again. Her appearance in the woods here and now was the farthest thing from his imagination, beyond surprise. His joy went beyond his understanding. His mind sputtered in the moment, unable to comprehend or calculate how she could have come to this very spot at this very instant.

Karin gripped him fiercely around his neck. Her heart soared. Her journey had seemed foolish from the start, a flight from the world as much as anything, and a dream beyond reach. And yet here he was.

Hansi's mind engaged. The instinct to survive fought his heart. He realized she wouldn't have been fleeing these men unless she was in great danger. And now they were in it together.

"Sister! You found me!" he announced.

He hoped they might just believe.

Hansi faced the soldier in the wet uniform directly. "I warned her to take care around the river."

And then, back to Karin, "Let's get you some fresh clothes." He tugged at Karin, as though the soldier's task was complete.

He turned to the soldiers. "Thank you for rescuing her. I will be sure to thank Leutnant Schmidt when I see him."

The circle closed in.

"You'll see him now," the soldier said.

Just then came the snapping of branches and a cry from the direction Hansi had come. Salzmann, ignoring Hansi's command, had followed and stumbled in his descent. One of the soldiers left the circle and returned with Salzmann and his suitcase.

That was it, then. Hansi's heart fell out of his body.

I've failed.

Chapter Forty-eight

The soldiers bound Hansi's and Salzmann's wrists with leather straps. Hansi was shoved up front between a pair of soldiers and they set off up the ravine. It was slow going on the slippery rocks. After the better part of an hour, in which Hansi was unable to see or speak to Karin or Salzmann, they finally reached the road on the Vianden side of the broken bridge, where the trucks Hansi had seen from the forest stretched up the road and around the bend.

When they stepped out of the forest down into the roadside culvert, Hansi's legs faltered at the memory of him and Manolo lying in the ditch on the opposite side of the road. All he had achieved and survived was swallowed by that despair. It would all end where it began.

The soldiers pulled them through the line of trucks onto the road, and then down to the bridge, where Hansi saw Leutnant Schmidt in an uncharacteristic agitation, pointing and stomping over the twisted and splintered lumber sticking up in the gap of the span. A few strides later, he saw the back of a man in a black trench coat and wide-brimmed fedora standing next to a kubelwagen.

A notion flickered in Hansi's memory just as their arrival drew their attention, and they turned. Hansi didn't see the surprise register on Leutnant Schmidt's face, for he was transfixed on Schlinge, whose appearance was like a demon from his worst nightmare.

Schlinge was as ugly and damaged as ever, but a smirk of satisfaction beamed through the scars.

And then, to complete Hansi's humiliation, the original Pierre climbed out of the jeep, holding a pistol. The other Pierre, the real one, had failed.

"You've proven yourself resourceful once again," Schlinge said. "And have performed a needed service to your new country. On its behalf, I thank you," he added.

Hansi was confused. He looked at Pierre. "You work for him?"

"We serve a common Führer," Pierre said.

"You're a liar," he said. "I should have known it from the beginning."

But the scene still didn't make sense. Schlinge, yes. Pierre, finally. But Karin?

A terrible feeling seized Hansi, erupting lava-like in his throat. He turned to her. "Did you bring Schlinge here?"

She shook her head. "No, I promise."

Before she could continue, Schlinge interrupted. "Allow me to enlighten you," he said to Karin. "Your friend—Hansi—got caught up in a plan he was not originally part of. For that, he bears reduced responsibility. Hansi was simply doing his duty, a quality we appreciate."

He turned to Salzmann. "His superiors sought to steal something that belonged to us."

"I'm not a something," Salzmann protested.

"We did not know that initially," Schlinge responded. "All we knew was that Luxembourg agents were intent on stealing something from Germany and delivering it to France. Of course, we could not allow that. And because we didn't know what they were stealing, we needed to let things play out. Hansi proved himself most successful in that regard. But now we have what is ours.”

“I failed,” Hansi said.

“You don’t have to look at it that way,” Schlinge countered. “Look around, what do you see? A fine-looking squad of engineers and beyond, a mighty army. Luxembourg is joining the Reich. The transition should be simple and easy. You people already speak German.”

“Never.”

“I’ll make it plain for you then,” Schlinge said. “You are still young. This mission, and your involvement in it— everything can be forgiven. Some trust must be regained, which you can earn over time. You are young and still moldable. Join us and I venture to say you still have—” He paused. “Join us and you will have a future ahead of you.”

“I’d rather die,” Hansi said.

Schlinge’s face turned serious.

“That can also be arranged.”

“No!” Karin shouted.

“Take them to the castle,” Schlinge said to Pierre.

Pierre flicked his pistol at Salzmann, whose face was deathly pale. “Get in!” he growled, pointing at the jeep.

Karin lunged at Schlinge and began pounding him with her fists.

“You promised me!”

Schlinge stood like a statue, bearing the blows until the wet soldier pulled Karin away.

Just then, a faint pop corresponded with the instantaneous appearance of a splash of red on Pierre’s jaw, and his head snapped back. He cried out. Then, as curls of yellow smoke billowed from a pair of objects in the center of their circle, the smell of sulfur swept through the gathering.

Hansi knew at once. Jacky had finally perfected his aim with the slingshot. And the Boy Scouts had thrown smoke bombs.

Knowing this was his only chance, he turned to Karin, still in the grasp of the soldier. Their eyes met for an instant, one filled with longing and knowing. Panic filled her expression as if she knew what was going to happen next. She fumbled in her knapsack as Hansi calmly took a step back. She found it! Reaching forward, she crushed the letter into his palm. If they could not speak, at least he could know....

In the last glance, Hansi said goodbye, and then threw himself off the edge of the bridge into the churning cauldron.

Chapter Forty-nine

In the burning cold of the rapids, Hansi was both free and yet seconds from death. The flow swept him downstream, or so he hoped, because he had no sense of up or down or distance. He tumbled and turned, held down by the river's force, all on a single breath stretched beyond its limit.

His hands, bound in front of him, were useless for swimming but helped defend against objects in the river. He bumped rocks and logs, scraped along sharp edges and smooth gravel, and bore blows on every part of his body. Still, he was fortunate to avoid the severest blow to the head, which would have sealed his fate.

He kicked and thrashed with a ferocity borne of suffocation. His lungs burned, and his entire body seemed gripped in an enormous vice whose force rose to such an intensity that he knew in the space of a few more heartbeats he would inhale the entire river and disappear forever.

Then, without explanation, the tempest ceased. He popped to the surface and felt warm air on his face. He sucked in a massive breath that rattled throughout his torso.

The current carried him on, bobbing up and down and rolling as he went. But now, despite too many gulps of the river mixed in, he stole sufficient breath for the panic to subside. Though his heart drummed in his ears and neck, he was able to focus his movements. After another minute's effort, he maneuvered to a gravelly shallow spot along the riverbank and stopped. He lay on his side and breathed uninterrupted. Never had the simple act brought such joy.

Resting only a moment, his attention turned to the leather strap around his wrists. Release turned out to be less of a challenge than he expected, for the strap was severed easily by one of the ubiquitous sharp-edged rocks.

He pondered the choices before him. He could continue downstream, disappear in the woods, and hide out until dark, assuming he didn't freeze to death in the wet clothes. It seemed dangerous, but doable. There would be a search. He could find help in the village. Perhaps after a few nights in barns and cellars, things would calm down. Then he could make his way on to Wiltz or back to Luxembourg City. He could find Papa and Maman. They could escape the war.

But shame would follow him everywhere.

He pondered only a moment.

I've been a fool.

Pierre had lied from the beginning.

How easy it was to trust him. I didn't want to do any of this. I thought it would be easy, even fun. How ridiculous.

Manolo was brave.

I have been afraid from the beginning. Pierre took advantage.

No more.

Chapter Fifty

Hansi heard a branch snap and looked up. Jacky was clawing through the underbrush.

"I hit him! I hit him, Hansi! Wasn't it beautiful?"

Hansi was looking beyond past him. "Keep your voice down."

Jacky complied for only an instant. "And those smokers, weren't they terrific? Just in time, too!"

As before, Jacky's enthusiasm worried Hansi. "How did you manage to join up with the scouts, anyway?" he asked.

"Easy. I know a shortcut."

"But the road was full of Germans."

"They don't much pay attention to me. And I found a drainage pipe to crawl through under the road. I told the scouts you were coming. They've been watching the work at the bridge. I joined them and saw you taken prisoner."

Hansi stood up and shook more of the water from his hands.

"Who was that girl?" Jacky asked.

"Someone—I used to know. How is Michele doing?"

"You saved her, Hansi. She was brave." Jacky turned and looked up the slope. "Come on," he said. "Let's go."

"You go on, Jacky. I'm not going with you. I'll catch up to you as soon as I can."

Jacky shook his head. "I'm not going to Vianden either."

"What are you talking about? Where are you going?"

"With you." He said it as though it was obvious and Hansi was stupid.

"Where am I going?"

Again, Jacky sounded irritated. "After Pierre and Salzmann. They left for the chateau, I'm sure of it."

Hansi let out a long breath. He had guessed as much. But his mission had never been so impossible as it was now that Pierre had Salzmann.

"Listen to me. If I go after them, you can't expect to save the day with that slingshot. Pierre is a Goliath, but you're no David."

Jacky wasn't hurt by Hansi's warning. He reached around his body and swung his knapsack forward. He opened the flap, pulled out a triangular cloth-wrapped object, and gave it to Hansi.

Hansi knew what it was before he unwrapped it. A pistol.

"Where did you get this? Does your mother know you have this?"

He shook his head. "I found it in Lieutenant Schmidt's room. I've been carrying it for a few days, wondering if it would come in handy. I figured you'd know how to use it."

Hansi turned the pistol over in his hand and checked the safety latch. He considered fleeing again to Vianden once more. It was senseless beyond imagination to go after Pierre, exponentially so with Jacky.

"You're a remarkable boy," Hansi said, turning the pistol over in his hand, "but I can't let you go with me, Jacky. I must do this alone."

"You're going to need my help."

Hansi couldn't disagree, but he could hardly consider the idea. Michele had known what she was doing, sacrificing herself, and had been lucky. Jacky didn't know what he was doing and would not be so lucky. Madame Poulet would never forgive him if something happened to her boy.

"I'm sorry, Jacky, but the answer is no. Look, you are courageous, without question. And you're right—I need to go after them. Pierre betrayed us all. And for some reason, Doktor Salzmann is important. If there's anything left to try, I can't let Pierre just take him back to Germany. But the more time we sit here arguing, the more of a chance he has to escape. I'm not leaving this spot until you promise me you won't follow."

Jacky clenched his fists and squeezed his face tightly as tears welled in his eyes.

"Nobody thinks I can do anything, but I can!"

"You can, Jacky. And you have. Your time will come. But right now, the best help you can give me is by going home and helping your mother and Michele, so I don't worry. Help them get packed and off to Wiltz. I'll come to you as soon as I can."

Hansi touched Jacky on the shoulder. The boy spun back to Hansi and buried his face against Hansi in a fierce hug.

After a moment Hansi spoke. "You can help me get back to the road," he said. "You know where it is, don't you?"

Jacky's pushed away and quickly wiped away the tears. "Of course."

Chapter Fifty-one

At the bridge, the sulfurous smell lingered longer than the smoke itself. When the bombs rained down on them, the soldier that had captured Karin by the river reacted instantly. He snatched her, forced her to the ground, and held her there until the chaos subsided.

The old man had dropped to the road and covered his head with his suitcase. The Gestapo agent Hansi seemed to know, who was apparently working with Schlinge, sank to his knees as blood poured from a wound caused by the stone projectile. The officer commanded a squad of soldiers to fan out in the woods to pursue the attackers. Schlinge had stood like a statue throughout the entire series of events.

"Get Klaus up here," the officer ordered. "Tell him to bring his medical kit."

The wounded man wiped blood from his eyes and shook his head, trying to clear his vision. Soon, the one called Klaus arrived and applied a cloth compress.

Schlinge glanced at Karin and stepped forward.

"May I trouble you, Leutnant Schmidt, for a man to secure the fraulein? Only until we locate my driver," he added. It was then that Karin realized Schlinge's driver was missing.

Schmidt agreed. With a toss of his head, the soldier holding Karin led her up the road to a flatbed truck that had been unloaded. Another soldier lowered the rear gate, and she climbed in. The bed of the truck was enclosed by wooden slats attached to metal posts like an animal pen. She sank down onto the rough boards carrying her own load of feelings.

Had Hansi survived? Was Schlinge's driver dead? Did I help anything?

One thing was certain—any agreement with Schlinge was as broken as the bridge.

Minutes passed while Karin pondered these questions and waited for Schlinge, expecting the worst. Defying him was one thing, killing his driver, and almost Schlinge himself, another entirely. Perhaps Mother would make the difference.

The sun overhead warmed her and then grew hot as her exile continued. She looked out into the woods. The road was cut into the side of the ridge, the stone walls more imposing than any prison. And a soldier had brought her guard a belt with his pistol, and a rifle. Escape was out of the question.

Her thoughts were interrupted by a soldier unlatching the gate. She jumped when it slammed open and reverberated through the frame. Then, two pairs of soldiers lifted the large, lifeless body of Schlinge's driver up onto the back of the bed. The back of his head slammed against the boards with a terrible knock. One eye was closed, the other half open, and his tongue could be seen in his open mouth. Karin's stomach seized and she retched a string of sourness.

She jumped up and began to climb the railing, anything to get away from him. Evil as she knew him to be in the short time since he'd snatched her outside Renee's flat, as a dead man whose skin hung loose across his face, he looked drained of all that. She felt a strange compassion mixed with sudden guilt and an overriding desire to flee.

Her guard reacted quickly by raising his rifle, cocking the lever, and pointing it at her.

"Sit down!" he barked.

For an instant, she wondered if a bullet would be proper justice, but her body was in control. She climbed back down and collapsed into the corner, clinging to the slats, shivering.

What have I done?

Some time later, the sound of a jeep broke through the voices inside that alternately accused and defended her. The first vehicle since she had been locked away, it puttered up the road and drew her attention away from herself and the body only centimeters away. The jeep's driver was the injured man, now with a white bandage around his head. Beside him was the old man with the suitcase.

Chapter Fifty-two

When he and Jacky emerged from the forest, Hansi was surprised to see the Germans on the move again. This was a bad omen for the task ahead, he thought, for it meant that the bridge repair vehicles had cleared off the main road and were no longer holding up traffic. And it also meant that Pierre and Salzmann might be making quick progress toward the chateau. In fact, Hansi wondered if he was already too late.

They had emerged from the forest about halfway between the village and the intersection of the road to the bridge. So, he would have to turn uphill again, march alongside the invaders as he had done many times already and slip across the road for the woods at the base of the promontory on which the chateau sat.

Jacky complied with Hansi's demand and said goodbye. He headed down the hill while Hansi joined the flow of the invaders in the other direction. The men and machines seemed to be making up for the delay, churning dust and diesel fumes into the air as they groaned, grunted, sang, and swore their way up the slope.

Along the way, a pair of soldiers caught sight of Hansi's unusual appearance. "Hey, Karl, I think the boy forgot his swimming trunks!"

"Or perhaps his boat sank!"

"I think he's just shy taking his bath!"

Hansi ignored them and took advantage of their attention to cross the road. They were more interested in their jokes than him passing through their column. He stopped, let them continue, and then plunged back into the trees on the north side of the road.

From his interrogation and release, Hansi knew that he had to find the backside of the chateau where the road curled around the promontory. If he made it in time, he would intercept them near where Pierre had climbed the pole and tapped the phone wires, out of view of both the invasion road and the chateau itself.

In the woods north of the invasion road, the chateau hill rose sharply. Hansi clawed through the thick undergrowth that clung to the sides of the slope and climbed. At the same time, he began to circle back eastward in a broad arc, hoping to meet the chateau road.

Fear, thicker than the underbrush, scraped at him with every step. Fear had frozen him when Manolo needed him most. On the road from Kleindorf with Salzmann, fear had pulled the trigger. But now, for the first time, he had time to think, to prepare. If given the chance, could he pull the trigger with intention?

He had gained considerable height above the invasion road, steam pouring off his wet clothes, when he came to a ridge he hadn't expected. On the other side, he saw a gap in the trees that seemed too hidden to be the chateau road. But he couldn't be sure because the sun was higher now than when he had been released. He would have to descend to find out.

Traveling downhill was rapid, but Hansi was surprised at how unsteady he was. The exertion from climbing had strained one set of muscles, the descent another. He stumbled more than ran through the underbrush, snapping branches and sliding on winter's wet leaves that lingered in the low spots.

The ground leveled off unexpectedly, and Hansi found himself on a fern-covered, two-rutted forest lane. To his right, the road descended north along the curve of the hill, extending beyond his view. To the left, it rose gently as it followed the same arc. Something told him he should continue to climb. He followed it and started running, compelled by the near panic of being perhaps too late, tapping some last reserve of strength. As he ran, water gushed in his shoes, but his feet were becoming numb from cold and exertion. He ran against time, against fear, and for Manolo.

His decision was rewarded. The lane rose up a bank and joined a road. He looked up and down—it was before dawn the morning of his release and the terrain had been hard to distinguish.

There! The telephone poles!

Confident now that he was on the chateau road, the next problem was that of stopping them. But there was no time. Down and around the curve, he heard the high-pitched whine of a downshift. The snub nose of the kubelwagen would appear around the bend at any instant.

Hansi crossed the road, jumped across a thin slurry in the culvert, and climbed up to cover behind a tree at the edge of the forest.

The strain of the jeep's engine grew louder as it neared. There was a dip in the road just below him before the road grew even steeper. If he was lucky, they wouldn't be going very fast and wouldn't see him until the last moment. That would be his chance.

Hansi reached behind to bring his knapsack forward. Like him, it was soaked through. The flap opened, Hansi looked down, and his chest seized with dread. *The pistol!* He had tucked it away and forgotten it. Now, at the bottom of his knapsack, its wrapping was equally soaked. The roar echoed up the valley. Hansi thought all was lost. He knew nothing about guns, but he was pretty sure a wet gun was useless.

He unwrapped the pistol. To his surprise, the moisture was less than he expected, beaded in tiny droplets on the metal surfaces. Half-precaution and half-panic, he smacked his hands against it, but there was no time. If it was ruined, he would have to bluff it.

Then Hansi remembered. As the sound of the engine swept over him, he rotated the pistol on the axis of the barrel and reached down. The index finger of his right hand, wrinkled and numb, found the safety. He switched it off.

The sun was high above the trees when the jeep appeared. It was going faster than he expected. He pushed away from the tree, suddenly in a hurry. The bank was steep, and so he stumbled, and then fell headlong toward the road. His shoulder hit the slope hard, wrenching his arm, loosening his grip on the pistol.

Hansi rolled to his side and twisted, swinging his legs below him. He splashed down in the culvert.

Where is it?

The jeep rattled closer. Hansi swept his hands up and

down the ditch, slicing his hands over sharp stones.

The jeep's engine relaxed slightly.

He sees me. Hurry!

Frantic, Hansi crawled up and down, feeling for anything.

The jeep squealed to a stop.

Hansi's hand slid over something different.

A door opened.

Hansi stood up and lifted his arms to the road.

Water poured from his sleeves and elbows. But the barrel was pointed directly at the man who had just climbed out of the jeep. Just in time. Hansi had him. Pierre turned his palms up and lifted an eyebrow.

Jacky's aim had not only been true, but the stone had done more than expected, as evidenced by the large bandage around Pierre's head. Still, his expression had not changed. He stared intently, as though the force of his stare would cause Hansi to lower the pistol.

You think you're always in control. Not this time.

"Don't move!" Hansi, steadying the weapon with both hands, stabbed the pistol at Pierre.

Pierre slipped a half-grin and nodded.

Hansi took careful steps out of the culvert onto the road in front of the jeep, bringing Pierre into full view.

"Listen to me, Hansi," Pierre said.

"Shut up!" Hansi snapped. "Raise your hands, carefully."

Pierre complied. His fingers were half-bent, relaxed, like supple branches blowing in a soft breeze.

"Two steps away from the jeep. Careful now."

Pierre smiled and nodded, moving as Hansi ordered.

"Turn around. Everything slow!"

Pierre submitted. "Please, Hansi."

"On your knees. Now!"

Pierre bent down. Hansi felt a measure of relief but doubt lingered. Muddy runoff had dribbled out of the end of the barrel when he twitched it at Pierre. And fear nibbled at his resolve.

"Professor, get out and help me."

"I can't with these straps."

"You must try."

"What do you intend to do?"

"Finish this and take you to France," Hansi answered.

Salzmann unlatched the door and climbed out. He reached into the rear seat for his suitcase.

"Come here, Professor, now!"

"Not without my suitcase."

Hansi had no time to argue. He could not risk looking away. He was nearing a precipice and gathering the courage to leap off it. The pistol in his hands was like a gangplank, and he was edging further and further toward the abyss.

"Will you permit me one last request, Hansi?" Pierre asked.

"What is it?"

"An explanation."

"I've had enough of your lies. Professor, please come here."

"I understand completely how you would feel that way, believe me. Your resolve has been remarkable, truly.

But you have been deceived and need to know the truth."

"From you, ha! Hardly."

"Do you remember that night you spent in the chateau? And how you were freed?"

"Lies," Hansi said. "Makes sense when I realized you were all Gestapo. You still needed me to find Salzmann. You had to free me."

"And we did, and you succeeded, and here we are again, at the same place. How do you expect us to get Salzmann to France? Simply walk? With invaders flooding every corner of the country? No, we use the same method. We hide in plain sight among them. In a few days, a week, things will calm down. We can get in our jeep and drive to Paris."

Salzmann stopped. "It makes a kind of sense," he said.

"Then what about the other Pierre?" Hansi argued. "He had a page from Hugo just like yours. With half a code. And he said you missed something."

"Oh?"

"An unwritten code. Something you should have given on the radio at the church. He said when you failed to supply it, the French knew."

"So then why did they continue the mission?"

Hansi didn't know, but he was dizzy from all the deception. All he was certain was that death followed him ever since he met Pierre. No more.

"Professor, check him for weapons," Hansi ordered. "He's surely got a pistol."

"The Gestapo are clever, but so are we," Pierre said. "Deception works in both directions."

"Then tell me something," Hansi said. "How is it that Schlinge knew you?"

Pierre didn't answer. Hansi had not mentioned him before, and certainly not by name.

"And how is it that I know him, you wonder? It doesn't matter. I do. And I know that he can't be deceived by just anyone. Professor, please."

Salzmann edged closer, but his movements were tentative, like he was approaching a poisonous snake.

"Speaking of our mutual friend," Pierre continued. "I expect him around that curve at any moment. Then what will you do?"

"It won't matter, because you'll be dead."

Pierre didn't flinch. "Then why haven't you done it already?"

Hansi shifted the grip on the pistol. To answer would expose the weakness in his plan. If Salzmann could recover Pierre's pistol, he could, with Pierre's back turned, switch to it and finish the task, free from the doubt of whether enough water had drained from the mechanism of his own gun. A few moments more and he would do it.

"Are you quite sure about this, Hansi?" The question was from the professor.

"Think about it for a moment, Herr Doktor. How did the Germans know where Michele and I would cross the border? Where to find us at your hotel, or on the road out of Kleindorf? How was it that Schlinge and Pierre were such good friends at the bridge?"

"They're spies. They're good at these things."

"The answer, Professor, is that I told him. I told him

everything. You see, I'm the most stupid of all. I trusted Pierre. He used me and everything I told him. My friend is dead, another nearly, and your wrists are tied. And do you think they care about what you know about how to build the super weapon? Of course not. There's a bullet waiting for you up that hill."

"I have truly underestimated you, Hansi." The voice was Pierre's. He was still on his knees, back turned, but had twisted his head to the side. "You are far more intelligent than you give yourself credit. You never should have made it into Germany, much less out of it with the doctor here. Or to this moment. You are a worthy adversary, and you have my respect. Too bad you aren't on the winning side."

"I don't care about winning," Hansi said.

"There's just one thing I don't understand, however." Pierre's voice was measured and confident. He didn't sound like a man about to die.

"Professor, check him!"

Salzmann shook with nerves. He shuffled forward, directly into Hansi's line of fire.

"From the side!" Hansi snapped.

The professor obeyed, nearly stumbling. He clutched the suitcase like a shield until the last moment.

"What are you waiting for?" Pierre asked. The question hung in the air like the steam that still rose from Hansi's soggy clothes and penetrated like the cold to Hansi's heart. Pierre's cleverness was no surprise. It carried power to evoke fear, and Hansi felt it now.

Salzmann drew near, set the suitcase down, and hesitated.

"Go on, professor." Hansi encouraged.

Tentatively, the professor touched Pierre under his outstretched left arm and padded down the side. His hand came upon something that caused him to draw back like he had received an electric shock.

"Reach carefully inside and remove it," Hansi instructed. "If he so much as flinches, I pull the trigger."

"I'm considering two answers to my question, Hansi." Pierre said.

"Shut up, I said!"

"You've survived the river, and so perhaps you are worried about your own weapon. Will it fire?"

"Professor!"

"Don't rush me!" Salzmann barked.

Pierre strained his head even further. A single eye, darting intently, searched for Hansi at the edge of his periphery.

"Or is it, Hansi...that you are simply afraid to do it?"

The question hit Hansi like a shot.

He shifted the grip once more. Pierre's silhouette danced in his view. His hands began to shake.

"Salzmann, hurry!"

The next moments rushed by in a blur. Hansi remembered seeing Pierre's upraised hands reach behind him. He snatched Salzmann's head like a ball and twisted it suddenly, and with such violence that Hansi heard, if not felt, the snap of the old man's neck. Salzmann's body melted. As he fell, Pierre shifted his grip to the old man's coat and simultaneously spun away, using Salzmann's body as a shield. In the next instant, Pierre was on his knees, facing Hansi, with his pistol drawn.

Hansi pulled his own trigger. To his surprise, the pistol barked. The recoil sent his arms skyward.

Pierre snapped backward. His head smacked back on the pavement, making a hollow sound, but he was still alive. Somehow, he had managed to hold onto his Luger and keep it from hitting the road, which almost certainly would have dislodged it from his grip. He lifted his head. His face was twisted with rage, but he was still in control.

Hansi pulled the trigger again. His pistol clicked lifelessly.

Exposed in the center of the road, pistol empty, he was an easy target for Pierre.

Then he saw Salzmann's suitcase, the tallest thing between himself and the German. Hansi dove, Pierre fired, and the shot ripped the air overhead.

Hansi smashed onto the pavement and suitcase at the same time. The sheer energy of survival took over. He churned on his belly, using the suitcase as a kind of bulldozer to plow and overwhelm Pierre. He was suddenly on top of Pierre, thrashing with a single purpose: to reach the Luger.

Pierre fought back. Despite the shot and Hansi on him, he had managed to keep the Luger out of reach with an outstretched arm. He brought it down like a hammer. Hansi, clawing his way up Pierre's body, sensed it and twisted his head at the last instant, avoiding all but a glancing blow that seared like a lightning bolt on the back of his shoulder. The strike had brought Pierre's arm within range now, and Hansi shifted his attention to it, moving his grip as though he were climbing a pole. To his surprise, Pierre's resistance ebbed. Hansi smacked the German's wrist against the pavement, first once and then again, and Pierre's fingers curled open. The Luger bounced out of reach under the jeep.

Hansi let go and reached back for the suitcase. Salzmann's prized possession, Hansi would use it as a club.

He didn't need to. When he turned back, the German's body was limp, his head twisted awkwardly, eyes blank. Pierre was dead.

Hansi fell back onto the road. The sky, blue overhead, was dotted with light puffs slipping steadily east. A column of steam from Hansi's body rose to meet them.

His hand touched a sticky wetness on the pavement, causing him to draw it back. He crawled over to the jeep, retrieved Pierre's pistol, and climbed up. Looking back at the scene, he learned the truth. A hole at the center of Pierre's tunic told him his aim had been true.

<h1 style="text-align:center">Chapter Fifty-three</h1>

Karin lay in her bed, eyes closed. A Mahler adagio whispered from the phonograph, tugging at her anxious heart with little effect. As exhausted as she was in the day and a half since leaving the bridge in Luxembourg, sleep did not come easily. She had been transferred from the truck to a jeep, to a locked compartment in a postal car of a military train that retraced her journey back to Berlin.

In the capital, a pair of Gestapo agents, each one the equal of Schlinge's dead driver, shoved her into another black Mercedes and zoomed her home.

Ursula was shocked beyond words at the delivery of her daughter at their doorstep with strict orders to remain within the walls of her townhome until further notice. Karin was all too happy to comply, preferring the smaller confine of her own room.

Ursula demanded to know what happened and peppered Karin with questions, despite Karin's locked door and refusal to respond.

"Don't let Heinrich be the first to tell me," was the most effective of Ursula's pleas. "I can't help you if you don't tell me."

Karin needed Ursula's help. She needed her mother's help. She could only count on the former.

If only I could talk to Oma. She'd pray. She'd know what to do.

It was dark beyond Karin's curtains, but she had no

idea of the time. Sleep was no closer.

Another knock on the door, softer than earlier. "Please, dear, let me in."

"It's not locked any longer," Karin replied.

Ursula stepped into the darkness and hesitated. "You know you can't listen to that—." She hesitated.

"Jew music?" Karin mocked. "Why not? Will you turn me in?"

Ursula crossed and sat down on Karin's bed. "No, dear, but he's here, downstairs. Don't add to your troubles."

"I don't care," Karin said.

"He wants to talk with you."

"Don't let him arrest me, Mother, please! I've done nothing wrong."

"What did you do? I can't help you with him unless you tell me what happened."

"I lied to you. I'm sorry. I didn't go to Cousin Trudi's."

"You went to—?" In the light from the hallway, Karin saw her mother's expression—the tense jaw, wide eyes.

She nodded. "But I didn't find him. Not at first anyway, not by my own efforts."

She explained the full story.

"Karin, dear Karin! Good heavens!" Ursula took Karin in her arms and cradled her. Karin was tense at first. With Schlinge downstairs, she would need strength and resolve, along with cunning. Ursula was surprising her, doing the one thing she didn't expect—being her *mother*.

"Don't worry, dear," she said. "I know Heinrich. He's

no different than any other powerful man. Nod and agree and promise to obey. The crisis will pass. He has larger game in the forest to hunt. Trust me. We can get through this. We adapt and survive."

Karin felt strangely encouraged and strengthened from an unexpected source.

They went downstairs.

Schlinge was in the parlor, sitting on the sofa. Oddly, he was in a plain gray suit, no black leather coat, no fedora, no gloves. When they entered, he stood with great effort and extended his hand to each one in turn before sinking back down more heavily than he would have liked.

"May I speak first?" Karin asked.

He nodded.

"I'd like to say, well, I'd like to—sincerely—apologize for the loss of your driver. I acted impulsively, desperate as I was to find Hansi before you did. And I didn't realize how foolish that was. When I pulled that lever—."

Schlinge put up a hand.

"I'm truly, truly sorry and prepared to pay whatever consequences I need to."

Ursula twitched with alarm.

Schlinge raised his hand again and cleared his throat.

"Fraulein—Karin—that's enough. That is, I appreciate your apology and accept it without reservation."

He began a smile, though to Karin it seemed strained. He glanced at Ursula, and the smile warmed.

"We can put this behind us. I propose this. Let us return to our original agreement, shall we?"

Karin jumped up. "You have him? You have Hansi?

Oh yes, I will! I agree. Whatever you want—a Work Year in Poland, labor camp, anything—the answer is yes! Let him go, and the answer is yes!

Schlinge extended his hand, but slowly. Impulsively Karin took it. His grip was soft, and he did not shake.

"You'll swear by the Führer this time, yes?" She regretted the impulse as soon as she'd said it.

But Schlinge was looking down.

"I'm sorry, Fraulein," he said softly. "But Hansi is dead."

Chapter Fifty-four

The scent of fresh bread penetrated Hansi's deep sleep. A voice sang softly from another room.

Maman? Was he dreaming?

He imagined her in the kitchen, dancing from table to cupboard, shelf to sink, cabinet to oven. Her white apron, handed down from her own mother, and hers before, a mere symbol. She would be dusted from sleeve to slipper from the cloud of flour stirred up by her joy. The bread would need no butter—it would dissolve on its own in his mouth. A dab of jam would make it better. Hot coffee, to wash away the sweetness, would make room for more.

Hansi wriggled out from under the heavy comforter and leaned out over the bed. In the night, the silver crucifix had worked its way out of his shirt and now swung freely around his neck. He clutched it for a moment, running his fingers over the contours of the body on the cross, and then stowed it safely back inside. His bare feet met the cold tile floor where his bedroom rug should have been. The blackout curtains made it impossible to tell if it was day or night, but Hansi knew the layout of the room by heart. He crossed the room and reached for the door but felt only air. A few steps more, and it was there.

He paused. Her voice echoed somewhere in the distance.

The kitchen? It seemed far away. And strangely, Maman's singing was much improved. No matter, Hansi thought; she sang for herself. Her music and skill were stronger for Hansi than any medicine he had ever needed.

The door swung open, and his heart ripped down the middle. He stared through the stiles of a sagging railing down into a wide country kitchen where his Aunt Milly stood bent over the table, stirring a bowl.

And he remembered. He was not in Luxembourg City in his room across the hall from the kitchen in their tiny flat in the Grund. He was in the small village of Wiltz, where he had arrived the night before, exhausted, but grateful to meet Papa. It had all been a dream. Maman was dead.

That night, after a cold supper of baguette and hard cheese, Hansi and his father slipped out of the house together, breaking curfew. Behind the chicken coop, a tired old shed that seemed to be held together by straw, old feathers, and pungent droppings, lay a large, canvas-wrapped bundle bound by a rope. It was partially covered by split firewood. Without being told, Hansi knew what to do. He pulled away the wood and grabbed a loop of rope at his end of the bundle, trying not to visualize the features of the body wrapped inside. For the two of them, it was too heavy except to drag up the trail that led into the forest behind Aunt Milly's farm.

Only in the cover of the trees did Papa speak. Hansi couldn't understand why, but he had been nearly silent all day. Something was eating at him. Something beyond grief for Maman, or even Manolo.

"I've been a fool," Papa said, pushing the shovel into the soft earth between two young trees. "But no more." He laid the first clods against the trunk of one. Hansi aimed the flashlight at the space so Papa could see.

"What do you mean?" Hansi asked.

His father continued to dig.

"I've worked for over a year to prepare for this war. Manolo and I recruited all over the country. Villages from north and south, identifying others, just like us, willing to resist the Nazis. We found many, both men and women, willing to help. Even if just to share information. We didn't want to end up like Poland." Winded from rapid stabs with the shovel, Papa paused and wiped his forehead. It had erupted with perspiration.

"Do you have a telegraph machine?" Hansi asked.

His father shook his head. "Too dangerous."

He jabbed the blade of the shovel into the air.

"We are small, but strong. We have no army, but we are resilient. We could bend without breaking. We could hold out until the French counterattack."

Hansi could hear the doubt in his voice. "It's all right, Papa."

"We've been fools," he repeated. "They've crushed us. When I think of what I did, sending you with Manolo...." His voice faltered. He let go of the handle of the shovel, it hung for a moment in the air, and then clanked to the ground. With it crumbled his father's control. He collapsed against a tree, hiding his face from Hansi.

Hansi stood in silence. The light in his hand seemed suddenly like a weapon that threatened to expose his father's private sorrow.

He stepped forward to close the distance. Despite the

darkness, he could see the outline of his father's shoulder, jerking up and down. Hansi stretched and let his hand come lightly to rest on it. His father sniffed and snorted, for only a moment, before turning back. He snatched his son with both arms and clamped him hard in his grip. His voice was barely audible.

"You could have quit at any moment. Why did you carry on, son?"

The question, once released, seemed to break the tension. His father straightened his back with one hand behind him, pushing out the last of the stress.

"I had to, Papa. I owed it to Manolo." Hansi explained what happened. The last days had taught him not to be ashamed. He held nothing back, confessing to his father how afraid he had been. How he blamed himself for Manolo's death.

His father shook his head. "No, son, don't blame yourself. Manolo knew the risks."

"But the mission failed. I failed." Hansi looked down at the bundle. "We were supposed to deliver Salzmann to the French, and here he is."

"The professor escaped because of you, son. Whatever secrets he carried died with him. At least the Nazis won't learn them."

"He was an arrogant, selfish blowhard," Hansi said, "but he didn't deserve this. He said what he knew would shorten the war."

"Wars end when they end. What you did saved all the people the false Pierre would have eventually rounded up." Papa nodded at the house. "They have you to thank."

"Not Manolo," Hansi said.

When they had finished burying Salzmann, Madame Poulet was waiting in the kitchen. A candle lit the room. She had stretched a single cup of coffee into two with hot water from the teapot. Aunt Milly was asleep upstairs. Michele was on a bed that had been moved from upstairs to the edge of the main room. Jacky, always by her side, had fallen asleep on the rug between the bed and the fireplace.

With the Germans swarming everywhere, they decided to act like a family. Papa had a plan for fixing Madame Poulet's papers. He would alter Maman's card with a photo of Madame Poulet. Michele and Jacky were young enough not to need anything but to be listed with her. There was no time to grieve the mutilation of Maman's identity card; the times required it.

The steaming liquid felt good on Hansi's throat. The chill of the river seemed to have lingered, at least in his memory. He doubted it would ever leave.

Hansi took his cup with him to Michele's bedside in the main room. She was asleep. The bandage covered her head like a stocking cap, but her expression was serene. The worry and fear had drained away. The blanket rose and fell with the calm rhythm of her breathing.

His father joined him.

"We forgot this," he said, holding Salzmann's suitcase.

"Let's burn it," Hansi said. He took the case and stepped over the sleeping Jacky.

Kneeling at the hearth, Hansi clicked it open. The

stench was an instant reminder of the man, his excesses, and his eccentric devotion to the unimportant details of a fearful life he just couldn't leave behind.

Hansi picked at one of the crusted shirts.

"We can wash those." The voice was Madame Poulet's. "And the case might come in handy. We're going to need everything. Dump it on the floor. Put the case outside; let it air out. I'll wash the clothes."

Hansi complied, which at least saved him from handling the items one by one. When the case was empty, he held it in midair, stunned by what he saw.

"What is it?" Jacky had come awake and joined Hansi at the fireplace. He was staring at the inside of the suitcase.

Hansi moved it away from the hearth to the shadows in the corner. The case gave off a faint light, *from the inside.*

They gathered around it. The huddle blocked even more light. The lining of the case glowed—not brightly, but with fine lines, lettering, short phrases, and strange formulas. Every centimeter of surface inside the case was covered with a radiant ink used to create the symbols.

"It looks like radium paint. They use it to make watches," Papa said.

"What does it mean?" Jacky asked.

Hansi closed the case and latched it shut. He returned it to its place in the corner.

"It means that a mad scientist was not so mad after all," he said. Then he returned to the couch, let himself sink deep into the cushions, and closed his eyes.

www.ingramcontent.com/pod-product-compliance
Lightning Source LLC
Chambersburg PA
CBHW031837310726
48972CB00005B/1315